D1267718

FOR POSITION ONLY

Craig Keller is that tall, gorgeous, sexy, and ridiculously rich S.O.B. that really *could* sell the chrome off a bumper. Though our friends and families warned us to avoid him at all costs, Royce's leading man reels us in against our will with his sophisticated charm and professional finesse. Once firmly under his spell, we witness the underside of his tortured soul. We root for him as he tries to work out his own salvation, taking every wrong turn along the way. But, after he turns his back on love, he inadvertently learns to love himself. *For Position Only* is an emotional roller coaster of glamour, greed, loss, love, and transformation.
—Lori Swick, author of *Comfort and Mirth* and *Dreaming: The Sacred Art*

The powerful story of a man's inspiring, introspective journey of ruthlessness and remorse, romance, and redemption, set against the frenetic backdrop of the high-powered Los Angeles marketing and advertising world. Adele Royce captures the souls of her characters. I only put this book down when I *had* to.
—Don Daniels, former president, South Florida Writers Association, and author of *Rhyme and Punishment*

Adele Royce, in *For Position Only,* takes us not down the primrose path but through the dark night of the soul. We ache for the man whose heart, newly awakened after tragedy years ago, now bleeds in pain for the love of the woman of whom he believes himself unworthy. This unforgettable journey of two beautiful and damaged souls, drawn to each other in the depths of their broken hearts, will captivate you with its exquisite beauty.
—Rebecca Augustine, author, *Love without Cause: Create Inner Transformation, Renew Your Thinking, and Be Love in a World That Doesn't Deserve It*

The heart of the story is round two in the rocky romance between the deeply conflicted Craig and the elegant and talented Jane. The main characters are tremendously vivid. Although the story is told from Craig's perspective, and he is an overpowering personality, the reader will find his parents, coworkers, and friends both fascinating and lively. The story's female villain is deliciously evil. The ad agency setting rings true, especially the preparation behind launching a successful advertising campaign. The author has obviously been there and brings the reader along. Get yourself some really good chocolate, turn off your phone, and settle in for a tasty treat of a read.
—CarolJean and Philip Kier, authors

FOR POSITION ONLY

# FOR POSITION ONLY

## adele royce

DAGMAR
MIURA
LOS ANGELES

Published by Dagmar Miura
Los Angeles
www.dagmarmiura.com

For Position Only

Copyright © 2021 Madweek Marketing LLC
All rights reserved. No part of this book may be used or reproduced in any manner whatsoever without prior written permission except in the case of brief quotations embodied in critical articles or reviews. For information, address Dagmar Miura, dagmarmiura@gmail.com, or visit our website at www.dagmarmiura.com.

This book is a complete work of fiction. All events are fictionalized, and although the names of real people are used, their characterization in this book is fiction. References to historical events, real people, or real locals are used fictitiously. Other names, characters, places, and incidents are the product of the author's imagination, and any resemblance to actual events or locals or persons, living or dead is entirely coincidental. All attractions, product names or other works mentioned in this book are trademarks of their respective owners and the names and images used in this book are strictly for editorial purposes. No commercial claims to their use are claimed by the author or publisher.

Cover photo by Merrell Virgen

First published 2021

ISBN: 978-1-951130-53-4

*For my husband and family, and in the memory of my beloved kitty, Meeko, who was constantly by my side as I wrote this book. I will always ache for your fluffy gray presence.*

*And for all the souls searching for a deeper meaning—those who are painfully aware of the certain sadness inherent in the human experience, no matter his/her status in life. Never forget, there is always a path home.*

*Craig Axel Keller—c'est moi.*

# One

*N*EVER GET ACCUSTOMED TO *defeat*. That's what I told myself every morning since that day—the worst career day of my life. I call it the worst *career* day because it certainly wasn't the worst *day* of my life. It's important to know the difference. That day in the office, I was blindsided—it was a complete ambush.

I was working diligently on a client memo after a particularly steamy session with Hayden Towne, the agency siren. That day we had a two-hour lunch that involved a bottle of Dom and a long drive up The Pacific Coast Highway towards Malibu. Her scent still enveloped me when I returned to the office, despite numerous hand-washings and teeth-brushings.

Someone was knocking on my door with persistence. "Come in, Cassandra," I called to my assistant, not even paying attention to the sound of the door opening and closing. I continued to tap away at my keyboard until the curious silence taunted me enough to stop typing and turn around. There stood Hayden near the door, in the same royal blue dress that I had gathered up around her waist only an hour earlier.

"What's up?" I said, getting to my feet and stepping cautiously around my desk. There was an insouciant smirk on her face as she moved closer—so close I felt my nostrils flare at the smell of her perfume, which still lingered faintly in my mouth. I placed my hand on her waist with familiarity, thinking I was in no mood to see her so soon after our mid-day frolic. "You back for more?"

She swatted my hand away. "You wish. You're going to want to sit down for this, Craig," she announced, shooting me a smug grin with those perfect teeth. She moved sideways around me and flounced over to the white leather couch in my office sitting area. It was opposite the fireplace, above which my most treasured Chagall painting hung. Hayden always jokingly referred to the area as my casting couch because we had done it there so many times. Hayden patted the seat next to her like *she* was managing partner of *my* advertising agency, not the other way around.

I slowly approached her, wracking my brain for the reason she wanted this impromptu tête-à-tête. It was obviously not about sex. When I reached the couch, she tossed her bleached blonde hair and gazed up at me with those heavily mascaraed tanzanite eyes. "Sit," she offered, patting the seat again.

I relented and parked myself next to her. "What's going on, Hayden? Did we lose a client? Just come out with whatever it is." I hated guessing games and I didn't trust the way she was looking at me, the tone of her voice, or anything about her demeanor at that moment.

She erupted in a wicked laugh. "You're about to lose a lot more than a client." She handed me a folded letter, sat back, and observed me, hands crossed over her chest with a purple-lipped sneer.

All I read was the first line, "Please accept this as my letter of resignation," before tossing the letter on the coffee table. I glared at her. "You can't resign. You have a contract and it's not up for another year."

"A contract without a non-compete," she gleefully reminded me. "Which makes it worthless." I recalled her insistence that I omit the non-compete clause. I didn't argue because I was doing Don a favor—Donovan C. Keller, my father—by hiring her. Her father was Stephan Towne, California's District Attorney and, because Don had won a lifetime of cases defending well-known mobsters in our hometown of San Francisco, the relationship between the two men had always been adversarial. Don ordered me two years ago to hire Stephan's daughter when a vice president of accounts position became available. It was his attempt to ease their relations.

"What are you saying, Hayden … did you get another offer? Whatever it is, I'll match it." There was no way I would allow her to walk out the door, no matter how talentless she was. Don would strangle me.

She cocked her head to one side and drew her platinum locks behind one ear with two fully extended fingertips. Hayden always wore red nail polish. I pictured those shiny red nails slithering around my pants just an hour ago.

"Being the sexist pig that you are, I knew you'd think that; but actually, I'm starting my own agency."

*Sexist pig?* I had to hold back my anger at that swipe. "How are you going to start an agency with no clients?" I scoffed, rising from the couch just to put distance between us. "That's a bad move, Hayden. Anyone will tell you that."

She immediately stood and straightened to her full height, shoulders back. Hayden was just under six feet tall, and today she was wearing five-inch heels, which put her at my height. "Oh, I'll have plenty of clients—in fact, I already do."

That's when the nickel finally dropped. She was leaving my agency and starting her own—*with my clients.*

THE YEAR FOLLOWING THAT unpleasant day had been painful—so painful that I was considering laying off half my employees. My pride wouldn't allow it; however, and I didn't want word to get out that I was struggling, even though the rumor mill was already churning. I ended up breaking down and begging Don for the cash to keep my company afloat another year. He reluctantly gave in, but the transaction earned him license to further humiliate me with lectures about 'learning when to keep it in my pants,' 'thinking with the wrong head,' and 'being asleep at the switch.'

The biggest irony was that I started my agency, Keller Whitman Group, much the way Hayden started hers—only I stole clients from my former mentor, Warren Mitchell, about a decade earlier. It took many long walks on the beach in deep meditation to discover the law of Karma. Hayden had beaten me at my own game. She got me where she knew it would really hurt. And why? At first, I thought it was for money and power—the same reasons I killed Warren's business. But I found out later it had more to do with helping her father take down the Keller family. She cleverly executed her plan the day she started working for me—and consensual sex was her way of keeping me oblivious to her behind-the-scenes maneuvers. I never got why people said Hayden was the female version of me until that day in my office.

THAT WAS WHY TODAY was so important. If I blew this meeting, I would have no other recourse but to close my agency and start over—*but doing what?* All I ever knew was being an ad guy. At forty, I was too young to consult and too old to work for anyone else. I was too notorious in the industry to be anything but the boss. I pictured myself sitting at home, unemployed, crafting my memoir, pitifully savoring the fragments of my life when things were different—when I had everything because I was Craig Axel Keller. My nickname in town was 'The Axe,' because I was brilliant at cutting deals. I pitched and won the biggest clients, had the highest reported revenue of any competing ad agency. My weeks were overflowing with power lunches in L.A.'s trendiest restaurants. Women crawled all over me—wanting a tiny slice of what I had, no matter how I demeaned them. But life was different now. I was teetering on the edge of obscurity. *This meeting had to be perfect.*

I pulled on the silk olive-green robe that hung near the shower, and sifted through my long, rectangular walk-in closet. I passed my hand along the vast assortment of custom-made Italian suits, color-sorted from dark to light. As I did this, the tassel cord belt on my robe kept coming untied, causing the robe to gap open. Each time this happened, I would yank the two ends of the cord, pull them together and tie them in a knot. The cord situation was getting on my nerves, which were already frazzled. The robe was a frivolous purchase from my last trip to Rome. I always loved the way Italians dressed. It was what originally attracted me to my ex-wife, Alessandra. She was born in Rome and had the innate sensibilities and taste in fashion that imbued most Italians from an early age.

I took the time every morning to go through my suits one by one to determine which conspired with the plans on my calendar. Once I selected the suit, I moved to the ties, then to the shirts, shoes and, finally, belts. The shoes determined the belt, so belts were always last.

It was important I select the right combination today because I was meeting with Warren for the first time in at least two years—since I bought out his agency. I was going to have to prostrate myself to sell him on an idea. I needed to wear something that was understated yet elegant; confident but not arrogant. A dark navy suit said class but still demanded attention. The tie was another story altogether. I went through the display of silk ties, a wall of shelves with infinite tiny square compartments cradling each individual tie, again arranged by color, so I could easily move to the palette of choice. Red would scream power, but it was such a cliché. I wouldn't own a red tie unless it had some sort of pattern. Solid red ties were for wannabe politicians and car salesmen. I moved to the blue section and found one that only whispered power, because it was pale blue with a tiny thread of red woven inconspicuously into the fabric. This was the right one.

Once I was fully dressed, I gave myself a once-over in

the full-length mirror. Not bad, I thought. I had inherited Don's looks, which was both a help and a hindrance. It subjected me to labels like 'pretty boy,' and 'girly' when I was younger. People immediately focused on my light jade eyes and the long lashes that any woman would die for. I had to work harder to prove my masculinity. By college, the braces that had rendered me a complete nerd in high school gave me teeth that rivaled a toothpaste model. I discovered my looks were an asset in every way, both in school with female professors and out of school when applying for jobs.

I leaned into the sink and washed my hands one last time. It was the seventh time I had washed them since getting out of bed, not including my morning shower.

As soon as I was satisfied that I looked the part to win Warren over, I sauntered toward the front door of my Malibu home. I glanced at my living room, which was just off the entryway, and noticed one of the black pillows on my massive crème-colored suede sectional was not evenly spaced with the other pillows. I sighed and advanced to the offending pillow, almost tripping over one of a trio of zebra-print ottomans. After I moved the pillow to the appropriate place, I realized the dimmer switch on the chandelier was left on—it was barely lit. The chandelier was a holdover from my old apartment in Brentwood. It was custom designed, made of Murano glass and imported from Venice. It was the centerpiece of my living room, with its long octopus-like rolling limbs, extending outward as though holding up flame-lit tips. While it was a bitch to move, I wanted it for my new home. I located the light switch and pushed it into the off position.

Before I passed the entryway to the front door, I stopped and picked up a framed photo of my older brother, Donovan James Keller, or DJ, as we called him. I did this every morning—and felt the same tingling in my hands—the crippling sensation of knowing I would never see him again. I started the photo ritual many years ago—it was something Alessandra had scolded me for. She thought it was masochism—an act of 'emotional cutting' as she always accused.

I quickly replaced the photo and exited my home to find the black Bentley convertible. I took a long look at it and ran my fingers along the side of the door before opening it and peering inside, immediately smelling the clean car scent. It was my home away from home. I eased in, scanned the rearview mirror as the colossal wrought iron gate slid open. Then I backed out of the driveway and headed east toward Santa Monica. It was only around eighteen miles—a twenty-five-minute drive in light traffic, which seemed to be flowing at a fast pace today. I didn't want to show up at Warren's office with disheveled hair, so I skipped putting the top down.

In the good old days, when business was flourishing and a certain euphoria radiated through my soul, I would put the top down as soon as I was off the freeway, and play a little game, counting how many women's heads I could turn. My usual projection was around ten, but sometimes it was lower. It depended on where I was.

I noted the change to the building's façade as soon as I pulled into the parking lot of Mitchell Vance & Mercer. It used to be Warren Mitchell & Partners before I took them over and forced Warren out. He formed Mitchell Vance & Mercer about a year after that. Warren hadn't taken defeat sitting down. He had pretended to go into retirement, all the while accumulating clients so that he could open his new agency and hire back two of his original executives—both partners now. Warren had even managed to buy his old building back.

I parked and immediately pulled out a bottle of hand sanitizer from my console, squeezing a glob into my hands and thoroughly rubbing them together. It felt cold and gooey. The pungent scent of alcohol filled the car as thickly as my vulnerability.

The possibility of rejection gnawed relentlessly at my gut. I was shocked that Warren would take a meeting with me after what I had done to unravel him in the past. He was kind to me—treated me like a son. And, in return, I nearly crushed his business. I knew this meeting was a long shot, but I had to take the risk. There was no other choice left.

I just had to sell it right. That's what Don had taught me throughout my life. He was the greatest salesman I'd ever met and schooled me properly when it came to the art of persuasion. I never called him Father or Dad. He was always Don to me. My parents were Don and Julia, not Mom and Dad. I always wondered what it would be like to call anyone Mom and Dad.

When my children, Axel and Anabel, were born, I vowed they would always call Alessandra and I Mom and Dad. But it was a battle with their grandparents, who still insisted they be called Julia and Don, even by my kids. At the end of the day, Alessandra won that battle, and they were stuck with Nonna and Nonno.

I entered the building, and an attractive receptionist looked up and smiled. "You must be Craig Keller," she said. "Please have a seat. I'll let Warren know you're here."

"Thank you," I responded, returning her smile, and finding a chair in the tidy lobby. *Always be friendly to the administrative staff. That's the only way they will remember you.* I clutched my briefcase as though it were filled with cash and stared blankly at a bouquet of red silk Gerber daisies sitting on the coffee table. I vaguely wondered why Warren wouldn't spring for real flowers like I did. It was expensive but said so much more about the success of an agency. Subtle touches like that eluded Warren.

I heard high heels clicking down the hallway and almost felt my heart stop. *Could it be Jane Mercer?* I was dying for a glimpse of her but didn't know how I'd address her after everything that had happened between us. The owner of the high heels turned out to be another associate—a woman in her early twenties—probably a junior account executive. She passed a file to the receptionist and clacked her way back down the hallway.

After about five minutes, the receptionist called to me, "Mr. Keller, Warren's ready to meet with you. I'll show you to his office."

"Great," I responded and got to my feet.

I followed the receptionist down the hallway and noticed she had a decent body. Not great, but decent. She stopped at a door with a plaque on it that read 'Warren Mitchell' and I felt a twinge in my stomach—past misdeeds echoing through me—brewing like a thunderous cloud ready to burst. *He might turn me down, but what if he doesn't?*

The receptionist knocked at the door, opened it, and poked her head inside. "Warren, I have Mr. Keller here."

"Thanks, Pearl," I heard Warren's voice call from behind the door. *Pearl.* Not a name I expected. Pearl glanced in my direction and opened the door wider, gesturing for me to enter.

Warren was at his desk, but stood and approached as soon as I walked in. I noticed his full head of salt and pepper hair was greyer and longer than I had remembered. It gave him a hip-intellectual look. He was also a lot more casual than I recalled; he used to be a suit-and-tie guy, but today he wore a simple checked, open-collared, button-down shirt tucked into belted suit pants. He was not smiling.

"Keller," he said finally, voice shrouded in distrust, and motioned for me to sit in one of the chairs opposite his desk.

I preferred to sit at his conference table, so we were on equal footing, at least physically. I always positioned people across from my desk when I wanted to show power and superiority. "Warren, how've you been?" I selected the chair on the side where I could still see the door. That was something Don had taught me—always sit where you can see the door. "Thank you for taking a meeting with me."

"Consider it a professional courtesy," Warren responded, slouching a bit in his chair, still not smiling. "You've piqued my curiosity if nothing else."

"Whatever the reason, I appreciate your time." My voice came off fake polite. I placed my black leather messenger bag on the chair next to me and spotted the familiar framed black-and-white photographs of the men he worshipped: JFK, Steve Jobs, David Ogilvy. The fact that Ogilvy mentored Warren came up a lot in conversation when Warren was mentoring me. It was a technique he used to put me in my place. It never worked.

"You can start by telling me why you're here," Warren urged. "The last time I saw you in this office, Keller Whitman Group was buying me out. Since I have no plans to go public anytime soon, I can't imagine the reason you're here."

"Then I'll cut to the chase," I replied, thinking that was the best way to deal with Warren—the only way. I found that out quickly when I went to work for him right out of college as a copywriter. In those days he was fond of hitting me with the adage, *I don't care how you made the watch, just tell me what time it is.* "I have a business proposal for you." I could hear the apprehension lodged in my throat.

Warren shrugged and looked unmoved.

"There's a relatively new agency that's rapidly gaining market share," I said. "Have you heard of Towne Ink?" I felt my neck stiffening at the mere mention of Hayden's agency and my hand instinctively flew up to adjust my collar.

"I know the name," Warren answered, looking barely amused. He casually fingered a red blown-glass paperweight in the shape of an apple and spun it around on his desk like a top.

"You know the managing partner worked for me at Keller Whitman Group, right?"

"You mean Hayden Towne? I heard she did a lot more for you than just work," Warren quipped, swiveling his chair to one side.

I didn't flinch. I never did when confronted with something that would be embarrassing or incriminating to anyone else. Don taught me that showing shame or regret was weak. But the truth was, I was crumbling inside—the mere image of Hayden caused a black bile to bubble up in my abdomen. And although sleeping with Hayden was one of the most regrettable things I had done in my life, especially since she duped me and made off with half my clients, I couldn't undo it. She was still there, like a loaded pistol that could go off at any time and without warning.

"When she left my agency, she stole a sizable chunk of my business," I explained. "And she's continued to do it by partnering with a large service provider and channeling her efforts into a fully digital marketing space." I paused a moment to let Warren process my words. With Warren, you had to give him time in between small nuggets of a larger info-dump.

"I've spent the past year researching how to take my agency in the same direction without dropping the traditional advertising elements that made us successful in the first place," I continued. "It hasn't been easy."

Warren laughed. It was a snarky laugh unaccompanied by a smile. "I'm assuming you didn't come all the way over here to warn me about your old girlfriend, Keller. But if you did, I'm really not concerned."

A sharp pain sliced through my chest. Warren was not buying my spiel. I could hardly blame him, but I was not about to give up. I had too much to lose and Warren was my only hope of saving both my business and reputation. I leaned in and lowered my voice. "You should be. We all should be, Warren. She's way ahead of us—has an army of data-analyzing, social media savvy junkies working for her now. *They* are the future of advertising. At the end of the day, *they* will be the ones understanding consumers' deepest desires and winning everyone's business, not us."

I sat back and waited for Warren's response. I had a feeling that last bit would appeal to Warren's analytical side. He was always obsessing about numbers and statistics, never about the overall picture of what we were doing: Selling the American dream to whomever would listen—the suckers of the world. We were the whores pumping our seed into the psyches of those with disposable income. And the only thing that mattered was how deep you went and how often you came.

He rubbed his chin and raised his eyebrows at me. "What are you after, Keller?"

"A partnership," I answered, returning his stare but feeling sick inside at what was at stake. "Towne Ink poses a significant threat to our conventional methods and they're doing it by being more consumer-centric."

Warren's expression changed to one of intrigue—although I couldn't tell if he was pondering my audacity or my courage—there was a fine line. I felt like I might be pulling him in—at least enough for him to hear me out. I shifted in my chair and crossed my legs.

"They're focused on content and distribution platforms," I said. "Neither of us is doing that effectively. But if you and I were to join forces.…"

"Hold on a minute, Keller," Warren interrupted, now looking dumbfounded. "You came here proposing a partnership—with *my agency*? Why on earth would I do that?" He abruptly got to his feet and paced the floor, stopping and staring out his office window at the thick layer of smog masking downtown Santa Monica. A full minute had passed before he finally turned to me and said, "What's in it for me?"

"Everything," I answered, focusing all my energy on sounding confident. Warren had a scathing look on his face, one I'd come to know well over the years. I was going to have to work quickly to keep him on track. "Are you comfortable your clients won't notice you aren't evolving as fast in the digital marketing landscape the way some of these up-and-coming agencies are?"

He just glared at me, hands on hips, saying nothing.

"I'm not," I admitted. "That's why I'm proposing we combine efforts—keep our top talent but reduce the overall headcount so we can focus resources toward the data and analytics business—that's the only way we'll be able to drive personalization. Isn't that what you want?"

Again, Warren said nothing. I started to feel my argument was falling on deaf ears. Warren just didn't seem ready to look past our history and see the writing on the wall. He had to admit that effective digital marketing and analysis were the current feeding frenzy of the advertising world. I also came to understand the parental side of Warren when I was his protégé. No matter how badly I'd screwed him over in the past, he would always long to have that bond with me back. I silently prayed that's what he wanted—and no matter how nonchalant I acted externally, I wanted it, too, badly. I needed him to be the father I never had—the type of father who would forgive my misdeeds and embrace me once again—love me unconditionally like Don never could. So, I held on. "I know you're skeptical. I would be, too."

"Skeptical doesn't even begin to cover how I feel about doing business with you," Warren replied irritably.

I took a deep breath. "I know there's baggage, but we're in a position to dominate the market. I have the most talented creative director in the city, and he's poised to knock out any number of stellar ad campaigns. I also have the rarest gem in media planning."

Warren now focused his steely grey eyes on mine. I was trying to read him, but his countenance just wasn't giving him away. I kept going. "We take the talent from both our rosters, add a highly functioning, tech-deep marketing team, and we have all the building blocks to create a powerhouse of an agency ... one that'll drive client business much further than we could if we operated independently—as competitors."

There was no way Warren could deny that my creative director, Alonzo Costa, and media planner, Bobbi Silverstein, were the best, not just in a huge city like Los Angeles, but on a national level. Those two alone were worth millions in revenue, and he would have them at his disposal. The client revenue I had left in my arsenal, even after losing so much business, would be icing on the cake.

Warren retorted, "It's not your staff I'm worried about. It's you. You're one of the most deceitful, unscrupulous people I've ever met, and I'd be a fool to trust you again. Are you forgetting everything that happened in the past?"

Warren was referring to my rather lengthy history of stealing his clients, employees, and partners. The only thing I hadn't stolen from Warren was his wife, although recalling Caroline Mitchell from the photos plastered all over Warren's office, at one time I would have had no trouble going after her, too. She was a beautiful blonde, after all. I just wished there were some way to express to Warren that I'd changed. I'd been humbled by the loss of half my clients at the hands of someone even more unscrupulous than me.

"Warren, I know I've been one of your biggest adversaries in the past, but Hayden Towne is an adversary to us both now. And she's winning." I tried to keep my tone above the level of pleading.

Warren frowned and eyed me with suspicion. "What happens to Keller Whitman Group?" he asked. "Are you just going to close your doors? What about all the equity you've established in your name alone?"

I had his interest now. He never would have asked that question if he wasn't interested. "Keller Whitman Group goes away," I answered without emotion. "Ben Whitman's moving on and the rest of the partners have no idea how to take the agency to the next level. It's all been on me and I'm ready to cut them loose."

"Are you asking for a spot on the masthead?" Warren asked.

"I expect to be added—but to the end of the lineup," I answered, thinking I would never accept that; however, today was just about whetting Warren's appetite for a deal. "It's not going to hurt your agency's reputation to have the name Keller attached to the brand."

"You're forgetting one important detail," Warren expressed, leaning back in his chair, crossing his arms over his chest, and studying me. I knew he was trying to evaluate my trustworthiness. "What about my partners? They have equal weight when voting on any changes to our agency. Both Jeffrey Vance and Jane Mercer would have to agree to a new arrangement."

"Does that mean you're willing to pitch it to them for a vote?" I asked, feeling success within my grasp.

Warren didn't answer my question. He sat for a moment as if considering it. "You know neither of them is a fan of yours, especially Jane."

I knew Jane would be a tough sell. I had had an affair with her years ago, while I was married, and I treated her terribly. Then, when I bought out Warren's agency, I treated her even worse and basically strong-armed her out of her job. Unfortunately, Jane was part of my long and checkered history with women. I went into therapy to sort out these problems. I was making progress, albeit slowly. Still, I hated what I had done to hurt Jane. In the end, she hurt me, too. But she would never believe me if I told her. I sighed. "What do you want me to say? I know how Jane feels about me but she's a professional, and I have a hunch she'll see value in this alliance."

We stared at each other in uncomfortable silence until Warren finally spoke. "I'll need numbers from you—hard numbers on client revenue, and they'd better be impressive. Throw in the salaries of your creative and media people plus what you'd want as a draw. All I can commit to is looking it over for now. If it meets with what I have in mind, I *might* share it with Jeffrey and Jane."

This was it. I had him. I couldn't wait to call Don—to share my triumphant sales pitch. Warren bought it and that's all I expected from this first meeting. I felt my neck release almost instantly, the tension diminishing. I stretched my hand across his desk to shake his hand, which he rejected, leaving me in the awkward position of having to take my hand back without looking tragic. "I'll have that information for you by end of day," I said, rising to my feet and grabbing my messenger bag.

Warren escorted me to the door, and I walked confidently to the front office, knowing I had just conquered the most difficult obstacle—convincing Warren this was a good idea. I arrived at the front desk where Pearl sat, thanked her, and said goodbye.

That's when I saw Jane entering the building. Our eyes met and she did a double take, her pretty, pink lips parted slightly, and her eyes narrowed. "What are *you* doing here?" she demanded in a tone I would have considered insubordinate if she still worked for me.

"Meeting with Warren," I answered coolly, feeling my heart race.

"I can't imagine what you have to meet with Warren about," she returned.

I shrugged. "Ask him." I knew my tone conveyed indifference when I should care what Jane thought. I should care a lot. I needed her vote. But I couldn't help it. Don had ingrained it into my brain—never bow down to anyone, no matter who they are. Plus, there was something so withering about seeing her for the first time in two years and having her so unhappy to see me. I don't know what I expected but it seemed exaggerated. It was difficult to recall the time when she thought I was the most attractive man on earth.

"That would mean I'm actually interested," she replied, "which I'm not."

Before I could respond, she shouldered her way past me and disappeared down the hallway. I must have caught Pearl's attention when I turned to watch Jane walk away because she was staring at me with a puzzled expression. I gave her a half smile and shrug, then exited the building.

Heading back to my office downtown, I called Don. "Donovan Keller's office." It was Shari Blackman, Don's assistant.

"Shari, is he available?" I'd known Shari since I was a child. She was a tough but kind-hearted woman who doted on my father and never left his side until he went home for the evening.

"Yes, dear, hold on a moment," she responded.

"Craig." the crunchy voice broke in. I could tell from his tone whether he wanted to hear a long story, a short one, or nothing at all. It sounded like he had some time on his hands.

"Don," I started brightly. "I just finished meeting with Warren."

"Well, son? How'd it go?" Don still had an Irish accent, even though he was the grandson of Irish immigrants and had been born and raised in the Bay area. His strict Irish Catholic roots were important to him and since he was raised close to his highly accented grandparents, he never lost his own.

"It went well," I responded. "I'm confident this is going to happen."

"Did you bring in all the good stuff? You know, everything I told you—the reasons that would make it an impossible offer to refuse?"

"I brought in all of it. He's asked for preliminary numbers to review with his partners."

"Good job, son," he commented. "It'll be a relief to finally get you off my payroll—you're much too old to be sucking money off your old man."

Of course, he would not be able to resist a jab or two at me. "I don't like it any more than you do."

"Well, I hope you've learned something from all this," he concluded. "Keep me posted." And the line went dead.

I wished I could have had more time to explain how I had steered the meeting—to make him proud of me. My mind suddenly went back to Jane and the look on her face—such utter disdain. She appeared the same, except with a little more confidence. She had the shiniest auburn hair that hung long and loose down past her shoulders. But those green eyes captured me again, just like the first time I saw her. She was so young and innocent then—so insecure, and I wanted her in a way she would never understand. I could have consumed her. She was like a brilliant jewel, devastatingly sexy in an uncontrived way. All I wanted was to possess her—to control her. And there was something in her look today that made me want to do it again.

With both hands on the steering wheel, I took a deep breath and blew it out slowly. These were the feelings I needed to bring up in my next session with Dr. Truer. But for now, I at least had my foot in the door with Warren.

WAITING FOR MY SESSION with Dr. Truer was always awkward. I met with her twice a week, on Mondays and Thursdays, and I never knew what to do or think when I was in the waiting room. Usually, I was still in the frenetic work mode of conference calls, emails, and constant requests for approval on client issues. Dr. Truer's whole office building smelled like old, sick people, and her office was particularly bleak. An old radio was chained with wiring to the floor, so no one could steal it … as if anyone would want to. Dusty old dolls, teddy bears, and board games in boxes with frayed cardboard edges sat in a wooden box to the side of the room. Back issues of *Psychology Monthly* beckoned from the coffee table with headlines like 'Silence Your Inner Critic' and '10 Life Skills Even You Can Learn.' I pulled a small bottle of hand sanitizer from the pocket of my suit jacket, feeling like I needed to douse my entire body with it.

While this was not the type of place I would normally inhabit, Dr. Janice Truer was the best psychologist in the city. She had been a close friend of Don's for years. While he never told me, I suspected Don had referred numerous mob clients while in San Francisco. I'd heard from Don that she had relocated and set up shop in L.A. I figured she would be frank, wise, and helpful. I never told anyone I was in therapy, especially not Don. He would see it as a sign of weakness.

I heard Dr. Truer's heavy, uneven footsteps draw closer and her inner door open and shut. She opened the door to the waiting room and stepped out. She always appeared to have stuck her finger in a light socket, with that frizzy blonde mop of hair sticking out in every direction. Her pale, freckled face was slightly shiny and her eyes glassy. Still, she had a warm smile that assured me everything was under control.

"Craig," she greeted me, holding the door open like she was welcoming me to a cocktail party; but there were never cocktails, only words … discussion … talking … stuff I normally avoided.

I stood and crossed the threshold into her office, which was furnished like an antiquated living room with its behemoth wooden bookshelves surrounding her desk and credenza. A rust-colored couch sat directly across from her desk. It had been worn thin by decades of patients, neurotically fidgeting, twisting, shifting legs, and undoubtedly many who treated it as a temporary bed while they spat emotional vomit all over Dr. Truer's kind, encouraging face.

Dr. Truer sat across from me in a marigold La-Z-Boy and kicked her feet up on the matching ottoman, like it was she who had had a rough day, not me. I wondered how she could sit there and listen to everyone spewing their dire crises and not slit her own wrists. She was the one who kept people from slitting theirs, from jumping off the ledge.

"Well," she said with this sort of self-effacing smile she always gave me when our sessions began. It was her way of saying, 'I know you don't like this, but we have to start somewhere and I'm expecting you to lead the conversation.'

"Yeah, so … I guess we can pick up where we left off last week," I responded.

Dr. Truer reached over and picked up a notepad and pen from a side table. "We were talking about your father," she said in a somber tone.

"You mean Don," I corrected her.

"Of course. Yes, we were talking about your relationship with Don. You started to tell me about something that happened to your brother and how it affected your relationship with Don—and your relationship with women."

I took a deep breath. This was a topic I had been fearing. It was *the* single worst day of my life—my adolescence—and it certainly set the tone for my future. We had barely scraped the surface of what happened to DJ. The subject came up in the last session, after I revealed Don's method of childrearing and his fondness for corporal punishment. His belt had cracked against my backside so many times as a kid, my skin was tough as rawhide. Dr. Truer had asked why I didn't get emotional when I talked about it. She said it was like I was reading a script or a story about someone else's life, not my own. She called this *dissociation*. Tonight, however, I was not sure how I would feel about telling this story.

"Are you okay?" Dr. Truer was asking me. I must have been staring into space.

I cleared my throat. "Yes, fine. I was just thinking about DJ."

"Tell me about him."

"He was five years older than me," I disclosed, picturing DJ with his glossy straw-colored hair, large honey-brown eyes, and earnest look on his chiseled face. He looked more like Julia than Don, but he had been given Don's namesake and was well on the road to becoming a replica of his father. Don was making sure of that.

Dr. Truer was looking at me expectantly, although still with the kind, empathetic look in her eyes. Sometimes I just wanted to wipe that look off her face and tell her to be real.

"He was in his first year of law school when it happened," I began, recalling exactly where I was when I heard the news. I was a senior in high school, but DJ had encouraged me to ditch class and sail on Don's yacht, with DJ and a bunch of his law school buddies. They had raided Don's bar and mixed strong rum cocktails which I guzzled while intermittently taking hits of pot.

"There was an accident while DJ was yachting out on

the San Francisco Bay," I said, the police images of DJ's bloody, mutilated body infiltrating my brain.

"What kind of accident?" asked Dr. Truer.

Suddenly the stinging pain of being awakened by police, naked, in bed with a woman I didn't know, seared through me like fiery cinders. I found out later she was a hooker who had been passed around by DJ and his friends. It was my seventeenth birthday and DJ must have told them all I was a still a virgin. They felt it necessary to get the younger Keller wasted and deflowered ... a hazing of sorts.

"I ... um, he fell overboard and was chopped in pieces by the yacht's propeller." As I uttered these words, I recalled the lengthy investigation and how everyone, including the four crew members and captain, had been interrogated for months.

My eyes met Dr. Truer's and her look was one of concern. I couldn't stand when she did this. I quickly looked away, focusing my eyes on one of the books sitting on the shelving behind her: *Man and His Symbols* by Carl G. Jung.

"Can you tell me a little more about what happened?" she asked, her voice gentle and controlled. She had begun making notes on the pad.

"I would but I don't really know," I responded. "No one saw the incident. All of our stories corroborated."

"Does that mean you were on the yacht when your brother fell overboard?" She squinted and cocked her head at me, as though she were studying my reaction.

I nodded. "Yes."

"I don't mean to push you, Craig, but that had to have been a very traumatic incident in your life, one that likely changed you forever. If you're comfortable, we should explore that for a moment."

She was not going to let me off the hook. I was going to have to tell her something. "Honestly, I don't remember a lot about that day, other than I got really drunk and was passed out when my brother died. The police woke me up and told me what happened. The rest is a blur. A lot of questions, Julia crying, Don in despair."

"What happened after that?"

I shrugged. "We moved on, but the family was never the same. Don was supposed to pass the torch to DJ—he would take over Don's law firm. There were high hopes for DJ, but they were shattered that day—shattered forever."

Dr. Truer nodded, her eyes focused on mine. "How did the accident affect your relationship with your parents?"

"On some level, I think Don blamed me at first, but he couldn't really because I was unconscious. I think he felt that I should have been cognizant of DJ's whereabouts. I think it frustrated him that he couldn't lay blame on me— on someone."

"What makes you say that?" she asked, shifting her feet on the ottoman. "Did you think you needed to take the blame?'

I shrugged and stared at my feet. "What really killed Don was hearing through the mafia grapevine that the hit was ordered from prison—a mobster named Sal 'two-toe' Marinelli. Don had screwed up his tax audit defense and left him open to a federal RICO and money-laundering charges. It cost him not only life in prison, but he also lost all his legit businesses."

I paused to look at Dr. Truer, who, after making more notes, signaled me to continue.

"Allegedly, Marinelli arranged for a hooker to proposition DJ. DJ always had a weakness for cheap women, and he gave her access to the yacht. She managed to sneak a hit man on board while everyone was intoxicated. Once on board, the hit man coaxed DJ to the aft of the yacht and threw him overboard. As soon as he was sure DJ was, in fact, shredded by the propeller, he disappeared."

Dr. Truer had a hard time hiding her horror—I could tell. For once, she was speechless. Her eyes watered.

"So, you see, indirectly, it was Don's fault. The blame could be placed squarely on his shoulders. He would never admit it, but it's there. It's there every day I see him, talk to him; it's there."

Dr. Truer gave me an empathetic frown. "Craig, I

understand how a tragedy like this could tear up a family, but accidents *do* happen—is it impossible to consider that perhaps no one is to blame?"

I straightened up in my chair and felt my eyes widen. The possibility that no one was to blame had never occurred to me. I didn't know how to respond. Dr. Truer and I just stared at each other because neither of us would speak and I knew it was because she wanted a response. In the end, I won.

"What happened after you lost your brother?" she asked—a redirection of sorts.

"Of course, they got rid of the yacht, but I'm a dreadful reminder of it all. I mean, it happened on my birthday, for God's sake. When that day comes around each year, no one's in the mood to celebrate anything, especially me." I instinctively took the bottle of hand-sanitizer from my pocket, squeezed some into my palms and rubbed them together before continuing.

Dr. Truer's eyes followed my hands.

"In case you haven't figured this out yet, I was never the favored son. I was never like DJ. He was scholarly and ambitious, and I was a silly dreamer. I went into advertising and, while my parents paid for my tuition as an undergrad at Stanford, they were horribly disappointed in the career I chose. I didn't want to step into Don's shoes and, because my parents lost DJ, they lost everything."

"What's your relationship with your parents now?" she asked. "Do you still harbor feelings of guilt over the accident?"

I felt my fingers tingling as I glanced down at my watch. It was only 7:35. "I'd like to stop now," I said abruptly. Dr. Truer's eyes moved to the clock, which was situated to my left, hidden by a fake potted plant. She could see it, but I couldn't. I often saw her eyes dart to the clock throughout our sessions so that she kept track of time.

She smiled. "Okay, Craig. But just so you know, I have to bill you for the full session."

"Fine," I answered, rising to my feet.

"I'll see you Thursday," she called after me as I briskly

made my way out of her office, out of the old, sick-smelling building and into my car. As I slathered sanitizer all over my hands and wrists, I glimpsed the rear-view mirror and noticed my eyes were watery. *Damn, I can't do this.*

THE TREADMILL SPEED WAS soaring as I absentmindedly flicked the speed button, feeling the muscles in my legs respond to the machine's demand. My feet thudded against the rubber platform with a relentless cadence. I broke a sweat, beads forming at the base of my spine and on my forehead. I wanted to cleanse my mind and body of the day's events—to shed the impurity. Tonight, it would somehow take longer—I could just feel it. I wondered how long and how fast I would have to go. I pressed my finger again on the speed button and felt my legs responding, my heart pounding, my breathing becoming increasingly difficult, *in through the nose, out through the mouth. Go faster—don't stop!*

After the treadmill, it was on to weights … tonight was arms and back night. Abs were always last. I spent every evening in my home gym. When I bought the estate in Malibu, I wanted everything self-contained and within reach. I found a house at the edge of the ocean. I could walk along the beach every morning and evening and then retreat into my home. I rarely went out in the city anymore because, when Alessandra and I divorced, the paparazzi had become unbearable. They were manageable in the past, and back then it was fun. It helped business that I was seen in every tabloid, at different parties and events. I was still married and, therefore, nothing was ever negative. But during the divorce, Alessandra had seized the opportunity to poison my image and it remained poisoned ever since. The previously dashing, flirtatious Craig Keller was now a predatory womanizer.

IT WAS AFTER 10 p.m. and I needed a shower. I had exhausted every muscle in my body. This was why I would never be anything but in excellent shape. Even at forty, there was not an ounce of fat on my body. It still looked and felt the same as it did when I was in my twenties. In fact, I didn't look much different, either. It was my mind that had been polluted. I silently wished there were a workout for that—something that could sponge the rot from my soul— the sickness wrought by sexual deviance, marital infidelity, and the cruel disregard of others' feelings. Sometimes I felt like Dorian Gray, but there was no gruesome hidden painting, further deteriorating with every sinful, disgraceful act, protecting me from scrutiny. There was no proof—nothing tangible I could see to understand the impact of my words and actions.

The shower water was now hot and steaming and I scrubbed my body with soaps of all varieties; I kept multiple bars, gels, and liquids in my shower. I had a process. First, I started with the bars and then I put on the scrubbing gloves and went over my entire body with each gel. There were five in all. Then, I moved to the liquids—this was the rinse cycle. Finally, I would wash my hair twice and condition it. The women I allowed near me all said I smelled like soap.

After toweling off and applying numerous unscented lotions and creams, it was time for bed and a glass of Scotch to lull me into oblivion. I had one every night as soon as I was seated upright in bed, silk pajamas on and legs tucked under the covers. I always kept a bottle of my favorite Scotch, Bruichladdich Black Art 1992, in my bedroom. I had a whole collection of these bottles, neatly lined up behind the bookcase. It was really a compartment hidden within my bedroom wall. If you moved the bookcase, there was a safe nestled in the wall. The combination was DJ's birthdate, 12-10-1975 and the wall pulled out like a door containing inside shelves. I kept the good stuff in the safe along with other valuables.

I took sip number one and felt immediately relaxed. By sip number two, my cell phone was ringing. It was after midnight and I quickly glanced at the phone screen. "Erin" was flashing. She must be drunk and wanting sex. There was no way I was going to answer. I made it a rule to eject any woman from my house prior to midnight. I simply couldn't handle anyone sleeping in my bed, messing it up and then becoming a burden the next morning. When I entertained females, I usually made sure they were out by 11:30. I turned the ringer off and tried to erase Erin from my mind. I had met her at a fundraiser for Alzheimer's—she was wearing a tight red dress and came on to me while I was bidding on some bauble at the silent auction. I remember her leaning forward, her large breasts exposed as she eyed the dollar amount of my bid.

"Are you bidding tonight?" I asked, focusing my eyes on her breasts instead of her average-looking face. It was caked with heavy foundation—so much so that it cracked in the corners of her mouth and in the crow's feet around her eyes.

"I'll bet you say that to all the girls," she answered, smiling up at me, further cracking her face paint. I guessed she was in her late thirties—that age when women tend to act desperate in front of attractive men in their same age group. "Are you here alone?" she asked.

I looked around me and back at her. "It seems that way. And you?"

"I was," she said, still grinning. I hated it when women were this brazen, although I knew she would be an easy one to get into bed, to put up with the biting and the eventual dismissal from my lineup. That's what they were these days—a part of the current lineup. I was no longer dating. That required effort. And I was so picky about women that I'd tired of the constant searching—the unceasing evaluation of potential partners. The only touchy thing was taking the mediocre women—those who didn't meet my criteria—to my house.

Once they were there, they presumed they could return, so I had simply resorted to taking them for drives in the Bentley. It was easier that way. There would be no memorization of my address—no getting into my space. I knew of a spot in Pacific Palisades, off the Pacific Coast Highway—where I used to take Hayden. If I drove to the top of a steep and winding hill, there was a secluded area where no one would see my car—there was no chance of getting discovered or arrested. I kept condoms and a clean towel in my car, in the event I met someone.

I had mistakenly allowed Erin into my house. She waltzed through it viewing the art on my walls with acquisitive eyes, thinking perhaps she could be Mrs. Keller. I always laughed at those women—the ones who never got that being Mrs. Keller was the absolute quickest way to hell.

I took sip numbers three and four consecutively. I was starting to get sleepy. I would not return Erin's call. She would call exactly three more times, and the pitch of her voice would get shriller with each successive call. The final phone message would include some declaration of love for me, which had little to do with reality. It would also include a barb about seeing someone else. I was so completely bored. Without the help of sip number five, I fell asleep.

# Three

**B**EN WHITMAN WAS IN my office, yammering on about some ass he was chasing, like he always did. I often wondered why I ever partnered with him in the first place. He was so shallow and uninteresting with his constant pursuit of office women, his inability to bring projects over the finish line, his lack of passion and energy. We were in the same fraternity at Stanford and I had a soft spot for him when we started the agency. That's why I took him in as a full partner. Still, he never added value—never had any good ideas. He was basically window-dressing—a good-looking mannequin in an expensive suit. He needed to go. I stared at him silently, watching his mouth move but not listening to what was coming out of it.

Cassandra called, interrupting his tedious soliloquy, and I answered on speaker phone. "I have Warren Mitchell for you," she said loudly. Ben's eyes immediately darted up to meet mine. He wore a surprised expression.

"It's about a board we're serving on," I explained without skipping a beat. "Will you please excuse me?"

Ben left without a question as I picked up the phone and told Cassandra to put him through. "Warren," I said into the receiver. I was hoping he had good news for me.

But his voice was measured. "I wanted to let you know I spoke to Jane and Jeffrey about your initial proposal," he started.

"And?" I asked, feeling my neck tense up slightly.

"Jane had nothing but positive things to say about weighting our business more heavily on the digital side … on consumer-centric analysis. Her only concern is partnering with you."

I felt a stab in my gut at Jane's negative assessment of me. "What about Jeffrey?"

"Well, Jeffrey knew you in a past life, Craig. He was not at all enthused about seeing you again … working with you … trusting you as a partner of this agency."

"So, where does that leave us?" I questioned, feeling the sting of being shunned by Warren et al.

"I still think it's a good idea, especially with the addition of Alonzo Costa and Bobbi Silverstein. Jane was excited about the prospects of having them on our team."

"But?"

"But they're still skeptical about your character, Craig." I heard Warren exhale into the phone, like he was already weary. "I honestly think you should pay each of them a visit and discuss the proposal with them personally," he continued. "I can't promise it'll change their minds but perhaps there's some way you can make them believe you're worthy of this new alliance."

"And what about you?" I asked, wondering why Warren didn't admit to sharing their distrust, especially after I'd burned him twice.

"I want the biggest success for this business," he responded. "I know one thing about you, Keller … you never give up and you have fire in your belly. Not many others have that. It's a rare quality and I'd rather be on the same side than competing against you."

I swallowed hard. "When should I approach Jane and Jeffrey?"

"As soon as possible and I'd do it discreetly, at our

offices. I don't want my executive team seen in public with you when you're hounded day and night by tabloid news reporters. I don't want rumors flying about mergers and acquisitions, especially after you bought me out once already."

"I understand. That wouldn't be good for me either. I'll call them to arrange private meetings right away."

After we hung up, I realized what I was up against. Jeffrey was fiercely protective of Jane. I knew that from when they were both briefly employees of mine. I wondered who I should meet with first and decided it should be Jeffrey. Jeffrey would compare notes with Jane and advise her. Jane was like climbing Everest. She could wear me out or kill me before I made it to the summit. I hated that she was positioned to evaluate me, after our volatile history. I hated that I needed her to be on my side.

OVER THE NEXT TWO days, I had managed to get on both Jeffrey's and Jane's calendars—Jeffrey on Thursday and Jane on Friday. It was exactly how I wanted it to roll out. If I could just get Jeffrey on the right side, Jane might be more inclined to accept me. I knew no one would embrace it, but I didn't need that. I just needed acceptance and a deal.

My approach would be to appeal to their desire to put Mitchell Vance & Mercer on the national map, even if they didn't go public. Having two superstars and my successful track record, they could move the agency into a new realm. People would seek out their agency for creative and media expertise. But between Jeffrey and Jane, I needed different strategies. What might work on Jeffrey would likely not work on Jane. I needed to impart enough enthusiasm to Jeffrey, so he would buy into it and already be working on persuading Jane before I even got to her.

I thought about Jeffrey's personality: whipsaw smart, creatively competent, brutally honest … and snide. He would need to get in enough digs to make him feel like he drove a hard bargain. I would have to swallow my pride to get Jeffrey's approval and Jane's submission.

ALONE IN BED WITH my glass of Scotch, I went over the plan for meeting with Jeffrey the following morning. I took sip number one and glanced at my bullets. I always did bullets for meetings so that I would remember key points to keep the conversation on track.

- Compliment Jeffrey's work, specifically citing his top three campaigns—focusing only on those he worked on closely.
- Reinforce the real threat of competitive agencies, especially in the face of competition from Towne Ink and their expertise in digital marketing and analytics.
- Address the trust issue head on—there was no way Jeffrey would not respect openness and honesty, based on what I knew of him.
- Imply that it will be great to have an additional creative mind to collaborate with Alonzo.

The last bullet was going to be tricky. On the one hand, Jeffrey would be flattered to think a creative genius like Alonzo would want his input; on the other hand, Alonzo would balk at any interference with his art, especially from someone of Jeffrey's ilk. To Alonzo, it would be like asking Chagall to work with Warhol.

I would have to manage Alonzo on the back end—his arrogance knew no bounds, but he wasn't stupid. After all, I had plucked him off the streets from a life of crime and drugs over a decade earlier.

I first noticed Alonzo's magnificent murals on the corner of Colyton and Palmetto downtown. They shimmered with the kind of saturated color reminiscent of Marc Chagall in all his resplendent glory. The messages were hopeful, clever, and original. I combed the streets looking for the creator of this singular art and was led to Alonzo. He was homeless, living out of a cardboard box on Skid Row. I set him up with an apartment, sent him to University of Southern California to properly learn graphic design and hired him as an intern. Upon graduation and with the experience under his belt, he quickly climbed the ranks and earned the creative director role. His work got attention—lots of attention—and he swiftly became a rock star in the advertising industry on a national level.

I knew he had offers all over the country with agencies like Ogilvy and BBDO, but I made sure he was eternally bound to me. He signed an extensive contract when I took him off the street, basically agreeing that he was not allowed to work anywhere else unless he had seven figures to repay me, an amount that accumulated in interest over the years. There was no way he could leave.

I was on sip number four already and thinking about Jane. I would have to try a completely different approach with her. *What was Jane motivated by?* I had a difficult time answering that question, which puzzled me further. When I first met her, I knew her so much better. She was like every young woman, dazzled by my looks, money, and power. But in the end, she stood up to me like no other woman ever had. She grew to be so smart and confident she could see right through my bullshit. I really needed to think this through with Jane—look at it as an ad campaign. *What message would resonate with her on an emotional level?* I took my last sip, set the glass down on my nightstand, turned off the light and went to sleep.

"TELL ME ABOUT YOUR wife, Craig," Dr. Truer suggested.

It was Thursday and I went straight from my meeting with Jeffrey to my session with Janice. I just wasn't in the mood for therapy. I felt like the meeting with Jeffrey went well, but he acted non-committal. As predicted, he was intrigued by the idea of working in a more collaborative fashion with Alonzo, but the trust issue was still high on his list.

"How do you feel about Jane?" he had asked cautiously.

I wasn't sure how to answer.

"I respect her work," I told him. I was reluctant to lay it on too thick. That would be transparent.

"But do you respect *her*?" he returned sharply. "Because if you don't, there's no way we'll be able to work together."

"Yes, of course I do," I had answered. But I could tell Jeffrey was still unconvinced. Jane had filled him in on our history and it never sat well with him. He would always view me as an asshole, and I could hardly blame him.

"Craig—did you hear me?" asked Dr. Truer, breaking into my thought bubble.

"Sorry, doctor, I was thinking about something else—something work-related."

"If we're going to make progress in here, you need to tune out the noise. We were talking about your wife, Alessandra," she responded, eyeing me carefully, as though she were expecting some big reveal.

"Ex-wife," I corrected her. "What do you want to know?"

"Why don't we start with basics—like how you met, how long you were together, how you felt about each other, and why you divorced."

I inhaled slowly. "We met in Paris. She was a runway model. I was introduced to her through friends and we had a whirlwind romance for the next three months. I was in Paris buying art—Chagall paintings, but I ultimately had to return to L.A. to run my business."

I paused to think about Alessandra, how slender and frail she always was. She was taller than any woman I had met before at 5'11 and we made a striking couple. I loved to watch her walk because she had this sort of glide, like a ballerina on pointe.

"I was about to leave," I continued, "but something made me ask her to come with me—I wanted to take her back with me to California. I remember thinking how Don and Julia would love her—she was everything they liked: classically beautiful, elegant, understated, and well-mannered. She still had an accent from growing up in Rome. I knew she was the only woman my parents would accept, so

I asked her to marry me."

Dr. Truer was regarding me thoughtfully. "Were you in love with her?"

I knew that would be her next question. I thought back to that time and how quickly it went—how young I was, only twenty-six, but how experienced sexually. "I wouldn't exactly say I was in love. I guess I was just tired of the game. I ran around with lots of women before her."

"How many women?" she pressed.

I shrugged as a collage of faces, breasts, legs, and other body parts flooded my memory. I had had so many women, sometimes two or three at a time. "I don't know—hundreds, maybe."

Dr. Truer's expression briefly skated the razor's edge between shock and disgust, but it quickly became placid. After all, psychologists were not supposed to judge. "Craig, that's a pretty significant number, don't you think? How old were you when you lost your virginity?"

The memory of that day on the yacht and DJ's death came back to haunt me as it did in the previous session. I didn't want to think of that woman, but I had to, because that day, that time with her changed my life. "I was seventeen," I uttered reluctantly, trying to wipe her out of my mind. "She was way older."

"Were you in a relationship with her at the time?"

"No, *okay?* Dr. Truer, there was no relationship." I could feel my collar restricting me at the neck and I pulled on it slightly to get some relief.

"You seem agitated right now."

I nodded. "It was the day DJ died. His friends fed me strong drinks and paid that hooker to take me to bed and pop my cherry," I explained, suddenly feeling like I needed hand sanitizer. My fingers were now tingling, and I felt dizzy. "The next thing I knew, my brother was dead, and she was next to me."

Dr. Truer's expression changed to sadness and empathy. "Your first sexual experience must have been the worst in your life. Have you ever heard of the term, *la petite mort*?"

I shrugged. "No."

She shifted her legs on the ottoman, crossing them at the ankles. "Literally, it means 'little death', but it's an expression used to describe the brief loss or weakening of consciousness."

"What does that have to do with me?" I asked, looking askance at Dr. Truer.

"Well, in the contemporary world, it refers to the sensation after having an orgasm, which is likened to a death of some sort. Your first sexual encounter involved you having an orgasm and awakening to the death of your brother. The incident with the woman on the yacht must have impacted your relationship with women throughout your life."

I didn't respond. I couldn't remember the woman's face, but I always remembered her scent. It was repugnant to me—cloyingly sweet like cheap, overly perfumed hand lotion. Her whole body reeked of this smell and it made me sick. There were times when I encountered that same smell and it drove me to leave a room in fear and disgust.

"Let's go back to Alessandra for a moment," Dr. Truer suggested as she picked up her notepad, scratching it with her pen. "You said you weren't in love with her and that you married her to both please your parents and to put a stop to your sexual promiscuity. Am I right?"

"Yes," I conceded.

"Did marrying her accomplish what you wanted?"

"For a little while. Of course, Don and Julia loved her, but that was predictable," I said, recalling the time I brought her to meet them. Julia fawned all over Alessandra's clothes and Don treated her like a goddess. "I had finally done something right."

"Were you physically attracted to her?"

I shook my head. "Maybe at first, like the first time we were ever together," I said thinking back to our wedding night. "Alessandra was a virgin, and I was a player. She had made me wait to have sex with her until our wedding night and I recalled being with as many women as I could throughout our courtship, almost as though preparing for the shackles to be fastened and locked. I knew every trick in the book, but when it finally came time, I had to hide my expertise in bed, so I wouldn't turn off Alessandra."

I was not looking Dr. Truer in the eye. I instead fixed my gaze on the bobble head doll of Elvis Presley she kept on her desk. It was situated right underneath an air conditioning vent and it shook slightly whenever the air kicked on.

"It's interesting that you saw marriage and monogamy as a kind of jail," she observed. "Do your parents see marriage in the same way?"

I thought about Don and his reckless womanizing. Julia doted on him regardless, obediently following his orders and putting up with his violent antics. She must have secretly known of his exploits. "I don't know how they see marriage," I finally answered.

"Did you have sex with Alessandra often during the course of your marriage?" Dr. Truer asked.

I tore my eyes away from the Elvis bobble head to look at Dr. Truer. "It was perfunctory. I swear I got her pregnant twice because we did it exactly twice." I glanced down at my feet uncomfortably. "That's an exaggeration, but it's not too far from the truth."

"So, your needs were not being met in your marriage," she stated matter-of-factly. "That had to be difficult for you."

I knew what was coming next—the questions about my infidelity, which started about three months after our wedding. I decided to come clean about it before she had to ask. "I cheated on Alessandra," I admitted. "It started early in the marriage and continued until she asked for a divorce."

Dr. Truer nodded and took some notes. "Did you two ever discuss the cheating? I mean, did you admit to being unfaithful?"

"I didn't have to—she's a bright woman. She knew the entire time, but she stayed for the kids—we both did—we're Catholic."

"So, you never actually talked about it?" Dr. Truer was not going to let this go, that was evident.

I shook my head. "She accused me all the time, but I

never confessed to it." I then saw Dr. Truer glance at the clock to my left and I knew our session was almost over. *Thank God.*

"Craig, I'd like to delve into this more when we meet next week. It seems there's a lot to explore and I hope you're able to open up about it in here."

I took a deep breath and then nodded.

"Good, then I'll see you Monday," she concluded.

In my car, drifting toward the freeway, fingers still wet with hand sanitizer, I almost had to stop twice because I thought I might throw up. The nausea came on so suddenly, I figured I must have eaten something that disagreed with me. I so seldom felt that way.

Dr. Truer had uncovered some rough territory. I knew it was only a matter of time before I would have to reveal the most personal things about myself and I was dreading it.

The only thing I dreaded more was meeting with Jane the next morning.

EARL WAS AT HER desk when I entered the lobby of Mitchell Vance & Mercer.

"Mr. Keller! My, we're seeing an awful lot of you this week," she greeted me, smiling in a flirtatious way. I gave her one of my most flirtatious smiles right back.

"And who are you here to see today?" she asked, eyes scanning me with approval.

"Jane Mercer," I answered and felt a little twinge in my stomach. I had selected a suit Jane would love. It was jet black and paired with a pale blue shirt with thin black pinstripes. I wore subtle knotted platinum cuff links and went tieless thinking it might disarm her a bit, make her feel like our conversation was more casual. Jane responded better when I wore black, something I sensed in the early days of our relationship. My bullet points were ready, but an unrelenting nervousness crept over me. *What if she throws me a curve ball?* I rarely felt this type of anxiety prior to a meeting—with anyone. *Just stick to the main points and you'll be fine.*

"Of course, let me call her—please have a seat."

I sat and anxiously flipped through *Advertising Age*,

which was filled with the usual gossip about competing agencies, the latest PR wins, and stories about who lost ground on Facebook and YouTube. After about ten minutes, I checked my watch and then glanced up at Pearl. She was typing away on her computer, oblivious that I had waited longer than the standard five minutes. I pictured Jane, sitting in her office, pleased with herself that she was able to make me wait. I shifted in my chair and, just as I was about to express my impatience, Pearl's phone rang.

"Of course, I'll show him to your office right away," she said. When she hung up, she glanced at me and smiled. "Ms. Mercer's ready to see you."

I followed Pearl down the hallway, past Warren's and Jeffrey's offices. Unlike everyone else, Jane's door was open, and she was standing in front of her desk, looking beautiful and serene. I felt a shot of adrenaline pulsate through me. She wore a sleek lavender dress that hugged her body and I had to stop myself from staring right at her nipples, which were protruding from underneath the material of her dress. She must be cold, I thought. Her long hair was pulled into a low side ponytail and she wore a navy and lavender printed silk scarf. Her tiny diamond stud earrings sparkled ever so slightly. I always admired the way Jane dressed. It was smart but sexy. She never tried too hard.

Pearl motioned for me to enter and then left us alone. It was just Jane Mercer and me. My neck felt stiff and I had the urge to loosen my collar.

"Please come in," Jane greeted me with a forced smile. "I've been looking forward to this meeting all week." There was sarcasm in her voice.

"Really," I responded, with the same sarcasm. *Control yourself, Craig. She's doing exactly what you expected.* "Me, too," I said, trying to sound more congenial.

I looked around as Jane shut her office door. She had a sizable office, with a round conference table, a small couch, and some leather chairs. The art on her walls was mostly ads from campaigns she had worked on with Warren. Framed photos peeked out from behind her desk on a credenza, but

I was too far away to absorb the content.

Jane ambled over to where I was standing and gestured toward her couch. "Please sit down," she offered and then took a seat across from me in one of the leather chairs. I watched her sit, crossing her lean legs. They were smooth and bare, and she wore navy high-heeled leather pumps.

"Would you like something to drink?" she asked. Her eyes scanned down my body and back up to my face, like she was sizing me up, perhaps remembering the times she'd seen me naked. I secretly prayed that was what she was thinking—hoped that her attraction to me would help seal the deal.

"No, thank you," I replied, lowering myself onto the couch, realizing Jane's chair had taller legs, giving her a psychological height advantage. I needed to get to the point with her quickly. I was so distracted by her very presence and hated to admit she had gotten to me on some level—it happened a long time ago and all the memories came flooding back.

"So, Ms. Mercer, I know you've spoken to Warren about my proposal," I began, noticing Jane wore a wedding band with pavé diamonds adjacent to what appeared to be a decent-sized princess-cut diamond ring. She must have finally married the violinist—the guy who took a swing at me when I saw her with him before they were married. My jaw was bruised and swollen for at least a week after that incident. I never returned the punch—it was deserved.

"I have," she answered, looking me directly in the eye.

"I met with Jeffrey yesterday," I added, hoping she would let on that perhaps Jeffrey swayed her in the right direction. "He seemed open and enthusiastic about a potential alliance." I probably should not have used the word 'enthusiastic' because Jeffrey was anything but; however, confidence was my only hope of getting her on my side.

She shrugged. "I haven't spoken to him."

I was having a tough time remembering the bullets I'd written, and it had me flustered, although I made sure my expression remained neutral. There was something about her look, something about her body language that conveyed reproach. I took a deep breath. "But you understand the concept and its advantages," I offered.

"You're correct. I also understand its disadvantages," she answered. Her smugness had me gritting my teeth and feeling anger boiling up underneath the surface. I watched her uncross her legs and cross them again the opposite way. Her dress was cut just above her knees and I felt like she was trying to tease me. She made me crazy—she was such a tease when she worked for me. I remembered going home after taking her to dinner—forced to masturbate in the shower because she said no to my advances. She wore a miniskirt that night and I couldn't stop myself from imagining those lithe, toned legs wrapped around me. I wanted her so badly. She was just sticking it in my face.

I cleared my throat and focused my eyes on hers. "The proposal comes with an exclusive collaboration you won't be able to find anywhere else."

"You mean, the same collaboration we had when I worked for you before?" she said with a little smile on her lips. "I can't think of anything worse."

"Then why did you accept a meeting with me?" I threw back sharply, knowing I was losing my temper and it was perilously close to showing. *Was it so you could watch me squirm in your presence? Is that what gets you off these days?*

"I accepted the meeting as a courtesy to Warren," she responded casually, leaning back in her chair. Those hard nipples were staring at me again. I thought about the violinist and wondered whether musicians like him were more talented in bed. I imagined him manipulating her body the way he played a violin, and I felt a stab of pure envy. *How did he get her, anyway?*

I breathed in deeply and tried to soften my demeanor. "So, this is merely a courtesy call?" I asked. "You should have just declined the meeting rather than waste our time."

All I could think of was yanking that lavender dress up to her waist and tearing off what little she was wearing underneath. Then I would take her over my knee and slap her bare ass until it was red as a candy apple. She would scream in pain until I forced her onto her knees. I would grab her by that ponytail and thrust myself into her mouth—shove it in so deep, it would touch the back of her throat—trigger her gag reflex—so she could no longer talk—so she could no longer disparage me. I wondered what Dr. Truer would think of my sick, violent sexual fantasies—she would probably have me locked up.

"Jane," I said, keeping my voice measured even though I was seething inside. "Would you like me to grovel? Would that make you happy? Do you want another apology? I thought we were done with all that." I noticed her jaw tightening, her lips pursed, and I knew I was going too far with my arrogance. I didn't care anymore. "It's really your choice," I continued in the same level tone. "You can stay in your plodding, steadfast cocoon and become redundant within a year or you can partner with me. The bottom line is, you'll be making the biggest mistake of your career if you reject this. You could be pulling in three times what you're drawing now. Don't blow it because of personal feelings."

She was now glaring at me, pink lips parted, eyes flashing, brows furrowed. But she said nothing.

I rose to my feet, eyes cast down upon her. "Talk to Warren, talk to Jeffrey, talk to whomever you want. But don't play revenge games with me, Jane. You're smarter than that."

I briskly made my way out of her office. Once in the car, I hastily reached for the hand sanitizer. I was done with this. I was no longer married to the outcome—Jane had taken care of that. I felt reckless in her presence—like I could throw everything away and it wouldn't matter. It wouldn't matter because she hated me. She would always hate me.

IT WAS MY TURN to take the kids for the weekend. I got them every other weekend in the settlement, but it was never enough for me. I was not at all candidate for a 'Father of the Year' award; however, I loved my children—loved them even though they were conceived through a loveless marriage. I glanced at my dashboard clock—it was almost 7:15 p.m. There was heavy traffic on the I-10 West and was bound to be stop-and-go on the 405, too. I wouldn't get to Bel Air before 8:30, and Alessandra would be pissed that I was late again. I didn't want to deal with anyone else's reproving words. This would top off a great week.

Even worse, I couldn't get Jane out of my head. I wondered why she didn't say anything to set me straight. It wasn't like her to keep her mouth shut in the face of my cutting commentary. She normally liked to spar but something had changed. I was almost disappointed.

One thing was certain: there was no way I would be able to get the deal done now. It was over before it even started. And it was my own fault. If I had just sucked it up in Jane's office, everything might still be on the table. I just couldn't control myself around her. Now I had to go back to making strategic moves within Keller Whitman Group, a thought that caused me distress. Ben needed to go quickly. Strong and Richards too. I would have to find partners as good as Warren, Jeffrey, and Jane in a sea of hacks I'd already tried on in the past. I would draw up a new org chart over the weekend and start over. The thought of having to ask Don for more money to fund my agency through another transition gave me a stomachache.

Just before I made it to the 405, Warren Mitchell's name was flashing on my Bluetooth screen. *Here it comes—the big rejection.* I took a deep breath and answered the call, "Craig Keller," I stated in my coldest, most professional voice.

"Keller, it's Warren." He sounded serious, but that's how he always sounded before he spat out whatever he wanted to say.

"Warren, I might as well save you the big conversation. I know what this call's about and there's no need to get into it. I've decided to work independently, within my own agency to make changes and move forward. I'm sorry it didn't work out."

There was silence on the other end.

"Warren?"

"I'm still here," he said. "I'm a little confused. I called to tell you Jeffrey and Jane both conditionally voted to accept your proposal. And now you're backing out on the deal? How does that happen?"

I couldn't believe what I was hearing. *Jane voted to accept the proposal?* There was no way after our hostile exchange in the office earlier. *What was she up to now?* Or did she just want to make me work for it? That woman was a mystery on so many levels. I felt my car swerve a bit as I hit the 405 on-ramp.

"Keller?"

"Yes, I'm here. I guess I thought the decision would be different. I'm not backing out on the deal at all. I'm incredibly pleased everyone voted to accept the proposal."

"Good. But, Keller, there will be some stipulations on your partnership, and we need to go over them together, with Jeffrey and Jane in the room."

"I'm happy to go through negotiations as a group," I responded, hitting the brakes as traffic merged and scanning my left side mirror.

"No, Keller—you're not hearing me. The stipulations will be non-negotiable."

"What kind of stipulations are you referring to?"

"That's why we need to have a meeting first. If you disagree with any of them, the deal's off," he delivered in a deadpan tone.

*Here's where Jane will try to stick it to me.* I knew there would be a catch. "When do you want to have this meeting?" I asked.

"In my office over the weekend. There's no need for our staff to further speculate about what's going on with all your recent office visits. We can have the meeting privately with all four parties in the room."

I thought about Axel and Anabel, and that I'd have to leave them with Sylvia for a couple of hours. Sylvia was my housekeeper and occasional nanny when I had business during custody weekends. Alessandra would not be pleased. One of her biggest complaints in our marriage, other than

45

my indiscretions with other women, was that I spent too much time working and not enough time with our children.

"I have my kids this weekend, but I'll work around your schedule," I finally answered. I thought it was a nice touch to mention my children—to have him think me a good father.

"Great," Warren said. "We were thinking 1:30 p.m. tomorrow. Does that work for you?"

"I'll make it work," I responded before disconnecting.

ALESSANDRA WAS PREDICTABLY VEXED when I showed up late and mentioned Sylvia needed to watch the kids on Saturday. She made me vow to tell her if I planned to have anyone other than me look after them. It was her way of watchdogging me—controlling what I did. I knew it was really about her jealousy over my dating habits since we broke up. She thought I slept with women while the kids were in the house, which was an utter falsehood. I never argued, however. It just wasn't worth it.

"I have an important meeting that could make or break my business," I explained to her, glancing around my former home uncomfortably. Everything looked familiar but there was no more warmth. I would always leave the house feeling empty.

I watched Alessandra shake her head, her shoulder-length dark tresses flipping from side to side. At thirty-five, she still appeared youthful with her full red lips and olive skin. I remembered kissing those lips for the first time and feeling nothing inside. She was beautiful but never sexy to me. She was the kind of woman other women thought men found sexy.

She shrugged with indifference and leaned against a red lacquered bookshelf. I remembered purchasing it on a trip to Singapore. "Your business meetings are none of my concern."

"My business allows you to live in a Bel Air mansion," I replied, catching my eye on the trio of elaborate Murano glass wall sconces lining the entryway. I found them in Venice, while shopping for a Chagall painting. It was a good thing our pre-nuptial agreement specified the Chagalls would remain in my possession.

My eyes met Alessandra's once more. "Your entire existence depends on what happens with my business, so you *should* be concerned, Alessandra—you should be as concerned as I am, if not more so."

"You never change, you know that?" She shot back with a toss of her hair. "You never fail to throw it in my face that you have to support us—oh, poor multi-millionaire Craig has to support his family because he fucked up his marriage by running around with every woman on the planet."

I sighed and looked down at my feet. "Look, I didn't come here to start a fight. I was just honoring your wishes that I inform you when someone other than myself is watching the kids. It should only be a couple of hours."

I was now just weary. I wanted Alessandra to get the kids and their things, so I could leave immediately, rather than watch her sulk over wounds that never healed. I wondered if she would ever just move on. Her anger and resentment would chip away at her life. She was still young enough to find a better husband. I didn't understand why she wasn't even dating—not that I knew of, anyway. She wanted to be a martyr and stay single. Of course, it would benefit me financially if she found a new husband. There were plenty of men in L.A. as wealthy as me—men who would love to marry a woman like Alessandra.

"Fine," she responded tersely as she marched away. "I'll get the children."

ONCE WE WERE HOME in Malibu, I brought the kids snacks and we sat in the game room and watched *Cupcake Wars* on Food Network. It was Anabel's favorite show. Axel wasn't paying attention; he was deeply engrossed in his Minecraft game.

"Hey, buddy," I called to Axel. "Do you have homework this weekend?" I liked when Axel asked me to help with his homework. Although a straight-A student, he had occasional trouble with Geometry, which had always been my forte in school.

"No, Dad," he responded, briefly lifting his gaze to meet mine and then becoming absorbed again in his tablet game. He shifted lazily on the bulky beanbag chair.

I had dedicated a rather large, square room on the lower level of the house to be the kids' game room. It was a full floor down from the rest of the living space and there were no windows. The previous owners must have used it as a movie theater, because there was a small studio where audio-visual equipment would have been. I turned the studio into a bathroom. A large screen used to face a few rows of theater chairs. I had them ripped out and the floor leveled. The chairs were replaced with casual furniture and the walls adorned with old movie posters. A mammoth wide-screen television replaced the movie screen and speakers throughout the ceiling gave the sound a theater-style quality.

I felt so guilt-ridden after the argument with Alessandra that I decided to turn my phone off for the evening and focus solely on my children. Anabel was lying next to me on the plush grey suede couch, head on a stack of red and black pillows. Her feet were in my lap. I was massaging them and noticed she wore red nail polish on her toes.

"Does Mommy know you're wearing nail polish?" I directed to Anabel, trying not to sound too stern; but it baffled me that Alessandra would have allowed her ten-year-old to wear such a grown-up color.

Anabel didn't look up. She just answered, "Yes, Daddy."

"Then if I call Mommy right now and ask her, she'll say yes?"

Anabel now glanced over at me and propped herself up on her elbows. Her long straw-colored hair was tangled around her neck. Sometimes it was hard for me to look at Anabel because she reminded me of DJ. Axel, who was two years older than Anabel, looked just like me. It was odd that the Keller genes were so strong—neither of my kids resembled Alessandra's family. It's like her genetic makeup was inconsequential in the conjuring of these two young miniatures of my brother and me.

"Well?" I asked again. "Tell me the truth, Anabel."

She blinked her light brown eyes at me and then admitted, "I found the polish in Mommy's bathroom."

"So, you just lied to me. That's disappointing."

"I'm sorry, Daddy," she mumbled, pulling her feet from my lap, and tucking them under her body. She peered up at me as though she were trying to gauge how much trouble she was in. "Are you going to tell Mommy?"

"Not if you take that stuff off your feet right away and promise me you won't touch Mommy's things again unless you ask her first."

"But I don't know how to get it off," she said picking at her toes, trying to chip the polish.

I sighed, thinking perhaps one of my 'lineup' left nail polish remover in one of the guest bathrooms. It was Brianna, the waitress from Chi Spacca in Hancock Park. I'd given her a huge tip and my phone number one night, and she wouldn't stop calling me. She was always leaving things behind, which turned me off. I usually warned women about this sort of thing—threatened that if they purposely left anything at my house it would be promptly thrown away.

"I might have something—come with me," I said, taking her by the hand and corralling her up the stairs, to the guest bathroom Brianna used the last time she was here.

I sat Anabel on the toilet lid while I sifted through the cupboards underneath the sink basins. Sure enough, there were all kinds of girl products, including makeup, tampons, and a razor. *What was Brianna thinking when I never once allowed her to stay overnight?* I rolled my eyes and pushed the items towards the back of the cabinet, so Anabel wouldn't see them. But I did find nail polish remover and cotton balls.

I knelt on the floor and took Anabel's left foot, gently cleansing the garish red polish from her little toes while she watched with a wide-eyed expression. "Daddy," she suddenly asked, "Do you miss Mommy?" It was one of those questions she used to ask more when the divorce was fresh, but I hadn't heard it for a while.

"Of course, I do," I replied. "I miss all of you."

"Then why don't you come home?"

I continued to rub off the polish, thinking about what I would tell her. "Honey, we've been over this before. Mommy and I love each other, but we can't live together right now."

"Will you *ever* live together again?" She was almost pleading with me.

I had removed the last trace of red polish from her toes and began to put Brianna's things away, not answering Anabel's question.

"Will you?" she repeated.

I took Anabel's hand to help her up. She was already over five feet tall without shoes. The top of her head came to my chest now. She would undoubtedly grow sky-high coming from such tall parents. DJ was tall, too. He was only an inch or two shorter than me. I pulled her close and held her there for a minute, running my fingers through her long blonde locks.

"You know I love you, right?" I said as she dug her face into my shirt. "And I'll always be there when you need me." I could feel her crying now, sobbing into my shirt, her slender shoulders shaking.

"Anabel, what is it, honey?" I asked gently, caressing her back.

"I ... I just want to see you more," she muttered between sobs.

I felt a pit in my stomach. When she finally turned her face up to me, I almost did a double take, she looked so much like DJ, with his same earnest expression and what were the start of his chiseled features. In a few years, she would mature into the female version of him. I wasn't sure how I would handle that.

"Mommy's always in a bad mood," she wailed. "I never do anything right."

"Sweetheart, she's just stressed," I said, thinking I would have a little talk with Alessandra about her attitude. *What the hell did she have to be stressed about?* It's not like she was a working, single parent. Her anger at me was affecting our daughter and I couldn't have Anabel take the heat for what I had done. I would simply not let that happen. "It has nothing to do with you."

"You don't know what goes on because you're never there," she tearfully protested.

"I think you need some sleep. Let's get you cleaned up and to bed and tomorrow morning, guess what I'm making for breakfast?"

She suddenly beamed up at me, tears still in her eyes. "Polka-dot pancakes?"

Anabel loved 'polka-dot pancakes,' which were really blueberry pancakes. I made them almost every Saturday for the kids when I lived with them full-time, and I knew it would cheer her up. I smiled and nodded. "You bet."

"I can't wait, Daddy," she cried, hopping up and down and throwing her arms around me again.

Once I was able to get Anabel and Axel to bed, I proceeded to the shower for my vigorous nightly ritual. In bed, sipping Scotch, for once I wasn't thinking about work. I knew the big meeting with Warren, Jeffrey and Jane loomed before me, but I couldn't get my mind off Anabel and, by association, DJ.

I always had a soft spot for my daughter. I wondered if Alessandra was jealous of Anabel on some level because it was obvious how much I loved her. Anabel was a living breathing connection to DJ, and her life was just beginning. I was more protective of Anabel than anyone because she personified hope for the future ... like no one else could.

# Five

I STROLLED INTO THE MITCHELL Vance & Mercer lobby Saturday and passed Pearl's empty desk. It was almost 1:30 and Warren's door was closed. I heard muffled voices coming from inside the office and I knocked on the door.

It was Jeffrey who answered. "Craig," he greeted me stiffly, like he was not at all pleased to see me again. "Come in."

Jeffrey and I had a congenial relationship most of the time—at least before he found out what had gone on between Jane and me. He always wore a smart-assed expression with his hipster horn-rimmed glasses and spiky hair. Today, he was wearing a nerdy sweater vest over a long-sleeved button-down shirt, giving him a collegiate look.

Warren and Jane were seated at his round conference table leaning into each other, obviously engaged in prequel dialogue. Jane's back was to me. Warren looked up as I approached.

"Craig," Warren called, waving me over to the conference table. It was the first time he called me Craig since the last time I worked for him years before. I never said anything to him directly, but I hated that he called me Keller. I preferred

Craig or Mr. Keller. Keller on its own reminded me of some football star getting a beat-down by his bullying coach.

I approached the table with Jeffrey and waited to see where he sat. He took the seat to Jane's immediate left. Warren was on her right. Great, I thought. The two fathers are flanking their little girl, shielding her from predatory me. I walked around the table and took the seat directly across from Jane, Warren to my left and Jeffrey to my right.

My eyes met Jane's briefly, and I felt my stomach flip-flop, the familiar rush vibrating through me again. Her expression was placid, and she said nothing. Today she was wearing a white pantsuit, the double-breasted jacket buttoned all the way up. The memory of running my hands all over her naked body, the feeling of her soft skin, was suddenly taunting me, making my concentration difficult. *Never mind Jane; focus on your objectives.*

I cleared my throat, "Well, here we are," I began, glancing at Warren. I assumed he would lead the meeting.

"Yes, thanks to everyone for giving up their Saturday to do this meeting." Warren placed his palms flat on the surface of the table. "It's my understanding that we're all in agreement we should be working together, pooling our dynamic set of resources to build one foundation, which will be the basis of our future agency."

Warren paused to look each one of us in the eye and then continued. "We have buy-in from each of the partners on the proposed structure and org chart as Craig outlined for us; however, there are a few points of contention we need to work through as a group." Warren shifted his gaze to me. "The first point is your draw, Craig. It's a bit higher than we expected."

I met his gaze without reaction. There was no way I was going to accept less money as an equity partner and partial owner, especially with everything I was bringing to them. Regardless, I waited patiently for Warren to comment further.

"I realize you're used to a rather lavish lifestyle and there's nothing wrong with that; but you're suggesting a draw that's at least thirty percent more than the most senior

person at this table, so we need to make some adjustments."
As he uttered that last line, he pulled his chin in, like he was
afraid of how I might react.

"What are you proposing?" I inquired. He would have
to throw out the first counteroffer, so I could take it apart
accordingly and put him on the defensive. That was a nego-
tiation trick I had learned long ago.

"To make this more equitable, we were thinking you
would give up twenty percent of your draw."

I had a hard time hiding my disgust, but I allowed
Warren to continue in the event he had more to say on this
topic. I was already formulating my rebuttal.

"Is that something you would entertain in the interest
of making this deal happen, Craig?"

I uncrossed my legs and leaned in. "I'm just curious as
to how you arrived at that number," I commented, fighting
to keep my voice slow and controlled. "It seems rather arbi-
trary." I would let Warren dance around this explanation. I
knew him well. He was excellent at maximizing client profits and hiring and retaining talent. What he sucked at was
paying himself and his partners appropriately. He was so
conservative, always keeping cash flow higher in the event of
potential hard times. My style had always been not to worry
about hard times because I was always looking ahead, shifting the business toward the highest gains. Warren would
stick with the good hand, while I would double down.

Jeffrey and Jane turned to Warren simultaneously, like
they were viewing a chess game as passive spectators. Warren was no longer making eye contact with me. He was
instead examining a file sitting in front of him. "Craig," he
said finally, looking up at me again, "we got to the number by
breaking down our combined client base, profits and losses,
and accounting for additional employees and overhead."

"Let's talk about that for a minute," I suggested coolly.
"You've seen my current client revenue, but you haven't seen
my prospect list. I tend to nail fifty percent of all prospects,
which is phenomenal when you consider how most agencies
perform in this market. Based on estimated revenue growth,

the anticipation of new business and the development of higher-level clients, I see no reason to shift anyone's draw anywhere but upward."

That got Jeffrey and Jane's attention. They turned in unison toward Warren.

"Oh, come on, Craig," Warren argued. "No one gets fifty percent of their prospects—that's just not possible. Plus, the acquisition of clients is the easy part. The real money is in client *retention* and we all know your track record is not exactly stellar in that area."

"I'll prove it," I replied with conviction. "We can either use your number and give me fifty percent of every new client I bring in, or we use my number and distribute new account revenue based on your established precedent." I leaned back and stretched my legs.

Warren paused to consider the math. He had a lot to lose if he accepted my offer, but I'd let him figure that out. He just wasn't a risk-taker. He looked to Jane and Jeffrey for input. Jeffrey shrugged and turned to Jane.

That's when Jane leaned forward, elbows on the table, hands folded under her chin. "I think you should prove it," she remarked with that little smile.

I smiled right back at her, briefly reminded of my fantasy of slapping her ass and force feeding her a blow job. "I'm happy to … anyone else?" I asked looking around the table from Warren to Jeffrey.

Jeffrey piped up with a frown. "If you acquire fifty percent of all prospects and lose them within a year's time, then your draw should drop accordingly."

Warren placed his elbow on the table and tilted his forehead into his hand, eyes lowered. There was a long, awkward pause. "Let us think that through and get back to you," he recommended finally.

"Fine," I said with a shrug. "What are your other points of contention?"

"One involves your art collection," Warren baited.

"What about it?"

"I've researched the cost of housing even one of your

Chagall paintings in the office and it's too much of a liability. The insurance is crazy, and we can't afford to keep your collection here." He wore an apprehensive expression, as though waiting for me to explode.

My current inventory of Chagall paintings had reached twenty-two. I kept them locked in a temperature-controlled room within my office building—the art library. It was a place I often took young women to impress them before they joined the agency. It's also where I had originally seduced Jane. I stole a quick glance at Jane, who was pretending to examine her manicure.

"Understood," I replied. "I'd already planned to pull the paintings for my home gallery. That said, I would like a few of them in my office. I'll take full responsibility for insurance and liability. It'll be a personal expense."

"Then I guess we're good on that," Warren responded, as though he didn't anticipate my response. "Jane and Jeffrey, do you have anything to add?"

Jane shook her head and Jeffrey pushed his glasses up his nose but said nothing.

"Craig?" Warren asked me.

"I actually have one more thing to discuss." It was something I had been thinking about ever since I had initial dialogue with Warren. It was going to be tricky to present. All eyes turned to me.

"I've been thinking about the agency's branding," I stated. "And the agency name is the crucial first step in communicating our brand, especially since it's new. Now, we could go with the original name Warren and I discussed, which would be Mitchell Vance Mercer & Keller but ... I think we can do better. It somehow lacks punchiness with the final two names ending in 'er.'"

Jane's eyes narrowed, and her lips pursed, likely surmising what I was about to propose.

"If you move the names around," I continued, "it just sounds better as Mitchell Keller Vance & Mercer." I paused to adjust my jacket lapels while awaiting their collective reaction.

There was a dead silence in the room. I wasn't about to budge on this, and I knew Warren would have to agree. Branding was everything to him. "Any thoughts?" I persisted.

"You know damned well what my thoughts are on *that* subject," Jane challenged, looking to Warren for back up.

Jeffrey shot me a scowl. "Why should your name precede ours when you're the new-comer here?" he chimed in with irritation in his voice. "That's not fair."

"I'm not talking about what's fair or about anyone's fragile egos," I answered, tone clear and even in the face of Jane's and Jeffrey's uprising. "I'm talking strictly about what makes the most sense from a brand standpoint and we all know how important that is. It's the business we're in."

Warren took a deep breath, his eyes moving from Jane to me. He leaned back and folded his arms across his chest. "If you're going down that path, then Keller Mitchell Vance & Mercer sounds even better." He then placed his hands on the table and leaned toward me. "But there's no *fucking* way that's going to happen."

Our eyes locked and I knew Warren was trying to decide how to break it to Jane that she would be last in the lineup, where, based on seniority, she rightfully belonged.

"I think in the interest of proper branding, we should go with the best name," Warren began slowly. "And, although I prefer the name we initially discussed, Craig's right. Mitchell Keller Vance & Mercer has a better ring; but, since this is an equal partnership, we'll have a vote. All those in favor of Mitchell Keller Vance & Mercer, raise your hand."

I raised my hand first and Warren's hand went up right after mine. Jane looked sullen, like she wanted to strangle me, and just sat with both hands under the table. Then Jeffrey surprised me and grudgingly raised his hand.

Jane hit him with a look that conveyed horror and betrayal, her mouth gaping open. "Why would you say yes to that?" she exclaimed.

Jeffrey shrugged. "I'm sorry Jane—but I'm a creative guy, and that name's just better. If I'm willing to take one for the team, you should be, too."

Jane tossed her hair and turned her attention to me. "I guess you got everything you wanted, as usual." And with that, she hastily grabbed her files, stood, and exited the room. I couldn't help but check out her ass as she stomped out the door. She looked so hot in those white pants.

"She'll be fine," Warren asserted, straightening the files in front of him.

"Are we done here?" Jeffrey asked, flipping his tablet and keyboard shut and rising to his feet.

Warren nodded. "Craig, can you and I talk privately?"

"Of course," I responded.

We waited for Jeffrey to leave and then Warren shut the door behind him. "There's one other thing you and I need to discuss, and I didn't want the others to hear because it's extremely sensitive." He sat down at the conference table again.

I cocked an eyebrow at Warren. "What's that?"

Warren looked uncomfortable, like he didn't know how to start. He ran his fingers through his long greying hair. "You see, there are some things in this office that won't be tolerated," he said studying my face. "I've heard a lot about what goes on at your agency and I run my business differently."

I said nothing and waited for him to continue.

"The culture we've fostered here embraces diversity and inclusiveness, respect and good manners."

He sounded like an Eagle Scout giving a speech to a group of wayward juveniles. "Warren, just come right out and say what it is you won't tolerate," I retorted.

"You can't chase women around this office," he blurted out. "In fact, I want your word that you will not flirt with, harass, date, or otherwise say anything sexual to any of the women who work at this agency."

I bit my lower lip. Of course, he would bring this up. My reputation preceded me. I waited for him to continue.

"I mean it, Craig. I'm going to put a clause in your contract that if I get even one report that you've said or done anything to make a woman at our agency uncomfortable, you'll have to go. And that means our deal and the partnership will be null and void. Do you understand?" Warren had this cautionary look on his face.

I nodded slowly. "Yes."

"Good, because there's one other thing I want to discuss and then we can drop the subject forever." He got up, paced back and forth near the conference table, and then sat behind his desk once again. I rose from the conference table, moved to a chair across from his desk and lowered myself into it.

"Go ahead," I urged after a long pause.

"It's about Jane." He lowered his eyes for a moment and pretended to pick something off his collar.

"What about her?"

"I know something went on between you and Jane, and I know it was not all *your* fault." Warren flashed both palms at me for emphasis.

I sat nonchalantly without responding.

"I get she was attracted to you at one time, but she's a married woman now, and she and her husband are planning a family. It's particularly important that you respect her."

I frowned and pulled in my chin. "Did she say something to you?"

"No. But I want you to pay close attention to how you behave around her. I know she can be emotional, but you need to do everything in your power to treat her as an equal partner no matter what went on between you two in the past. Do I make myself clear? She's off-limits."

"You've already made your policy crystal clear so why would Jane be any different?" I asked, thinking I was really going to have to psych myself into looking at her as I would a man, not the gorgeous, sexy woman I wanted to attack whenever I was near her.

"I had to say it, Craig."

"You have my word," I answered, holding out my hand to Warren. We shook hands and I stood to leave.

"I'll be in touch," Warren called as I sauntered out, feeling pretty good about the meeting overall.

Heading down the hallway, I ran right into Jane as she was coming out of the ladies' room. She stopped and glowered at me for a few seconds before I spoke.

"Ms. Mercer, I have a question for you."

She crossed her arms over her chest and continued to glower but remained silent.

"If you hate me so much, why would you have voted for this new arrangement in the first place?"

"It's not because I wanted it, *Keller*," she responded, lower lip jutting out. "It's because all the things that make you a despicable human being will make us successful."

With that comment, she side-stepped me and flounced down the hallway.

W ARREN DID EXACTLY WHAT I thought he would do
with my draw. He accepted my original proposal,
which was a big compliment. It showed he genuinely
believed I would make more money on prospects than anyone else there could.

We agreed that first I would cherry pick the employees I wanted to bring with me to the new agency, speak
to them and urge them to get on board. Next, we would
put together a joint press release announcing both the dis-
solution of Keller Whitman Group and the formation of
Mitchell Keller Vance & Mercer.

I decided to speak to Bobbi first. She was, after all, one
of Keller Whitman Group's day-one employees. I had per-
suaded her to leave a huge gig at Ogilvy in New York, and
she became my trusted advisor on everything media related.
She had also become a loyal friend—someone I could rely
on to always tell me the truth. I used Bobbi as the office
barometer; she kept tabs on how employees and management worked together, kept me aware of dissenters and
defectors, and warned me of upcoming client disasters. I
heavily depended upon Bobbi for just about everything.

The only time Bobbi failed me was with Hayden. Bobbi was even more surprised than I was. It was a debacle that left us scratching our heads. *How did she manage to pull one over on both of us?* I thought I knew why. I never considered Hayden a threat because I was still sleeping with her. And although Bobbi never let on, she knew I was sleeping with her. Throughout the two years Hayden worked at my agency, I was preoccupied with buying out Warren's agency. I still kicked myself for not being more suspicious of Hayden's motives. And while she was available most of the time, she wasn't even that good in bed. She was beautiful but strangely sexless and uninteresting—one of the women I fell back on when I was bored or lonely.

"Oy, you're *dissolving* the agency!" Bobbi was incredulous as she snapped her Nicorette gum at me. Bobbi had been a heavy smoker her whole life and, since she was not allowed to light up at the office, she incessantly chewed Nicorette throughout the day. "After all we've built. What the hell for?"

"Because it makes sense," I responded. She had been in my office for a full fifteen minutes and still couldn't grasp why I would want to close Keller Whitman Group and start a new venture with Warren. I didn't want to tell her the real truth—that it was as much a financial decision as anything else.

"But we can do all that stuff here," she argued. "We don't need to move to another agency. What about the other partners? What are they going to say about this?"

"I don't care what they say—I don't have to. I'm managing partner which means I have majority ownership. They don't get a vote in what I do with this business. I established that years ago before I ever opened the doors here."

Bobbi was going to be stubborn. I'd seen this behavior before, but she would come around. She was past retirement age so I was not afraid she would seek out another agency. I was more concerned she might give up agency life and start consulting. I just had to make the new arrangement so attractive, she couldn't say no. Bobbi didn't like change. But we had a solid relationship, and I was confident she would come with me.

"Well, I don't know, Craig," she said, shaking her head, several strands of long silvery hair falling from her bun. I nicknamed Bobbi the 'silver dollar' because she saved us so much money. She beat salespeople to a pulp and negotiated media rates no one else could get. She also made sure they gave so much added promotional and editorial value; it almost eclipsed the rates we paid. Clients loved Bobbi and she was worth her weight in gold—and silver.

"Bobbi—look at it this way, nothing changes for you except the venue. You can bring your entire team with you. You'll still be working with me and you'll get to see your buddy Jane Mercer every day."

I knew Bobbi had a certain fondness for Jane. She came at me hard when Jane resigned from Keller Whitman Group, blaming me for losing the best account VP we ever had. I was pretty sure Bobbi didn't fully understand my history with Jane—our affair that went awry.

Bobbi suddenly smiled. "I loved working with Jane— that kiddo's a good girl, you know."

"Yes, I know," I agreed, thinking of Jane's work ethic, and sharing Bobbi's admiration.

"When do we move?" she asked.

"Does that mean you're saying yes?" I answered, leaning forward, elbows on my desk.

"You never doubted I'd say yes, did you, Craig?" She was now grinning at me as though we were co-conspirators. "But aren't you worried the other partners might band together and compete with us?"

I drew in my chin and frowned at Bobbi. "Are you serious? Whitman's too lazy, and the rest are incompetent. If they're lucky, they'll get low level jobs at minor agencies— the ones we don't care about."

Bobbi nodded, popping her gum loudly, "I suppose you're right about that."

"As soon as I talk to Alonzo, I'll speak with each client individually. Then, I'll put the rest of the agency on notice."

I KNEW ALONZO WOULD be slightly more difficult to get on board. Instead of meeting at the office, I invited Alonzo to lunch. I insisted on driving to the restaurant and, on the way, I filled him in on my plans. Of course, he immediately began whining about losing his stature and having to report to Jeffrey.

"You mean, I'd have to report up to a creative guy whose concepts remind me of kindergarten arts and crafts?" he snarled. "If that guy tries to stick his nose into my work, I'll lose my fucking shit."

"He never did when you worked together under my roof," I replied, studying Alonzo's tattoo-laden arms and thinking Warren would have a hard time with the excessive amount of pot and other substances he and his team ingested. I wasn't sure I could convince Warren to give Alonzo a kitchen pass on drugs and alcohol at the office like I always had. Warren was hard lined when it came to stuff like that. Always was.

"I don't know, man. I mean, I'm sure I don't have to remind you of the zillion Addys, and Clios I've racked up for you," he pointed out, sniffing petulantly. Addy and Clio awards were the Emmys and Oscars of the advertising industry, and most agencies clamored to win them each year.

I had taken a special route to make sure we passed the corner of Colyton and Palmetto where I originally noticed Alonzo's murals. Once there, I pulled the car over and put it in park. I turned to look Alonzo in the eye, but he was staring out the window.

"What's this?" he burst out in panic. "Why are you taking me here?" When he finally turned to face me, long black hair streaming down his shoulders, peacock blue sideburns quivering, there was fear in his eyes.

"I'm sure I don't have to remind you of where you came from and who helped you get where you are now," I offered coolly. Sometimes Alonzo just needed a kick in the ass to get him in line. "If you'd like me to provide the current number, I'm happy to do so."

I always referred to the seven-figure amount with accumulating interest he would owe if he ever left as 'the current number.' We had this conversation every six months or so whenever Alonzo became so full of himself, he needed a beat-down back to reality. It usually happened around awards season. Of course, if Alonzo wanted to, he could declare chapter seven bankruptcy to get around our monetary arrangement, but he was too stoned all the time to figure that out. He was also emotionally bonded to me after everything I had done for him.

"Tell me, Alonzo, are you in or are you out?"

Alonzo sighed, lowered his eyes and then said, grudgingly, "You got me, man. I'm in."

"WHEN YOU SAY YOU'RE aggressive with women, what do you mean?" Dr. Truer probed.

I shifted on the threadbare couch and crossed my legs, already feeling the discomfort of coming clean with Dr. Truer. I wasn't sure how to explain it without sounding like a maniac—a sadistic freak.

"I—um, I don't know—I'm just aggressive." *Just say it, Craig. That's what you're paying her for—if you didn't want to get into this area of your sickness, you shouldn't even be here.*

"Do you want to be more specific?" Her glassy eyes were focused on mine.

"You mean, you want to know what I do when I'm alone with a woman?" For some reason, Jane came to mind. I thought about the first time I was with her. I pictured her naked with that smooth, fair skin, welcoming me to tear her apart. "To start, I like to be in control," I explained, remembering how easy it was for me to get Jane to meet me alone in a suite at Shutters on the Beach in Santa Monica, where we had the first of several sexual encounters. "It turns me off when a woman comes on to me or makes the first move.

I don't like to be taken by surprise. When I see someone I want, *I* pursue *her*."

I recalled seeing Jane for the first time at an industry party. She had taken an embarrassing tumble on the pool deck and I came to her rescue. From then on, we engaged in a flirtatious game of cat and mouse. I pretended I wanted to hire her and, at first, she fell for it; however, at the end of the day, we both knew what I really wanted.

Dr. Truer was sketching notes on her pad. "And when you get her alone?" Dr. Truer didn't bother looking up from her pad. I assumed that was a method she used to avoid embarrassing her patients.

I took a deep breath. "It varies, depending on what kind of mood I'm in. Sometimes I like to rip clothes." The memory of shredding Jane's expensive dress in the hotel suite was coagulating in my mind. She had dressed to impress me, having no idea I would destroy her clothing, fling it to the side, and devour her. Despite being appalled by my aggressive behavior, she stayed. She stayed until I was finished with her. "Sometimes I like to play games and be teased. But it always ends up the same way."

"Which way? How does it end up?" Dr. Truer looked up and frowned at me.

"It ends with me biting them, biting into their flesh until it hurts." Again, I recalled seeing Jane completely nude for the first time and having a difficult time figuring out where to bite her first. I started with those exquisite nipples and continued down her flat abdomen to her thighs and back up again. "I mark them for myself, so they can't be with anyone else—at least while they're with me." I had been staring uncomfortably at my feet until I finally uttered these shameful words. I lifted my gaze to Dr. Truer, who was examining me with a placid expression.

"There's a term for that," Dr. Truer explained. "It's called odaxelagnia. When did you start doing this?"

I didn't know there was a term for what I did. I thought about all the women who walked away from me with bruises lining their bodies. I never left marks that could be seen in public with clothes on. It was a technique I learned early on when I started biting women: Never bite them on the neck or the arms or below the knees.

"I don't remember," I answered trying to think of the first woman I ever bit but my mind was blank. The only woman I could come up with was Jane. "Sometime in my early twenties," I said with vague recollection.

"Did you do this with Alessandra?" Dr. Truer looked like she was trying to restrain her horror.

"Never," I confirmed. "She would not have allowed it."

"And when you cheated on Alessandra, did you do this with your affair participants?"

"Always," I said, again envisioning Jane.

"That's an extremely violent way to engage with a woman. Have you ever been accused of rape or assault?" she asked, a serious expression clouding her face now.

"Never, because I always obtain consent," I responded. "Some women enjoy it, and consider me, I don't know, maybe *rough* is the right word. Women have described me as rough in bed."

"Have you ever considered the reason you bite women during sex? Do you feel angry toward them?"

"Angry ... why? For what?" I asked, wondering where she was headed.

"That's what I'm trying to get to. Let me ask you this, are you still angry with the woman from your father's yacht?"

"I try not to think about her," I answered, the saccharine smell of her skin filtering through my nostrils. The smell was so real, it triggered my gag reflex, causing my mouth to jut open with a contraction. My eyes watered and I began to cough.

"Are you okay?" Dr. Truer asked, eyebrows raised. "What just happened?"

I was now coughing uncontrollably. I grasped a nearby water bottle, twisted off the cap, and began to gulp down the water until the choking subsided. Water spilled out and dribbled down my chin and onto my green silk tie. I immediately examined the tie and wiped it with my hand, still coughing.

Dr. Truer just observed my actions with concern. "Calm down, Craig," she said. "I know this is tough for you."

She waited until the coughing fit finally subsided, and I was able to breathe normally.

"Tell me, Craig," she said gently. "If that woman from the yacht were standing here right now, what would you want to say to her?"

My hands tensed up, my jaw and neck tightening. "I wouldn't want to say anything," I finally managed in a rasp. "I'd want to kill her. I'd want to make her pay for what she did to me. I was seventeen years old, for God's sake. She had to be in her thirties. You want to talk about sexual assault? *That* was sexual assault or statutory rape or whatever you want to call it—not only was I underage and too wasted to consent, I was too drunk to do something—*anything*—to prevent my brother's death." My voice rose, and my hands began to shake. I had lost control.

"Craig," Dr. Truer said after eyeing the hidden clock to my left. Her face had returned to an expression of empathy. "We need to pause for today, but I want to check in on how you're feeling now."

"How the hell do you think I'm feeling?" I threw back, eyes burning. I put my thumb and forefinger between my eyes, pretending to feel a headache coming on. I didn't want Dr. Truer to see tears—that I was capable of crying. I never cried. The first time I cried, Don beat the hell out of me with his belt. Crying was not to be tolerated in the Keller family. DJ and I learned that early.

I couldn't wait to get out of the sickening, musty office. As soon as I was in the car, I poured hand sanitizer all over myself. I even patted my cheeks and rubbed it all over my face and neck. When I got home, I did double the cardio and exhausted myself by lifting every weight I owned. I did a ten-minute plank. Then I stayed in the shower for an eternity—until the hot water ran out—anything to cleanse this awful, terrifying regret. *How do I feel, Dr. Truer? Like I'd rather die than talk about this any further.*

# Seven

CCORDING TO DR. JANICE Truer, part of the process of letting go was moving forward. And after some time into my new venture with Mitchell Keller Vance & Mercer, I was feeling like things were sailing along at a swift pace. News of the freshly merged agency had traveled quickly throughout the city, and we heard through several sources that Towne Ink was feeling vulnerable. I was sure Hayden would focus on retaining the clients she stole from me, as well as the acquisition of new business that we would be going after. It was going to be a bloody battle and I was ready—ready to do whatever it took to slay her.

There were a few hiccups in moving new teams into Warren's building—a few disagreements and hurt feelings through the shifting offices and dedicating space but, overall, I considered it a smooth transition.

When I originally signed the contract with Warren, he advised there was an option for an additional 20,000 square feet of space within his building, so we were able to house an entire digital marketing and analytics team.

Slowly, I began to feel a camaraderie among partners, too. Jane was the exception. No matter what I said or did, she just wouldn't warm up to me. The first few weeks were the most difficult. I had a tough time seeing her as an equal partner, just as Warren had predicted. I often had to stop myself from interrupting her when she was saying something I disagreed with, dismissing her ideas as silly or naïve. The other part was purely sexual. I was keenly aware of her clothing and hairstyles, the way she looked and smelled— so squeaky clean—I wanted to mess her up—to tear her clothes and pull her hair—to bite into her flesh without mercy. Her blatant show of distaste both attracted and infuriated me, and she kept her distance as though I were an ugly, garish piece of artwork. I stopped trying to get into her good graces. She was like a fresh bouquet of gorgeous red roses rife with sharp thorns—a barricade I had no hope of penetrating.

The other obstacle was the HR director, Veronica Scarsdale, who watched me like some agency cop. I knew her when I worked for Warren right out of college. An attractive African American woman in her late fifties, Veronica was Warren's administrative assistant way back then. She had always been suspicious of me, but now her suspicions were echoed and amplified by tabloid headlines. I knew Warren had filled her in on the stipulations within my contract where it concerned the female employees at Mitchell Keller Vance & Mercer. It was obvious in the way she shot me acutely evil glances, like I was already guilty of violating some policy. It wouldn't surprise me if Warren had all my company emails blind-copied to Veronica. I was careful of what I put in writing.

She also kept a close eye on Alonzo, who showed up each day reeking of pot smoke, red-eyed, with colorfully exposed 'sleeves'. I had advised Alonzo to be discreet about his drugs, so he got into the habit of waking and baking now—coming in pre-toasted rather than blatantly using in his office during work hours.

Partner meetings were held every Monday morning in the small conference room. Warren used to believe in round tables to ensure everyone was on equal footing. After I joined, however, he purchased a rectangular table and always sat at the head, with me to his immediate right. Jeffrey would sit across from me and Jane next to him. It was an informal seating arrangement that had morphed into something permanent. Warren began to defer to me on everything concerning strategy; Jeffrey on everything related to creative; and Jane on accounts. Warren had quickly reverted to our old relationship in which he viewed me as a *wunderkind*, his right hand and protégé. Warren and I were the only ones allowed to sit at the adult's table and the other two were extraneous add-ons. The arrangement suited me fine, but I knew the others resented my intrusion into their egalitarian three-partner safety zone.

At one meeting, the discussion turned to a client who was up for review. It was a tough one because the client had been with Warren's original agency, batted over to my agency during the acquisition and then back to Warren's old/now-new agency. Wild Paint was a trendy cosmetics company that originated in San Francisco in the early 2000s. It had grown into a national brand within five years and was now standard stock in every major department store within the U.S. and Canada.

"Word's out that Towne Ink is bidding for this account," Jane mentioned, eyeing me with disgust as the words escaped her lips. It appeared she still considered me pond scum for sleeping with Hayden, which I couldn't help but agree with. *What could I say?*

"Anyone else you know of?" Warren asked, ignoring Jane's transparent expression.

"Not sure, but we're going to have to pitch new concepts and develop an updated media plan focused on the hardcore digital elements," Jane answered, again fixating her glare on me. "This is the type of baggage we're going to deal with on all your previous clients. I'd love to know what your go-to strategy will be with Towne Ink out there trying to devour everyone and everything."

Again, Jane shot me a look of reproach. I thought about Hayden going after Wild Paint and it immediately occurred to me that she would sleep with the CEO, Rex Brass, to cement a contract with her agency. Hayden used that tactic anytime she could. Rex had a weakness for cheap blondes, and he cheated on his wife constantly. He was not a bad-looking guy himself and would consider it added value to have Hayden at his beck and call, in her tight pencil skirts and low-cut blouses.

"Craig, what should our angle be?" Warren asked.

I smiled at the irony in Warren's question. I also knew his deference toward me pissed off Jane and I loved it. She just had this sour look on her face that reminded me of someone who had accidentally bitten into a rotten apple. I didn't care.

"I think we should approach it exactly the way Towne Ink is, but do a much better job," I suggested evasively, thinking I would have to use a different ploy in this case, one that no one in the room would respect or endorse, but one I knew would save the account.

"You know Hayden better than any of us," Jeffrey said, giving me an all-knowing smile. He was aware of my indiscretions with Hayden while he worked for me, as well as those of every other partner at the former Keller Whitman Group. Of course, Jeffrey had been the exception—he shunned our antics and steered clear of Hayden. Still, she was on everyone else's dance card then and we had passed her around like a bottle of tequila.

"Of course, which is why I'll handle the strategy personally," I announced.

Jane immediately bristled. "That's not the way we work around here. This is a collaborative process, and we all need to be involved."

I didn't even address Jane, which I knew would also drive her indignation into high gear. I instead turned my attention to Warren. "It's up to you but, as Jeffrey mentioned, I know her methods better than anyone here. And I know Rex Brass better than anyone here. I'm happy to set us up for success on this one, but it needs to be done in an extremely specific fashion."

Warren looked from me to Jeffrey to Jane and then back to me. "Will you at least tell us what you have in mind?"

I shook my head. "Not until after I've done some initial fact-finding. What I would suggest is we start working on the new concepts and the alternative media plan, strongly based on digital elements. If we could have a shell of those documents to review within the next week, I should have a good feel for our approach at that time."

"Fine," Warren agreed immediately. I watched Jane scowl at me again and I thought about her lips. I remembered how they felt when I kissed her, how turned on I got when I bit into them and made them swell with bruises. I remembered her willingness to take whatever I gave her—to give me whatever I wanted. She was so young and uncomfortably tolerant, ready to do anything I asked, even if it insulted her own soul. She was not like that now.

I smiled right at her, a grin-fuck of sorts as we moved on to the next client on the list—another situation in which I would take control and leave little Jane Mercer pouting. I reveled in her powerlessness and how effortless it was to sustain it. Then there was the other side of me—the side who would fall at her feet just to see her smile or throw a kind word my way. I wondered whether I would ever just own my ambivalence.

LATER THAT DAY, IN my office, I went through my contacts and found her: Lisa Boscio, Chief Marketing Officer of Wild Paint cosmetics. I picked up the phone and dialed her direct office number. She answered right away.

"Craig Keller, what a lovely surprise," she exclaimed in her deep voice with the New Jersey accent. She had tried to neutralize that accent over the years, but it stubbornly remained, like a huge dark mole on her face that would never fully disappear no matter how many times it was lanced into obscurity.

"Lisa," I intoned smiling flirtatiously into the phone. Lisa was divorced, early sixties, with a squished face and a burnt-on Jersey tan. She had the worst eye bags I'd ever seen—both upper and lower lids were packed with fluid—but oddly, even though her eyes were somewhat obscured by the bags, they had a strange popped out quality—sort of like an aging version of Betty Boop. Lisa was the skinniest fat chick I'd ever met, only because she appeared smallish, but not at all toned or fit. Her calves resembled little sausages that dimpled in places when she walked.

I attempted to wipe her image from my mind and continued. "It's been way too long since we've seen each other, especially now that I'm officially on your account again. How about dinner this week?"

I could feel her excitement mount in the form of heavy breathing into the receiver. "I would love to," she answered.

That was all I needed. I took Lisa to dinner. She was predictably over-dressed and wore an expensive strapless gown that belonged at an uptight New England garden party or wedding, rather than a dinner at Maude in Beverly Hills. Still, I was on a critical mission.

I quickly got her verbal support to keep our agency and cancel the review, even though the decision was fueled by vodka. Once I had this, the rest was up to me.

I toyed with her at the table, ordering dessert with only one spoon and feeding her mouthfuls, leaning into her, knowing my scent was arousing her. I watched her wrinkled, sun-damaged face twist up into joyous laughter at my wit and charm. Her pokey eyes resembled black coals pressed into puffy dough. Her shoulder-length jet black hair was flat-ironed and sprayed to such an extent that it didn't move. Though she was repugnant to me, I had the charisma volume tuned to its highest setting.

That night, I drove her to Malibu and welcomed her into my house, discreetly placing the framed photo of DJ face down as I swiftly passed the entryway, silently telling DJ, "You don't want to see this." I led Lisa to my living room but purposely not into my bedroom. There was no need to taint my bed with her ghastly old lady perfume. I gently pulled her down with me onto the living room floor while she floundered around in a sea of black and white taffeta. She wanted me to kiss her—wanted romance but I just couldn't do it. Once I had the hideous prom gown off her body, I fiddled with the many hooks on her strapless bra, which seemed more like a harness. She unsuccessfully tried to help me get it off. As soon as I had the bra unfastened, I unfurled her deep-tanned, speckled breasts. They dangled into my palms like cow udders. I vaguely pictured her sunbathing topless somewhere in Pirate's Cove, repulsing the young surfer boys. She wore a one-piece girdle with pants attached. It required inordinate effort to peel off the girdle, roll it down to her knees and past her ankles. Once the spandex contraption was off, she spread her legs and lay there, like some fat opera diva, expecting me to perform.

It was difficult for me to even get hard for a woman like Lisa, but I did—mostly with the help of Jane Mercer's image. I pretended it was Jane and that she had just struck me with another surly look in our partner meeting. I decided not to bite into Lisa—her crepe-like skin would probably bruise easily or even bleed—which could potentially stain my cream-colored area rug. The other part, of course, was that I was doing this to save business—she needed to walk away feeling like I wanted her—not that I had attacked her. Once a condom was in place, I closed my eyes and drove my tongue into her mouth, again pretending she was Jane. I pounded Lisa Boscio's brittle, sagging body, all the while picturing Jane's fair-skinned, taut freshness. And when I finally came, I shouted at the top of my lungs, so Lisa would believe it was her I wanted. It took me an hour-long shower and at least eight teeth brushings to eradicate her odor before I could finally enter my bedroom and get to sleep.

THE NEXT MORNING, I drove to work thinking about my dastardly deed. I told Sylvia to call in extra staff to clean the living room, especially the couch and floor where Lisa and I lay the night before. Lisa had more influence on Rex Brass than anyone else and she would most certainly convince him that Mitchell Keller Vance & Mercer deserved Wild Paint's business. I would call her today at exactly 5 p.m. to check in and see how she was doing—fool her into believing I wanted to see her again.

# Eight

**B**OBBI WAS IN MY office bright and early, jabbering about office politics. I sipped my cappuccino and listened with interest. This is how I started most days—with Bobbi giving me the lowdown in her amusing New York Jewish way. She must have been behind on her Nicorette gum count for the morning because she seemed a little more hyper than usual.

"You know, this place could use a bit of humor," she declared, pulling a piece of gum from the pocket of her long full skirt, and popping it into her mouth.

"How so?" I asked with a smile in my eyes. It was tough for me not to burst out laughing at Bobbi's way, even if she hadn't yet said anything funny. Bobbi was funny most of the time without knowing it.

"That Veronica—she's a real turd in the punch bowl, you know." Bobbi was now chomping her Nicorette, the occasional spit ball flying out of her mouth. Thankfully, she was far enough away so the saliva rockets were not hitting my desk. "She called me into her office the other day to tell me I'm no longer to refer to my male employees as '*boychik*.'"

I raised my eyebrows. "Really? Did one of your

employees complain?"

"Of course not," she claimed. "Veronica overheard me. You know, she slinks around here like a double agent, so you'd better keep your *schmuck* in your pants, if you know what I mean."

I instinctively straightened up in my chair, crossed my legs, but said nothing.

"I'd better not call you the *sheyna punim* anymore either—she'll probably have me written up for being insubordinate to the partners."

Bobbi always called me *sheyna punim* or simply *sheyna*, which was Yiddish for handsome or something. It wasn't meant to flatter me. Bobbi flattered no one. She simply called things as they were.

"Tell you what, Bobbi, you can call me whatever you want," I said, now grinning at her. "I'll take care of Veronica."

"I don't know, kiddo, she's not too sweet on you, either. I can just tell." Bobbi gave me one of her all-knowing looks, chapped red lips pursed.

I decided to change the subject to someone more interesting. "How's Jane these days?" I asked nonchalantly before taking a sip of my cappuccino.

Bobbi shrugged. "Jane's a bit serious, too—more serious than she was before but maybe it's her marriage. That kid has a lot going on at home."

*Finally, a detail I wanted to hear.* "What do you mean by that?" I asked, purposely moving my attention to one of the Chagall paintings I had on a side wall. It was one I had hung in my old office above the fireplace—*Circus Dancer*—it depicted a topless woman with long red hair clasping her arms around a horse's neck.

"Well, she tells me things, here and there—you know, she confides in me," Bobbi answered following my gaze, turning her own attention to the same painting. "Between you and me and the rest of us liars, I think she's having problems with her husband."

Bobbi paused to get my reaction, but I remained stone-faced, still observing the painting. I knew Bobbi would continue because she just couldn't help herself. No matter how much she adored Jane, she was a relentless gossip and unable to resist the urge to divulge juicy information on others' personal lives. All I had to do was stay silent and listen. I turned from the painting, sat back, and took another sip of my cappuccino, this time with my full attention on Bobbi.

"You see, Derek—that's her husband—wants kids. He's putting a lot of pressure on her because she works so much. They've even been to the doctor to see if either of them is, you know, barren."

"You mean *reproductively challenged*," I replied with a wink. "That's for Veronica."

"Okay, whatever, reproductively challenged," she said slowly and clearly as though she were being tape-recorded. "Anyway, there's nothing wrong with either of them, but Jane doesn't want kids right now because she's, you know, at the height of her career. They also have a big house, and an even bigger mortgage and Jane doesn't think they're financially ready for kids."

This information was all remarkably interesting to me. I pictured Jane at home with the violinist, lying on her back naked with pillows stacked underneath, a basal thermometer sticking out of her mouth, suddenly crying out for the violinist to make a deposit.

"And what do you think of that?" I goaded, dying for more information about Jane's pathetic suburban marital life.

"Well, I think there's a lot of conflict," Bobbi said, leaning forward. "I overheard her on the phone with her friend—you know her best friend—the Puerto Rican woman with the national talk show."

"Marisa Silva?" The only reason I knew Marisa at all was through Jane. Marisa was my worst enemy at one time—she was protective of Jane and had once blackmailed me so that I would back off. She also nosed into Don's business in search of a negative publicity hook a couple of years ago which resulted in a not-so-subtle thwarting from one of Don's old mob client's henchmen. Marisa was abrasive in an East coast way and hardly my favorite person.

Bobbi nodded. "Yeah—that's the kid—Marisa. You know, she's Jane's best friend. Her and the other one—the blonde."

"You mean Kat," I replied. Katherine Blakely was another of Jane's BFFs—and she was someone I had also slept with a long time ago. With Kat, things got messy and complicated and I was quite sure she still hated me and blamed me for causing her divorce.

"Yeah, that one," Bobbi responded. "Anyway, I over-heard Jane talking to Marisa about how unhappy she is at home and how bored she is because it's all about making a baby, which she doesn't want."

I almost spat out my coffee on that one. Little Jane was sexually unfulfilled. *How about that?* It was hard to hide my ecstasy upon gleaning this new bit of information. I just had to draw it out further—so I stayed silent, praying Bobbi would continue without a prompt. She didn't disap-point me.

"She told Marisa she was going to stop being intimate with her husband and halt the whole baby-making process until their marriage was back in order," Bobbi remarked, shaking her head. "Poor kid just seems over her head with everything."

I marveled at this. Jane was going to stop having sex with her husband to save her marriage. Not that I cared about Jane's marriage in the slightest, but someone should tell her that's a sure way to wreck everything. Women should never say no to sex with their husbands. I thought she knew better. If she were really into the violinist, she would have just started using birth control, not halt the sex altogether. I ran my tongue over my lower lip.

"Well, Jane will figure it out—she's a smart woman," I contended in a tone that meant I was done with the conver-sation for the day. I had enough fodder to savor for a while.

"She is, you know, that kiddo's very bright," Bobbi muttered while replacing her Nicorette gum with a fresh piece and bounding out of my office, skirt flowing wildly behind her.

WITHIN A WEEK, WILD Paint dropped the review with competing agencies and renewed our contract. We were sitting in the partner meeting when I decided to announce it. Jane brought Alonzo in specifically to discuss his preliminary creative concepts for Wild Paint. I preempted them with my news.

"Wild Paint has decided to renew us for another three years," I announced. "I received confirmation a little earlier."

Warren cocked an eyebrow at me. "How'd that happen so fast?"

I shrugged casually. "I convinced Lisa Boscio to keep us on. I reminded her of all the new developments, the superior team—our track record in pushing gross sales. It wasn't too difficult."

Jane's mouth dropped open. "I find that hard to believe. Lisa Boscio was the one who ordered the account to be put up for review in the first place. You know, she's tight with Rex, so he went right along with it."

"Well, they've changed their minds," I countered with an informal wave of the hand.

Alonzo shot Jane an accusatory look. "You mean I spent my entire weekend working on new concepts and we don't even need them now? Someone could have fucking told me, you know ..."

"Language please," Warren interrupted sternly. Warren himself cursed like a sailor, but only among the partners. He tempered his words around the rest of the staff unless he was thoroughly angered by something. Then the expletives flowed out of him like hot lava.

Alonzo was known for his foul-mouthed tirades when something didn't go his way. I decided to intervene, so Warren would not think me complicit. "Calm down, Alonzo, you didn't waste your time," I said. "I told Lisa you were working on new concepts—she wants to see them. And we absolutely need to follow up with the fresh media plan. This news just eliminates the extreme sense of urgency. Let's spend the extra time refining the new concepts. We have the business, but we still need to fight to keep it."

Jeffrey and Warren exchanged glances.

"I don't know how you did it, but great work, Craig," Warren commended me with a proud smile.

Jane was looking down at her phone, scrolling through her emails and ignoring the huge compliment Warren just paid me. I thought back to my conversation with Bobbi and how Jane must be obsessing over domestic issues. I wondered whether she had in fact, stopped having sex with her husband, and if she ever fantasized about me. I pictured her masturbating in bed while her bourgeois husband was fast asleep, dreaming of his first-born. Jane would be in a sexy black silk chemise without panties, her fingers moving skillfully between her legs. She would get hot thinking of me inside her—building to a steamy climax. She would have to stifle her urge to scream loudly when she came so she would not wake her husband.

As we rose to exit Warren's office at the close of the meeting, I lingered slightly behind Jane as she made her way to her office. I followed behind her, secretly admiring her body, her hips swaying from side to side in a khaki dress with no sleeves. She wore red patent leather high heels, and I imagined her naked in my office, wearing nothing but those shoes, me behind her, feverishly banging her against my desk.

I don't know whether it was the fantasy of Jane naked in those red shoes, or the recent revelation from Bobbi that she was having problems at home, but when she got to her office, I stopped and stood in her doorway. Her back was still to me, so she didn't know I was there.

"Hey," I called to her boldly.

She spun around. "What do you want?" she asked straight away, as though she were waiting for me to do this at some point.

"Would you like to have lunch and discuss Wild Paint?" I asked in an offhanded way.

She frowned, pretty lips forming a pout. "I can barely

stand seeing you in meetings; what makes you think I'd want to eat lunch with you?" she snorted.

*Because I can't stand that you hate me so much, Jane—damn, you're a hard-ass! What the hell is it going to take to get you to lighten up?* I decided to use a different tactic.

"You have to eat anyway, and, at some point, we need to work together on this account. Don't you think Warren would appreciate our collaboration?" I knew dropping Warren's name would be effective in getting Jane's attention. She was well-aware that Warren's respect for me was growing by the day and I knew it made her nervous.

She glanced at her watch and then at me reluctantly, pausing for a moment. "Maybe. What do you have in mind?"

I felt my heartbeat quicken. *She might say yes.* "I was thinking Gjelina in Venice. We could leave now and be back by two or two-thirty. What do you think?" I knew by the way she was looking at me she would say yes. Something about her had suddenly shifted. She didn't seem as hostile; her negative energy had diminished slightly.

"Okay," she finally replied. "Are we going in one car?"

"Of course," I answered giving her one of my most dashing smiles. I couldn't help it. I was going to lunch with *Jane Mercer.* Finally, I would have her all to myself for a couple of hours. And she looked radiant today.

We walked together to my car and I opened the door for her. I watched as she climbed in, gracefully backing her body into the seat first and pulling her legs and those wondrous red heels into the vehicle.

I got in and turned to ask her, "Want to drive with the top down?"

She shrugged. "Either way."

I was surprised. Most women didn't want to mess up their hair in a convertible. I pushed the button and waited for the top of the Bentley to settle and lock into place, my heart bursting with excitement.

We drove in silence to the restaurant, listening to a song by King Princess, and I couldn't help but smile. Just having Jane next to me gave me a sense of power and freedom. I never understood my intense feelings for her, but they were always there. Especially today.

When we were seated in the restaurant, I took a good look at Jane. She was so beautiful with her long shiny auburn hair, slightly wind-blown, slinking down past her shoulders; and her eyes—sexy green jewels planted exquisitely amid clear whites—sparkling in the dimly lit restaurant. It was difficult for me to resist the urge to take her in my arms and kiss her on those glossy pink lips.

She scanned the menu and looked up at me. "I'm hungry."

"Would you like to get a pizza?" I asked. "They're good here." I was so happy to be having lunch with Jane that the work excuse I used to lure her out suddenly felt far away. It only mattered that I was finally alone with her.

She smiled, which melted me. *I got a smile out of Jane.*

"Sure—you pick," she replied.

"How about this squash blossom, zucchini, cherry tomato, burrata and parmesan masterpiece?" I said, clearly enunciating each word, which made her laugh. She nodded so I waved the waitress down.

"Are you interested in a glass of wine?" I asked to test the waters. She might loosen up if we had a drink.

"Are you suggesting a liquid lunch?" she responded. "We both have to work this afternoon, you know."

"Oh, come on, Jane. One glass is hardly day-drinking. Besides, we're celebrating our success with Wild Paint."

She shrugged and cocked her head to the side. "Whatever, Craig. You always get what you want, anyway, so there's no use in my protesting."

"Now that's not true … that I get *everything* I want."

When the waitress returned, I ordered two glasses of Barolo, plus the pizza and two salads. "So, Ms. Mercer," I began. "How've you been?" I desperately wanted to touch her, but I kept my hands to myself. Thank God I was seated across from her. I was suddenly reminded of Warren's threat about what would happen if I ever made Jane feel uncomfortable. It was a sobering thought.

"I'm just fine," she answered in her semi-professional

tone. "And you? Do you like the new arrangement?"

"It's working out great for me," I responded. "How do you feel about it?"

She took a deep breath. "I'm getting used to it. It hasn't been easy, to be honest."

I nodded, noticing when she leaned forward, I could see a small piece of the beige lace bra she wore underneath the dress. I couldn't help but think about her breasts. I was feeling the beginning of an erection. *Damn it, how does she do this to me?* I crossed my legs uncomfortably, praying the angst would go away before I had to stand up again. *Cool it, Craig, stay focused on work.* "Is Alonzo treating you okay?" I asked, thinking the mere mention of Alonzo could kill a boner on impact.

"Oh, please, Craig, we both know he's resented me ever since I worked for you at Keller Whitman Group," she responded, shaking her head. "He could tone down the arrogance, you know. But then, he's a disciple of *yours*, so that's never going to happen."

"You think I'm arrogant," I returned, feeling slightly wounded. I wished she had a higher opinion of me.

"No, I *know* you're arrogant, but that's given you an edge in life—I mean, look at how you handled Lisa Boscio—no one's ever been able to tame her evil ways—except you."

Images of Lisa, nude, with her spotted, deeply tanned skin, laying with her legs spread in my living room, sprang up in my mind. The memory returned of her horrible smell and desperate face gazing longingly up at me ... I felt nauseated and wondered whether I should bring it up with Dr. Truer. Part of me didn't view it as an element of my sickness; rather, it was merely a business transaction.

Before I could answer, I heard a familiar voice emanating from the adjacent table. It jarred me enough to turn to its source and then I saw her—Hayden Towne—*live*. I cleared my throat and pretended I didn't see her, but it was too late, she was standing next to our table now, glaring at me.

"Well, well, well," Hayden sneered. "If it isn't my favorite couple."

I quickly glanced at Jane, who was now staring in disgust at the malevolent she-devil. It was such a buzz kill to see Hayden when I was so absorbed in Jane's beauty. Hayden was a painful reminder that I slept with the worst type of female animal on the planet. She was still striking—attractive in a cheap way with her bleached blonde hair, violet-blue eyes, and dark purple lips. She wore a tight black dress that had an open keyhole in the front—exposing her cleavage to the world.

Neither Jane nor I said anything as the waitress cut in, setting two glasses of Barolo down on the table.

Hayden's eyes followed the wine glasses as she continued her scorn. "This looks awfully cozy—I guess I busted your little tryst." Her smile exuded viciousness.

Jane was the first to speak. "It's hardly a tryst. And though it's really none of your business, this is a working lunch. I also happen to be married."

Hayden laughed in her mean-spirited way. "Oh please, do you think that'll stop this one?" she spat, glaring at Jane while gesturing toward me. "In case you didn't know, Jane, your lunch companion's the biggest whore in the city."

"Second biggest," I interjected, now fuming at her explosive commentary. I didn't care what she said to me, but Jane was another story altogether.

She turned her scrutiny from Jane to me. "Really, Craig? That's not what I've heard. Does Little Miss Muffet here know you *fucked* Lisa Boscio to get her business back?"

I felt my jaw tightening and I narrowed my eyes at her. *How did she find out? Or did she just assume I did it because it would be something she would have done if Lisa played for the opposite team.* There was no way I could let Jane find out what really happened.

"You should watch your mouth in public," I said coldly, my eyes meeting Jane's briefly to gauge her reaction to Hayden's accusation. Jane's brows furrowed, and her eyes widened, like she wasn't sure what to believe.

"You should watch your *cock* in public," Hayden shot back, pointing to the crotch of my pants. Jane's mouth dropped open, obviously shocked by Hayden's unchecked vulgarity.

A rather disheveled-looking man in his late twenties suddenly appeared, wearing an ill-fitting suit. He sported a sparse-looking bouquet of facial hair—like he was attempting to grow a beard and mustache, but his face wasn't cooperating. He also had a loosely defined unibrow. Since he didn't hear the first part of the conversation, he looked eager to be introduced and thrust his hand toward me. "I'm Marius Durand," he offered with a faint French accent. "Vice President of Accounts at Towne Ink. Aren't you Craig Keller? I've been wanting to meet you for, like, ever."

*Of course—another star-fucker to contend with.* I said nothing, staring blankly at his hand. I stole a glance at Jane, who still appeared to be processing the raunchy conversation. It couldn't have felt more awkward.

"Marius, go get us a table on the other side of the room, or outside, preferably," Hayden ordered, snapping her fingers, and pointing at the hostess, predatory sneer in full effect. He scurried off like a frightened rabbit. Hayden leaned over to Jane and said in a loud voice, "If I were you, I'd wear protection—in fact I'd double bag it with this man if you don't want to bring home an STD—you know he's nailed the entire female population of L.A. county and beyond."

Jane pursed her lips and looked as though she might throw up. As soon as Hayden had stormed off, Jane's eyes met mine and she shook her head, slowly, looking thoroughly disgusted by the display.

"Jane, please don't let her ruin our lunch. You know how she is," I said trying to think of something to say that might reverse what had just transpired. "She's just unhappy our agency was able to save Wild Paint."

"Tell me, Craig. Tell me how *you* saved Wild Paint," she demanded, eyes now flashing with anger. "Tell me how you miraculously convinced Lisa Boscio that putting the account up for review was a bad idea."

The waitress placed our salads in front of us, and the pizza on a round, elevated stand, but I no longer had an appetite. "Great, thanks so much," I said, giving the waitress a tight-lipped smile.

As soon as she had left, I looked Jane square in the eye. "You're letting her get to you. Don't do it. She's not worth it."

"You're not answering my question," Jane countered, flipping her long hair over one shoulder with her hand. "Tell me the truth right now, Craig Keller, or I'll go to Warren and tell him exactly how you *saved* Wild Paint."

I wasn't about to tell her. I just lowered my eyes and then looked back up at Jane, who was now holding her purse, poised to leave.

"Come on, Jane. Let's at least have something to eat," I insisted, trying to keep my voice controlled. But I was near panic. I had lost precious ground with the one woman who would never allow me to gain it back.

"I lost my appetite," she snapped getting to her feet. "I'll get an Uber back to the office."

"There's no need for that," I protested calmly. "Let me get the check and I'll drive us." I flagged down the waitress and requested the check as I watched Jane sashay toward the exit.

"Do you want me to wrap up this food?" the waitress asked, inspecting the table with a puzzled expression.

"That's not necessary," I responded quickly, getting to my feet, pulling two hundred dollar bills out of my pocket and handing them to her. "This should cover it." I knew I must have over-tipped her by at least fifty dollars, but I didn't care. I was about to lose Jane to an Uber.

I hurried out of the restaurant and spotted her standing by the curb, phone in hand.

"Jane," I called to her, but she didn't turn around. A black Toyota Corolla was pulling up next to the curb and she quickly opened the door and got in, slamming the car door shut. Watching helplessly as the car pulled away and disappeared down the street, I sighed and started to walk toward my car. Then I had another thought. I re-entered the restaurant and found Hayden and her bootlicking French minion at their table. I strode right over to them and Hayden looked up while chewing her food.

"I'd like to speak with you privately," I told Hayden, my gaze boring down on her like a hot lightning rod.

"I'm busy," she muttered, still chewing. "Some other time."

"No. Now." I commanded calmly but so forcefully, she jumped slightly in her chair. She turned those tanzanite eyes up to me and gawked, but slowly wiped her mouth with a napkin and stood.

I gestured for her to walk in front of me toward the restaurant's entrance. Once we were outside Gjelina, I led her around the corner where there were no windows, and I backed her up against the exterior cement wall. I leaned forward, so my face was not even an inch away from hers and stared ruthlessly into her eyes.

"Don't *ever* speak to Jane that way again. Do you understand me?" My voice was level but fraught with a menacing quality.

"Oh, did I offend your girlfriend?" she asked with mock concern.

"Your entire being is offensive to *everyone*," I responded.

"I remember when you weren't so offended," she said with a vindictive smile. "What are you worried about? That I might outshine your little protégé?"

"Oh, come on, you couldn't outshine Jane Mercer's shoes. She's got you beat on every level and you know it." As I said this, I put my face even closer to hers, whiffing a mouthful of hairspray.

One side of Hayden's gaping purple mouth tugged down while she cupped my package in both hands, attempting to squeeze my balls. Before she could cause any real damage, I roughly grabbed her hands and pinned them behind her, backing her against the wall. I quickly lifted my thigh and rotated it to one side in case she tried to give me the knee.

"Here's what's going to happen," I ordered sharply. "The next time you see Jane in public, you're going to avoid her. If I hear you've said anything or gone anywhere near her, you'll hear from me again. And, trust me, you don't want that."

"Are you … threatening me, Craig?" she stammered, pupils laced with fear.

"You bet I am." I said before slowly releasing her hands.

She hugged them around her body like I'd hurt her, but I knew it was just an act. Hayden was an Amazonian man-eater with long, strong legs and broad shoulders. It astounded me that I was ever attracted to her, but I had long since accepted the fact that I was just lonely. After I divorced Alessandra, Hayden became a diversion. She had a pretty face, but when I found out how vile she was, I couldn't look at her again without feeling sick to my stomach. I didn't wait for her to regain her composure before turning my back and heading toward my car.

She called after me. "You'd better keep Lisa happy because I'll be seeing Rex again."

"Based on personal experience, I have nothing to worry about," I shot back without even turning around. She just wasn't worth the effort.

# Nine

ANE WASTED NO TIME relating my misdeeds with Lisa Boscio to Warren, who promptly called me into his office. When I entered, his mouth had tightened into a straight line and he seemed to be clenching his teeth as he paced the floor. "Keller, you want to tell me what went on at lunch today?" he demanded, inspecting me with his steely grey eyes. He had this way of blinking numerous times when he was angered by something.

"I'm not really sure," I answered. I would never volunteer information until I knew what I was being accused of.

"You mean to tell me you didn't run into Hayden Towne at a restaurant this afternoon? And what the hell are you doing having lunch off-campus with Jane anyway? Didn't I tell you to stay away from her?"

"Which issue would you like me to address first, Warren?" My neck stiffened.

"Did Hayden Towne publicly accuse you today of sleeping with Lisa Boscio to influence her boss and keep us on at Wild Paint?" He had stopped pacing now, and was standing straight in front of me, eyes piercing mine.

He was so close, a hint of his sharp, serious cologne

drifted into my nostrils. I felt like I was in court, under oath, about to perjure myself. "Yes, she accused me of it, but she says a lot of things that have no basis in reality."

"Whose reality are we talking about, Craig? Yours or everyone else's? One minute we're scrambling to get new concepts ready to save a major client and the next you're sailing in with news that the account is no longer up for review. How else, in this industry, does that happen?" He had momentarily gone back to pacing the floor of his office but had stopped in front of me and was again glaring, expecting an answer.

I sighed deeply. I had been caught. And there was no way he was going to let me off the hook. I would have to tell the truth. "Okay, Warren. I'll admit it. I had drinks with Lisa and—well, one thing led to another and—we, uh—we ended up at my house. Right after that, she called to tell me they changed their mind about the review."

"Jesus, Keller," Warren erupted. "She's a client. You bedded a client to save the account?"

"Oh, come on, Warren—in this business, it's by any means possible," I argued. "We're talking about $150 million in ad spend alone for their international campaign. Plus, you never mentioned clients were off-limits here, just the female employees."

Warren scratched his head in disbelief. "I didn't realize I needed to be that specific, Keller. I just assumed you'd have an actual code of ethics preventing you from doing something like this."

"We were in danger of losing the account," I disputed. "Hayden used her feminine wiles to get to Rex and I knew if I got to Lisa in the same way, *we'd* win. Besides, she wanted it, not me—you've seen Lisa, haven't you? Do you think I *wanted* to do that?"

Warren just stood there, stone-faced, but he listened.

"We wouldn't have stood a chance if I turned her down," I continued. "Plus, I didn't see any better ideas floating around the table. What's the big deal since we have the desired result?"

"The big deal is now she's going to expect you to sleep with her again. What happens then, Craig? Are you going to take her home every time she asks? You know it'll end up going bad and we'll lose the account anyway." Warren's expression was a fusion of disgust and anger.

"You leave that to me," I responded coolly. "I can handle Lisa Boscio and no one else around here will even know. I can make this go away as fast as I made it happen and she won't have any bad blood against me or the agency. Trust me."

Warren put his hand on his forehead and frowned as though he were thinking about it. Then he looked up and reluctantly nodded. "Okay, I'll trust you this time. But listen to me and listen, good. Sleeping with clients is forbidden. I'll have another clause added to your contract stating such. Now tell me what went on with Jane."

I thought back to Jane having been subjected to Hayden's contemptible words and humiliating discourse, and I cringed. She was so far above that sordid dialogue. "I asked Jane to have lunch as a peace offering," I replied. "You know she's not my biggest fan, so I didn't see any harm in trying to improve our working relationship. If you're concerned, please ask her whether I was a gentleman. She'll have to say yes. I couldn't help that Hayden barged into our lunch and ruined it. But with Jane it was completely innocent. I gave you my word on that and I'm not about to break it."

Warren leaned against his desk and crossed his arms over his chest like he was assessing me, trying to figure out whether I was telling the truth. He finally sighed and said, "Fine. I believe you. But you've been officially put on notice about client relations."

"Thanks, Warren," I said, taking the opportunity to exit his office. I breathed deeply, relieved that he had let me off the hook this time.

FROM THAT MOMENT ON, Jane avoided me. She stopped being hostile, but a certain coldness emanated from her. It was like she was so sickened by my behavior, she no longer wanted to acknowledge me. I finally gave up on trying and treated her exactly the way she treated me—with an icy, professional respect.

LISA PREDICTABLY THOUGHT SHE would have another crack at sex with me, but I killed it early. I called while she was still in her office and she blatantly flirted with me on the phone, like we were secret lovers avoiding a delicious scandal by acting clandestine.

"Craig," she cooed. "When can we review more of the new ad layouts?" She was speaking in code like someone might be listening in.

"That's what I need to talk to you about," I answered. "We'll have to temporarily halt creative production." If Lisa wanted to communicate in ad-speak, great. I was more than fluent in the language.

"What? But why?" She sounded like a little girl whose mother took away a favorite toy.

"I'm getting back with my ex-wife," I explained, thinking there was no advertising equivalent for this excuse. "We're doing it for the kids," I added. When you brought kids into any situation with Italian women, they always understood.

"Well, I guess it's my loss, then," she said. "I can't stop thinking about you—about us at your house. You mean to tell me that's never going to happen again?"

"Never say never, Lisa," I responded. Leading her on to believe I was sacrificing our affair because of my children was the only way to go. The thought that she might have a chance with me down the road would keep her hanging on. *In your dreams, Lisa.* I hung up feeling satisfied that she believed my lies.

Warren developed a new respect for me because the affair never came up again and we had no further problems with Wild Paint. I surmised he must have secretly been okay with using me as a gigolo to resolve a client issue. Warren had high ethics, but he was as serious about making money as I was.

OCTOBER SNUCK UP ON me, and I sat in my office one smoggy, overcast morning pondering my last few sessions with Dr. Truer. She had moved me to once a week because I was no longer in crisis mode. We were now exploring my personal relationships and what she described as my inability to love anyone. She had asked me straight up whether I had ever been in love and I, sadly, had no idea what to say—I wasn't even sure how I would be able to tell whether I was ever in love. I didn't think so. I did tell her I loved DJ and my children, but she said that was not the same as being in love with a woman. It's like all the love I had in my heart was flushed into the San Francisco Bay along with DJ's blood, rendering me incapable of giving love to a woman.

My thoughts were interrupted by Bobbi, who came bounding into my office for her morning chat. She plopped down in a chair opposite my desk as I sipped my cappuccino. Little did she know how much I cherished these sessions. Bobbi, as therapy revealed, was the closest thing to a friend I'd ever had. Although she worked for me and really shouldn't count as a friend, she had an energy I loved. I needed her to brighten my days. I needed her in general.

Today, however, she looked serious, like something had gone dreadfully wrong. "Craig," she said like she was about to lay some big news on me. I prayed she wasn't resigning. I simply couldn't cope without my daily dose of Bobbi.

"What is it?" I asked, uncrossing my legs, and leaning toward her.

"It's Jane," she said softly, as though she didn't want anyone to hear. Bobbi never lowered her voice for anyone.

I felt my heart racing, imagining the worst. "What about Jane? What happened?"

"She found out last night her husband has been unfaithful," Bobbi answered with a glum look on her face.

I put my cappuccino down and sat up straight in my chair. "What? There's no way—I mean, that guy's in love with her."

"Derek cheated on Jane and confessed to her last night," she responded. "But that's not the weirdest part about it … he cheated with," she gulped hard, "he cheated with Hayden Towne." Bobbi's thin red lips were stretched against her teeth in disgust.

I felt my blood run cold imagining the violinist being with the amazon when he was married to the most exquisite creature on earth. "Are you sure?"

"Totally sure. She's all broken up about it, poor kiddo. I didn't even know what to say to her." Bobbi popped a Nicorette into her mouth and began chomping loudly, spit flying everywhere. I was so shocked by the news; I didn't even flinch or search for where her saliva might have landed.

"How would Hayden even *know* Jane's husband?" I asked, now curious as to how this could have happened. I pictured Hayden performing one of her porn-star-disgusting moves on the violinist. I remember commanding her to stop when she tried to do these things with me, which caused her to rage at me later. She accused me of being uptight, prude, gay, etc. because I found it so distasteful. Maybe it was just because it was her.

"That viper went for him after a performance," Bobbi explained, sinking into the chair. "She supposedly waited for him backstage, introduced herself and asked him to have a drink. She told him about her company and that she would do free work for the LA Philharmonic as a trial with the hope of representing them later for a retainer. He claimed she put something in his drink, and he woke up in bed with her the next morning, but Jane doesn't believe him. I mean, who would do that?"

I thought about Hayden and realized she would absolutely do that. There was no question. "What's Jane going to do?" I asked, thinking about how I had threatened Hayden to stay away from Jane. She had exacted her revenge by getting to Jane's husband. *What a scum bag!*

"She said they can't afford to live in separate homes right now, so they're in separate bedrooms. She really isn't sure what to do. I told her she should see a marriage counselor.

And even worse, Jane's grandfather is in the hospital right now. You know she was raised by her grandparents. The poor kid's only family is disintegrating before her eyes." Bobbi shook her head and slouched a little.

I never knew Jane was raised by her grandparents. Come to think of it, when I first met her, she just seemed wholly alone and without support, other than what she got from her friends. What was even worse was the thought that I took advantage of her at that time. I wished there were some way to take it all back. I also felt helpless that I had no relationship with her after the whole Hayden scene in the restaurant and her discovery that I slept with a client to keep an account. I'm sure, to Jane, Hayden and I were in the same sleazy category.

"Do you think there's anything I can do to help?" I asked on the off-hand chance she might say yes.

Bobbi just shook her head. "She needs her girlfriends now."

"Bobbi," I said quietly. "I know Jane doesn't think much of me, but I do care about her."

"I know you do," she responded with a curious look in her eye. "That's why I'm telling you." She leaned forward and added with a cautionary expression, "Of course, she swore me to secrecy."

Of course, I thought wryly, Jane always had a certain naïveté when it came to trusting Bobbi with secrets. I don't think she ever quite understood the relationship Bobbi shared with me. If she knew I was aware of this latest bombshell, she would be humiliated.

As soon as Bobbi had left the office, I fumed over what Hayden had done. I went home that night furious and spent two hours in the gym. I was able to hold a plank for twelve full minutes—a new record. I emerged still angry over how Jane had been hurt by my nemesis.

Later that night, in bed with my Scotch, I took a sip and considered the situation. I wondered if there were any way to help Jane. I turned it around in my mind over and over but came up with nothing. She wouldn't talk to me, so there was no way I could bring it up. She wouldn't accept help from me anyway. By sip number five, I had resigned myself to listening to Bobbi's updates and doing nothing—being useless to anyone emotionally. After all, I was used to it. That was my way.

THE NEXT MORNING, WE had a huge pitch presentation to a new client. This one was an entertainer, an old crooner named Kenton Fox who was openly gay. He had a major following and decades of hit singles. I heard he was also being courted by Towne Ink, among others, so today was important. I had selected a navy wool suit by Tom Ford with a navy and white thin-striped tie. The suit jacket had the trademark two pockets on the right side, one pocket on the left, which was stylish—and would appeal to a gay enter-tainer—without overdoing it.

I worked with Alonzo directly on the spec work. We had three concepts to present, all geared to the Las Vegas target since they were doing a residency at the Regal Oasis Casino Resort on the Strip. I knew the resort well because Don was close to its owner, Luuk Van Ness. I recalled many covert meetings between Don and Luuk after DJ died. I was never sure why they had those meetings, but assumed it had something to do with the mob-related nature of Luuk's casino business. Since that time, things had changed in Las Vegas. The Strip used to operate like the Wild West, before it became home to corporate giants—a highly regulated, legitimate business.

The Kenton Fox gig was huge, and Mr. Van Ness wanted the debut to ring loudly throughout the city. He sent the entertainer to us because he specifically wanted a Los Angeles-based ad agency. After all, a solid percentage of Las Vegas customers came from Southern California.

I sauntered into the large conference room where Alonzo and two of his creative team were setting up the AV. One of his two creatives was not exactly my favorite. His name was Sherman Bouldridge, and I'd asked Alonzo to remove him from the meetings or fire him because he seemed inane and incompetent; however, Alonzo balked at this suggestion, offering as his argument, "I can't do that, boss—he's stupid, but he knows shit."

I recalled rolling my eyes and responding, "I'm not even going to *ask* what that means." In the end, I relented and had to get used to Sherman haunting our meetings with his aimless presence.

They were using a small wireless LCD projector to cast images onto a wide screen. I remembered the days of using color printouts spray-mounted to black poster board, and I smiled. Things were so different now.

Alonzo jolted slightly when I entered the room. "Hey, Boss," he said. I noticed he was wearing a white long-sleeved button-down shirt to cover his tats. His blue sideburns and long black hair sparkled freakishly under the fluorescent room lights, but some level of hipness and eccentricity was expected of an LA creative director—especially one as infamous and meticulously on-trend as Alonzo.

"You ready?" I asked, eyeing Alonzo's nimble fingers, tinkering with the AV equipment. Creatives were not normally expected to be so handy when it came to electronics. Alonzo defied all customs when it came to this stereotype. He sought out new technology and owned the latest in every gadget. He even personally attended the Consumer Electronics Show in Las Vegas every year. I thought about how valuable he was to the agency and burst with a sudden pride at having discovered him—at having helped develop him into who he was now.

"I got it, Boss," he replied with a confident grin. Smiling was a rarity for Alonzo, but when he did, it was sincere.

Jane, Jeffrey, and Warren entered the conference room at the same time, and I studied Jane's face. She wore a somber expression; however, her eyes looked clear and bright—there were no signs of a tearful evening, as far as I could tell. She didn't make eye contact with me; she was instead deep in conversation with Jeffrey, who had his hand on her shoulder, a look of concern on his face. I felt a stab of envy at how close Jeffrey and Jane were—at how much she trusted him. I'm sure she shared with him what happened with the violinist. It killed me that I was such an outsider in her life. I crossed the room to where they were and greeted them.

Jane gave me a perfunctory smile and said hello. There was that thorny rose bouquet again. She wore a sleek black pants suit with a sky-blue blouse underneath. Her hair was pulled back into a ponytail and I was again taken with her beauty. She always looked so sharp and clean.

The client arrived with his manager—a short, thin bald man named Del Jasmer. He had been Kenton's manager throughout his career and the rumor was that they were a couple. Our team rose as soon as Pearl walked the pair into the conference room, and we welcomed them with enthusiasm. I half-expected Mr. Van Ness to have sent his Chief Marketing Officer to attend this meeting—his son Hendrik—a mysterious man whom I'd never seen nor met; however, this time it was only Kenton and Del.

Kenton looked utterly ridiculous with his orange-tinted sunglasses and what appeared to be a dark brown toupee on his head. He was in his early seventies and had seen his share of sex and drugs. His face was stretched hideously tight from plastic surgery and he wore a long purple jacket with a white ruffled shirt underneath, jeans, and tennis shoes. The whole effect was flamboyant in an Elizabethan kind of way. But he had a huge budget and was projecting serious revenue for the show's three-year run. If we landed this account, it would mean a sizeable retainer and a lucrative long-term contract.

Usually in pitch presentations, the agency team sat on one side of the room and the client on the other, so we could all see one another. Since there were only two on the client side, we split things up. I sat on one side with Warren and Alonzo, plus his creative team. Jane and Jeffrey sat on the other side with the client.

We had an order of doing things in these meetings. We would start with introductions around the table and then Warren would do an overview of the agency. Next, I would give the preamble to the spec work, throw out some research data to support our positioning, and then hand it off to Alonzo for presentation. Alonzo was passionate in the presentation of his work but lacked the finesse of a corporate ad guy. That's where I came in—I would often interject commentary whenever I sensed Alonzo was about to go off the rails.

Jane and Jeffrey were there to answer questions after the presentation regarding process and account leadership. When a discussion about a media buy was on the agenda, Bobbi would also attend. We had been at it for a while as a team and had become comfortable in our respective roles.

As Alonzo presented the concepts, I watched him closely. He had a nervous twitch whenever he presented, but no one would likely notice it but me. He had this odd habit of knocking on the conference table as though it were a door when he finished imparting a nugget of information.

"We engage the audience on an emotional level with one image," Alonzo described, showing the preferred ad, which was third in the lineup. We always put the agency-favored ad last so the first and second would seem not quite right. The second was usually a throw-away. The ad was a full bleed closeup of Kenton on stage, face contorted, singing his heart out into the mic. "We want them to see the ad and virtually hear the songs that have charted their lives for so many years." *Knock, slide change.*

I often wondered if perhaps Alonzo was signaling the change of a presentation slide with the knock, but it was never consistent. At one point, he was glaring at me with what I'd come to recognize as an SOS, so I jumped in.

"I think what Alonzo's saying is that the right image does the total selling job of the prospect's imagination," I pointed out, glancing at the concept. "One image tells the story—and when that happens, you only need minimal copy—maybe no copy at all—just your logo and a call to action."

Kenton kept gazing at me with these googly eyes from behind his orange-tinted frames. I thought he might be looking at everyone this way, but he had somehow singled me out and had locked his eyes on me.

"We don't like that picture," Del piped up as Kenton shook his head in disdain.

Of course, they would consider the concept literally, I thought. All clients did that with speculative work. It was always tough for them to imagine what the concept would become when it was finished—after it was run through a battery of refinements to make it perfectly whole and complete. "We'll shoot original photography," I responded. "The image here is FPO—for position only."

After Alonzo presented and the clients had a chance to express their opinions, it was evident they were leaning toward the concept we favored. Warren, looking pleased, turned the conversation over to Jane for the account leadership discussion.

"The overall strategy, creative direction, and account management will involve everyone in this room," Jane explained. "We'll also put together a team to manage your account on a day-to-day basis."

"You mean, we'll get the junior squad," Kenton interrupted in his shrill, nasal inflection. "That's not what we want. That's why we're coming to you with our business. We want personalized attention from the top executives, not junior-level staff. We can get that in New York."

"Let me clarify this for you," Jane added quickly, tilting her head toward Kenton, her shiny ponytail bouncing slightly to one side. "You'll have everyone in this room making the most important decisions, but the day-to-day management will be a dedicated team."

Kenton shot me a look. "Will *you* be on the dedicated team?"

I cleared my throat, eyes briefly skimming Jane's. "Absolutely," I stressed. "I'll be working with them."

"But will we have direct access to *you*?" he pressed in a way that told me he wanted something more than just my attention.

I was going to have to handle this in a way that wouldn't

wreck our chances of being hired. This old queen was attracted to me and, as uncomfortable as it made me, I needed to use it to secure the business.

I gave him one of my most dazzling smiles, one usually reserved for a beautiful woman. "To be honest, we usually don't have partners get too far in the weeds on accounts. And that's a good thing—believe me—you don't want to use up your retainer having me run down job requests or set up photo shoots. That said, I'll make an exception with this account, knowing it will be one of our most important. So, to answer your question, yes, you'll have direct access to me regarding the more global issues as they come up."

Kenton was now licking his lips in anticipation. *What a pig—and right in front of his partner.* I shifted my attention to Warren, who was almost smirking. I wanted to kick him in the teeth right about now. Once the meeting had ended and they left the conference room, Jeffrey dismissed Alonzo and his team and shut the door.

"What the fuck was that?" Jeffrey turned to me with his eyebrows raised. "The guy did everything but give you a hand job in front of us."

"Jeffrey, please," Jane protested, shaking her head. "That's just gross."

Warren suddenly leaned in, a sarcastic look on his face. "Looks like we have another Lisa Boscio on our hands."

"Did you really mean to give them *direct access?*" Jeffrey asked me, now laughing hysterically. "That guy's going to be sexting you in the middle of the night when something big *comes up.*"

"Laugh as much as you want now," I countered, "but Hayden Towne will get nowhere with them."

"Of course, she won't," Warren quipped. "She doesn't have anything *they* want."

I ignored Warren. "Once she's knocked out of the running, there's only one other agency who's courting them, and I guarantee they don't have what we have."

"You mean they don't have *you*. I'll buy you a rape whistle," Jeffrey snickered. "Do you have a color preference—or maybe we should order an assortment to match your ties?"

Jane was not laughing. In fact, her face reeked of pain and agony. I cringed at my own insensitivity. *Why the hell did I have to bring up Hayden?* I was surprised Jeffrey didn't stop me.

"Let's wait until we secure the business before we do anything," I responded.

"I don't know, Craig," Warren said, now grinning, "I'd say we should go ahead and order the rape whistle now. Or maybe a bull horn would be more appropriate."

I stood and exited the conference room, taking long strides to my office. I was walking so fast, I almost failed to notice Jane trailing right behind me. She must have been in a hurry to get back to her office, too.

I stopped at my office door and put the key in the lock. I didn't look up at Jane—just wanted to let her pass me in peace but she stopped and lingered for a moment as I rotated the key in the lock and opened the door. I turned toward her and leaned against the doorframe. She looked composed but not serious.

"Must be tough to be in such high demand," she commented, eyes on mine.

"That's exactly what I tell myself every night when I go home to an empty house," I responded.

"Am I supposed to feel sorry for you?" she asked, leaning to one side with her files pulled close to her chest.

"Never," I answered. "I'm a guy and we tend to feel sorry for ourselves."

She lowered her eyes and sighed like she was reminded of something depressing.

"Hey, Jane," I said, peering down at her. "If there's anything you need—anything at all—you know you can always come to me." I didn't know what made me bold enough to say this to her now, but I did, even though Bobbi made me swear to act like I knew nothing.

She lifted her eyes up to mine with a puzzled expression. "What do you mean by that?"

"I'm just saying," I confirmed in my professional voice.

"You looked pretty upset when we left the conference room. So—if you need help with this account, or with anything. I'm … here for you."

She just stared at me, still with a confused look, as though she didn't know whether to believe me. I smiled, wanting desperately to touch her face, but restrained myself. When she didn't respond, I turned and walked into my office, leaving my door open with Jane in the hallway, likely still trying to process the fact that I was being kind. Maybe she just didn't expect it. Maybe I didn't either.

# Ten

ATURDAY CAME AROUND AFTER a long week, and it was a weekend without Axel and Anabel. On these weekends, I usually got up, drank coffee, and took a long walk on the beach. Then I would take an extra hot shower and head into the office. Saturdays were a perfect day to work because they gave me a chance to catch up—to strategically think through challenges without interruption. I often went in on Sundays, too. The office had always been a refuge for me, especially when I was married. It was my escape—free time to do what I wanted. I loved weekends like this.

I arrived at the office around 3:30 and entered the deserted office lobby. This was going to be a great day—no distractions. I thought about my partners, all ensconced in their domestic lives and suddenly Jane came to mind. She must be working through her demons with the violinist. I pictured her at home on the couch weeping while her husband gave pitiful excuses about being date-raped by Hayden. I had to admit, as lame an excuse as it was for committing adultery with a beautiful woman, it was not entirely outside the realm of possibility. Hayden obviously went after him specifically to get to Jane. *But why?* Hayden only slept with men when there was something in it for her. In this case, I couldn't figure out her motive—unless it was simply out of rotten spite. She had always been jealous of Jane—jealous of my feelings for her. There had to be some way I could make Hayden pay for this outrageous blow to Jane's marriage, but I hadn't yet come up with a plan. My initial threat had already been disregarded. If I came back with anything, it would have to be serious—serious enough to bludgeon her into subservience for good.

I entered my office, turned on the lights and opened the curtains. Then I made myself a cappuccino, settled in at my desk, and turned on the computer. I had a process on weekends. First, I cleared my desk of every paper and file and put them in a pile on the floor next to my chair. I would flip on my office Sonos system and play the Sirius XM Chill channel. It was the only music, besides classical, I could ignore. There were no serious lyrics to detract from my mission. Then, I would pick from the pile on the floor, one paper or file at a time and go through it thoroughly, reading every word thoughtfully, making notes and decisions.

After a couple of hours, I stretched my arms and legs and yawned. I was getting a lot done. Tackling emails was next. That's when the sound of the copy machine interrupted my flow of work. Someone was here, making a hell of a lot of copies. I was so curious to know who would be in the office on a beautiful Saturday in November that I got up from my desk to investigate.

The copy machine was humming at a relentless pace, but it was left unattended. I examined the documents and saw creative briefs and job requests passing through.

I glanced down the hallway and noticed Jane's door open with the light on. I advanced to her doorway and saw her standing by her conference table, engrossed in ad layouts. She was wearing an olive-green military jacket over a grey T-shirt and jeans with high-heeled boots. She didn't look up until I got her attention.

"I thought I was the only one who worked weekends," I commented from her doorway.

She jumped, obviously not expecting anyone else to be there either. "Oh, it's you," she replied, putting her hand to her throat, and breathing deeply. "You scared me."

"Sorry. But I *am* glad you're here," I said with a half-smile, "In the event I need to use the rape whistle, I know it won't fall on deaf ears."

She smiled back at me. Was it my imagination or was her smile almost *affectionate?*

"What are you doing here, Craig Keller?" she asked, turning to face me. Her long hair was loosely curled. "I mean, I'm sure you have better things to do on a Saturday, especially when the weather's this nice."

"You'd be surprised," I responded, entering her office and approaching her slowly, cautiously, as though she were a rare animal on the verge of extinction—one I wanted to examine up close without startling and scaring away. "Weekends are when I do my best work. Plus, I have the whole building to myself. Except for today."

"Sorry to ruin your private work experience," she remarked. "I promise to be quiet."

"What are you working on?" I asked, peering over her shoulder at the ad layouts on the conference table. I was close enough to smell her clean clothes and skin.

"Wild Paint," she answered, stepping aside so I could clearly see the ads. "I'd love your opinion, if you have a minute," she added.

"Of course. Tell me what we're looking at." I was flattered she would ask.

"I'm veering toward this one," she stated, pointing to an ad with a beautiful woman leaning against a bathroom sink in what looked to be a nightclub. Her back was to the camera, yet her face was clear in the mirror's reflection. She was in tears, but her mascara was not running. Wild Paint touted its top-selling mascara, which was both water-proof and easy to remove. The headline read, 'Cry all you want.'

"It's a good concept, but do you really want to show a woman crying? I doubt that's going to move product."

"Everything happens in the ladies' room," Jane countered,

looking me in the eye. "You wouldn't know because you're not allowed there."

*You're wrong, Jane.* I was briefly reminded of a woman from my past taking me into the ladies' room to watch her urinate. I remembered washing my hands at least eight times and emptying a full bottle of hand sanitizer after that experience. "Then why did you ask for my opinion?" I was trying not to lower my gaze to her body, and those snug-fitting jeans.

"Because you're smart—you know everything," she answered in a flip tone.

"Except what goes on in the ladies' room."

"But don't you get it?" Jane was getting more passionate about the ad and I wasn't sure why. "It's about their mascara being waterproof—tear-proof."

"I get the concept, Jane, but I'm just not sure women want to see other women cry—that's all. Do you?" I asked, studying the ad.

"We all cry—we cry in the bathroom, we cry in the bedroom, we cry in our offices. Women fucking cry, okay?" She waved her hands around wildly as she made this declaration.

"Okay, okay—women cry. What do you want me to say?" I glanced at the ad again, baffled at Jane's outburst and rare public use of the F-bomb. When she didn't answer, my eyes met hers and I saw tears.

"Hey … are you okay? Did I upset you?" I sighed. "What did I do now?" I gently touched her shoulder and then pulled my hand back as though I had accidentally grazed a hot stove.

"It's not you," she whispered, turning away, and pulling a tissue from a box on her conference table. She blew her nose loudly.

I didn't know what to do. It was obvious the situation with the violinist was on her mind and clouding her judgment with the Wild Paint ads. "My apologies," I said contritely. "I'll go." I quickly exited Jane's office and returned to my own.

I sat at my desk, consumed by the scene in Jane's office.

*What was it about me that always upset her?* I never knew how to deal with a woman who cried. Maybe that's why the ad made me uncomfortable. And, again, I was being insensitive when her life was in such disarray. I wished, somehow, she would let me in and just tell me what she wanted—what she needed—anything to clue me in on how to deal with her.

It was around 8 p.m. and I was ready to leave for the evening. My desk had transformed into a eurythmic arrangement, which would offer peace when I returned to Monday's chaos. As I gathered my things, I heard a knock at my door.

"Come in," I called. The door opened, and Jane appeared, looking sheepish. "Need something?" I asked, with cool professionalism. I had no desire to rile Jane's emotions again.

"Yes, I was wondering if we can have dinner," she inquired in a way that told me she was afraid I might say no.

"You mean, tonight?" I had no plans, as usual, but I didn't want Jane to know.

"Yes," she replied, "Unless you already have plans. I'm sure someone like you always has plans." She was nervously wringing her hands.

"I do have plans," I lied. "But I think the bigger question is do you think it's a good idea? Look what happened when we tried to have lunch."

"If you already have plans, then it's a moot point," she retorted. "Sorry for bothering you."

"Jane, wait," I called after her as she flew out the door. I hastened to the doorway to find her already half-way down the hall. "Jane—I'll change my plans, okay?"

She stopped and spun around, a stubborn look on her face. "I wouldn't want to infringe on your single life," she muttered.

"Stop it," I protested, advancing toward her. At that moment, I wanted to grab her, carry her into my office where I would promptly tear off her clothes and throw her on my desk—prove to her that she was the only plan I wanted. "You're not infringing on anything." My voice was calm. "But I do ask that we go in separate vehicles. In the event you have a sudden urge to desert me in the restaurant, you'll have a getaway car."

That elicited a slight smile and she nodded. "Okay. Where to?"

I paused to think for a second. "How about Michael's? It's within walking distance so we can get some fresh air after being cooped up in here all day."

That got a big smile. "Yes," she responded right away and then hesitated. "But how are you going to get a reservation? Doesn't that place take months to get into?"

"I have connections. Get your things," I said gesturing toward her office. "I'll call Michael's now."

She obediently scurried down the darkened hallway, boot heels clicking against the hard wood floor.

WE WALKED ALONG SECOND Street and took a right on Wilshire. I breathed in the chilly night air and turned up the lapels of my black light wool coat, one I caught Jane eyeing with admiration. I had had it custom made the year before because I needed something to throw over casual clothes on nights like this. Underneath the coat, I wore a chocolate cashmere sweater, dark jeans, and Grenson leather oxfords. It was the most perfect night—in the high fifties, clear, crisp, and starry. I had the overwhelming urge to take Jane's hand as we walked, but I resisted.

"Do you ever think of leaving L.A.?" Jane asked suddenly as we rounded the corner of Third Street and Wilshire.

"Never," I responded. "I have kids, so I can't leave—at least not anytime soon."

"But do you ever think about it?" she persisted, taking small steps at a brisk pace to keep up with me. I instinctively slowed my stride.

I had no idea why Jane was asking me this unless she was thinking of leaving herself. "Why do you ask?" I cleared the way through a throng of slow walkers. Again, I had the urge to take Jane's hand and lead her through the crowd, but I thrust my hands into my coat pockets instead.

"I … don't know," she responded. "Sometimes I just wonder what else is out there."

"Maybe you should travel more," I suggested. "It's great to travel and then come home—makes you appreciate your roots." At that moment, I stole a glance at Jane and caught her staring up at me, wistfully. She looked away as soon as our eyes met.

Michael's was packed but they found us a table in the garden which, I had to admit, was one of the most romantic spots in Santa Monica. Jane was now oddly silent but seemed in better spirits. I couldn't help but think I was violating Warren's policy when he had told me several times to stay away from Jane socially. And I knew bringing her to a spot like Michael's on a Saturday night was not the best decision. But we were here, so I would have to control myself.

When we were seated, and the waiter came to take our drink order, Jane immediately piped up. "I'll have a Grey Goose martini up with olives," she announced, like she'd been thinking about it all day. She looked at me expectantly.

I gave her a wry smile as if to say, 'here we go.' "Make that two," I requested, and we were off.

After the martinis were delivered and we each took a sip, someone was standing at our table. It was the restaurant owner. "Craig Keller, as I live and breathe."

"Michael," I responded, shaking his hand. "It's been way too long."

"And who's this lovely young lady?" Michael was gazing at Jane as though she were in my current lineup.

"This is Jane Mercer—she's a partner at the agency," I added quickly.

"Partner indeed," he said, stretching his hand to take hers. "They're just making 'em younger and prettier these days. Nice to meet you, Jane."

"It's a pleasure," she answered, smiling sweetly.

"Watch out for this guy," he warned, grinning slyly, and shifting his attention to me. "If you don't mind, I'd like to give you a special menu tonight—I see you already have drinks."

I turned to Jane. "You okay with that?"

She shrugged. "Sure."

After martini number one, Jane spilled her guts.

"You know, my husband cheated on me," she blurted out, fingers tapping impatiently against the wooden table. "He cheated with *Hayden Towne*." As she said this, she glared at me as though I were somehow responsible—like I had conjured Hayden through some odious method of witchcraft for the sole purpose of meddling in Jane's marriage.

I pretended not to know. "Wow—that's terrible," I commented, taking a small sip of my martini, and reaching for the hand sanitizer in my pocket. "I'm sorry to hear that."

"It's true. And, get this," she continued, "he insists that she *drugged* him—you know, like put something in his drink to get him to go home with her." As she lobbed this last bit of information at me, her eyes became wild with anger. "I mean, that's the oldest excuse in the book."

Jane's voice had become shrill. I looked around to make sure we had not caught anyone's attention and cleared my throat. "You know, Jane," I began, lowering my voice and choosing my words wisely. "Hayden's pretty aggressive. Is it possible she really did drug your husband?" I doused my hands with the sanitizer and rubbed them together.

"What was he doing having drinks with her to begin with?" she shot back. "I'm sorry, but he's not a child. He's a man and he's responsible for his own actions. We all are."

As soon as she made this statement, the waitress came by and she ordered another martini. I saw where this was going. "Jane," I spoke gently after the second drink had been delivered. "I know you're upset, but maybe you should slow down on the vodka."

"I'm fine," she snapped with a touch of indignation. "I thought we were supposed to be having fun tonight."

"If we're going to have fun, then I'd suggest we change the subject. Do you agree?" I felt my knee touch Jane's under the table, and I pulled it quickly away, so she wouldn't think I did it on purpose.

She took a large slug of her martini and licked her lips. "Okay, fine."

Michael had dish after dish sent to us with paired wine and I started to worry about Jane. She was drinking too fast and began slurring her speech. When they brought her another glass, I had to intervene.

"Sweetheart, I think you've had enough of that," I commented, realizing I was speaking to her in the same tone I used with Anabel. "Drink some water." I pulled the wine glass away from her and pushed the water forward.

"Shh-weetheart?" she trilled, full of outrage. She reached over and grabbed the wine glass, quaffing the whole thing rebelliously in two gulps. Her eyelids were starting to flutter, and she looked sleepy.

I wasted no time pulling a batch of crisp hundreds from my pocket, thumbing through it and leaving it on the table. I was not about to ask for a check and risk anyone seeing Jane this smashed. I had to get her out of the restaurant right away.

"Come on, let's go," I commanded, scooping up her handbag, pulling her out of her seat and dragging her to the restaurant entrance. I wished I could leave her with someone and get my car, so she didn't have to walk. She could barely stagger at this point. Jane never could hold her liquor. I clutched her in front of me and tried to walk, restraining her upper body—attempting to avoid touching her breasts—while directing her lower body with my legs. It was tough because I was so much taller. She was on the verge of pitching forward and falling onto the sidewalk.

By some stroke of good fortune, we made it to the agency parking lot, I dragged her toward the car, her stiletto heels grating against the asphalt like nails on a chalkboard. When I located my vehicle, I poured Jane into the passenger seat where she promptly passed out cold. I pulled the seatbelt over her inert body and fastened it.

*What a mess!* I had really done it now. I had no choice but to take her to Malibu, something Warren would admonish me for—he might even fire me. *But what else could I do?* She was in no shape to walk, let alone drive. If I dumped her in the office to sleep it off, the surveillance cameras would catch me red-handed—Warren reviewed them every Monday morning. I thought about going through her purse to find her driver's license so I could deliver her to her home address. Then I realized the violinist might be home and wondering what she was doing out with me—drunk. I had already been clocked in the jaw once by the man for canoodling with Jane in the past.

I sped north on the Pacific Coast Highway toward Malibu with the top down, so the cold night air might wake her up. Her long auburn hair was whipping in the breeze while I cranked the loudest radio station I could find. They were playing "Ain't Talkin' 'bout Love" by Van Halen, and the late Eddie Van Halen's iconic guitar solo reverberated loudly. I silently prayed Jane would come to; but whenever I glanced in her direction, she was still out cold. Miraculously, the traffic lights all stayed green. We were almost there.

When I pulled up to the house, I knew it would be difficult to drag her from my car to the door. She likely weighed only about 115 pounds, but she was dead weight, which was tough to move. I opened the car door and unfastened her seatbelt.

"Jane," I called loudly. "Can you wake up for me? Wake up—wake up, Jane." *Nothing.*

I pulled her by her upper body, trying not to injure her, and managed to dislodge her from the car. Her head rolled around like it might snap loose from her neck; her long hair hung like a mop around her face. Then I gathered her up in my arms like a child and carried her to the porch.

I shoved my key into the door and unlocked it. The security alarm was beeping with a deafening hum. *Damn*—I had forgotten to turn it off in advance with the phone app. I had to carry her to the control panel to shut it off. Finally, I transported her to one of the guest bedrooms, the one right next door to my bedroom, and plopped her corpse-like body onto the bed.

I stared down at her, thinking there was nothing more repulsive than a drunk woman—except for Jane. She just looked angelic lying there on her back like Sleeping Beauty.

One by one, I unzipped and pulled off her boots, and drew a soft blanket over her. I wished I could put her in the most comfortable pajamas I had, but that would require removing her clothes and I couldn't risk her thinking I took advantage of her—not in this state. I stooped down to kiss her on the forehead goodnight but stopped myself because it seemed too weird.

I backed my way out of the room like I was exiting a murder scene and turned off the light. Once outside the room, I closed the door behind me and inhaled deeply. Then I opened it again. *What if she woke up and freaked out? She sure as hell wouldn't know where she was.* I decided to close my own door to put a barrier between us.

After an inordinately long shower, I got into my pajamas and tucked myself into bed. I usually passed on Scotch the nights I was out drinking because I didn't want to mix anything with the good stuff. But tonight, I hadn't taken more than a couple of sips of vodka and a little wine because I was so worried about Jane. Now, I needed something to calm my nerves, so I pulled out the bottle of Scotch, and considered how much should be poured. I really needed a stiff one, but I didn't want to sleep too soundly in case Jane woke up frightened.

I lay there for at least an hour, propped up on my pillow, taking sip after sip of the Scotch. It was already after midnight and I couldn't sleep. I was obsessing over the smooth, creamy figure I fantasized about every night, who now lay only footsteps away. I wondered how I could possibly have this beautiful creature so close but so far from me. I imagined what it would be like if she had been sober—if she had somehow forgotten her troubles with the violinist and remembered how much she wanted me at one time. It was a fantasy only destroyed by Warren's ominous threats and the shackles he had forced upon me early in our business relationship.

In the wee hours of the morning, I dreamed of her. I felt her smooth, flawless body in my arms, and her beautiful mouth pressed against mine as I probed my tongue into it.

She was on top of me, running her fingers through my hair with one hand and moving the other softly down my neck, to my chest hair, pausing there before leaning over to kiss me, first on my chest and then back to my mouth. I moved my hands from her breasts to her waist, and then along her hips, tracing my fingers down her thighs. She gently took my right hand and positioned it directly between her thighs, so I could feel how much she wanted me. It was the best dream of my adult life.

# Eleven

**T**HE SUN'S RAYS DRENCHED my bedroom with a tortuous palette of early morning hues—mauve, tangerine, indigo, and violet. It reminded me of one of my treasured Chagall paintings, 'Mazin, The Poet.' It was a rare portrait of the artist's poet friend seated at a table with a book of poems resting in his lap. The only objects contrasting with the meditative mood of the painting were the multi-colored book and the bottle to the far right. I smiled.

I originally had the skylight installed directly above my bed, so I could see the stars on clear nights. Mornings at the beach were usually overcast and foggy—thick with the marine layer until noon, but not today. There was a rare glimpse of a cloudless sunrise and I couldn't help but feel calm and happy, for the first time in years. I didn't want to get up. Then, I rolled over and saw her. It was Jane—sleeping beside me, *naked*.

*What the …? I couldn't have.* I thought back to everything I was doing and feeling—seemingly dreaming I was with her. *But was it real?* She was naked, next to me. *What had I done?*

I broke into a cold sweat and scrambled to get out of bed,

feeling for leftover dampness on the sheets—evidence—but could find none. I was naked, and my pajamas were strewn across the floor on one side of the bed. I grabbed the bottoms and pulled them on quickly, afraid she would wake up and accuse me of rape. As I shakily tied the drawstring on the pajama bottoms, the murky memory of Jane crawling into bed with me in the middle of the night returned. The Scotch had me so woozy, I couldn't remember exactly what happened. I gazed upon Jane lying on her side with her back to me. The covers had inched down, and I examined the gorgeous length of her spine. I pulled the covers up to her neck, so she wouldn't wake up feeling cold or exposed.

I stumbled into the kitchen and ran through my options while I brewed coffee. This was it. Warren would kill our partnership. I retrieved the *New York Times* from my front yard and sat on the couch, opening the paper, and nervously sifting through its contents. I usually read the *Times* online, but weekends were for the hard copy because I liked to feel something tangible between my fingers. Today, I could barely concentrate on what I was reading. I sipped my coffee, absentmindedly shuffling the papers and eyeballing the clock. It was already 10 and Jane was still sleeping. I didn't understand how she could sleep with all the natural light streaming through the skylight.

Finally, she emerged. There she was, living breathing proof of my breach of contract, standing there with her long hair hanging in a sexy tangle around her face and shoulders, wearing my olive-green Italian silk robe, which was way too big for her. For the first time in my life, I didn't care if someone wore something of mine. I wanted her scent on the robe. In fact, I hoped she would drench it in perspiration because I would never again have it cleaned.

The worst thing was that I wanted her even more now—whatever happened or didn't happen. It's like she unleashed something that had been pent up for years. These feelings were eclipsed by the reality that she was a ghost of my wrongdoings and self-sabotage.

"Good morning," she said smiling brightly, as if nothing

were out of the ordinary, like she was meant to wake up in my bed on a Sunday morning and help herself to my silk robe.

"How do you feel?" I asked.

"Fabulous," she replied, eyes lowering to my exposed chest and torso, her lips parting slightly. I still wore only silk pajama bottoms with the drawstring waist.

I examined her face, searching for any sign of a hangover. Shockingly, I could find none. She must have washed her face and used the exclusive emollients in my bathroom to make her skin so clean and natural. "That's very surprising, Ms. Mercer, considering the condition you were in last night. Do you remember *anything*?" I held onto a thread of hope that perhaps she was so out of it, she blacked out what we may have done through the night.

"Um—which part?" she replied with a coy grin. She wanted me to spell it out for her. I decided to avoid the question altogether.

"Would you like some coffee?" I asked, running my fingers through my hair.

"Sure," she answered, tripping around my house observing the art and furnishings, touching things here and there, eyes wide with fascination. "This place is unreal. Is this really where you *live*?" She picked up the photo of DJ I kept in the entryway and studied it with curiosity. "Who's this?"

I exited the room without comment, went into the kitchen and returned with a tray containing a cup of coffee, cream, sugar, and a bowl of strawberries. I set it on the coffee table in front of her.

"Thank you," she said, watching me intently. She was already comfortably ensconced on my couch, feet tucked under her like she had been living with me long-term. I sat a few feet away from her on purpose.

As soon as she reached for the coffee cup and took a sip, the tassel cord on the robe untied and her perfectly rounded right breast sprang out, her light pink nipple pointing upright like a pencil eraser.

I immediately looked away, feeling the beginning of an erection. *Why does she do this to me?* I shifted my legs, so she wouldn't notice. When I finally turned my attention back to her, the robe was still open. I cleared my throat. "Jane," I said in a husky voice, "your robe … my robe … you should cover yourself."

"Oh," she said glancing down at her exposed breast and blushing slightly. "Sorry."

I watched her fasten the robe again. "You have to tie it in a knot for it to stay put," I offered, thinking about sinking my teeth into those beautiful white breasts, sucking on them for hours … days.

Once the robe was fastened, she stood up and moved to where I was sitting.

"Is everything okay?" she asked, planting herself directly in front of me and leaning forward so she could look into my eyes, which I averted again.

"Yeah," I responded, barely glancing up at her.

"You want to talk about last night?" she asked with a voracious look on her face, like she wanted to rub it in that I was so weak—I couldn't control my urge to plunder her body.

I glared at her. "You know I could get into a lot of trouble for what happened last night."

Her brows furrowed, and she cocked her head as if she had no idea what I was talking about.

"It's in my contract that I'm not to touch *any* of the female employees at the agency or my partnership goes away."

"But I'm not an employee," she protested, blinking at me. "I'm a partner—we're equal. I don't count."

"I have it in writing and I signed it. I'm not to date or otherwise do anything with the female employees and *especially* not you, Jane. Warren made that clear."

"But … you wanted it, too," she accused, voice incredulous. "It was consensual, so what's the big deal?"

My temper was rising at her ability to be so blasé about my partnership. I got to my feet and moved toward the window, put my hand on the back of my neck, which was stiff with tension, and paced the floor, feeling the cold, hard marble under my bare feet. "You were so drunk last night, I had no choice but to take you home," I explained, struggling to keep my voice controlled. "As soon as we got here, I did the appropriate thing and put you to bed—fully clothed—in a guest room. When you wandered into my bedroom naked and got in bed with me, I was asleep."

"You woke up pretty quickly," she remarked, advancing toward me, a frown on her beautiful face. "We didn't do it, you know—not all the way. We were close, but it never happened. You kept saying we shouldn't."

Although relieved, I had a tough time believing that *I* was the one who had stopped us from having intercourse. My anger was again bubbling up at her for putting me in such a precarious position at work. "So, you decided to use me to get back at your husband? I have no desire to play that game with you."

"What are you saying, Craig ... you didn't want it to happen?" She was now standing an inch away, peering up at me with those big green eyes, which tapered slightly at the corners. I towered over her by more than a foot when she wasn't wearing heels. "I know that's not true," she added in almost a whisper. As she said this, she slid her hand under the waistband of my pajamas and felt me, as hard as a rock now and a dead giveaway about what I wanted. *Damn her.*

"It's not true, is it, Craig?" she continued to taunt, while running her fingers up and down in my pants.

I closed my eyes and let out a deep sigh with my mouth open, feeling my jaw twist to the side. I was ready to explode because she was touching me there again. "Oh my God, Jane. What are you trying to do to me?" I couldn't stop at that point. My mouth was on hers, our tongues ensnared, tasting each other's saliva. I hastily untied the tassel knot, hands trembling in anticipation before I yanked the robe off her body. She pulled the drawstring on my pajama pants and drove them half-way down my legs before they fell to the floor.

I stepped out of the pajamas, squatted to her height, and swept her up. Her legs straddled my body as I carried her back to the bedroom where we thudded onto the bed, still attached to each other. I felt her nipples grazing the hair on my chest, the heat of her flesh against my lower abdomen. I had the urge to bite her, but I didn't. I suppressed the need to hurt her in some way for hurting me—for making me lower my guard.

I positioned myself on top and entered her body, feeling the excruciating goodness of plowing into such a tiny space. She moaned, grabbing me around the neck and pulling me closer, thrusting her narrow hips upward so I would go in deeper. I put my mouth on hers, probing my tongue in it, and she responded with passion. Not long after, I came hard inside her, feeling relief at last.

My concentration was off the next morning. I kept an eye on the clock, knowing there was a partner meeting at 10, and dreading it. I was going to have to see Jane again—this time in the context of work. I wondered how I would feel—how she would act—whether our body language would give us away to Warren.

When we assembled in the conference room, Warren and Jeffrey were already seated, discussing some client's social media plan. I took the seat to Warren's right.

"Good morning, Craig," Warren greeted me. Jeffrey just looked up and nodded. He had quickly gotten used to the idea that I was an equal partner with my name before his on the masthead.

"Good morning," I responded, trying to sound casual.

They continued their conversation. "They're pissed off about negative reviews," Jeffrey spouted. "But they don't want to actively request that their clients post positive comments because the content's too sensitive."

I realized they were discussing a very high-profile divorce law firm we had been representing for the past few months.

"Why don't we have the digital department work with them on streaming content—for their website and social media channels—you know, so the negative reviews get swallowed up by generic posts about all the things that surround divorce?" I suggested, drawing on my own situation with Alessandra and the vast material that would be relevant to someone seeking a divorce attorney. "For example, 'how to help your children cope with joint custody'—something like that."

Jeffrey shook his head. "They don't want to do *any* social media—they think it makes them look cheesy."

At that moment, Jane appeared in the doorway, looking stunning as always in a navy pinstriped sheath dress with red suede pumps. She wore her hair straight today and it flowed down her back like a shiny curtain panel. I secretly wondered how she could walk after what we did over the weekend, but she strolled into the conference room with ease and took the seat across from me. Her familiar clean scent wafted as she sat down. Our eyes met briefly, and I swore I saw a subtle look of—*what was it?* I couldn't put my finger on it.

"Good morning, Jane," Warren called to her. "How was your weekend?"

My eyes quickly darted to my phone and I scrolled through emails, pretending I was looking for something.

"It was *just* fabulous," she said with sarcasm. Since Jeffrey likely knew about Jane's personal problems with the violinist, her tone was appropriate.

As Warren spoke, I slowly shifted my gaze from my phone to Jane and saw she was now engrossed in the contents of *her* phone. Then she suddenly glanced up at Warren. He had asked her a question.

I wasn't listening to her response. I just watched her mouth as she spoke, thinking about where it had been yesterday, for so many hours. I sighed deeply. This was not going to be easy. I couldn't even sit in the same room without wanting her again—couldn't be in the same zip code.

It wasn't until three days later I realized I hadn't worn a condom. Not at night when she caught me on autopilot nor the day after, when we spent the entire afternoon in bed. I wore condoms without fail my entire sexually active life, except with Alessandra. But it didn't even cross my mind to use one with Jane. She finally left around seven that evening, and I didn't want her to go. In fact, I wanted her to stay for-ever—to be there when I came home at night—to quell the treacherous loneliness and somehow make me whole. The one thing I noticed after she left was that I hadn't thought of DJ for an entire twenty-four-hour period. That was a record. Jane was somehow the only one who could fill the empty void left by DJ after he was killed.

I didn't understand what it was about Jane that made me feel like this. It had never happened before with any other woman, including my ex-wife. I needed her in a way that scared me. It filled me with fear that she would ulti-mately leave because I was not good enough for her. I would never be. And we both knew it.

# Twelve

*I* ARRIVED AT DR. TRUER's office early Thursday evening. I normally got there right on time, so I wouldn't have to inhale the musty waiting room scent. Today, I sat there nervously scanning my phone, eyes occasionally darting at the old radio wired to the floor. For once, I urgently needed Dr. Truer's help.

I had spent the entire week obsessing over and avoiding Jane. Even when we saw each other in meetings, I sat far away from her and tried not to make eye contact. Then at night, I'd go home and work out for hours, attempting to get her out of my head. After my shower, I'd go into my closet to get a clean pair of pajamas—the olive-green silk robe hanging in front of me. I'd leave it hanging there, taunting me. I had a game in which I would try to put on pajamas and make it out of the closet before I touched the robe. Then I'd quickly return and pull it off the hanger, cover my face with it and try to pick up the scent she left behind. The smell of her glorious skin was growing fainter and fainter with each passing day.

After every robe episode, I would settle into bed and sip my Scotch. I'd think about her until I could get to sleep. I didn't even masturbate because it seemed absurd when I had just had the real thing. I could only conjure images from the previous weekend and savor them—praying they wouldn't fade, unceremoniously, from my mind.

Dr. Truer ushered me into her office and I had barely sat down before announcing, "I need to talk to you about something that happened last weekend—about someone."

Dr. Truer's eyes lit up slightly; it was the first time I'd ever spoken without prodding and prying. I was never comfortable talking in therapy but today was different. "Tell me what's going on, Craig," she said, with the empathetic look on her face. "You look rattled."

"Well, I—there's this woman I work with at the agency. She's a partner."

"Oh? What's her name?" she asked, grabbing her notepad, resting her legs on the ottoman.

"Jane," I answered. "Jane Mercer, and I had an affair with her more than four years ago when I was still married."

Dr. Truer's eyes widened a bit. "Okay."

I took a deep breath. "I've had a rocky relationship with her ever since that time. I was awful to her. I used her. Then she ended up working for me at my old agency and I—I tried to get her to be with me and she refused. I punished her—no, I really tortured her. And she ended up resigning." I paused to take a sip of water from the bottle in front of me. I crossed and uncrossed my legs.

"You used your power to punish a woman because she wouldn't be with you? That's sexual harassment, Craig. You know that don't you?"

I nodded, remembering when Jane said no to going home with me. I was dying to be with her, but she stood her ground. "I was angry—angry I couldn't control her."

Dr. Truer adjusted her feet on the ottoman and sat in silence, observing me. I sipped the water again, nervously twitching my foot.

"Just like when you were angry at the woman from the yacht—the one you couldn't control when your brother died."

I stared blankly at Dr. Truer and shook my head.

"No—Jane's nothing like the woman on that yacht. You're way off here. Try another angle, Dr. Truer."

Her expression changed briefly to one of surprise. "I'm not saying the circumstances are the same, I'm saying your anger at being out of control may be what drives your aggression toward women."

"But I'm not *angry* at Jane," I protested. "I was angry at *myself* when she quit. It's when Hayden bamboozled me out of half my clients, but none of that mattered compared to what I did to Jane. She—she was just so good, and I was horrible to her. I was a monster."

Dr. Truer edged her glasses up her nose from the side and took notes. "I'm guessing she's not a big fan of yours now. Did you abuse your power with other women at the office or was Jane just special?"

"I feel like you—you're judging me." My mind went back to the intense mutual lust—the unavoidable tension and chemistry that saturated the air between Jane and me—in the office, in restaurants, in the bedroom. The whole world ceased to exist when we were alone. Jane *was* special. I never looked at it as an abuse of power because I saw her as my possession—someone who belonged to me from the moment I saw her.

"I'm sorry, Craig. I don't mean to sound judgmental," she said with an apologetic look. "I'm glad you feel comfortable calling me on that. This needs to be a safe zone for you to express yourself without anyone's judgment. Please tell me about Jane."

I took a deep breath and visualized her. "She's—um—she's beautiful. She's smart and funny and she excites me. I can't tell you how often I think about her. I can't stop thinking about her. It's been years and I've never been able to put her out of my mind." I felt the pain of her swelling in my chest as I spoke, so much so that I grabbed my collar and tried to loosen it.

"I'm curious as to why you never brought Jane up until now," Dr. Truer said.

"She's off-limits," I answered, my signed contract coming

to mind. "I was told by my boss, the managing partner, that I was not to go near her, or any of the female employees, but he was specific about her. She's also married."

"Do you want to tell me what happened last weekend?" she asked, watching me intently.

I focused my eyes on the Elvis bobble head, which was now gyrating frantically in the flow of the air vent. "I—we slept together. I wasn't planning on it. It just happened. She came to my office on Saturday. We were the only two working in the entire building. She wanted to have dinner. She had a lot on her mind. Her husband was unfaithful—with the woman who stole all my clients. She got drunk—so drunk I had to take care of her. I drove her to my house and put her in a guest room."

I suddenly snapped out of my Elvis daze and my eyes met Dr. Truer's. "She came to my bed in the middle of the night. I had too much Scotch. I woke up not knowing what we had done." I had to catch my breath for a minute, I tugged at my collar again, this time hastily loosening my tie.

Dr. Truer eyed my body language uneasily, like she was afraid I might implode right there on the couch. "Take it easy, Craig. Sip some water and continue whenever you're ready." I followed her orders and took three sips from the water bottle sitting in front of me. I tried to breathe slowly to calm myself. Dr. Truer leaned toward me intently, her feet dropping off the ottoman like two lead balloons. "Did you make love to Jane?"

"Not fully," I said, feeling uncomfortable revealing details to Dr. Truer. I pictured Jane's naked body lying next to me. "But I wanted her desperately."

Dr. Truer looked at me expectantly.

"I waited for her to wake up and then I—it was awkward. But there was something so natural about it, too. I can't describe it. I wanted her there. I wanted her period—and we—she stayed until that evening."

Dr. Truer looked me in the eye. "You chose to make love to her, *fully*, then," she said as though she had just cracked some code.

I nodded.

She blinked at me empathetically. "Where does the relationship stand now?"

"I don't know. I've been trying to avoid her but it's impossible because we work in the same office—we're both full partners. It's—I don't know what to do."

"Do you want to be with her?" Dr. Truer asked, sitting up straight on the La-Z-Boy.

A spear of surprise shot through me. "You mean, again? Of course, I do. It's just impossible because—because of everything we're both in jeopardy of losing."

"I don't mean do you want to make love to her again—that's obvious. Do you want to be with her, Craig? Do you *love* her?"

I pictured Jane and her contagious life-force—how passionate she was about everything—how much I loved to be with her—how good she felt in bed—how she made me a better person—how being with her was like holding a rare, sparkling jewel and then having to give it up, abruptly, causing a spate of emptiness and pain. I *did* love her. I loved someone finally. It was Jane.

"Yes," I said quietly, still absorbed in thought. I looked up at Dr. Truer, with her empathetic stare and felt my eyes water slightly. "I'm in love with Jane."

Dr. Truer studied me with knitted brows, like she was thinking through a problem. "You've told me for months that you'd never been in love with anyone. And here you are, in love with this woman. Have you ever told her?"

"Of course, not," I admitted. "She's married, and I'll lose my job. What am I supposed to do?"

"I'll lose *my* job if I tell you what to do," she returned while eyeing the hidden clock.

THAT NIGHT, I DRIFTED home, having no memory of how I got there. I was consumed by my revelation in therapy that I was in love with Jane. Dr. Truer's question loomed in my mind like a black cloud. *Have you ever told her?* I could never be that honest with Jane. Her life was too fragile now to burden her with anything else. Plus, I was not sure how she felt. I knew she wanted me. Sexually, there was no doubt in my mind what or whom she wanted. Still, I had no clue about her relationship with the violinist—whether she wanted to work things out after his infidelity. After all, she married him—exchanged vows and now they had both broken them. I knew what that was like. When I broke my vows, it felt like handcuffs being removed—I was free to do whatever I wanted after that because there was no chance the handcuffs would ever reappear—no way things would work out with Alessandra after I broke that bond. That's the way I saw it, anyway.

I wondered how Jane viewed our intense weekend affair. I wished I could ask, but I would run the risk of finding out it meant nothing to her. And there was the other small detail: my partnership was now on the line if Warren were to find out about my dalliance with Jane.

"I'll never tell," was what Jane whispered to me over and over after I had tasted and probed every inch of her body for hours. She kept saying I had to trust her. And the truth was, I had no reason not to trust her. I just didn't want to put my livelihood into the hands of a woman—one I'd slept with. Women were unpredictable—especially Jane. I was never sure whether she'd turn on me and want revenge. I'd seen that behavior before with other women.

While we didn't do a lot of talking that Sunday, I remembered fragments of discussion. She asked why I wore pajamas to bed. I don't remember my answer. She said she pictured me sleeping naked. I asked her why she was picturing me at all. And then she didn't answer. She kissed me instead. There was no further mention of the violinist, or what she was planning to do about her marriage.

Late in the afternoon, we ordered two Chinese chicken salads and ate them with chopsticks. I had never allowed food in my bed, but that's where Jane wanted to eat. I didn't object. Jane could have anything she wanted. I couldn't for sure say how many times we did it—only that at the very end, we had nothing left to give each other. I was satiated beyond belief and so was she.

Around 6 p.m., she asked if she could shower. I led her to a guest bathroom, even though my dream of all dreams was to have her in my shower—with me. I longed to soap her up—to rub her entire body clean. But I was not ready to have her see my obsessive shower routine and the wall of shelving that displayed a variety of liquids, soaps, and scrubbing tools. She would think me a freak. And she'd be right.

When she emerged from the guest bathroom, smelling sweet and clean, dressed in the clothes she wore Saturday, I asked if she'd like a ride back to the office. She shook her head, preferring to take an Uber. I remember feeling bereft—she would be missing from my life again.

We stood in silence outside the gate to my home entrance, waiting for the car. It was dark outside—the sky a velvety blue—a cool breeze whistled softly but persistently through the palm trees. I felt as though I were in a trance—floating outside my body—watching the scene unfold before me as though it were the end of a very satisfying movie, the credits rolling upward as our images slowly faded.

When the car arrived, I took her hand and kissed it tenderly. Our eyes met, and she smiled. "See you tomorrow," she said softly. And she was gone.

THE UPCOMING WEEKEND, I had Axel and Anabel, so I knew I'd be occupied and not over-thinking things with Jane.

When I arrived at Bel Air Friday evening, I found Alessandra all dressed up, her dark hair swept into a high bun. She was wearing a little black dress with the diamond necklace and matching bracelet and earrings I'd bought her for our tenth anniversary. It was one of those gifts that somehow assuaged my guilt over the numerous affairs I had perpetuated over our decade together. She looked the way she always looked, classically beautiful but unsexy.

"You look nice," I remarked, as I entered the expensive home where I was no longer welcome. "Hot date tonight?"

"That's none of your business," she returned coolly, brown eyes glinting under the chandelier lights in the entryway.

"It is if he's marriage material," I quipped. I was in no mood to spar with my ex-wife.

"I'm going to need some extra money," Alessandra announced, "Anabel starts sixth grade at The Archer School for Girls next year. It's not going to be cheap."

I drew in my chin and examined her face, which was slightly flushed like she was expecting a fight. "Why wouldn't she just stay at Brentwood? Her grades are good, and the classes there are tougher than college-level courses."

"You don't even know your own kids," Alessandra scoffed, tilting her head back and emitting a small, angry laugh.

"That's not true," I argued. "Anabel told me she's happy where she is."

"That's not what she told me," she snapped, taking a step toward me, and inching her face closer to mine. I caught a hint of her perfume, one I never liked. It was some expensive fragrance with heavy notes smelling of musky figs.

I recalled Anabel in tears, bemoaning her mother's short fuse. "Have you ever considered that Anabel goes along with everything you say because she's afraid of you?"

Alessandra's mouth fell open. "You have no idea what you're talking about. Maybe you should be more involved in your kids' lives. You might actually find out something about them."

"I'd love to, Alessandra, but you fought me in court, remember? You told the whole world I was unfit to be a parent and that's why I only see them twice a month."

"That's bullshit and you know it, Craig," she shouted, pointing her perfectly French-manicured index finger in my face. "You could have had them more if you wanted— you didn't bother trying because chasing women was more important to you—it always has been—admit it."

I took a step back, cast my eyes down at my feet but said nothing.

"Admit it, Craig," she yelled, now fuming at me.

"Please lower your voice," I pleaded, fighting to remain calm. "I don't want to fight." I was exhausted and just wanted to collect my children and drive to Malibu.

Alessandra pursed her lips, still frowning, but she stopped badgering me. She turned and marched down the hallway towards the children's rooms. I prayed they didn't overhear our argument, but I knew in my heart that children hear everything.

Anabel came bounding out first, wearing a red corduroy jacket. I had bought it for her a few months back, thinking it would look cute as we got closer to the holiday season. She ran right up to me and threw her arms around my waist. "Daddy!" she cried.

I loved when she did this. It was so heart-warming to be with my daughter—to know someone loved me unconditionally. "Hi, Princess," I said stroking her blonde hair. I stooped down to give her a kiss on the cheek. She smelled like fresh peaches.

Axel lumbered over next, carrying his iPad—no doubt getting ready for a video game marathon. "How's it going, Buddy?" I called to him. "You have a good week at school?"

He shrugged, blinking his green eyes at me uncomfortably. I always thought the divorce was tougher on Anabel, but it's only because Axel never showed emotions—never expressed himself verbally. He reminded me of myself at age twelve.

I decided I wanted to do something with each of my children this weekend, not just as a group. We usually saw a movie together or went to Disneyland or Knott's Berry Farm, the zoo or something like that. This weekend, I wanted to bond with them individually. I would take Axel to see the Lakers on Saturday night. I had courtside seats courtesy of Staples Center, one of our clients. I would leave Anabel with Sylvia for the evening. During the day, I would take Anabel shopping. She was a fashionista in the making, and I knew just where to go: Maisonette clothing had a pop-up shop this weekend over in Van Nuys. Anabel had dropped a hint a few weeks earlier that she loved Maisonette. I would take her there and to Costa Grande Mexican Restaurant on Sepulveda for lunch. Guacamole and chips were Anabel's favorite.

On the drive home, Anabel sat in the front seat while Axel stretched out in back. I cranked a song by Chvrches on the radio and Anabel adjusted her seat, so she could lay back while I drove, a blissful smile on her face. She suddenly leaned down and reached between her feet, fishing something from the floor of my car.

She held it up to me with a puzzled expression. "Whose is this?" she asked.

I glanced quickly at the object and realized it was Jane's lipstick. It must have rolled out of her purse when I gave her a ride the other night.

"One of my colleagues must have dropped it," I answered. "We had a presentation last week and I gave the team a ride—I'm glad you found it."

She inspected the small black container that looked more like a bullet than anything else. She pulled the cap off the lipstick and twisted it upward. Then she looked in the car mirror and painted her lips with it.

"What are you doing, Anabel?" I asked sternly. "That's not yours, and you're way too young to be wearing lipstick. I told you, that comes later—much later."

I don't know why I was so exasperated. Maybe I wanted Jane's lipstick all to myself—as a memento to savor. I wanted something that touched those beautiful lips every single day. I would keep it at my house with the thought she might return some day and use it. I had already decided I was not going to give it back to her anytime soon.

Anabel ignored me and painted it heavier, pursing her lips together to mix the waxy pink lacquer. She turned toward me and puckered up, blowing a kiss in an exaggerated fashion. I couldn't help but smile because she looked just like DJ. And that was exactly something he would do. DJ was a clown at heart.

I recalled him at age twelve, around Christmastime,

impersonating Elvis. Julia had this long red velvet robe and DJ had borrowed it so he could perform a show for us. He stuffed a pillow in the front where his abdomen was and a pillow in back where his butt was. He tied the sash low around his hips, underneath the pillow so it looked like his gut was hanging over it. Then he arched his back in an overstated manner, did a side-step, and proceeded to belt out "Hound Dog" into an imaginary microphone. Julia laughed uproariously and I, at age seven, just gazed at him in adoring curiosity. He was an oddity to me—someone so full of life—so demonstrative in every movement. I desperately wanted to be like him but knew I couldn't. Just being his brother would have to be enough.

"Daddy, don't you think I'm pretty?" Anabel asked, jarring me out of my DJ stupor.

I glanced over and saw her puckering up. "Okay, you need to wipe that stuff off right away," I scolded, grabbing a tissue out of the car's console, and handing it to Anabel. "You look ridiculous."

"You don't think I'm pretty?" she asked again, giving me a sad, pouty face with the pink lips.

I rolled my eyes at her. "Never mind—just get that stuff off your face."

Instead, she leaned over and kissed me on the cheek, planting a huge pink lipstick stain on me. I just shook my head. She was going to be formidable as a teenager.

ON MONDAY, JANE WAS absent from the partner meeting. She never missed the meeting. I was uncomfortable asking anyone until Warren finally said something.

"With Jane out of the office this week, we'll have to pull Victoria for Wednesday's client presentation." Victoria was VP of accounts and often subbed for Jane when she couldn't be in two places at one time.

"Did Jane go on vacation or something?" I asked, attempting to sound casual. I felt a stab of insecurity—something that was alien to me until Jane came along and disrupted my highly ordered, sanitized life.

Warren made a face. "No, death in the family, unfortunately. She's out on grievance."

I couldn't help my reaction, which was one of concern. I wanted so badly to find out who died and then I remembered Bobbi's comment about Jane's grandfather being in the hospital.

"Her grandfather, right? Are we doing anything for her—I mean on behalf of the agency?" I was trying not to sound too anxious.

"We're sending a rather large pastry platter from Freedman's to the *Shiva* home," Warren answered. Freedman's was reputed to be one of the best Jewish delis in Los Angeles.

As soon as the meeting ended, I hastened to Bobbi's office. She was busy on the phone, grinding Nicorette gum into her molars while ball-busting some hapless media victim, boring down on them to get the rates she wanted. Her gum smacked relentlessly before she made a point.

"You can do better than that," she growled. "Do you think this client is made of money or something?" She rolled her eyes at me and tossed her pen on her desk. I sat across from her and waited patiently for her to finish pounding the poor soul on the other end. She finally hung up and looked at me expectantly. "What's up, *Sheyna*?"

"Jane's grandfather passed away?" I knew I was in danger of showing my true feelings in front of Bobbi, but I couldn't help myself.

Bobbi grimaced. "*Oy*, it's so hard for that kiddo right now," she groaned. "I mean, first with the hubby and now this. I don't know how she's coping."

I pictured Jane grieving over her grandfather and a feeling of sadness came over me. "What did he die of?" I asked finally.

"Had a series of strokes," she answered. "Had one six months ago and just didn't get better—Jane had to move him to hospice over a month ago." Bobbi shook her head, thin, chapped red lips pressed together in sadness.

"Are you going to the service?" I asked, thinking about

my weekend with Jane and wondering how much of what happened was her needing to escape—first the pain of her broken marriage and second the caring for her ill grandfather.

"The service is tomorrow, but I was planning to visit the *Shiva* home in the evening," she answered. "If you'd like, we can go together. Jane's grandmother lives in Los Alamitos so it's a bit of a drive."

"How about if I drive?" I suggested.

Bobbi nodded. "Fine with me. That'll save me an Uber."

Bobbi was a true New Yorker and never bought a car. She insisted on taking public transportation and had recently discovered Uber and Lyft, which she thought were brilliant new concepts.

THAT NIGHT, I COULDN'T stop thinking of Jane. I pulled out my phone, wanting to text her but then decided not to. I just poured my intensity into the gym, where I ran for an hour on the treadmill, jumped rope for another half hour and did a circuit of pushups, reverse crunches, and squats. I pumped upper body weights until my muscles gave out and my arms were shaking. I finished with a fifteen-minute plank. I felt drops of sweat trickling off my forehead onto the mat as I obstinately held the plank, my abdominal muscles searing.

My shower lasted for what seemed like forever because I stood for at least twenty minutes with the hot water just running over my back. For some reason, I couldn't move. Once I realized the time, I went through my cleansing processes and finished up.

In bed with my Scotch, I took a sip and savored the memory of my lost weekend with Jane. I recalled her sleeping to my left and wondered why she picked that side. I imagined that was how she slept with the violinist and suddenly, I felt pangs of jealousy that he had gotten to her first. I usually slept right in the center but, ever since that night, I moved over to the right—like she might at some point return and reclaim her just space in my bed.

By sip number two, I wondered how badly Jane hurt—if

she was beside herself with grief. I pictured her face, twisted up with tears, crying herself to sleep. I wondered if the violinist were with her—whether this loss would drive them back together. Sometimes that happened. A death or a new life brought people together.

# Thirteen

THE DRIVE TOWARD LONG Beach on the 405 was jam-packed with rush hour traffic. It was also Thanksgiving week, so the freeway was a sea of cars scrambling to get to the airport.

Bobbi was busy yapping in the passenger's seat, loudly chomping and popping her Nicorette gum. A long time ago, she tried to light up a cigarette in my car, but I had rebuked her so harshly, she never tried it again.

"What a *schlep*," Bobbi remarked, peeping out the window when traffic came to a halt.

"How come her grandparents live so far south?" I questioned.

"Jane grew up there—in that exact house. Maybe she'll want her grandmother closer to her now," Bobbi mused.

"Have you talked to her?" I asked. "I mean, since her grandfather passed away."

"Not really," she answered. "I just got texts here and there, with directions and times."

"Was it her paternal or maternal grandfather?" I asked, now curious as to who raised the amazing Jane.

"Paternal," Bobbi responded. "So, they're Mercers."

"I've never been to a *Shiva* home," I commented, abruptly changing lanes to get around a slow-moving truck. Bobbi's whole body jerked to the right when I made this move because she refused to wear her seatbelt. She always connected it before she got in so the alarm wouldn't beep incessantly.

"Oh, it's a lot of talking and eating," Bobbi explained, readjusting her seat. "You'll be fine."

When we arrived, I couldn't help but be struck by the age of the neighborhood and house itself. It was in suburban Long Beach, which was quite different from Malibu. I looked around at the old, decrepit mulberry trees planted near the sidewalk, which was heavily cracked, probably from earthquakes of yore. I pictured Jane as a young girl, walking home from school without a hint of knowledge of the spectacular woman she was about to become. I suddenly wanted to see her as a girl—to know what she looked like and what she said—to know what kind of a child she had been.

There was a basin of water at the home's entrance with towels next to it. Bobbi instructed me to wash my hands in the basin, which didn't seem sanitary to me, but I did it anyway, immediately drenching my hands with hand sanitizer afterward. Bobbi hadn't noticed; she was opening the front door, which was unlocked.

"Bobbi, don't you think we should knock first?"

"*Oy, putz*, you don't know anything, do you? I've sat *Shiva* a few times in my day. Stick with me and you won't look like a *schmuck*."

As soon as we were in the door, I surveyed the room, my eyes adjusting to the dim interior. There was a musky, moldy odor. All I could make out were a lot of burning candles, along with people speaking in hushed voices. Black cloths covered what I figured out were mirrors, and huge platters of food sat on every surface.

I stayed close to Bobbi like she was sponsoring me. "What are we supposed to do now?" I whispered.

"We need to find Jane," she responded, taking my hand,

and leading me through the crowd. "There are a lot of people here."

I followed Bobbi through the decaying old one-story house, marveling that this was the house in which Jane grew up. I felt a sense of curiosity that she had no parents and, based on the condition of the house, little financial security.

We toured through old-school saloon doors, leading to a quaint citrus-pocked kitchen with dilapidated appliances that couldn't be from this century. On the wall hung an old-fashioned push-button phone sprouting a long beat-up and stretched-out cord. It reminded me of the set of a seventies' sitcom. The kitchen door opened to the outside where a lot of people were standing near a burning fire pit. Then I saw Jane. She was next to the fire pit with an older, heavy-set woman with a grey beehive hairdo.

"There she is," Bobbi exclaimed, shouldering her way to Jane and bursting into the conversation they were having with some man in a dark suit. I found out later he was the rabbi.

"Kiddo," Bobbi said in the demurest voice she could muster. "*Alav Ha-sholom.*"

"Bobbi," Jane uttered as she was pulled into an embrace. "Thank you for being here."

Jane's eyes were closed so I couldn't gauge the pain she was experiencing. She wore a long-sleeved black dress. Once Jane withdrew from hugging Bobbi, she saw me for the first time.

When our eyes met, I felt her utter grief like a shooting pain ripping through my gut. She wore no makeup but still looked gorgeous—almost tranquil in her despondency. All I wanted was to comfort her. She advanced to where I was, not taking her eyes off mine and I just stood there. I was not sure whether it was appropriate to hug her, so I kept my hands by my side.

That's when I noticed the violinist hovering next to Jane. He looked rough. His eyes were rimmed with dark circles like he hadn't slept in weeks and his hair looked disheveled, spiking out in different directions. I never understood what

Jane saw in the violinist because she seemed so superior to him. He reminded me of an actor from some vampire series—not that I watched them. Alessandra was into those shows. He put his arm around Jane to mark his possession and glared at me with hostility.

"What are *you* doing here?" he demanded in a sour tone.

"Derek, please," Jane chastised. "It's okay." She turned to me. "I'm glad you came."

"I'm so sorry, Jane—I'm sorry for your loss." I didn't know what else to say and certainly was incapable of emulating Bobbi's Hebrew greeting to the attending mourners, but Jane didn't seem to mind or notice.

"Thank you, Craig," Jane responded, just gazing up at me. The violinist lingered near us awkwardly, like he couldn't understand why Jane would give me the time of day, but I didn't leave. There was something in Jane's eyes that wanted me there—an invitation to stay.

Suddenly, the woman with the beehive broke into our conversation with Bobbi right behind her. It was obvious Bobbi and the woman with the beehive had met before. Out of the corner of my eye, I saw the violinist slink off.

"Isn't someone going to introduce me?" the old woman screeched in a loud voice that reminded me of a wild animal. I almost winced at the decibel level.

"Grandma, this is Craig Keller," Jane said softly as though cueing her grandmother to lower her voice for the sobriety of the occasion. "He's a senior partner at our agency."

Jane's grandmother examined me from head to toe as though she were trying to recall where she'd seen me in the past. Her eyes were puffy and red.

"You just missed the other ones—Walter and Jimmy," she announced. "They just left."

"Grandma, you mean Warren and Jeffrey," Jane corrected, in the same soft, polite tone.

"It's a pleasure to meet you, Mrs. Mercer," I said, holding out my hand to shake hers. "I'm sorry it's under these circumstances."

Instead of shaking my hand, she threw her arms around

my neck, pulled me down toward her and planted a kiss on my cheek. "You're a tall one—all *fupitzed*," she bellowed. "You smell good, too. What is that? Some highfalutin' cologne?"

I couldn't help but smile at her unintended comedic riff.

"*Hello*—inappropriate, Grandma," Jane interjected, shaking her head.

"And look at those teeth," she commented, ignoring Jane's admonishment. Instead, she grabbed Bobbi's hand and pulled her into our circle. "Are those real?" she asked, pointing at my mouth.

"The last time I checked," I answered, shooting an amused glance at Jane, who looked embarrassed but said nothing.

"What color are your eyes?" she inquired, now inspecting them closely. "Haven't I met you before? You look familiar."

"The man's a celebrity," Bobbi croaked. "You've probably seen him in some magazine."

"Jane, you didn't tell me a celebrity was sitting *Shiva* with us," she said throwing an annoyed look to Jane, who still wore a mortified expression. Grandma Mercer turned back to me. "You look hungry. You're much too thin. Have something to eat," she demanded, surveying the area, and taking me by the hand. "Bobbi, you, too. Let's get some food for these two—Jane, make yourself useful."

I looked helplessly back at Jane. "Oh no, thank you, Mrs. Mercer. I'm really not hungry."

"Nonsense," she protested, corralling me to a table with huge platters of meat, cheese, fruit, and pastries. "You need to eat something. *Esn meyn kind!* And call me Barbara. Bobbi, come over here—there's *milchig* and *fleishig*."

Bobbi turned up at my side, leaned over and whispered in my ear, "Just eat something—it's what we do here." Then she began piling things onto a plate. She handed the full plate to me, along with a fork, knife, and napkin.

"I can't eat this," I muttered to Bobbi under my breath, staring distastefully at the mass in front of me. It was full of things I never ate.

"You call that a plate?" Grandma Mercer had snuck up behind me and was now scrutinizing what Bobbi had stacked. "I've seen birds eat more than you."

I smiled and said politely, "Thank you, but this is plenty of food."

"*Oy*, the *goyim*," Bobbi commented, giving Mrs. Mercer an all-knowing smile. "Leave him be."

I felt Jane at my side, her arm linked through mine, and she pulled me off to a more secluded part of the backyard. I just followed her, holding the full plate and utensils in my hand awkwardly. The yard was spacious and there was a rusty old swing set in one corner. I pictured Jane as a child, in the swing on warm summer afternoons.

Once we were alone, Jane took the plate and utensils from my hand and set them down on a side table. "You don't have to eat if you're not hungry," she said pensively.

"Are you sure?" I asked, noticing Jane's skin was clear and dewy. She didn't need makeup. "Your grandmother seems pretty serious when it comes to food."

Jane smiled. "We all are," she admitted. "But don't worry—I'll tell her I watched you scarf the whole plate down."

"Are you okay?" I asked, suddenly feeling the urge to kiss her.

She nodded, tears forming. I couldn't help myself at that point; I put my arms around her and pulled her close to me. I lowered my head and nuzzled my face into her long shiny hair, inhaling her clean scent deeply, not wanting to let go. Surprisingly, she didn't resist. I felt her head turn to the side, her body quiver slightly as tears flowed down her face. We stayed this way for what seemed like an eternity and everyone else seemed to vanish. It was a private moment I didn't want to end.

Finally, I released Jane from my grasp and studied her face. Her eyes were still wet with tears. I brushed off the tears gently with my fingertips and leaned down, kissing her tenderly on the forehead. "You're going to be okay," I whispered.

"What's going on here?" The violinist broke into our affectionate twilight.

Jane backed away from me quickly but didn't take her eyes off mine. "Nothing," she answered. "Nothing at all."

"It looks like something to me," the violinist accused, staring me down like a dog ready to pounce. I recalled his rough shot to my jaw a few years earlier. I had let him do it without remonstration because I felt deserving of his wrath. I felt differently now.

"Don't make this about you," I responded flatly to his implication, drawing myself up to my full height. Then I turned back to Jane, who was still peering up at me, almost as though she wanted me to save her—to gather her in my arms and run far away from this house of pain—to rescue her.

"You call me if you need *anything*," I said. "I mean it." I took her hands in mine and squeezed them.

She nodded. "Thank you for being here."

I let go of Jane's hands and drifted through the crowd, which was building. I spotted Marisa and Kat, two women I had no desire to run into, and realized it was time to grab Bobbi and get out of there. When I located Bobbi, she was with Grandma Mercer, smoking. Both women were puffing away, intermittently taking bites of cheese Danish. I recognized the Danishes from the plate Jane had so kindly disposed of for me.

"There's my *sheyna punim*," Bobbi rasped as I approached. She quickly stomped out her cigarette in the grass. "You ready to go?"

I nodded and turned my attention to Grandma Mercer, who was also stomping out her smoke. "Mrs. Mercer, I just wanted to again offer my condolences at this difficult time. I—we love Jane."

Grandma Mercer gave me a strange look, as though she were trying to figure something out. "Thank you, *boychik*," she responded. "My Janie's a good girl. And she was so close to Bruce." As she uttered the last words, I saw tears in her eyes.

"Jane's my saving grace," Bobbi interjected, giving Mrs. Mercer another hug and kiss.

As we found our way out of the house, I noticed a distinguished-looking man enter with an older Asian woman at his side. His eyes struck me with familiarity. They were almost exactly like Jane's. I instinctively turned around and saw Jane standing there, frozen, staring at the man with a look that was somewhere between shock and horror.

Bobbi grabbed my arm and pulled me with her. "Let's move or we'll be here all night," she commanded.

Once in the car, headed back North on the 405, I posed an inquiry to Bobbi. "Who was that man—the one who came in as we were leaving?"

"I'm pretty sure that was Aaron Mercer—Jane's father," she answered, grimacing.

"I didn't realize he was alive," I said, recalling the look on Jane's face, almost like she was seeing a ghost.

"He left her when she was eight. Was a mean bastard—a real *shicker* and nasty as hell to Jane. I'm sure she hates him and hasn't seen him since."

"Should we have left her there to deal with that alone?" I asked, worried now about Jane having to go through an unexpected reunion with someone who obviously hurt and abandoned her for good.

"What are we supposed to do about it?" she asked incredulously, popping a Nicorette into her mouth. "Sometimes it's best to leave family drama where it is—at home. We did our part. We showed up."

My heart filled with a sense of heaviness. *What kind of man would leave a little girl alone?* She was only eight for God's sake—younger than Anabel. I couldn't imagine leaving Anabel—saying an uncaring or callous word to her. I treasured my daughter and only wanted the best for her. I ached to think that Jane had been so cruelly maligned as a child. It made me long to make things better for her—to give her what her father took away—which was obviously love—the one thing every child needs to grow and succeed in life.

It unexpectedly struck me that my own adolescence and the life I left behind after DJ's death were similar. I felt in some odd, paradoxical way, Jane and I were the same. We shared a bond of loneliness and rejection. I put my hand on my jacket lapel and found that it was still damp with Jane's tears.

# Fourteen

THANKSGIVING WAS A DAY away, and I sat in my office trying to concentrate on work. I had passed Jane's door several times knowing it would remain closed and locked, her office dark inside until she returned. I resisted the urge to call and see how she was. This holiday season would be the most difficult for her, simultaneously grieving a loved one and going through a marital crisis.

Right before we closed the office for the holidays, I got a surprise visit from Marisa Silva, Jane's best friend. Pearl buzzed my office and announced she was in the lobby waiting for me. There was an excited quality to Pearl's voice. I wasted no time strolling out to meet her, wondering why on earth she would want to see me. We had a history. I didn't suspect it would be pleasant.

"Marisa," I greeted her without warmth. She stood and approached me, wearing a snug olive pantsuit with a crème silk blouse underneath. Marisa was a beautiful woman but not at all my type. She was just one of those women who grated on my nerves—too aggressive for my taste.

"Craig Keller," she began, voice clipped. "Thanks for seeing me. I would have called but I happened to be in the neighborhood and decided to stop by instead."

"Would you like to step into my office?" I couldn't help but notice people pausing in the lobby, gawking at Marisa. The agency had its share of high-profile, famous clients, but Marisa had her own talk show and was an international celebrity. She was the Latina version of Oprah. The employees likely thought her a prospective client.

"That'd be great," she responded, again in the staccato tone, as she followed me down the hall.

Once we were in my office, I closed the door and gestured for her to sit down in one of the chairs opposite my desk.

"This won't take long," she said with a look that told me she meant business. She took the seat across from me as I walked around and sat behind my desk.

"Let me guess," I began coolly. "This is about Jane."

"You've always been an astute man, Craig." Her voice dripped with sarcasm as she tossed her long black hair, leaning back in the chair.

"Well, given we have nothing else in common, I just took a long shot." I was in no mood for this impromptu meeting.

"I saw you at the *Shiva* home last night," she accused, like I had done something horrible.

"Congratulations," I replied in a sardonic tone. "I was there with a work colleague offering condolences to Jane and her family."

She shook her head and blinked—a look of disgust on her face. "Well, in case you didn't know, you caused quite a stir with Jane's husband and that's why I'm here."

I thought back to the violinist and his reaction to my being there. He must have complained to Marisa after I had gone. *What a pussy.* "I didn't mean to—I was only there to support Jane, along with the rest of the partners."

Marisa shifted irritably in her chair and leaned forward. "What are you doing, Craig?"

I took a deep breath. "I'm not sure what you're after, Marisa, because my only intention was to be there for Jane. If her husband was upset, there's nothing I can do about that, now is there?"

"You can stay away from Jane," she threatened, lips squeezed together. "She's extremely vulnerable right now. She's going through something personal with her husband and she just lost her grandfather. She doesn't need you there, sniffing around and causing trouble."

I leaned back in my chair, crossed my arms over my chest and said nothing. Marisa was on a mission to protect her friend, but she didn't know the half of it. If Marisa found out what happened the night we went to Michael's, she'd be more than a little furious.

"Well?" she pushed. "Are you going to stay away from her?"

"I work with her," I answered. "There's only so much I can do to avoid her."

"I'm not talking about work and you know it," she shot back, pointing her index finger at me.

"Then why are you in *my* office talking about this?" I asked. I knew my ability to remain calm was pissing her off—I could tell by the frown lines between her eyebrows—they were deepening with each word spoken.

She turned and looked around my office and at the door, as though someone might hear us, dark hair spilling over her pantsuit jacket in swirls. She turned back and gave me a stern look. "I'm just going to spell it out for you, Craig. Jane has a thing for you—she has for years—none of us have ever understood why, but she does. She's not thinking clearly right now so it's up to you to be a grownup and respect her need to heal."

"I'll do my best," I responded, thinking Jane had obviously told her friends at some point she had a thing for me. I wondered how much of what happened was due to her vulnerability and how much had to do with her feelings for me. I hated that Jane's friends all saw me as a nemesis and someone who was trying to destroy her life.

"You'll do more than that," Marisa snapped before getting to her feet and flouncing to the doorway. Before she left, she turned around one more time: "I mean it Craig—stay *away* from her." She thundered out like a freight train, leaving my door open.

Marisa had blackmailed me with video of Jane and me together many years ago. It's how she got me to leave Jane alone the first time I messed with her. I wondered whether that was what she had on me. I put my elbow on the desk and sank my head in my hand.

SOON AFTER MARISA FIRED off her hostile invective in my office, I drove home to prepare for my incoming guests: Don and Julia. They were staying through the holiday weekend. Alessandra's family had been in town since the previous weekend. Our deal was that I would get the kids on the evening of Thanksgiving through the weekend, so they could spend equal time with both sets of grandparents.

There was much to do at the house; and I had it fully staffed with Sylvia, my cook Camilla, and back-up cooking and cleaning crews. Don and Julia were fanatics about perfection and cleanliness and would not hesitate to show their displeasure if anything were out of place.

Wednesday evening, I sent a car to LAX for them. Nervously pacing the living room, stopping at the floor-to-ceiling windows which overlooked the ocean-facing back yard, patio, and large infinity pool, I examined my reflection. I looked tall and slim, with broad shoulders—a product of my intense nightly workouts.

Then I heard the doorbell ring, turned, and waited for Sylvia to answer, which she did immediately. The sound of Julia's voice lilted from the hallway and I felt the hairs on my neck stand at attention. Julia was the kinder and warmer of my two parents, but something had changed after DJ's death. She had become distant. And after I divorced Alessandra, our relationship had almost completely disintegrated. I talked to her once a month at most and our conversations were short, shallow, and stilted.

Sylvia had ushered them into the house, and they were suddenly standing before me. Julia smiled before Don did.

"Craig," she called, approaching me slowly and with grace, like she was being filmed for a movie role. *Meryl Streep in 'Death Becomes Her'*. She was wearing a red knit St. John skirt suit that had a nautical look—navy pockets and gold buttons down the front. She wore smart low-heeled navy pumps. When she got near me, she put both hands on either side of my face, not kissing me, but just examining.

"You look well, darling," she intoned softly, her eyes grazing my face like a plastic surgeon, checking on how her creation was aging. She seemed pleased with the result.

I looked past her to Don, who was handing Sylvia his overcoat and hanging onto his cane possessively. Don had walked with a limp ever since he hurt his back in a car accident. Now he never went anywhere without the cane—he had started calling it his third leg. It had an ivory eagle for its grip, and the rest was black lacquered wood.

"Don," I said, freeing myself of Julia's hands and advancing to where my father was standing. He wore a formal, charcoal grey suit, like he had jumped onto the flight straight from work. I knew better than to hug him. He distained hugs and kisses of any kind—he thought it was weak and unmanly. "How was the flight?"

"Flight was good, son," he responded, surveying my home with a discerning eye. He was likely checking for dust, which he would never be able to find. I made sure of it.

"Why don't you relax and settle in? We'll have dinner around eight," I suggested, glancing at my watch, and gesturing to Sylvia to get Don and Julia's bags to their room.

"Of course, darling," Julia replied while following Sylvia. "I can't wait to catch up on everything."

When she said 'everything' I knew what that meant. It was time to talk about my romantic life. Sometimes I felt Julia was worse than the relentless tabloid reporters—pawing for information on my private life.

MY LOVE LIFE WAS the first thing Julia brought up at dinner, as soon as we clinked glasses of an old Château

Lafite-Rothschild, Pauillac, which cost upwards of $1,000 a bottle, but it was Don's favorite. After all, it was Thanksgiving, and I was prospering at the agency. That was obvious.

"Are you seeing anyone, Craig?" Julia asked before inserting a forkful of pumpkin ravioli into her mouth. She was exactly who Anabel would look like when she got older—after she'd had a husband and children and a full life. I tried to fast forward Anabel to that time in her life—in her golden years—and I prayed she would be happier than Julia—more aware of who she was. It was true, Julia was more interesting than most, with her numerous volumes of published poetry. She wrote about deep things but concealed that depth when in social situations or at any time when she was with Don. Sometimes, when we were alone and free from Don's influence, her warmth would reluctantly emerge—like a pilot crawling out from shattered wreckage in the middle of a jungle.

"No one special," I responded to Julia's inquiry. "I've been busy with the agency—in fact, I'm aggressively *not looking*." I added for emphasis. They appreciated my work ethic and would grudgingly accept that as an excuse as to why I was not with anyone.

"You know, son, the worst mistake you ever made was divorcing Alessandra," Don grumbled with his mouth full, before taking a sip of the rare, expensive wine. He let out a slight belch while still chewing. "She's a treasure and you'll be lucky to find someone half as good."

I thought about Alessandra and her lack of sexuality, her uninspiring personality, and her disparaging attitude toward me, and I cringed. There was no way I could explain how I really felt to Don and Julia. They just had their minds made up about Alessandra—they cavalierly dismissed the unhappiness I felt in the marriage and nothing would change that—nothing ever.

ON THANKSGIVING DAY, WE drove to Marina Del Rey and had an expensive brunch at Café Del Rey. I tried to keep the conversation light, but Julia kept bringing it back to depressing realities about my broken marriage, separation from my children, and how I was generally an ostracized member of society. She had this habit of throwing in hints that I had embarrassed her in front of her society friends with the numerous tabloid photos during the divorce.

Back at home that evening, we prepared for our Thanksgiving dinner. I dressed in a hunter green pullover sweater with black jeans and Grenson leather boots. Don and Julia, who were stuffy and always into appearances, dressed in their usual finery. Julia even questioned me when I emerged from my bedroom.

"Where's your suit, darling?" she asked, lips pursed. "It's Thanksgiving—how about dressing for a sense of occasion?" As she said this, she gestured to her own outfit, a black cocktail dress with long, translucent sleeves. Multi-colored embroidered flowers were splashed all over the tulle bodice and full skirt, which puffed out like a ballerina. Her large, dangly diamond earrings sparkled around her face.

"Because I wear a suit every day," I answered, scanning my own clothes, which were highly stylish and hardly inexpensive. "Besides, it's only the three of us."

She shrugged, but I could tell it displeased her that I refused to change.

Our dinner was perfect from an aesthetic standpoint. Camilla and her staff were on point with their maple-glazed turkey with apple-sausage stuffing. The gratin potatoes with Gorgonzola cheese and shiitake mushrooms were creamy and decadent, as were the numerous sides and more expensive red wine.

After dinner, I treated my parents to the special Scotch and we sat in the living room, as Julia admired the Chagall masterpieces. There was no way they could deny their only son's success. I just wished they would acknowledge it.

Around 8 p.m., I heard the doorbell ring. Thinking Alessandra might have sent the kids over early, I bounded to the door, instead of letting Sylvia answer.

I caught my breath because it was Jane Mercer, standing

there on my doorstep, looking beautiful as ever, dressed in all black. She wore a cashmere sweater tucked into a skirt that was snug at the hips and flared out in two pleated panels. Tall black leather boots with stiletto heels completed her sleek look. I felt my heart skip a beat. I was so happy to see her. "Jane," I breathed, feeling like I was in a dream sequence.

"I'm sorry—I tried to call, and I texted but you didn't answer. I was driving up PCH and remembered where you live. I decided to take my chances. Are you—um—alone?"

I could see pain in her eyes and I immediately welcomed her. In fact, I was dying for her to rescue me from my staid parents and their eternal disappointment. "Please come in," I encouraged, standing to the side to let her into the house. She edged past me with reticence. "My parents are here," I told her as soon as she had crossed the threshold.

"Oh—I'm sorry—I should leave," she exclaimed, looking embarrassed and turning toward the door. "I should have known you'd have family here on Thanksgiving."

"No, Jane—please stay. I want you to meet them," I responded quickly.

"Are you sure? You just—well, when you told me to call if I needed something—and I was thinking I—um ...." She was wringing her hands as she said this.

"Of course," I uttered deferentially. I wasn't sure what was happening, but I wanted her more than ever at this moment, regardless of Marisa's warning that I 'stay away from Jane', regardless of the potential loss of my partnership should Warren get wind of our affair.

"I spent Thanksgiving with my Grandma—we went out for an early dinner but, you know, it's just not the same without Grandpa. She's so sad." Jane took a moment to draw a deep breath. "And Derek went to Seattle to see his family. So, you see—I'm alone and I ..." her voice trailed off and tears formed in her eyes.

I couldn't help but think about what a flat-out bastard the violinist was to leave Jane on her first significant holiday without her grandfather. *What a prick!*

"It's fine—I want you here—please stay," I urged, taking

her by the hand and leading her to where my parents were in the living room, Scotches akimbo.

"Don, Julia," I announced. "I'd like you to meet Jane Mercer—she's a partner at the agency."

They both smiled, set their Scotches down and rose to their feet, approaching Jane. My mother looked Jane from head to toe and gave her that fake luncheon-lady smile while Don, who wore a blue smoking jacket with black lapels and belt, grabbed her hand, squeezed it too hard and shook it with vigor.

"I'm pleased to meet you," Jane said. "Sorry to intrude on your Thanksgiving."

"The pleasure's all mine, lass," Don gushed in his usual boisterous Irish manner, shooting a lascivious glance at Jane's black leather boots. "You're not intruding on anything."

Jane looked as though she needed help and I took my cue. "We have a lot going on at the office right now," I explained. "Jane tried to call my cell, but I turned it off during dinner. Will you please excuse us? We'll go outside to discuss business."

With that I steered Jane out to the back patio with me. The only light was from the illuminated pool, which cast a green, shimmery, mischievous glow along the walkway. I led her around the pool, and we leaned against the outer rail, the one separating my property from the dark, restless ocean. We were silent for a full minute.

"You look a lot like your dad," Jane finally commented. "Your parents are both good-looking, but I don't know why that would be a surprise."

I smiled but said nothing. I was watching Jane's body language, which seemed relaxed, like she trusted me.

"I still can't believe this is where you live," she continued, gazing over the rail and then back at my house, which was openly lit up like a candle in the blackness of night. "Your family must love to visit you."

I thought about Don and Julia and how their mansion in Sausalito was at least three times the size of my home. I remembered Jane's humble upbringing and felt guilty—guilty at the luxury I took for granted. If this made Jane happy, I would give it all to her without question. That's how much I loved her.

"I've missed you," I said while still staring into the sunless ocean. The only noise around us was the sound of crashing waves lapping relentlessly at the sand and rocks before retreating with the tide.

"You have?" she asked, turning her body toward me.

I didn't respond. *What did she want me to say?* I felt awkward, like I was finally with the princess I always wanted but was too tongue-tied to talk to her like a normal person. This was yet another alien feeling for me—I never lost my confidence in the presence of a woman. *Never.*

"How *much* have you missed me?" she asked, glancing up at me in the darkness. Light from the full moon and the still, glittery sky gave Jane's face a soft radiance.

That was it—an invitation to kiss her, which I'd dreamed of since she was in my bed only a few weeks ago. But so much had happened since then. I loved her—I loved her fully and completely and had no reason to stop myself.

"Let's see, shall we?" I leaned down and pressed my lips against hers. She put her arms around my neck and opened her mouth to me. I dreamily inhaled her clean scent. All I wanted was to carry her into my bedroom, take her clothes off and make love to her all night. Neither of us halted the kiss, one which could have lasted a week. I pressed my body against hers, dipping her back slightly against the railing. My hand wandered to her breasts and I felt an immediate erection.

"Craig, your children are here." We were interrupted by Julia's impatient voice. I withdrew immediately from Jane, my erection depleting as soon as the words were uttered.

"Be right there," I called to Julia in a throaty voice. "I'm sorry," I whispered to Jane.

"Oh my God," she exclaimed, putting her hand to her mouth. "I'm humiliated."

"No, don't worry about it," I assured her. I was certain Julia saw everything, but I didn't know what to say. We had been officially busted by my mother.

"I can't go back in there," Jane cried, sounding panic-stricken. "I never should have come here tonight."

"Don't be silly," I responded, keeping my voice cool and controlled. "I'm forty years old. I don't explain myself to my parents." I took Jane by the hand and pulled her with me back inside the house.

Anabel was in the living room getting the inquisition from her grandparents. When Jane and I approached, everyone turned in our direction.

"Did you have a nice Thanksgiving?" I asked Anabel.

She looked fresh-faced from the cool outdoor air and her cheeks were slightly blushed. She nodded and ran over to me, throwing her arms around my waist and burying her face in my sweater. "I missed you, Daddy," she mumbled into the wool. Her breath felt warm against my chest.

I caught Jane with a sweet smile on her face—almost as though she had never considered me a real father until this moment. "Where's your brother?" I asked, caressing Anabel's shoulders.

"I'm here, Dad," Axel called from the hallway. He had obviously dropped his things in his room. For the first time, I detected a slight froggy sound in his voice, like it was starting to change.

"Anabel, Axel—I want you to meet someone," I said to them. "This is Jane. She works with me at the office." My heart swelled with pride to introduce them. Anabel blinked at Jane with curiosity.

Jane smiled graciously and held out her hand. "It's nice to meet you, Anabel." Anabel shook her hand without sentiment.

Axel appeared and gave Jane a distrustful stare-down with his serious light jade eyes, not speaking.

"Axel, where are your manners?" I scolded, looking down at my youthful doppelgänger expectantly. "Say hello to Jane."

"Hello Jane," he grudgingly muttered, unable to look her in the eye.

"Great to meet you, Axel," she responded, knowing better than to extend her hand to my son.

"You're the one with the pink lipstick, right?" Anabel charged, pointing at Jane's lips. Jane shot me an uncomfortable look. "That's the same color, right, Daddy?" Anabel then examined my face and declared, "It's on you now, too."

I instinctively put my fingers to my mouth and wiped it. Out of the corner of my eye, I caught Julia with a disappointed look on her face. This was turning into a disaster quickly.

"Daddy, *you* have her lipstick—the one I found in the car—it's in your room on your nightstand. Remember? I'll go get it."

Before I could stop her, Anabel tore off into my bedroom to retrieve Jane's MAC lipstick in a shade of Bombshell. I was struck with a certain shame that Anabel outed me for hoarding Jane's lipstick on my nightstand. I had examined it every night while sipping Scotch, twisting it up and down, obsessing over Jane's lips. I was also beyond mortified that my parents now knew Jane and I were more than work colleagues—not because I was embarrassed to be with Jane, but sorry she would be compromised before they even knew her. Jane just stood there looking like she wanted to flee through the nearest exit.

Julia gave Jane a cold look, evaluating her every move in the presence of her only son, the one she wished *hadn't* survived the yachting accident. Don, the eternal narcissist, had no clue what was going on and certainly didn't care, as long as his next glass of Scotch was imminent.

Axel didn't speak. He wore a quizzical expression, like he was trying to piece together what was going on between his father and the beautiful auburn-haired woman. Axel was a boy of few words, but he was definitely no one's fool.

Anabel returned and handed the little black bullet-shaped lipstick to Jane, who accepted it, turning it in her fingers contemplatively.

"Thank you, but this isn't mine," she said, giving Anabel a slight smile. She passed the lipstick to me. "I'm sure the owner will turn up at some point."

We exchanged a glance I couldn't even describe. I quickly dropped the lipstick into the left front pocket of my jeans.

"I have to go now. It was lovely meeting all of you," Jane said, bowing her head slightly to my offspring. She turned to Don and Julia. "Enjoy your holiday weekend."

Then she looked up at me. "Craig, thank you for being available," she said with the utmost professionalism. And she was gone.

I went to bed that night thinking about our kiss and her words. Something was happening here, and it wasn't my imagination—not just something I wished for and wanted desperately. It was happening.

I WAS THE FIRST one up Friday morning. Usually I could never beat Don, who rattled around for at least an hour before I awakened. Today was different. I had a reason to get up early—I was so happy. I wished I were waking up to Jane, seeing her in the olive-green silk robe, wrestling with the tassel cord to keep her breasts covered before I jerked the robe off her again.

I poured coffee and pulled the *Times* up on my tablet. After a few minutes of reading the news, I heard footsteps padding closer, muffled by the thick wool rug in the hallway. It was not Don's uneven limp with the cane, nor was it the kids, who wouldn't be awake for hours. Julia rounded the corner into the kitchen. She was already fully showered and dressed, wearing a dark-green sweater and black pants, the clothes draping elegantly on her slender frame. Her smart, shoulder-length blonde bob bounced from side to side as she walked.

"Good morning, Craig. How did you sleep?" She had a strained look on her face.

"Julia—you're up early," I responded. "Would you like some coffee?"

"I'll get it, darling," she said, voice quavering a little. She was never up this early. Never as far back as I could recall. I wondered what was on her mind.

I watched her pour coffee, empty a packet of sweetener into it and stir it with a spoon. She carefully lifted the cup by its handle and settled across from me at the kitchen table.

"Craig," she began, eyeing me pensively, yet with admiration.

I often caught Julia admiring my looks, like she was exceedingly proud of her tall, good-looking spawn. I wished she were proud of who I was, but the looks seemed more important to her than anything else. Appearances in general motivated Julia.

"You know I don't like to pry," she threw out as a disclaimer.

"Since when?" I replied with a laugh. "You *live* to pry."

"I'm serious," she answered without smiling. "I have to ask you what's going on with that woman from work."

"You mean Jane." I knew she would get there at some point. That's why she got up early. To her credit, she was protecting me from Don's interrogation. She obviously hadn't shared with him what she witnessed outside by my pool the night before.

I was not sure how to position my relationship with Jane to Julia. She would never fathom the bond we shared, nor would she ever understand a woman like Jane in the first place. The only type of woman Julia liked was Alessandra. Period.

"I'm just wondering if you're serious with that woman." She paused for a moment, which told me she was getting ready to lecture me. "Because if you're not, you probably shouldn't have introduced her to my grandchildren."

I loved how she skipped a complete generation and referred to Axel and Anabel as *her grandchildren*. I tried to breathe calmly and keep my temper under control. "Maybe I *am* serious," I answered coolly, looking her square in the eye. "Regardless, I know exactly what I'm doing with *my children*."

"Craig, darling, please don't take this the wrong way. I

know men have needs and, based on what I saw last night, your needs are being met by that woman."

"You mean Jane." *What was her problem? She couldn't say Jane's name? What was she afraid of? That Jane might be a real person and I could be in love with her?*

"But what would you have done had that been Axel or Anabel who caught you outside kissing that woman? It's bad enough they saw you with lipstick all over your face. What would you have said if they saw where your hands were? I mean, honestly, Craig, we raised you to be a proper gentleman. I don't know how that woman was raised but clearly good morals were not part of her upbringing."

"I'm going to say this one more time—*that woman's* name is Jane, and *her morals* are just fine. If you want to examine loose morals, look at me and then go look in the mirror because I'm *your* creation."

"Craig Axel Keller, you apologize this instant!" Julia's face was reddening. "I'm still your mother."

"You're right," I responded. "And I'm sorry I disappoint you in every possible way, but please leave Jane out of this. She's an exceptional woman who's a role model for every child—not just Axel and Anabel."

"A *role model*," Julia repeated in disbelief. "Really, Craig? She was wearing a wedding ring, for goodness sake. I suppose you were too busy with your hands all over her to notice that."

"I'm through talking about this. Think whatever you want but please refrain from saying another word about Jane."

Julia studied me for a minute in silence, obviously unsure of what just hit her. One thing I knew about Julia is that she always backed down in the end. It was from living with an alpha male all these years. She knew when she had gone too far.

"I'm sorry. I didn't know you felt so strongly. You just told us the other night that you weren't seeing anyone. You've never once brought her up in conversation."

"Maybe that's because I knew how you'd react." I tossed

the tablet down and rose to my feet, furious at Julia's pretentious, judgmental attitude. I was so angry, I could feel my hands shaking, so I did the appropriate thing and left the room.

LATER THAT DAY, I sent Julia with the kids to see a Disney movie while Don and I tackled eighteen holes at the Bel Air Country Club. I was still a member, even though I no longer lived in the neighborhood. Golfing with Don was amusing because he used a cane to walk, right up until the moment he would take a swing. He spent most of his time in the golf cart watching me, swearing like a sailor, and berating the universe whenever he missed a putt, which was rare.

Being with Don on the golf course was the surest way to get information. It's because he was off-guard and not thinking so seriously about work.

"Ever talk to Stephan?" I asked him in an off-handed way. Stephan Towne was Hayden's father and California's Attorney General. Don had had an adversarial relationship with him his entire career.

"Stephan? No, but that crooked bastard's always crawling around my business," Don spat while assiduously teeing off.

"Crooked?" I asked, trying not to sound too interested. That's how you had to play it with Don to fish for intel. He wouldn't give it up if he were on to you. It was a lawyer trick of his.

"He's up to his eyeballs in corruption—you know the bastard just got re-elected—took dirty money during the campaign—several million from a lobbyist with ties to Russian banks, for fuck's sake. It's been all over the *Chronicle*—there's an active investigation."

"Really," I said, positioning myself for a long shot. "I'm sure his daughter wouldn't want anyone to know about that."

"His daughter?" Don growled. "You mean the older or the younger one?"

"Younger—the one you had me hire."

"Oh yeah," Don responded, like he was just now recalling how he ordered me to take on Hayden as an employee to ease his relations with her father. "She doesn't still work there, now, does she?"

I rolled my eyes at Don's selective amnesia. "Not after she stole half my clients and started her own agency. *Remember?*"

Don stopped his golf game temporarily to search my face with his piercing jade-colored eyes. His forehead dripped with sweat in the warm afternoon sun. "Fuck's sake—that's right, son." He lowered his gaze as though recalling the whole situation and feeling slightly responsible for part of my downfall. "But look at you—you recovered nicely, didn't you? You're a Keller—and we never lay down, no matter how we've been double-crossed."

Don looked so pleased with himself, I didn't have the heart to tell him how badly Hayden had beaten me at my own game. He wouldn't be so pleased with that part of the story.

"When you say Stephan's being investigated, what does that mean? Can he be removed from office?"

Don shrugged but gave me a sly look. "If I were a bettin' man, I'd lay odds that it'll turn out much worse for that crooked bastard. He'd better pray his only comeuppance is to be removed from office, instead of indicted by a grand jury and thrown in the slammer."

"What do you have on him?" I prodded, knowing I was moving a little too far into Don's professional terrain but not caring. I was on a mission for damaging information on the Towne family.

"It involves a serious crime, son. And that crooked bastard's fingerprints are all over it." He turned and limped toward the golf cart, signaling me to do the same.

Just like that, I had all the ammunition I needed for the time being.

SUNDAY ROLLED AROUND, AND it was time for Don and Julia to return to San Francisco, Axel and Anabel to their mother's house. When the limo arrived to pick up my parents, Julia regarded me solemnly, like she wanted to say one last thing, but she didn't. She simply patted my face with her hand and said, "Goodbye, Craig. See you at Christmas."

# Fifteen

OBBI WAS IN MY office bright and early Monday, snapping her Nicorette and gulping coffee. She had never been married, and I could see why. What man would put up with the incessant smoking and consumption of nicotine gum? She always reeked of coffee and stale cigarettes. I tried not to get too close most of the time, even though I loved her dearly.

This morning's rant had to do with Veronica's new policy that shorted everyone's vacation by three days. They were bullshit holidays like Flag Day and Presidents' Weekend, but Bobbi was not happy.

"I work my *tuchus* off," she bleated, intermittently gulping at the coffee, and shoving the gum into her mouth, the sticky masses popping as she chomped. "I don't even take sick days, but I like my holidays off—all the other agencies get those days off."

I just sat sipping my cappuccino and waiting for Bobbi's rant to end. "Then take the days off—you know I don't care," I finally interjected.

"But it's not *you* who keeps track of it," she argued. "Veronica's the attendance Nazi—she'll charge me vacation time."

169

I yawned and browsed my computer screen.

"How was your Thanksgiving?" she asked as though she suddenly realized there was another person in the room.

"It was great—the parents were in—I'm glad it's over. Now I just have to get through Christmas." Bobbi knew I couldn't stand the holiday season. "How was yours?"

"Oh, you know, I don't get into the whole Thanksgiving thing," she said with a wave of her hand. "I went to a friend's house."

It struck me that Bobbi was lonely. Her parents were gone, and she had no husband and no children. I knew she had a niece who lived in New York. I should have invited Bobbi to my home for Thanksgiving—she would have been welcome comic relief with Don and Julia and their dysfunctional charade.

Later that morning, I attended the partner meeting. It was just Jeffrey and Jane sitting there when I entered the room. I wasn't sure how to act toward Jane at the office—now that we shared a secret. She looked effortlessly cool in a grey flannel pinstripe pantsuit. It had an asymmetrical collar. Her long hair was shiny and straight, pulled behind her ears.

"Good morning—welcome back, Jane," I greeted her, forcing my voice to a professional tenor. Jane gave me a smile, but it wasn't a warm smile. It was her fake work smile. I'd seen it many times.

"Thank you," she replied. "It's good to be back."

Warren entered the room and we sat in our usual formation to run through client updates. It was difficult for me to concentrate on work with Jane sitting across from me. At one point, she caught me staring at her, no doubt with longing in my eyes. I promptly looked down at my files and tried not to let my gaze drift near her again, no matter how much I wanted to. She was hard not to look at.

"Where are we on Kenton Fox's new campaign?" Warren inquired, casting an expectant glance in my direction.

"The photo shoot is Thursday afternoon," I announced. "They approved the photographer—German guy who's flying in from New York. He's costing a fortune, so we'd better get the right shot."

"Alonzo's going to be there to art direct, right?" Warren asked, skeptically.

"Of course," I replied. Sometimes Warren treated me like the kid copywriter I once was. It was irritating. "The only challenge will be what we do in post—you know how aging entertainers feel about post-production."

"This guy's going to be a real pant-load from what I can tell," Jeffrey remarked. "Craig, you're going to have to use your *charm* to get them to sign off on something." He winked at me after he said this.

"Would you like to be at the shoot, Jeffrey?" I offered this more as a courtesy because of Jeffrey's past as creative director. I know it irked him when Alonzo went rogue and didn't include him in major creative decisions.

"That's all right," Jeffrey responded. "This client's all yours and Alonzo's."

I gave him a sarcastic, tight-lipped smile. "I appreciate that."

At the end of the meeting, Warren assigned industry events for us to attend. Our usual tactic was to divide and conquer at the best events. Pearl would put all the invitations together and sort them from most important to least important. She would throw out the total losers—like Los Angeles Hotel Network—the events that drew only bottom feeders.

We only considered heavy hitters. This Friday evening, it was the Clio Awards, the Oscars of advertising, and we were up for awards in numerous categories.

"Whose turn is it?" Jeffrey asked, eyeing each of us around the table. Most of the time, we sent one representative.

"What do you mean, *whose turn?*" Warren scoffed, shooting Jeffrey a sideways frown. "We all need to be there—there are ten tickets. It's at the Dolby Theater this year." He turned to me. "Craig, let Alonzo know he's coming and it's black tie, which means no exposed tattoos and he needs to show up sober."

"I'll do my best," I answered, thinking Alonzo would show up stoned as usual, no matter what I said or did to discourage it. With Alonzo, it was best not to say anything and just hope to be pleasantly surprised.

"That's only five people," Jane pointed out. "What about the rest of the seats?"

"Tell Bobbi she needs to be there and have Alonzo fill the rest with senior level creatives," Warren barked at me. "Only those who've worked on the campaigns up for awards."

"Fine," I responded, watching Jane again and thinking about kissing her. I just couldn't get her out of my mind since she spent the night at my house. I wondered what she was thinking—about her life? About me? I never knew what was going on in that head of hers. I envisioned her trying to work it out with the violinist, but I just wasn't sure; she never let on to anything. My eyes lowered to her left hand, reminded of Julia's unpleasant commentary regarding Jane's wedding ring and, to my surprise, she was not wearing it today.

THE CLIO AWARDS WERE upon us and I decided on a navy Tom Ford tuxedo jacket with a black velvet bow tie, white shirt, and black pants. I liked mixing navy and black—the effect was classic but not too conservative. I thought about Jane and felt exhilarated at the mere thought of seeing her dressed up.

She didn't disappoint me. I spotted Jane and Warren on the red carpet and did a double take on first sight of Jane's outfit. She wore a black tuxedo, perfectly fitted to her slim body, with a crisp white tuxedo shirt underneath. The white shirt was unbuttoned perilously low, giving the impression she wore nothing under it. Her black bow tie hung asymmetrically around her neck, untied like she might have just had a quickie with someone. I fantasized that it had been with me, in the Bentley, pulled over on some side street near the Dolby theater, hastily inching my fingers into her unzipped, unbuttoned black pants, discovering some delightfully sheer lingerie but little else to protect her from my touch.

"Well, I thought Warren and I would be the most well-dressed men at this event," I said as I approached the two, "but it appears someone much more attractive stole our act." Our eyes met, and Jane gave me a close-mouthed smile that was both welcoming and heart-breaking in its sincerity. I had to remind myself of Warren's presence and that I needed to exercise self-control with Jane in every way.

"Aren't we a good-looking group?" Warren commented, eyeing my tuxedo with pride. He looked distinguished himself in a black tux with a red bowtie. "Where's everyone else?" he asked me.

I glanced at my watch and took my phone out of my pocket to check on Alonzo's whereabouts. "Excuse me a minute," I said stepping out of earshot in case I had to unload on Alonzo for being late.

I saw Jeffrey and Bobbi from a distance. The only people missing were the creatives. It figured. Alonzo's phone went to voice mail. "Alonzo, the fact that I'm getting voice mail must mean you're at the event and can't hear your phone. We're at the red-carpet entrance. Where are you?" I ended the call and stashed the cell phone in my pants pocket.

I returned to the group and smiled casually. "They're on their way," I fibbed. "Perhaps we should walk the red carpet now and meet the creative team inside the venue."

Warren shrugged. "We can wait a few more minutes." I knew he was waiting to make sure he saw how Alonzo arrived, i.e., whether he was sober and dressed appropriately. Warren strolled to another area of the red carpet to press flesh with some of his cronies. As soon as he was out of hearing distance, I gave Jane the once-over.

"Let's practice red carpet interviews," I playfully suggested, pretending I had a microphone in my hand. "Ms. Mercer, tell me, are you wearing anything under that blouse?"

She nodded, immediately going along with my flirtatious game. "Oh, yes, Mr. Keller."

"And what might that be?" I prodded her with amusement.

"Tape," she responded, smiling up at me.

I felt my eyes bulge at that response. "And *who* are you wearing tonight?"

"Vintage Ralph Lauren," she answered.

I leaned down and whispered in her ear. "Yum." I backed up and looked in her eyes.

"Yeah?" she asked, those beautiful lips parted. She wore red lipstick tonight which made her look like a super model.

I nodded with my eyebrows raised.

Warren had returned and was eying us suspiciously. The chemistry between us was so unmistakable, it was difficult to hide. But I had to.

"I think we should go, now," Warren said to me. "Jane, you lead. I'll follow you, and Craig, you'll follow me."

*Of course, he would insert himself between Jane and me.* I would have to stay quite a few paces behind, so I could still watch Jane strut in those tuxedo pants. The jacket hit her just above the curve of her hips. As we began the red-carpet walk, cameras flashed, and reporters threw out questions regarding our campaigns. After several interviews and lots of posing for pictures against the step and repeat, I ended up standing right next to Jane as cameras flickered.

She turned to me and smiled. My eyes darted down her blouse. I couldn't help thinking about her comment that 'tape' was all she wore underneath. I pictured those beautiful, ripe breasts with tape stuck underneath them, making them even perkier. I thought about getting her home afterward and pulling the tape off with my teeth, letting her hard nipples spring up against my cheek. *No, Craig, don't do this—you'll give yourself away—not in front of Warren.*

Out of the corner of my eye, I saw Hayden with her fawning minion, Marius Durand. I immediately took Jane's hand and pulled her along with me, so she was out of Hayden's sight.

"Where are we going?" she asked. "We're supposed to stay on the red carpet."

"Do me a favor and wait here," I answered. "I'll be right back."

I returned to the carpet and found Hayden and her henchman. Hayden was wearing a long silvery blue gown with a plunging neckline. It was made of some sort of sparkly chiffon. Her hair was pulled into a French twist and she wore a diamond choker—likely one daddy had bought her. The whole effect was that of a diabolical Cinderella.

When she spotted me, she gave me a wicked sneer but didn't approach. She knew better. I approached her instead. Her violet eyes narrowed at me and her overly mascaraed lashes squished together like fuzzy caterpillars. "We're up for two awards," she boasted.

"Really? In which categories?" I asked, eyeing her coldly. I could barely look at her face knowing what she did to Jane. The only thing that made me feel worse was what *I* was doing to Jane. At times I felt like I was no better than Hayden—taking advantage of someone in a weak place. As much as I couldn't stand Marisa, I knew she was right.

"One for Digital/Mobile and one for Digital/Mobile and Social Media Technique," she announced with arrogance.

"Really? What a coincidence—our agency's up for awards in those categories as well. I don't remember seeing any of your ads, but good luck with them. May the best man win," I offered with a cocky smile.

"Where's your little girlfriend?" Hayden jeered. "Off crying somewhere?"

*She had to go there.* The sudden urge to punch Hayden right in the face overwhelmed me. She giggled while Marius looked me up and down, unibrow undulating like a restless snake. "That's a nice tux," he remarked with a lewd grin. "Is it Tom Ford?"

"Of all the men you had to go after, why the hell did it have to be Jane's husband?" I demanded, completely ignoring her sycophant.

"Because I knew it would knock your girlfriend off balance—she can't handle turmoil at home and that'll translate into poor work performance, which is better for us." As she said this, she grinned at Marius and back at me, like she had hatched an ingenious plan.

*So that was it.* It was all about rattling Jane at work, so she'd fall behind on the job as our agency's digital marketing bench strength. It was something so heinous, only Hayden could come up with it. "That's interesting," I responded, "because your plan backfired—Jane's at the top of her game and has been all along. Your interloping in her personal life has had the opposite effect. So, thank you."

"Whatever," she shot back, "And in case you were wondering, Jane's husband was a better lay than you ever were, even while he was half-unconscious." Then she smiled her vitriolic smile with the perfect white teeth.

I leaned into her and spoke in an ominous tone: "If I were you, I'd be more concerned about how things are rolling out in San Francisco right now—I'm sure open investigations aren't going to help anyone in your family, including you."

I watched her face contort in astonishment and then rest in a scowl; her purple lips squeezed together.

Then I added, "I hope the impending scandal won't impact the judges' decisions tonight." I didn't wait for a response; I just turned away to find the rest of the agency. I remembered what Don had said about Stephan Towne, and I thought about how to use that information to discredit Hayden—to make sure her reputation was permanently tarnished, along with her 'crooked bastard' father, as Don had repeatedly referenced him. I had dropped the hint that I knew something, which would make her wonder what else I had. But I needed something beyond rumor—something concrete.

Jane was no longer waiting for me in the area where I had left her, so I made my way to our seats. Once I was there, Alonzo and his team of creatives streamed in. I just rolled my eyes and shook my head. I inhaled the acrid smell of pot smoke as they took their seats. Warren, who shot a pained look in Alonzo's direction, sat between Jane and me, clearly as a cock block but I was grateful to have a barrier to Ms. Sexiness. There was no way I would be able to keep my hands to myself if she were seated directly next to me.

Jeffrey sat on the other side of Jane, and Bobbi was to my left, grinding Nicorette and complaining about not getting the lobster rolls during cocktail hour.

"They always skimp on the good stuff at these things," she groused. "I swear, the only way to get anything decent is to wait by the kitchen."

"Shh—they're starting." I cut her off.

We ended up with four Grand creative campaign awards, two for Keller Whitman Group, which I accepted, and two for Mitchell Keller Vance & Mercer, which Warren accepted. It was an incredible sweep. Warren was ecstatic because we also beat out Towne Ink in both digital categories. While on stage accepting our awards, I caught a glimpse of Hayden leaned over in her chair, obviously cracking the proverbial whip on her luckless assistant, who seemed to be scrambling for reasons why they didn't even win a Bronze. I just smiled.

Alonzo was being hailed a superstar and soaring with pride. Our group dispersed as red light flooded the Dolby Theater after party, which was being held in the lobby. I found Alonzo nursing a cocktail and I pulled him off to the side.

"Congratulations," I said patting him on the back. "Don't get too wasted and, for God's sake, if there are cameras, always put your drink down and widen your eyes—they look like slits." It was hard to believe I still had to give such instructions, but Alonzo was like a child who needed to be guided.

He threw his arms around me and kissed me on the cheek. "Got it, Boss."

That's when Warren approached us with Jane. "Well, Keller, you pulled it off—I can't believe all the awards—you should be proud," he complimented, slapping me on the back and shaking my hand.

I caught Jane's eye and her expression was one of admiration. I returned her glance and smiled. There was something in her look that told me we were going home together tonight. There was no doubt in my mind. I felt almost breathless at the thought of being alone with her after a night of torture.

Jeffrey now joined our group, holding two of the awards. Bobbi was right behind him lugging the other two awards like she was hauling heavy furniture, grimacing with every step. I quickly turned up at Bobbi's side to relieve her of the burden.

"May I buy everyone a drink?" Jeffrey offered cheerfully.

"Of course," I replied. "Champagne?"

Warren checked his watch and said, "I think I'll take off—Caroline wasn't feeling well earlier and I'd like to get home. You guys stay and have fun."

*Thank you, God.* Warren offered to take all the awards with him and, as soon as he had gone, Jeffrey disappeared to the bar and I asked Jane to dance. It was a song by Beck. Jane nodded, and we found a place far into the dancing masses where we could groove to the music. Jane moved with such grace and confidence that she had me mesmerized as I watched her body sway, her hair hanging fiercely in her face, a seductive look in her eyes.

I couldn't wait for the song to end before grabbing her hand and pulling her through the crowd, no longer caring who saw us leave together. Jane didn't resist and, in fact, we both began to walk faster and faster, zigzagging our way through the well-heeled crowd and out the front entrance. We were soon running together, her stiletto heels clicking against the pavement, our hands still clutched tightly together until we reached the valet service. Out of the corner of my eye, I noted Hayden's sparkly chiffon swelling in the distance.

As soon as the Bentley pulled up, I flung open the door for Jane and she got in. I quickly went around to the other side and slid in next to her, pulled out of the parking lot at reckless speed and headed for the 101 freeway. We didn't speak as I raced toward Malibu, tempted to run red lights on PCH. I glanced anxiously in her direction and saw she was staring straight ahead, a mysterious smile on her face. The only thing dominating my mind was having her again—all to myself. I was like a giddy child on Christmas Eve, with a living room full of unopened presents and an overstuffed stocking.

When we reached my house, I skidded into the driveway at a crooked angle, like it was an emergency. I opened the door for Jane, anticipating with great delight what we would spend the night doing. Tomorrow was Saturday, so we could stay up all night. There was no doubt in my mind we would spend the entire weekend together. That's all I wanted.

Once inside the house, I swept her up, carried her into my bedroom and lay her on the bed. There, I took a good look at Jane, in the tuxedo with the half-unbuttoned blouse. She reminded me of an ad layout for an expensive fragrance—she looked so incredible at that moment, sprawled out on my bed, I didn't know where to start. I wanted to devour her.

"You know, Ms. Mercer," I teased, taking measured steps toward the bed. "If you want to dress like a man, I just might have to treat you like one."

"And what, Mr. Keller, would that entail?" she uttered, with those red lips parted sensually. She slid off the bed and stood in her heels, her long hair glistening as she inched her way toward me.

"It would entail being very aggressive about what you want," I answered, carefully removing her jacket, and hanging it on a chair, so it wouldn't get wrinkled.

"Really?" she asked softly. "I wouldn't want to 'steal your act'."

"Tell me what you want," I whispered before pulling her toward me by the front of her shirt and probing my tongue into her mouth. She responded with passion while I hastily unfastened each of the remaining buttons and slid the shirt backward off her shoulders. I withdrew from kissing her long enough to lower my eyes to her exposed breasts. Sure enough, there was tape holding them by either side. I stood back, so I could examine them fully. Jane did nothing to cover herself.

I slowly unbuttoned and unzipped her pants, pulling

them past her knees and onto the floor where she promptly stepped out of them. All she had on were filmy black panties, black high-heeled pumps, and the tapes around her breasts.

"May I?" I asked, eyeing the tapes.

"Please," she responded, smiling.

I delicately peeled the tape off each breast, uncovering the gorgeous light pink nipples, which were already erect, her breasts lowering to a natural curve absent the tapes.

"Now," I repeated, breathing deeply, barely able to contain my lust for the beautiful woman standing before me. "Tell me what you want."

She put her hands on my shoulders, grasped the velvet lapels of my tuxedo jacket, and looked me in the eye. "You know exactly what I want," she answered. "And I want to watch you do it."

She pressed down on my shoulders and I obediently lowered to my knees. I felt her hands on my head, guiding it between her thighs. She groped my hair and wound it around her fingers while I ran my tongue over the sheer material barely covering her. She moaned. I exhaled hot breath, pulled the material aside and tasted her smooth skin. She was dripping with anticipation. I felt her leg muscles tighten up as I orally stimulated her, cupping my hands around her from the back and pulling her into my face so I could thrust my tongue in deeper. I glanced up and caught her watching intently, eyebrows raised, mouth open, breathing heavily like she was ready to come. I closed my lips around her, feeling her entire body shiver and her legs shake uncontrollably. Her moaning became louder as she came.

I slowly got to my feet and wiped my hand across my mouth, eyes on hers. I backed away and removed my own clothing—the tuxedo jacket, shirt, cuff links, watch, belt, pants, shoes, and socks. Once naked, I lay on my back, on the bed, pulling her along with me. She got on her hands and knees and took me into her mouth. I could only handle a few minutes of being in her mouth before I pulled her up by her hair, so her face was close to mine, her legs straddling my body. I found her mouth and drove my tongue inside to meet hers. I picked her up by her tiny waist and lowered her onto me, feeling the intense relief of being inside her again. I rocked her back and forth, alternately playing with her breasts until I finally exploded inside her.

THE NEXT MORNING, I turned over and slowly opened my eyes to find the beautiful one sleeping beside me. It was raining and that never happened in Southern California, as the old seventies song proclaimed. The raindrops were pelting the skylight roof above the bed and, although the clouds looked sinister, the rain sounded peaceful and comforting.

I propped myself up on one elbow and examined Jane's divine sleeping face. She was on her side. I leaned down and kissed her lips softly so as not to wake her. "I love you, Jane," I said in a barely audible whisper. It was so easy to say when she was asleep and couldn't hear me. I listened to her slow breathing through her nose and felt her chest rise and fall. I traced my fingers along the side of her face and moved them softly to her tip-tilted nose and then to her lips. She must have felt my fingers on her mouth because her eyes suddenly fluttered open and she glanced at me.

"What are you doing?" she asked sleepily.

"Looking at you," I answered, now focusing on her big almond-shaped green eyes, which were drowsy in a sensual way.

She smiled and yawned. "Good morning."

"You're beautiful when you wake up," I commented, brushing the hair from her face. There was a faint hint of last night's makeup—a tinge of mascara and a faded red stain on her lips. I had kissed most of it off.

She responded by moving her smooth legs under the covers, so they were tangled up with mine. Her eyes lifted toward the skylight where raindrops continued lashing against it. "It's raining."

"I noticed. Do you like rain?"

She nodded and put her arms around my neck. "I like

*anywhere* you are," she mouthed softly before kissing me on the lips. I responded to her kiss, then gently pushed her away, so I could see her face again.

"I find it interesting we keep ending up here, don't you?" I asked, looking her in the eye.

"What do you mean by that?" she returned, rolling over and grabbing a pillow to thrust under her head.

I shrugged. "It's just an observation."

"It sounds like the intro to a 'where is this all leading' conversation," she responded, pulling the covers up to her neck and turning her face back up to the skylight. The rain was becoming more torrential with each passing minute.

"I think you know me better than that." I had to force myself to be cool, knowing how deeply I felt about Jane. I was dangerously close to showing it.

"On the contrary—I know nothing about you," she responded, glancing around my bedroom, her eyes stopping at my bookcase—the one with the secret compartment behind it containing my precious Scotch collection and expensive time pieces.

"Now that's simply not true, Ms. Mercer, you know more about me than most," I countered. The truth was she didn't know much about me at all. I never talked to anyone outside of Dr. Truer, so how could she know anything about me? *How could she possibly know how I really feel?*

"I don't know anything that can't be found on Google," she returned with a smile in her voice.

"You know where I sleep. I'm fairly certain that information's not available on Google—but I've been wrong before."

"Don't tell me I'm the only woman who's been in your bed." Jane was now sitting upright, pulling the duvet so it covered her. "Don't forget that I knew you in a previous life. I'm sure your bedroom has a revolving door."

"You're actually wrong about that. I don't take women into my bedroom." I left out the part about taking them into every other part of my house and frequently in my car. She would run for her life.

"Are you saying I'm special?" she asked, putting her hand

on my shoulder, and studying my demeanor. "Or maybe it's your bedroom that's special."

"You don't need me to tell you you're special, Jane," I answered. "But I guess we're getting back to a 'where is this all leading' conversation, right?" Jane's expression changed to one of sadness so suddenly, I wondered what I had said to upset her. "Are you okay?" I asked, raising my body so I was sitting up and facing her.

She nodded but said nothing. She lay her head back down on the pillow and stared up at the skylight. The rain was no longer coming down in sheets—instead, it resembled a car's windshield, covered with a solid sheet of water. "Is that thing safe?" she asked, still staring up at the skylight, wincing slightly, like she worried the weight of the downpour might burst it open and shell us right there on the bed with broken glass and rainwater.

"Very safe," I answered, gently tracing my finger over her shoulder blade, "Is there something you'd like to talk about?" I wanted desperately to get into a 'where is this all leading' conversation but didn't want Jane to know what I was after. She shook her head, still silent. "Because I'm happy to discuss anything that's on your mind," I added.

She turned, gave me a gloomy look, and swallowed hard. *Come on, Jane, I'm setting it up for you—just take the bait—say something—anything—and this game will be over. I will tell you everything. I will give you everything—because I love you, Jane. Please just say something.*

"I—don't know what I'm doing right now," she disclosed finally, tears forming. "I wish someone would tell me what to do—it would be so much easier."

It was not at all what I wanted her to say—it sounded like she needed a session with Dr. Truer, not another night in bed with me. I was clearly just making her life more complicated. I had no idea where to go with the conversation, which would obviously turn into an emotional one regarding her conflict with the violinist. I decided changing the subject would be best.

"Tell you what—why don't we get some coffee and I'll

make you breakfast," I suggested.

Her eyes scanned my bedroom to where her clothes from last night hung on my chair. "I don't have anything to wear."

"You can wear your robe," I offered, thinking of the olive-green silk robe with the tassel.

"*My* robe?" she asked, catching my use of the possessive right away.

I felt my heart quicken. *Jesus, Craig—be cool—you're acting like a needy woman.* "You know—the one you wore last time. Let me get it for you." I rose from the bed and felt her eyes follow me to the closet. Jane always had a unique curiosity about my body, especially when I was naked. I wondered if I were in better shape than the violinist, even though he was younger than me. I had to be with all the intense workouts and regimented diet.

I selected boxers and a navy Adidas track suit and pulled them on, zipping up the jacket, suddenly struck by the fact that I hadn't had a shower since the previous afternoon, before I donned the tuxedo. Under normal circumstances, I would never put on clean clothes before a shower, but I had Jane's scent all over me. It felt, strangely, like she had in some way cleansed me. I removed the olive-green robe from its hanger and chose another pair of boxers, thinking, perversely, it would turn me on to see her in them—and then to bury my face in them after she had gone.

When I returned to the bedroom, Jane was nowhere to be found.

"Jane," I called, heading down the hallway. I passed one of the guest bathrooms and the door was shut. I heard gagging sounds from inside. "Jane," I called, knocking on the door. "Are you okay in there?"

When she finally opened the door, her face was pale and her eyes watery. She had wrapped a towel around herself. "I just got sick," she announced. "Do you have a toothbrush, toothpaste and mouthwash?"

"Of course," I answered, now concerned. I wondered if she ate something that disagreed with her last night. Either that or she didn't eat at all. I noticed she didn't drink much at the Clios. Drinking was always a toss-up with Jane— you never knew how much she would have or how it would affect her. She was a lightweight most of the time, but she seemed sober last night. "Use my bathroom," I suggested, putting my arm around her slim shoulders, and leading her down the hall. I gave her the items she needed, along with the robe and boxers, and I left her alone.

I STOOD BREWING COFFEE and feeling peculiar, like something was standing between Jane and me having an intimate conversation. I did not want to upset her again, but I still wished she would tell me how she felt. Dr. Truer's words echoed in my mind, 'You have nothing to lose in telling Jane how you feel. If she doesn't feel the same way, you can at least move on with a clear conscience that you didn't miss out on the greatest love of your life.' Being that emotionally honest was contrary to how I had ever been and, when it came to Jane, I didn't know where to start.

Jane was now standing beside me in the kitchen wearing the robe with the tassel knotted. She lifted the bottom of the robe up to her waist to show me she was wearing my boxers. "It's a good thing I had a safety pin," she commented, whirling around so I could see where the waist was pinned in the back.

I smiled. "How are you feeling? I mean, you're not still sick, are you?"

"No, I'm better. I don't know what that was—maybe I just ..." her voice faded into silence.

I couldn't help but wonder what was going on in her mind. One thing was certain—she was conflicted. I was sure our sexual relationship was only augmenting her conflict and I felt immediately selfish in perpetuating an affair with her. But if the violinist were so important, she wouldn't be here with me. *Or would she?* Maybe she was trying to retaliate for his infidelity, but now the playing field was uneven. She had slept with me more than once. We were fully into an affair, a love affair, not just a one-night stand.

Jane was now standing at the floor-to-ceiling windows which overlooked the pool, coffee cup in hand. "Look—the rain stopped. Let's go for a walk on the beach," she suggested.

"You want to walk now?" I asked doubtfully. "The tide's pretty high."

"I don't care. Let's go."

"You might be a little cold. Let me find you a sweatshirt or something." I located a red Stanford hoodie which would likely swim on Jane and brought it back for her to wear.

She wasted no time, dropping the robe from her body and flinging it on the couch. I saw her naked breasts again. There was a level of intimacy developing between us that no longer necessitated modesty. I watched with lust as she pulled the hoodie over her head. I was right, it was huge on her, but she didn't seem to mind.

MY EYES SHIFTED TOWARD Jane as she walked beside me, bare-foot and with the hoodie draping over her, hanging mid-thigh. It was cold and balmy—the sky was grey—not the best day for a walk on the beach but it's what Jane wanted so I went with it.

When we got all the way to Pirate's Cove, Jane wanted to go into the water.

"Are you sure?" I asked her. "It's cold this time of year."

She ignored me and waded into the ocean, which was now up to her knees.

"Watch out for the rocks," I called to her. "Step on them the wrong way and they'll shred your feet."

"You're forgetting I grew up here—I'm familiar with beaches," she yelled back.

I sighed, watching her clumsily attempt to keep her balance with the ocean swirling furiously at high tide. It was dangerous, and she knew it. She wanted to do something dangerous in front of me. She, herself, embodied danger in every possible way. She was skating through unfamiliar waters and razor-like rocks. That's what we were both doing—tiptoeing around the truth—the inevitable sharp slicing of our feet and the outpouring of blood into the salt water—the unavoidable stinging pain—pushing our way through the ocean against the tide, finding our way to shore—to safety—wherever that was.

I thought about DJ and how he never had the opportunity to fall in love, to be with the woman of his dreams. I wondered what Jane would say if I just told her—if I just opened my heart and took a risk. *Would she turn me down?* I wasn't sure if I could take that. I was such a craven coward.

I felt Jane's hand tap my shoulder and I turned toward her, having temporarily zoned out. There was that beautiful, hopeful face—those bright green eyes and that smile.

"Do you ever worry about the high tide, living so close to the water?" she queried.

"Nope," I answered, watching the letters of the Stanford logo distort as they rippled around her.

"Do you ever worry about *anything*, Mr. Keller?" she asked smiling up at me.

*I worry that I don't have the guts to tell you I love you, Jane. I worry that I'll never be able to tell you how much you mean to me and that it will drive you away. I worry that something will happen, and I'll never see you again. I worry that, like DJ, you will slip away from me forever.*

"Not much," I finally answered. "Are you hungry?" She looked as though she were floating as remnants from the storm caused the ocean wind to kick up. The Stanford logo was now billowing around her as droplets of rain began to fall.

She nodded. "Starving."

"Let's get something to eat," I responded, pulling her by the hand and leading her in the direction of my house. As we walked, I put my arm around her and kissed her tenderly on the cheek. She abruptly stopped, faced me, and put her arms around my neck.

"Kiss me," she ordered and put her mouth on mine. She stood on her tiptoes, so I wouldn't have to stoop too far. We made out for several minutes right there in the sand. The rain was starting to come down harder, the percussive thunder clapping in the distance. I withdrew and began kissing her neck. I felt her hands lower to my shoulders, her fingers tugging at the zipper of my jacket—then grazing lightly underneath the jacket against my bare chest.

"Jane," I whispered, pulling her closer. "What's happening here?" I couldn't stop myself. I just had to know. "Please tell me what this is."

She didn't answer—she just stood back, took my hand and pulled me along, traversing the beach to my house in silence, the rain soaking through our clothes—soaking us to the bone.

I let us in through the back gate, which opened to the stairs leading to the pool. When we were at the back door of the house, I realized I never locked it when we left—I was so hung up on Jane. Once in the house, I did a double take. Alessandra was in the living room, pacing across the floor, an angry expression on her face.

"Alessandra," I uttered uncomfortably, standing in front of Jane to shield her. We were dripping profusely all over the marble floor and wet sand was stuck to our feet. My olive-green robe lay on the couch where Jane had casually tossed it. "You didn't tell me you were stopping by."

"That's because I couldn't reach you," she snapped. "It's about Anabel."

"What about her?" I asked, feeling my heart race.

"I had to take her to the emergency room this morning—she has a 104-degree fever. They think she has pneumonia."

I couldn't believe what I was hearing. "How in the world did Anabel catch pneumonia?"

Jane stood awkwardly behind me, and I momentarily forgot about her, letting go of her hand to hear the news about Anabel.

"They have her on a ventilator," Alessandra answered. "They need to keep her overnight. I don't know how she got it—started with a cold and then turned into bronchitis. When I couldn't get a hold of you, I drove here, and let myself in through the back door—which was unlocked. I called Sylvia and she said you must have gone out."

At this point, she stared coldly at Jane, eyeing the borrowed hoodie, now drenched, and her tangled, sopping wet hair.

"I'm sorry, this is Jane," I said. "Jane, Alessandra."

Jane was the first to speak, "It's nice to meet you. I'm sorry—it seems you two have a lot to sort out. I'll be on my way." Jane stepped around me and disappeared into my bedroom, her feet squishing and squeaking on the marble floor.

Alessandra's cold glare was now on me. She shook her head. "Another one of your whores? It figures."

"That's not fair," I scolded. "How was I supposed to know you'd show up?"

"You could be a responsible father for once and keep your phone on you at all times in case of an emergency."

*What could I say?* She was right, but her wrath was not going to help Anabel now.

After a few minutes, Jane emerged from the bedroom with her tuxedo on, her wet hair pulled into a ponytail. I felt bad because she looked disheveled without having the benefit of a change of clothes and a shower. Even so, she was still beautiful. Alessandra's disdainful expression only made matters worse. Then I realized Jane didn't have her car. "Do you need a ride?" I asked.

"Are you serious?" Alessandra blurted out, now furious. "Your daughter's fighting for her life right now and you're worried about giving one of your sluts a ride home?"

Jane turned toward Alessandra, looking as though she might slap her. "That's unnecessary," she said frostily. Then she turned to me, "I'll get a car service. I hope your daughter recovers quickly."

She walked with her head held high out my front door, leaving me standing there like a gutless jerk. Once Jane had gone, I laid into Alessandra. "What the hell was that about, anyway?" I demanded angrily. "You call someone you don't even know a slut?"

"She's here with you, so she must be one," Alessandra shot back.

I felt my neck stiffening. "What is *wrong* with you? Do you realize how awful your behavior makes you look?" Alessandra sat like a princess in her Bel Air castle, one which I paid for, and had the audacity to call Jane, a hard-working career woman, a slut. It made no sense.

"All I care about is my daughter right now and that's all you should care about, too—but you'd rather waste time defending one of your whores." Alessandra's eyes flashed as she tossed her hair in indignation.

"Do *not* say that about Jane—she's—I'm in love with her." I realized as soon as the words came out of my mouth what I had done.

"*Love?* Are you kidding me? You're in *love* with that woman?" Alessandra stared at me with an open mouth. "Since when? Have you had her around my children?"

I took a deep breath. "Yes—*our* children," I replied. "She was here at Thanksgiving."

"What?" she asked, now incredulous. "How come you never told me? That wasn't our deal."

"Our deal was that I only tell you when someone other than me is watching them. I don't owe you an explanation beyond that."

"Did she meet Don and Julia?"

"Yes." Now the news was out—and Alessandra was going to rake me over the coals for delivering this news—news I didn't even have the balls to deliver to Jane in person.

"That's just great, Craig," she yelled, stomping around my house, hurling a stack of magazines on the floor like a child throwing a fit. I wasn't sure if it was the fact that I loved someone other than her or that I never loved her. She had to know I never loved her. Women just know these things.

"Stop it, Alessandra," I scolded, calmly picking up the magazines and replacing them on the coffee table.

"Are you ready to go to the hospital now to see your sick daughter?" she demanded, mocking me.

I nodded, following Alessandra outside where we took separate cars to the USC Medical Center.

# Sixteen

"**A**NABEL, HONEY," I SAID, peering down at my daughter, who was attached to a ventilator. "Anabel, it's Daddy." Her eyes blinked open and she tried to say something. "Shhh—don't talk, Sweetheart," I told her. "Save your breath—you're going to be okay. I'll stay here with you until you feel better."

She just blinked again, and her honey-colored eyes widened. It broke my heart to see her in such distress. I leaned over and kissed her forehead, which felt hot against my lips. "Anabel—I love you so much," I whispered. "You have no idea. You're going to be okay. You have to be." She looked so small and pitiful in the hospital bed. I would have given anything to be the one sick and fighting to breathe. I just wanted to take her pain away—to suffer for her.

Alessandra was sitting in the chair near the hospital bed, arms folded, undoubtedly still sulking at the revelation that I loved Jane. I never should have told her, but I had bottled it up for so long, I couldn't help it. I hated myself for being so weak and not just telling Jane earlier. I fantasized about Jane being Anabel's mother and how she would be acting right now. I doubted she'd be sulking in a chair.

Jane was so down-to-earth and real. I secretly wished she were by my side right now, sharing with me the pain of seeing my daughter struggle. I knew she would be loving and wonderful.

ONCE ANABEL HAD FALLEN asleep, I stole away to the waiting room and dialed Jane's cell; she didn't pick up. Upon getting her voice mail, I wasn't sure what to say. "Jane—it's me. I'm sorry about this morning. I want to talk to you. Call me."

Hours went by and Jane did not return my call. Once the doctors had assured me Anabel was recovering properly, and visiting hours were over, I headed home for the evening and tried again to call Jane. This time, she answered.

"Hello," she said in a voice that sounded like she'd been crying. "How's your daughter?"

"She's going to be fine," I answered. "How are you?"

"I'm okay." There was a quietness in her voice that told me something had happened since I saw her.

"I missed you—listen, Jane, I'm sorry about how things went down this morning. I'd like to take you to dinner tonight and make it up to you."

"You don't need to make anything up to me," she said. "In fact, it's probably best you forget about me for a while."

"What's that supposed to mean?" I asked, feeling sick with dread that she was breaking things off because of Alessandra's bitchy comments.

"I just think it's best, Craig."

There was something in her tone—something unyielding. I started to panic. "Look, Jane, I know my ex-wife said some awful things and, after you left, I made that clear. But, you know, it has nothing to do with you."

There was a long pause and I heard her breathe into the phone. "I think our lives are a little too complicated right now to be intersecting," she said in a calm, even voice.

I felt my world crashing down on me. I couldn't lose her—no matter what little I had of her. She was so good—so beautiful and poignant at the same time. I couldn't lose her without a fight; she made me happy—happier than I'd ever remembered being. I couldn't let her go. But something inside me—some swelling level of fear kept me silent—I didn't argue. I said nothing. After another long, awkward pause, I finally spoke. "If that's what you want, I have no choice but to respect it." I felt like my heart was being squeezed mercilessly in my chest and I gripped my collar, trying to loosen it with one hand while I clutched the steering wheel with the other.

"That's what I want," she answered and hung up.

I SPENT THE REST of the weekend in and out of the hospital until Sunday evening, when Anabel was released and could go home to her mother's house. I drove to Malibu reflecting upon my complex relationship with Jane and wondering how I was going to recover. This feeling was something new, although, in some terrible, excruciating way, it reminded me of what I went through with DJ so many years before. I felt that sinking feeling deep in my soul that things had come to an end, that my life would be devoid of someone who meant so much—someone who could transform loneliness and desolation into joy and goodness.

I booked Dr. Truer for Monday evening, viewing it as an emergency session. I didn't work out and I skipped the exhaustive shower Sunday night, barely making it to work the next morning. I was a complete wreck, but I couldn't let it show. I just couldn't have my colleagues see me so emotionally destroyed.

I didn't see Jane at all Monday morning. She stayed close to her office and didn't join the partner meeting. Warren said she was working on a deadline and couldn't attend. I knew she just didn't want to see me. Warren was still basking in the afterglow of the Clios and had ordered a catered lunch for the entire agency to celebrate. I doubted I'd see Jane there, either.

Bobbi was waiting in my office after the partner meeting. For the first time, I was not in the mood for her.

"*Oy*, you look like hell, Craig," she commented, jaw dropping and Nicorette falling to the floor. She quickly knelt to pick up the gum and tossed it in a nearby wastebasket. "What happened to you?"

"My daughter's been sick," I responded, placing a stack of files on my desk, and wandering to the espresso machine like a rudderless zombie. "Want something?"

Bobbi shook her head and squeezed her eyes shut. "Is Anabel going to be okay?"

"Yes. She has pneumonia but is recovering well. She went home from the hospital last night." I couldn't tell Bobbi the real problem—that Jane Mercer broke me and all I could think of was the devastation of that blow. I should have known not to go there with her—not to let her into my life where there was no room for anyone else but me. I could not believe how silly and gullible I'd been, thinking someone like her would feel anything for me other than infatuation, followed by contempt. I sat at my desk and stirred sweetener into my cappuccino, gazing out the window at the layer of smog saturating the city beneath.

"I have some interesting news—not sure if I should be repeating it," she dropped coyly.

That meant she was going to spill the beans. "That's never stopped you in the past," I replied. "What now, Bobbi?"

"It's Jane—she's pregnant," Bobbi announced, pulling a few silvery wisps of hair behind her ears. "She doesn't want anyone to know."

I felt my heart skip a beat and put my hand to my chest. "*Pregnant?*" I repeated.

"She did a test over the weekend and went to the doctor this morning. That kiddo's going to have a baby."

I thought about the timing. I'd been sleeping with Jane over the past four weeks. We'd only spent two full nights together, but we'd had sex so many times during those interludes, it would be no surprise that I had impregnated her—especially since I never wore protection—not once. I wondered whether Jane had had sex with the violinist, too. Maybe she didn't know who the father was. *Poor Jane! No wonder she broke things off with me.* She was probably beside herself trying to figure out what to do.

"Bobbi—I appreciate that you keep me updated on things. But if Jane doesn't want anyone to know, what are you doing in here telling *me*? Please do me a favor and tell no one else this story." I realized at that moment Jane threw up at my house Saturday because of morning sickness. I knew that phase well from going through it twice with Alessandra.

"What?" she cried, sounding wounded. She rose from her seat in indignation, smoothing her long black skirt, hands on hips. "I would *never* tell anyone but you."

I gave her an open-mouthed sigh. "I mean it, Bobbi. She'd be furious if she knew you told me. Trust me, I know her."

I worried about Jane all day and thought about how I might approach her about this. She had to be carrying around this weight—literally—and not knowing what to do about it. All I wanted was to relieve her of stress.

Later that afternoon, I wandered down the hallway to the war room. This is the room we used to debate branding and positioning and to review critical ad layouts. The walls were all whiteboards with different messages scribbled on them and printouts of ads pinned up for analysis. Alonzo had asked me to stop by and review something. When I showed up at the war room door, I saw Jane sitting with him. They appeared to be arguing.

I stood in the open doorway listening to the content of the argument. Jane was wearing a camel-colored pencil skirt and leopard-print sweater with black boots. I tried to imagine her with a baby growing inside that flat abdomen and it was a difficult image to conjure.

"The client doesn't get to tell us where to put the logo," Alonzo growled. "That placement looks completely out of balance—just so you know, it's for position only—this isn't the final—I'm just showing it to you so you can see for your-self how bad it looks."

"Alonzo, they're not telling us to move the logo—they're

asking us to make it bigger," Jane argued. "You know this is always an issue with them, so why don't we start by giving them a layout with an appropriately sized logo?"

Neither of them knew I was standing there, so I decided to listen a little longer before entering the room.

"The logo will look fucking ridiculous that big—and I *will* have to move it if it ends up even a point size larger," Alonzo retorted, rapping his fist on the ad layout for emphasis.

I was not at all comfortable watching Alonzo bully Jane. He was such an asshole sometimes. Jane was holding her own, but I couldn't help but think dealing with Alonzo's ego was the last thing she needed right now with everything else going on in her life.

"The only reason you want the logo so small is because of aesthetics," Jane threw back and then pursed her lips. "To you, it's all about winning awards and the client knows it."

"Which client are we talking about?" I suddenly interrupted from the doorway.

They both jumped and turned in my direction. I caught Jane giving me the once-over and then looking down at her lap.

"Hey Boss," Alonzo said completely reversing his sullen tone to one of deference. "How long were you standing there?"

"Long enough. Who's the client?"

"Kenton Fox," Jane answered. She looked uncomfortable that I was there and had overheard their conversation.

I crossed my arms over my chest and leaned against the doorframe. "If they want a bigger logo, then give it to them. They're trying to sell tickets in a tough market."

"But Boss, it's going to look like shit—you want your name on something that looks like shit? Can't we just keep it like it is? Jane's the one who's supposed to be managing the client, but she never has the balls to stand up to them."

"That couldn't be further from the truth, Alonzo," Jane objected, eyes widening. "I fight the clients every day over artwork that you refuse to compromise. Most of the time, I agree with you, but not on this issue. You need to find a way to make it work. Period."

Alonzo just gave Jane an insolent glance and addressed me like she was no longer in the room. "Boss, it's *your* call. Are we keeping it *my* way?"

I gave Alonzo a stern look. "You're wrong—it's not my call, it's Jane's. But since you've asked, let me help you with this. No."

My eyes briefly met Jane's and she appeared flabbergasted. I turned and walked away.

"YOU MUST HAVE QUITE a lot on your mind right now, Craig," said Dr. Truer, leaning back on the marigold La-Z-Boy and kicking her feet up on the ottoman. "You want to tell me what's going on?"

I sighed. "I don't know where to start. I guess I should start with Jane."

Dr. Truer raised her eyebrows slightly. "Yes, tell me about Jane. Did you talk to her?"

I shook my head. "No—I couldn't—I tried but I just couldn't. I'm not really here to discuss that. Something else came up—something more urgent."

"And what's that?" she asked, picking up her notepad and pen.

"I found out she's pregnant and I might be the father," I announced, looking down, avoiding Dr. Truer's expression. I traced my fingers along the thin lines of the plaid pattern on my suit pants.

"How did you find out?"

"A mutual work friend told me this morning and I did the math. I never wore protection with Jane." I still didn't look up at Dr. Truer. I was somehow ashamed of being in the predicament I was in—that I could have been so careless with Jane, knowing this could happen. I was forty years old, for God's sake.

"Do you usually have protected sex?" she asked again, this time twisting her head sideways like she was trying to get me to look her in the eye.

"Always," I answered, meeting her gaze.

"Do you want a child with Jane?" she asked in a deadpan tone.

"What are you talking about?" Sometimes Dr. Truer said the most outlandish things.

"You either consciously or unconsciously chose not to use protection with her. I'm trying to explore why."

"I don't know. Maybe it had to do with wanting to be as close and intimate with her as possible—to have no barriers between us. Maybe I wasn't thinking about it at all. It really doesn't matter because she's married, and the child is probably her husband's."

"But what if it isn't? You're speculating because you really don't know anything about it. You see, Craig, all of this could be resolved if you would just grow up and be honest with Jane about where you are in this relationship."

"There is no relationship," I erupted. "She told me, unequivocally, to go away."

Dr. Truer's shoulders twitched. "That had to have made you feel awful," she remarked, now with a frown. "Do you know what brought it on?"

I shrugged with exaggerated sarcasm. "I had to guess—she said something about our lives being too complicated. It came on the heels of Alessandra walking in on us—making disparaging comments—the stress of my daughter being in the hospital with pneumonia—and then Jane finding out she's pregnant. I'd say that's enough to drive someone away from a dangerous entanglement, wouldn't you?"

Dr. Truer shook her head, blonde frizzy mop quivering slightly. "Well, Craig, you've gotten yourself into a mess. Now how are you going to *clean* it up?"

I was silent. Dr. Truer was judging me again, just like she did in the last session. I didn't have the energy to call her on it.

"The most striking thing about this situation," she continued, "is that you're a master at manipulating work situations in your favor. Why don't you apply those same talents to your personal life? What are you afraid of?"

I shifted uncomfortably on the couch and lowered my gaze to the floor. "It's not even the same thing."

"You can't figure it out because you're detached from your own emotions," she replied. "All I hear you talk about are Jane's feelings. It seems to me something's missing here—*your* feelings. Or do they matter?"

"I've been miserable—like the walking dead," I explained. "I'm not functioning. You don't understand, Dr. Truer, this is not like me. I'm not doing well with all this. It—it's just like …." For some reason, I could not finish the sentence.

"Just like what? Like DJ?" she questioned as though reading my thoughts. "Craig, Jane is *not* DJ. Jane's *alive* for one. If you love Jane and believe you could be the father of her child, don't you want to have a conversation with her?" Dr. Truer blinked at me and cocked her head, like she was talking to a child—a forty-year-old boardroom toddler.

I took a deep breath. Dr. Truer just didn't understand what was at risk. All she was thinking about was the heart-driven aspect—not Jane's marriage, my partnership—everything that could be lost if I acted on impulse now.

Dr. Truer talked for the rest of the session about the importance of expressing my emotions—especially toward Jane. She even ordered me via a written prescription to talk to Jane within the next 48 hours. She gave me a 5 p.m. appointment but said to cancel if I'd not yet spoken to Jane on some level about my emotions. She continued to hammer me about my office prowess and how I could be a mighty iceberg with work decisions but a puddle of water with Jane. It was so different—business was business—there was no emotion—nothing to be attached to—nothing to be heartbroken over.

Two DAYS LATER, I ran into Jane in the hallway. She had managed to elude me by skipping all meetings I attended or held. She always sent her number two, Victoria, with some excuse as to why she couldn't be there. But here she was, right in front of me, as chic as ever in a cream wool pantsuit with a red fishtail pattern embroidered into the border of the jacket fabric. She never failed to take my breath away.

"Hi," I said softly, feeling the ache of her presence, realizing there was a good chance she would never allow me to touch her again.

"Hi," she returned. "I'm glad I ran into you."

"And here I thought you were avoiding me," I responded, studying her face—trying to read her in some way.

Her eyes lowered for a second. "I need to talk to you." There was anxiety in her voice.

I nodded right away. "I need to talk to you, too."

She looked around to make sure no one else was in the hallway. "Can we meet after work?"

I felt my heartbeat escalating. "Of course, what time and where?"

"Um—I don't know—somewhere quiet and dark," she suggested. "I can't think of anywhere."

"How about The Room on Santa Monica Boulevard," I offered. "That's about as quiet and dark as you can get."

She gave me a half-smile. "Great. Seven?"

"See you then," I answered, knowing better than to suggest going in one car. She was just so over it with me. I could tell.

For the rest of the afternoon, I had a difficult time concentrating on work. I was supposed to prepare for a brand presentation the next morning to the corporate marketing team of Our Vows Dot Com, the most successful of online wedding resources. The pitch was to rebrand their website and magazine—Alonzo had been working on it for weeks. I was so screwed up about Jane that I fell out of the loop on the project, even though I was called upon to present some of the work. Alonzo had convinced everyone that my looks and stature made me a much more believable representative in the business of matrimony, which was utterly laughable; however, I would play the part. Jeffrey even suggested I resurrect my old wedding band and wear it for the meeting.

Around 6:45 p.m., I headed out to meet Jane at The Room. When I entered the bar, my eyes had to adjust to the grisly red lighting—because there was barely enough light to see anyone's face. Yet, it was an astonishingly appropriate place to meet Jane for our talk—a talk I was not at all prepared to have. I felt a lump in my throat for what she might say—for what I might say back, and for how the conversation would end.

I found us a swanky booth with a privacy curtain that could be closed or opened. I tipped the door guy generously, so we could have it as long as we wanted. I got the impression he received this request often because he gave me an amused look and said, "Enjoy yourselves."

From a distance, I saw Jane enter the bar and look around for me—likely unable to see in the ruby-saturated room. I stood right away to catch her attention and she approached me. My heart was beating faster. *Here it comes—ready or not.*

She sat down next to me and we just stared at each other in silence for a few minutes. I was not sure what kind of vibe I was getting—she just seemed so serious. "Would you like a drink?" I asked, wondering if she would order alcohol in her condition.

"I'd like a ginger ale," she answered.

*Good girl.* I signaled the waitress and ordered two ginger ales and a bottle of Grey Goose vodka. Jane gave me a look. I shrugged. "I didn't want to cheap out on the drinks since I got us the best booth here. I'm sure they keep a close eye on the average check in this place."

She smiled. "Look at you, always the savvy businessman."

"Jane," I started but stopped myself. I didn't want to make her uncomfortable by telling her how much I missed her—how miserable I had been since she told me to leave her alone.

"Craig," she said softly. "I have to tell you something."

I bit my lip as my eyes met hers. She looked incredibly beautiful, even with her face awash in the ghastly reddish pink bar rays.

"I'm listening," I responded, leaning forward so I would

not miss a word. The waitress interrupted to deliver our ginger ales and the vodka, with two extra glasses. I barely acknowledged the waitress because I was so focused on what Jane was about to say.

Jane waited patiently until the waitress had gone. "You see, some things are happening right now and I—well, I thought you should know." She paused and took a deep breath, glancing down at her lap. When she lifted her eyes to mine again, they were misty. "I filed for divorce Tuesday morning," she revealed. "It wasn't an easy decision, but I know it's the right thing to end my marriage."

"What?" I asked, raising my eyebrows in shock. "But why? Because of the thing with Hayden? Jane, don't you think you're overreacting?" Jane took a long sip of her ginger ale. "I mean it was just one time and you really don't know what happened. She's the type of woman who *would* drug a man—she'd do anything to get to you. You're letting her win."

Jane put up her hands to stop me. "Please, Craig—hear me out. This decision has nothing to do with Hayden. It has to do with how I feel about you."

I stopped dead in my tracks and felt my pulse quicken, but I said nothing and let her continue.

"When you and I got together, I realized how much I care about you—how much you mean to me. It's like all these feelings came back—from years ago but this time, they're so much more intense." She paused and scooted closer to me. I felt her warm leg rub up against mine. "Even if I could forgive Derek for his betrayal with Hayden, it wouldn't make me feel about him the way I do about you. It's just not the same thing."

I felt my mouth drop open. *Jane was leaving her husband for me.* It hit me so suddenly and with such grave force, I was rendered speechless. I reached for the bottle of vodka and poured some into a glass, feeling like someone was choking me with their bare hands. I shot the liquor down quickly and regarded Jane, still unable to say a word.

"Craig are you okay?" she asked, placing her hand on my arm, and looking apprehensive. "Did you hear me?"

I pressed my lips together and slowly nodded.

"There's something else you should know," she continued. "I'm pregnant and … it's yours."

I stared into her eyes as she uttered that last line and had a tough time not falling into her arms and kissing her with all the passion and intensity surging within my heart at that moment. But I had to stay strong. Jane Mercer was getting a divorce and having my child. She was asking to have a life with me—something I had been dreaming of for so long, it was almost inconceivable that it would actually happen. And, for some reason, I couldn't talk. I thought about the violinist and Warren's stipulations, the fact that I willingly played with fire and was now watching a young woman—the only woman I ever loved—with her life unraveling—because of *me*. It baffled me that Jane turned out to be the courageous one—that she was the one willing to give up everything to give me the one thing I always wanted. *But how could I accept it from her now?* I couldn't do it because it was so entirely sad and pathetic the way it happened. I was a thief, a home wrecker, and a dishonest, unprincipled business partner. I didn't deserve her. That's all there was to it and there was no way I was going to let her make such a huge mistake.

"Jane," I finally said. "First of all, congratulations on the baby." My voice was grossly cold and professional, a tone that took every bit of strength I could muster under the circumstances. "But I'm afraid it's a biological impossibility that it's mine."

Jane's eyes widened, and her lips parted. "But the doctor gave me the date range—it has to be yours because I didn't sleep with Derek for at least a month before he slept with Hayden and not at all after. You're the only one I've been with."

I inhaled deeply, trying to keep my cool so Jane would believe me—believe the spineless monster in front of her couldn't possibly have fathered her child. "Jane, I can assure you it's not mine. I had a vasectomy after Anabel was born. I couldn't get you pregnant if I tried." It was a wretched lie, but it was all I could think of at that moment.

I watched Jane's expression turn from shock to curiosity. "If that's true, then why did you use condoms when we were together five years ago and not now?"

"I was married then." I spoke tersely—I didn't know where it was coming from, but I felt more cold-blooded, more ruthless as the conversation progressed. I had one mission and that was to convince Jane that the baby was her husband's and that she needed to save her marriage—not ruin her life by running away with me. It was the only decent thing I could do for her now.

"But these past weekends—the time we've spent together—you can't tell me you haven't felt anything...." Her voice straggled off and her eyes were almost pleading.

"Oh." I let out a breathy laugh. "I've felt a lot of things—being with you is—well—you're a beautiful woman, Jane. I doubt any man would have resisted you. But that's not what you're talking about. You're talking about leaving your husband to be with me and—well, I just don't feel that way about you. It's not mutual."

Those last words felt like daggers in my heart—out-and-out lies that poured from my lips like I was a soulless robot programmed with a sickening script.

She suddenly glared at me, eyes flashing. "So, what you're saying is you were just using me the whole time?" she asked, incredulous. Then she shook her head and declared, "You used me again and this time, I had *everything* to lose."

I sighed but didn't drop sight of my goal. "The operative word is *again* Jane. You should know better. People don't change. We just become more bitter—more jaded—more cruel over time."

She shook her head as though she didn't believe what was happening.

"The good news is, it's not too late for you to put everything back in order," I forced out in a positive tone, like I was doing an ad pitch. "Your husband loves you, Jane, and now he has the baby you both want. Don't throw it all away for someone like me."

"You felt something—admit it, Craig," she insisted, tears now trickling down her cheeks. I wanted desperately to take her in my arms and tell her how badly I needed her, how downright shattered I was to be pushing her away like this, but the thought that I was destroying her life was too overpowering. Instead of responding, I slid a stack of cocktail napkins toward her, so she could wipe her eyes.

"You can't tell me you didn't feel anything," she persisted, voice shaking with emotion. "And the baby *is* yours—I know that, too. I don't know what you're trying to pull here but it's not working." Her voice had risen to a pitch that was getting attention from the resident barflies in The Room.

"Calm down," I told her, standing, and pulling the curtain shut around us. I sat down and turned to Jane, who was now sobbing, huge heaving long sobs like her life was ending.

"Jane, please don't cry," I urged, now with controlled gentleness. "You're wasting tears on the wrong person. There are so many things you don't know about me—you said so yourself last weekend. You said the only things you knew about me were on the internet—available to anyone with access to a search engine. You were right. It's because I'm incapable of talking to anyone about anything real."

"But you can talk to me," she cried, dabbing her eyes with a cocktail napkin. "Maybe I can't change how you see yourself, but I'm the one person you *can* talk to. I don't understand why you haven't figured that out."

"No, what *you* don't understand is that I'm incapable of being with someone—anyone, not just you. You want to know why I'm divorced? Go ask Alessandra. You want to know why I go home to an empty house every night? Because I'm emotionally bankrupt, Jane. I have nothing to give you. Do you hear me? I have *nothing to give you.*"

She stopped sobbing long enough to stare at me in disbelief—like I was an alien from another planet.

"I'm sorry," I said, pressing my hands into the vinyl seat covering to lift my body and move it away from hers. "I didn't mean for this to happen. Go be with the man who loves you and is every bit as capable of giving you what you need and deserve. It can't be me. It won't ever be me."

"But … what about work?" she asked lifting her head slightly. "I mean, I have to see you every day—I don't know if I can do that after everything that's happened between us."

"I'll take care of work. You won't have to worry."

"What do you mean?" she sniffed with a puzzled expression, her eyes and face still glistening with tears.

"Just leave that to me," I responded, coolly. I then stood up and pulled cash out of my pocket, tossed it on the table and looked down at Jane, gorgeous, raw, heart-broken Jane. She was staring straight ahead like she didn't know where she was.

When she finally focused her gaze up at me, she whispered, "Are you leaving me now?"

I nodded. "Take your life back, Jane. It becomes you." I turned quickly, pulling the curtain aside and sauntering out into the blood bath of light, taking long strides that increased in pace like someone was stalking me.

I DROVE HOME SICKENED. I thought I'd feel a strange sense of relief, like I had finally done the right thing, but I felt worse. And as I entered my cold, empty house, I heard my footsteps echoing on the marble floor, shoes clacking with an eerie tempo I never noticed before Jane entered and exited my life.

I stopped in the entryway and peered into the large round mirror that hung above a table with a red lamp on it. I studied my countenance intently—the light green eyes, the full, lengthy eyelashes, the pronounced cheekbones, and strong jaw. I turned to the side to observe my profile, which I had often been told was perfect. I opened my mouth and examined the impressively white teeth with the slightly longer canines that women found so irresistible. I then watched my brows furrow and my jaw tense up in anger. "Who *are* you?" I demanded of my reflection.

Instead of the gym, I pulled on swim trunks and did

laps for two hours. It was cold and dark outside, but the pool was heated and lit up in a deep shade of emerald—the color of Jane's eyes. I plunged in and felt the water bubble up around my body. I lingered at the shallow end, eyeing the length of the pool in the night sky. Then I swam toward the deep end, picturing Jane's face, seeing her eyes in the water, haunting me with their surreal glow before I came up for air. I swam lap after lap, absorbing the silence underwater—the intense silence that mangled reality, endlessly spinning a distorted chimera of power and suspense. At some point, I realized I had been swimming an eternity—my fingers were crinkled up like an aged parchment and my nose and throat felt inflamed. At that moment, I knew no matter how hard I tried, I would never get Jane out of my mind. I could never shed the feelings I had for her. She was permanently seared into my memory.

After a long hot shower, I put on silk pajamas, drank exactly five sips of Scotch, and fell asleep, tucked into the center of the bed.

# Seventeen

T HE MORNING'S SUIT SELECTION process was moving slower than usual, for today was to be a special day. *What does one wear for his final act?* I thumbed through the blues, passing them by altogether. I went through shades of green, grey, black, a variety of checks, houndstooth, plaids, pinstripes, and then I found it. It was one of the charcoal hues, wool with a subtle pinstripe on the pants and jacket. I selected a lighter grey snug cardigan with an accentuated black border trim to wear under the jacket and over one of my hundreds of white button-down shirts. A grey tie with amethyst and black dots finished the smart look. I would wear black lace-up Oxfords and a black belt. I selected a timepiece from my wall safe, an IWC Schaffhausen Da Vinci edition with an alligator watch band. Once I had fastened the strap, I took one more, long look in the mirror.

I drove the Bentley to work with the top down, counting the number of women who craned their necks to watch me drive—*five, six, seven—oh, there are two together—that makes nine in less than two miles.* I imagined their discussion: *Did you see that gorgeous man? Did you see his car? I'll bet he's loaded. I'll bet he has the most beautiful woman in the world. He must be the happiest man on earth.*

I smirked at the thought—*ten, eleven, twelve, thirteen*—I was rounding the corner into the parking lot of the agency that bore my name on the side of the building. *Thirteen is a new record. I must look good.* I glanced at my reflection in the rearview mirror. *I'm one good looking son-of-a-bitch, as Don always said.*

I strolled into the lobby and passed Jane Mercer's closed office door, not even bothering to glance in its direction. I stood in my office brewing a cappuccino and perusing the horizon out the window, observing only blue sky and fluffy white clouds. I wondered why it was such a clear day. No smog and no marine layer.

"It's about time you showed up," Bobbi crowed from my doorway. "Do you have a minute?"

I turned to face her. "Actually, no I don't." It was the first time I ever said no to Bobbi's morning briefings.

Her expression turned from gossipy to somber in a split second. "Oh—I guess you're busy," she said, looking dejected.

"You're right," I answered without emotion. "Close my door, please."

She backed out of my office rapidly, skirt billowing. She shut the door behind her.

I sat at my desk to review emails until it was precisely 10:30 a.m. It was time for the Our Vows Dot Com presentation, which I hadn't even looked at yet. I quickly pulled up the Power Point deck and scanned through it, landing on the final ad we were going to push down their throats. Then I closed the file, stood up and gave myself a final once-over in the full-length mirror behind my door. This was it.

When I entered the conference room, everyone was already seated, including the client team. It was a large group—maybe fifteen people. I immediately spotted Jane. There was one open chair left directly across from her and next to Warren. I quickly took the seat, scanning the table, acknowledging Alonzo and Jeffrey but purposely ignoring Jane.

"Craig Keller," Warren announced brashly with a proud

smile. "Our consummate award-winner. Ladies, and gentleman, Craig is the most important partner at this agency."

I noted the Our Vows Dot Com group looking my way and murmuring appreciatively, especially the women, who suddenly looked interested in the pitch meeting. Out of the corner of my eye I saw Jane, wearing a snug-fitting white dress with long sleeves and a bow tied at the neck. I tried to erase her from my mind and imagine she was some fat, sloppy guy sitting across from me. It was tough.

I turned to Alonzo and nodded. Alonzo began the preamble about the ad concepts. As usual, there were three and the last one was key. We strategically had Alonzo present the first two, knowing he would pass the baton to me and I would present the third—the one we wanted them to approve. I even asked Alonzo to present pedantically, so they would be bored to death by the time they got to the third and final ad.

I absentmindedly flipped through the printed deck sitting in front of me while Alonzo presented slides, tag lines and sample copy—rapping on the table intermittently as usual, for no apparent reason.

I wasn't even paying attention until Alonzo cued me. "Boss?"

I stood and strutted to the head of the table as Alonzo changed slides to the final concept.

"What is love?" I began, surveying the room, my eyes moving from one person to the next, skipping Jane completely. Everyone returned my glance with sudden interest but was silent.

"It's the promise of brightness and beauty—it's fantasy, it's sensuality, it's a chance at new life. It's fresh and gorgeous, like a light rain in spring." The room remained silent as all eyes were on me and, for some reason, I could no longer control where my eyes wandered. I was looking directly at Jane. She was the most beautiful woman I'd ever seen.

"Love gives us courage," I continued, eyes now locked on Jane's. "It makes us whole. It helps us forget tragedy. In fact, there's no more human way to numb the pain of loneliness—to mitigate the agony of rejection." I was speaking unswervingly to Jane now, like there were no one else in the room. I wasn't paying attention to the slide changes because I knew Alonzo was keeping up with me. I had no interest in what was going on outside Jane's penetrating stare.

"It's that inexorable, irrepressible power of love that gives us life, energy, and a reason to get up in the morning." I briefly glanced at the others in the room; they were fixated on me, like they were under hypnosis. I returned to Jane.

"When two people fall in love, they'll do anything to protect that love—that mystical, unfathomable feeling of finally being home. We try, in vain, to capture the elusive butterfly—to keep that love within our grasp forever."

Jane cocked her head, lips parted, and brows furrowed, but I kept going, not taking my eyes off hers for a minute.

"That's why we give diamonds. That's why we get on our knees and utter the most beautiful prose. It's a harmony that only happens once in a lifetime. And if you're lucky enough to find that rare, all-encompassing, true love, the only way to make it last forever is to set it free."

I turned to view the final slide, which was the ad—so beautiful and perfect. A wedding couple in a field of greens, spattered with daffodils—a blonde woman wearing a white lace wedding gown with the most exhilarated look on her face—a man fawning over her, about to kiss her but savoring her beauty first. I was ready to close the deal.

"So, you see, marriage is really an extraordinary kind of freedom. Marriage is the freedom to love forever."

The last sentence was the headline. I tore my gaze from Jane and looked from person to person. The women were in joyful tears, like it was their wedding day all over again. The men were in awe. They began to clap and nod.

Warren regarded me with an amazed expression. Jeffrey just shook his head and smiled. Alonzo studied me with pride. That's when I caught Jane standing and darting out of the room as quickly as she could. I breathed deeply, knowing what was coming next.

I DID THE NORMAL amount of schmoozing with the Our Vows Dot Com people and then slinked away at the appropriate moment. The ad campaign would move forward. It would be successful. It would probably nail the agency a Clio next year. But I didn't care about any of that. I was intent on one thing that day.

When I was back in my office, I began the process of moving out. I had a crew scheduled for 1 p.m. to remove the precious Chagall paintings from my office walls, wrap them properly and transport them in a temperature-controlled vehicle to my home. I hired another crew to move my furniture and other personal belongings. I sat at my desk while they boxed things up and I ran through emails, planning my exit for later that afternoon.

Around 4 p.m., Warren surprised me with a visit. I was going through files, trying to determine which items I might want to take with me, knowing my time was running out.

When he entered my office, Warren did a double take. It looked like thieves ransacked everything and made off with the valuables. "What the hell happened in here?" he asked, mouth gaping open, turning his rapt attention to me.

"Warren," I said, standing and facing him squarely. I was around six inches taller than Warren and I knew it intimidated him.

"Are you ... leaving or something?" he asked, looking shell-shocked at the condition of my office.

"I'm afraid so," I answered, voice devoid of emotion.

"But ... why? I mean, you can't just disappear, Keller. You have a contract, and your name is on the fucking building. Are you crazy? What's this all about? When were you going to tell me?"

"The contract is now null and void," I replied matter-of-factly. "I'll use your words here—I've violated the contract because I didn't adhere to the stipulations I signed—the stipulations you so patently outlined when we finalized the agreement."

Warren cleared his throat and glared at me, still astonished. "Which stipulation, Craig?"

"The one in which you mandated I never come near a female employee of this agency—flirt with, harass, date, or otherwise say anything sexual," I stated. "Those were the exact words you used."

"Now hold on a minute," Warren stalled as though he were thinking the whole situation through and trying to understand it. "I told you I never wanted to get a formal report. No one's reported sexual misconduct or harassment against you so, as far as I'm concerned, it didn't happen."

I drew in my chin and gave him a blank look.

Warren let out a deep sigh and closed his eyes. "Does this woman have a name?"

"She asked not to be identified. She's humiliated. I took advantage of her. She doesn't want to come to work and see me. She made that clear."

"You have to tell me who it is—come on. We've known each other a long time." Warren was beginning to look beleaguered, like he knew his words were falling on deaf ears.

"It doesn't matter, Warren. It's over. I'm leaving, and we'll figure out how to position this to the public, so it doesn't bring your agency down any further."

"But you can't leave now—we've just gotten started— you're building this business like I've never seen anyone before. I know we've had our differences in the past, but this is real. I admire you, Craig. No one on this team could have done what you did in such a short time. You're a superstar and we need you."

I sank into my desk chair and put my head between my hands. When I looked up at Warren, he wore a nervous expression. "You want to ignore what you made me sign because of what, Warren? Because I won two Clios before the agency's doors were open a full year? That's shallow, even for you."

"That's not it," he argued. "It's your energy—your intelligence. It's your charisma—I'm sorry I never saw it before because I was too busy competing with you. I was so busy being angry at you for stealing my business all those years ago." He paused to rub his forehead with his hand, as though a headache was coming on. "But I get it now—you got the business because you're better. No, you're the best. There *must* be some way to work this out. I mean, who is this woman? Is she someone we can talk to? Is she someone we can pay off—someone we can have sign a non-disclosure agreement? I don't care what we do, but you're the valuable one here. There's no one else, as far as I'm concerned."

I was astonished at Warren's willingness to throw his alleged unbendable ethics away to keep me there. He had become a star-struck sycophant, just like the naïve giddy women who used to comprise my typical lineup. As he was speaking, the movers were carting heavy boxes out of my office and out the front door of the agency into a huge moving vehicle. It was an absurd juxtaposition with Warren's groveling. The paintings were already on their way to my home. I was surprised no one had yet posed an inquiry as to why my office was being emptied out at rapid speed. They were likely working in robotic silos, not bothering to question anything odd or unusual going on right in front of their faces. I could have burglarized the place in broad daylight, and no one would notice.

There was nothing left to do but shake Warren's hand and say goodbye. "Thank you for the opportunity," I concluded. "I'll be in touch to discuss financial arrangements."

I exited the building not even glancing in Pearl's direction. She called after me, "Mr. Keller—I have phone messages for you." I continued walking to my car, got in and turned on the ignition.

My first stop should have been home to supervise the safe delivery of the Chagall paintings. Normally, I'd never let anyone touch them without my supervision—they were just too valuable. But some reckless instinct prevented me from caring, so I drove to Rae's Diner on Pico Boulevard. There, I sat at the counter and ordered coffee and a slice of apple pie with ice cream. I typically wouldn't touch anything sweet. It just was not on my diet regimen. It had been so long since I tasted something with real sugar, I felt queasy as I shoved another heaping forkful of pie and ice cream into my mouth. The waitresses all smiled flirtatiously at me.

"You eat up now, handsome," a heavy-set waitress with carrot-red curly hair grunted at me, winking.

I gave her a closed mouth smile because my mouth was overstuffed with the rich, fattening dessert. After two more cups of coffee, it was time to visit Dr. Truer. I paid my check and was on my way.

I arrived and entered the sick musty building, finding the waiting room to Dr. Truer's office. I was right on time and when she opened the door and welcomed me to her twisted brand of cocktail party; I inwardly smiled.

"Well," she said, once ensconced in her marigold La-Z-Boy. "Did you talk to Jane?"

I shrugged. "Yes, let's talk about Jane—my talk with Jane," I began defiantly.

"You finally talked to her? That's good news—please tell me how it went."

"I'm sure you'd love to know," I answered sullenly. "But it's none of your business. Your warped advice got me into a mess I can barely pull myself out of and I'm no longer interested in your quack opinions."

She gave me the empathetic look. "Craig, I'm concerned about how you're acting at this moment. I mean, look at your body language. You're extremely dysregulated."

"*Dysregulated?* Is that what you call this?" I asked, voice dripping with sarcasm. "From what esoteric psych book did you derive that term?"

"Craig, what happened to make you like this?" she asked, frowning like she was trying to solve a tricky puzzle.

"What happened is my life fell apart and there's no repairing it. It fell apart a long time ago when my brother was killed but no one ever picked up the pieces—least of all me. I've been walking around like a wounded veteran, breaking other people's hearts, and trashing their lives because I don't have a life, and I *never* will."

I saw Dr. Truer's eyes move to the clock on my left. I reached over and pulled away the fake potted plant, grabbed the clock and glared at it.

"I have forty-seven more minutes," I announced forcefully, turning the clock around to show it to her. She looked horrified. "Now finish the session, Dr. Truer—give me more of your professed wisdom and teach me how to live with this sickness—this crazy, incurable disease I lug around every day."

Dr. Truer was quiet, just observing me thoughtfully, but without the empathy. She now looked concerned, like I was spinning out of control before her eyes. I knew she must have seen this behavior before, given the league of mobsters she had seen over the years. *Or was I the worst?*

"Craig—I'd like to talk rationally about what happened with Jane. I'm assuming that's what has you so dysreg—I mean, so out of sorts. If you would please just talk to me about that ..."

"And do what with that information?" I interrupted belligerently. "Here's the long and short of it—I knocked her up—I denied it—I lied to her—I rejected her—I sent her back to her husband, who she was planning to divorce because of me. That's what happened. It's over. She's heartbroken and I'm somewhere near dead inside."

She was now back to the empathetic look, which I could no longer stomach.

"Do me a favor, Dr. Truer, and wipe that look off your face. I'm not pitiable. I'm not even someone who deserves that look—in fact, it infuriates me." I was now standing and approaching the door.

Before I put my hand on the doorknob, I turned back to her and delivered a parting shot. "And do yourself a favor and clean up this miserable, depressing building—clean up this sick-smelling musty office. Clean it up and buy new furniture—live a little. I'm sure you have the cash to pay for it."

And I left.

# Eighteen

*I* DROVE LIKE A MADMAN toward downtown as though laws no longer applied to me. I was an outlaw, waiting to be captured—a prisoner who escaped, recklessly spiraling into a frenzy without walls, boundaries, rules. I drove the Bentley with the top down and the windows open, my hair raging in the gust of the convertible wind speed. I ran stoplights, swerved past cars, and pressed my foot down on the gas pedal further and further, flying toward—*where, really?* I had no idea where I was going but knew I'd end up somewhere.

I did. It was on the corner of Central and 5th Street in Skid Row, close to where I originally found Alonzo. I peeled onto the side of the street corner and jerked the car into park. The area was well-lit. I didn't bother putting up the top, closing the windows, or locking the doors. I got out and walked Northwest on Fifth past Towne Avenue—to the real dregs—the insane apocalypse that was San Pedro Street. I wandered through the abyss in my custom-made Italian suit, marching to an unheeded cadence, lulled into the sad depths of humanity where real people suffered—sleeping on the streets and eating out of garbage cans.

San Pedro was where the nucleus of filth and homelessness stretched out for blocks. Mismatched and discolored tents lined the sidewalks along with dilapidated umbrellas the colors of faded rainbows. Trash bags stuffed with some poor soul's earthly possessions sat off to the side. Broken, abandoned bicycle parts, filthy blankets and useless possessions discarded from someone's basement appeared from every angle. I spotted a stray pit bull roaming the neighborhood, sniffing at a painter bucket covered with plywood, the stench revealing it was a makeshift commode.

A huge Chrysler pulled up and parked near me, and a greasy white guy blaring rap music rolled down his window. He was obviously a drug dealer, just waiting for a desperate addict. I was sure he wouldn't be alone long. I noticed there were no cops on these streets for even they were too smart to come here. There was no help, no order, no justice for the inhabitants of this anguished destination—one which boasted the famous mural on St. Julian Street that read, 'Skid Row City Limit. Population: Too Many.'

I turned back toward Fifth Street and ventured further west, feeling the light slowly vanish, the air become thicker and the streets less populated. I passed a huge mural featuring a black man in tears, the words 'American Dream' scrawled next to his face in crimson paint—the letters etched in a font that reminded me of dripping blood. I tossed my car keys against the mural, the metallic clanking sound echoing into the dense night as they hit the wall and fell to the ground. Enormous, bloated rats hovered at the base of the drainage ditches, burrowing, feeding off human waste.

The streets had become so dark, I could barely comprehend my surroundings. Then I saw him standing not far from me, smiling and beckoning. It was DJ—as young and bright and earnest-looking as he was the day he fell from the yacht to his death.

"Craig," he called to me, his straw-colored hair ruffling slightly in the night air. "Come with me."

"DJ," I breathed, feeling like I was on some hallucinatory drug. "Is it really you?"

DJ smiled and nodded. He looked ethereal and almost translucent in the darkness. He held out his hand and summoned me to follow him.

I slowly took steps toward him, but he was moving too fast.

"DJ—wait—wait up for me," I shouted. "Please don't go."

"I have to go now, Craig," he replied, waving at me in the distance.

"I'll be right there—please don't leave me—I need you, DJ—you left too soon." I was running as fast as I could, but he was almost flying, and I couldn't keep up. "DJ—it's cold and lonely without you—please come back," I cried out like a little boy. But DJ's image was already vanishing into the distance. I could no longer see him. He was gone.

Suddenly, I felt a swarm around me and, with the help of the moonlight, glimpsed the most gruesome of apparitions—something out of Dante's *Inferno*—without Virgil to lead me—distorted faces staring angrily at the unwelcome intruder—the good-looking suited bastard from another planet. One who worked in high rises with fancy paintings—one who slept with good girls because they wanted a piece of the Keller fortune—something that was so minuscule—so unimportant to me but that would help these people spend one night in a comfortable bed—where they could sleep—sleep a full night without being disturbed by a drug-addled zombie or beaten to a pulp by street vermin.

"How many of you have ever slept a full night?" I blurted out to the crowd of jagged characters—their faces resembling grotesque voodoo masks—those meant to scare away evil—only they *were* evil. They were the night owls who had not yet drank or shot up enough to put them out for the night. They stared in dismal hostility, not answering my blistering outburst.

They just thrust their hands out and demanded money, screaming into the jet-black darkness, howling at me like wild dogs in a discordant mantra. I put my hand in my pants pocket and pulled out my wallet, throwing it out to the people as I descended further into Skid Row, L.A.'s version of

Hades. One toothless man demanded my jacket, which I immediately peeled off and handed him.

I felt someone pull my sweater, heard the seams ripping and felt rough hands tearing it off my body. I didn't fight it. Then I ripped open my shirt, buttons popping and springing off me, and let it fly behind me, the material getting caught in greedy hands. Someone was tugging at my belt from the back, so I unbuckled it and stripped it away from my body, letting it fall to the ground. The pandemonium followed me—a brawl over who should have my belt. My watch was a different story. It cost upwards of $12,000. I unhooked the strap and threw it into the maelstrom of bodies menacing behind me.

A sad growling fiend of a man claimed my shoes, so I knelt and took them off, one at a time, along with my socks so I was barefoot, only in my suit pants, treading through the filthy, urine-soaked streets, feet shuffling along, becoming more scorched—sliced up with broken beer bottles and other debris. I knew my feet were bleeding, but I didn't care. It was a cold night, but I didn't feel it. I could barely sense pain anymore.

When I was at the end of Fifth Street, in the clotted sludge of Skid Row, something crashed hard against my back. Before I could turn around, someone smashed a bottle against the back of my head and then another hit my face, cutting above my right eye. I began to stumble and slip to the ground, extreme nausea enveloping me like a putrid curtain, my vision waning, finally fading to black.

# Nineteen

A SPLASH OF COLOR PAINTED the sky at dusk, as I lay on my back in the sand, examining the unpredictable cloud formations and colors—the sun slowly disappearing along the horizon—streaming shades of rose, azure, violet, blush, tangerine and gold, reflecting their shimmering spectrum on the ocean water at twilight. I was reminded of a Claude Monet painting.

DJ was lying on his stomach next to me, doodling something in the sand with a discarded popsicle stick. "You know what I miss the most?" he asked me.

"What's that, DJ?"

"I miss our big family dinners—you know—at the holidays."

I nodded and leaned over to see what DJ was doodling. It was a big heart with a cross woven through it—something we would have drawn as young children to delineate which girl we had a crush on at the time. "Those dinners were never the same without you," I responded. "They could never be."

"I hope you still have those dinners."

"We mostly have smaller versions of them now—just Don and Julia and me in L.A. When I was married, we used to go to San Francisco and see all the aunts, uncles, cousins—but it's tough to get my children there. Oh—that's right, you've never met my children. I have two, Axel and Anabel. You'd love them—Anabel looks just like you."

"I'm sorry I never met them," DJ answered, tossing the popsicle stick aside, turning over on his back and gazing at what was left of the sunset. It was becoming darker by the minute as the sun's fiery rays descended behind the ocean—preparing to say good night.

"I'm sorry, too, DJ—I'm sorry for so many things," I said, feeling tears in my eyes. "I'm sorry I didn't save you that day, DJ—will you ever forgive me?"

"Forgive you for what?" DJ asked. He shook his head. "Don't be sorry, little brother, it wasn't your fault. I never should have taken you out sailing that day. It was irresponsible. But what happened, happened. It was meant to be."

I suddenly sprang upright and stared at DJ, who was still engrossed in watching the sunset. "It was *not* meant to be, DJ," I insisted. "It was never meant to happen that way."

"Do you ever tell Mom and Dad you love them?" DJ asked, turning his chiseled earnest-looking face toward me, honey brown eyes wide.

"You mean Don and Julia?" I smirked bitterly. "As you're aware, they aren't sentimental people. But to answer your question, no."

"Maybe you should sometime," DJ responded, shrugging. "It couldn't hurt. And that 'Don' and 'Julia' stuff is such a crock. They never believed in it. They just did it because they saw themselves in a certain way at a certain time and, once they started it, they couldn't go back. Dad's pretty stubborn that way, you know."

"And this is new information?" I asked, now chuckling. "He's grown more stubborn over time—especially after you—um—left."

"You mean when I died," DJ corrected me. "I'm serious, Craig—Mom and Dad love you—you should give them a chance. Please promise me you'll give them a chance." His eyes were pleading, and he put his hand over his heart. "I mean it, Craig. Promise me." DJ now got to his feet.

I stared up at him and nodded. "Okay, DJ—I promise."

He patted me on the shoulder and then walked toward the water, disappearing into the ocean along with the forlorn colors that lingered in the ensuing darkness.

I OPENED MY EYES to a shock of peacock blue and the chronic beeping of a heart monitor. I heard muffled voices nearby. I could not open my right eye and my head and back were throbbing. The peacock blue suddenly shivered and disappeared, and I saw Alonzo's blurry face peering down at me. He must have been listening to my breathing, shoving his blue sideburns into my face.

"Boss—you finally woke up," he exclaimed, gazing at me intently, his dark eyes hooded by deep-set lids, like he hadn't been sleeping.

"Where am I?" I tried to ask, but my speech sounded garbled, as though I were unable to formulate words. My throat was sore and my mouth dry. I realized there was a long tube down my throat, preventing me from speaking. Although my surroundings were unfamiliar and unclear, I noted I was hooked up to an IV, and a heart and blood-pressure monitor. I was swathed in a blue hospital gown and a quick pat down with my fingers told me I was naked underneath. I turned my head to the side, and saw a young black woman was sitting in a chair next to the bed.

"You're at the Temple Medical Center," Alonzo replied, having obviously translated my incoherent drivel. "In ICU. You've been in a coma for days."

"How did you find me?" I muttered, still hearing the mangled enunciation. My hand tugged on the cord of the IV and I felt the itch of the needle moving in my vein.

"Here," Alonzo said, reaching for a black slate that had been propped up against the wall with numbers written all over it. I watched as Alonzo wiped the slate down before handing it to me with a piece of chalk. "Write down what you want to say."

I accepted the slate and chalk and awkwardly scrawled the message, barely able to see what I was writing. "How did you find me?"

Alonzo glanced down at the slate and frowned, like he was having difficulty figuring out what I wrote. Then he turned back to me. "Oh ... how did I find you? Well, it wasn't easy, Boss," he answered. "Your parents filed a missing person report because you disappeared—from the office—from your house—everyone was calling the office looking for you. Warren told us you left suddenly. No one knew where you were. They found a shell of your car on Fifth and Central—totally taken apart—missing tires, steering wheel, motor—completely stripped down."

I was only comprehending fragments of Alonzo's explanation of my whereabouts. I tried to think back to the faraway remnants of my surreal walk in Skid Row and the shedding of all my possessions barely came back to me. It puzzled me that I was in a coma—*for how long?* It felt like it could have been a lifetime—or only for an hour. I recalled nothing of where my mind had traveled in this time warp—I had gone away—to another world—one to which I would never return. I only vaguely remembered seeing DJ—somewhere, but I didn't remember where. *Could it be that he came to me? Or was that an illusion?*

I crossed out the word 'how' and wrote 'when' above it: "When did you find me?" I was still woozy, but desperate to piece things together.

"Today's Monday," Alonzo replied. "I always volunteer Sunday evenings at the Union Rescue Mission." He turned to the young black woman, who had remained silent, seated bedside. "You owe your life to this young lady."

I slowly and sorely positioned my head toward the young woman, whose face looked like an amorphous pool of chocolate syrup. Everything I tried to focus on seemed to be moving—vibrating. I felt a sharp pain seize the back of my head.

"I found you out on the street," she explained, her voice echoing with each syllable like she was talking through a tunnel, so it was hard for me to comprehend what she was saying. "You'd been beaten pretty badly. At first, I thought you were dead. My friends helped carry you to the Union Rescue Mission, so you wouldn't be out in the cold."

I hoisted myself onto my elbows to see if I could sit up, but my body was not cooperating. I fell back down and lay my aching head against the cold pillow. The chalkboard and chalk fell to the floor with a loud thwack. Alonzo swooped down to retrieve the board and chalk—he wiped it clean and then handed it to me.

"They got you here and I've been visiting you every day," the echoing continued. "They've been waiting for you to wake up. I saw Alonzo at the mission last night—he showed me your picture and I led him here. That's a nasty cut above your eye, mister. You got a big old shiner, too."

I wrote, "What's your name?" and then held it towards the voice, feeling my own throat burning.

I watched as the pool of vibrating chocolate came closer to me—the echoey voice becoming louder. "My name is Meseret," she answered. "But no one can pronounce it, so I go by Mary."

"Mary's been a friend of mine for years," Alonzo added, backing his way toward the door of the hospital room. "I need to get the doc to let him know you woke up—and I hope you don't mind, as soon as I found you, I called Bobbi—she was all messed up when you went missing. You know she sees you as the son she never had."

I was barely able to nod at Alonzo without understanding what he just said and took a deep breath, glancing at my rescuer. I decided to stop trying to write on the slate—I couldn't understand my own thoughts at this time. Mary continued to speak in echoes.

A mass of sea-foam green entered the room, and I realized it was the doctor with Alonzo trailing behind him.

"Boss," said Alonzo. "This is Doctor Gonzalez." I focused my eyes on Doctor Gonzalez's face, which was hazy but seemed dark and kind. He had tiny hands—little surgeon hands that looked nimble and quick as he waved them before my eyes. "You made it, brother," he said smiling. "We sure were worried about you."

"What's wrong with me?" I scribbled on the slate and held it up for Dr. Gonzalez.

The doctor paused for a minute to study the slate. "When they brought you here, you were in bad shape," he pointed out. "I had to operate on your right eye—if that cut had been a half-centimeter longer, you would have been blind in that eye. You also experienced blunt trauma to the back of your head. We did an MRI, and the skull was fractured, which caused possible injury to your brain. We administered a medically induced coma to reduce the metabolic rate of the brain tissue as well as the cerebral blood flow."

He paused and shined a light over my face, and I felt the glare hit my left eye. Then he continued.

"With these reductions, the blood vessels in the brain narrowed, decreasing the amount of space occupied by the brain. The plan was to relieve the swelling and decrease the intracranial pressure so that some or all brain damage would be averted. Your throat's going to be sore for a while because we used an endotracheal tube to safeguard the airway. I'll have it removed right away now that you're conscious."

Dr. Gonzalez waited for me to react, but I said nothing. It sounded like he was speaking in a foreign tongue.

"You came in here with no ID—we assumed you were indigent. But your friend Alonzo here identified you this morning as Craig Axel Keller," he said looking down at a clipboard, "Birthdate September 28, 1980. Is that correct?"

I did my best to nod, trying to rein in my disoriented mind.

Dr. Gonzalez smiled. "The important thing, Craig, is that you're going to be okay. You have some recuperation to do, but you'll heal. We're going to keep you here at least another week or more for tests and rehab. We need to give you the right amount of time to recover from these injuries. The neurologist needs to evaluate your brain activity and that eye needs monitoring."

He turned to Alonzo and Mary. "I'm afraid I need to kick you both out for a while. We need to remove the endotracheal tube so your friend here can breathe on his own. You're welcome to return tomorrow during visiting hours. He'll be out of ICU by then."

I suddenly thought of Don and Julia and grabbed the slate to write. "Call my parents," I wrote, holding the slate up to Alonzo.

"Of course, Boss," he replied. "Right away—do you have their numbers?"

I realized I had no phone, and all my contacts were stored there. I wrote underneath parents, "Donovan Keller S.F." My writing was crude and almost illegible.

Alonzo studied the slate. "Donovan Keller—San Francisco. You got it—do you want me to tell Warren?" he asked nervously.

I thought about Warren and tried to recall our conversation before I walked out on him—out of the agency towards my descent into Skid Row. The memory was still fuzzy. I was not sure how to answer. I needed time to process what happened—what I did to initiate such an impromptu leap into the void. I tapped the chalk against my father's name so Alonzo would understand that I only wanted my parents contacted.

He nodded slowly. "Whatever you say, Boss." He then exited the hospital room.

THE EXTUBATING PROCESS WAS painful and traumatic, causing me to cough violently and uncontrollably until the tube was out. The nurse affixed an oxygen mask to my face until I could breathe spontaneously. They moved me out of ICU into my own room where I could watch television and reacquaint myself with the world once more.

The next morning, I was able to sip warm chicken broth and eat a few bites of toast, although I didn't have much of an appetite and my throat burned. I did feel incredibly cognizant after a good night's sleep and some pain meds. Around 10 a.m., Dr. Gonzalez stopped by on his rounds to check on me.

"Good morning, my friend," he greeted me, smiling.

"How are we doing today?"

"Much better," I answered, noting my throat was still hoarse and my voice raspy.

He checked my vitals and recorded some things on his tablet. I heard a knock at the door and Alonzo entered with Mary trailing behind him.

"Morning, Boss," said Alonzo. "Talked to your parents last night. They were on an early flight from San Francisco today—they should be here soon."

"Thanks, Alonzo." I silently wondered why the hell they didn't come down as soon as they knew I was missing. They could have stayed in my house while I was MIA—their conspicuous absence was mind-boggling.

I turned to Mary, who stood beside Alonzo, giving me a huge toothless grin.

"Hi—Mary, right?" I asked. "Tell me your real name again."

"Meseret," she answered.

"*Meseret*—that's a pretty name," I commented in my throaty rasp, wondering how old she was. "What kind of name is it?"

"Ethiopian," she answered. "It means 'foundation.' My parents came here from Ethiopia, but they got on drugs when I was a baby and couldn't afford to take care of me. Then, I got on drugs—and here I am."

"Do you live on the streets?" I asked, thinking I needed to find a mirror—some place where I could assess the damage done to my face and eye. I was still having the hardest time picking my head up to talk to Alonzo and Meseret. I had no choice but to listen and be grateful she found me. She saved me.

She nodded. "Yes, and I work at the mission during the days. I work in the kitchen and help feed people."

"Where do you sleep?" I asked, dreading how she was going to respond.

"I have a tent out there," she nodded to her right, where the prison-like windows were. "It's not as bad as you think."

"Remember when I lived out there?" Alonzo asked me.

"I had a cardboard box—not a tent. A tent is a palace compared to what I had."

"You're the most beautiful person I've ever seen," Meseret commented, grinning shyly. "When I found you, your head and feet were bleeding—I thought you were Jesus. You looked like a gentleman. I knew you didn't belong here. You're too beautiful to be down here with us."

Dr. Gonzalez had leaned over and was now examining my eye. There was a bandage over it, which I hadn't realized when I woke up the day before. He gently pulled the bandage off and began cleaning the wound.

At that moment, Bobbi flew into the room, red-faced and chomping her Nicorette. "Craig—my *sheyna punim*," she shouted. "Oh my God—you have no idea how worried we've been." She observed me for a minute while Dr. Gonzalez dressed the wound above my eye and she immediately began crying—something I'd never seen Bobbi do—something I assumed she was incapable of. "Oh, Craig," she wailed. "I can't believe it—what happened to you?"

"Take it easy, Bobbi—I had a little accident but I'm going to live."

Tears continued to stream down her face as she took my hand and squeezed it. "It doesn't look like a *little* accident to me."

"I must look pretty awful to make the Silver Dollar cry," I grated, giving her a slight smile. It was all I was capable of in my condition.

She shot a concerned look at Dr. Gonzalez. "Is he really going to be okay?"

Dr. Gonzalez smiled and reassured her. "Yes, but he needs to rest. You guys can stay for a few minutes, but I'd appreciate if you don't keep him up too long. The more rest, the quicker the recovery."

Bobbi let out another howl and grabbed the tissue box on the tray next to my bed, hastily pulling out several sheets and wiping her eyes.

Dr. Gonzalez seemed satisfied that my wound was healing nicely and bandaged it back up. He took a step back, so he was standing in a circle with the others, all eyes on me.

I looked from Bobbi to Alonzo to Meseret and then to Dr. Gonzalez—my collection of strays—good strays with big hearts. "Thank you," I whispered.

"Craig—I'd like to speak with you alone for a moment," Bobbi requested, glancing at Dr. Gonzalez, Alonzo and Meseret, who were still hovering around my hospital bed. "Do you mind?" she asked them.

"Of course not," said Dr. Gonzalez before guiding Meseret and Alonzo out of the room, leaving Bobbi and me alone.

"Craig," she started as soon as they had departed. "I need to talk to you about something. It's very personal and I'm not sure where to start."

I felt another shooting pain in the back of my head and winced. I was not at all sure what Bobbi was about to lay on me, but she looked serious—more serious than I'd ever seen her.

"Just say whatever it is you have to say, Bobbi," I told her. I could feel my raw throat burning with each word.

"It's Jane," she began. "She's despondent—as soon as she heard you were missing; she's been beside herself. *Oy* was there *mishegas* in the office when you left! Anyway, Jane confided in me—she told me everything."

I felt my heart burst at the mere mention of Jane. I had blocked her from my mind because of the acute pain associated with everything involving her. Of course, it was about Jane—*Jane*—yet another mess I created before my ultimate meltdown and subsequent slide into nowhere-land. The reminder of Jane made my heartbeat quicken. I could hear the heart monitor beeping with more persistence. I vaguely considered the monitor as an inadvertent polygraph. I drew a deep breath and waited for Bobbi to continue.

"She had no one else to tell," Bobbi said gently, running her fingers through the ends of her long silvery hair. "She said her friends would be furious if they knew what happened."

My thoughts went back to Marisa's threats and I could only imagine the reaction both she and Kat would have if they found out I had impregnated Jane and then pulled the stunt I pulled.

"So, I don't want you to be angry with her for telling me about you—about you and her," Bobbi added.

"Go on," I urged. I wondered how Jane spun it to Bobbi—whether she was angry at me, hateful—even vengeful. I deserved it—all of it.

"I know you had an affair with Jane," she murmured quietly, like she didn't want anyone to overhear, even though we were alone in the hospital room. "I know she fell in love with you and now she's pregnant. I know you told her you had a vasectomy after the birth of Anabel." She paused for a moment. "And I know you were lying."

The heart monitor beeped fervently at the conclusion of this statement.

Bobbi tore her eyes from me long enough to gape at the monitor and then she looked me directly in the eye—the one working eye—with the gravest look on her face. *How would Bobbi know about my reproductive status?* Unless I told her at some point. *Beep—beep—beep—beep.*

"What are you talking about, Bobbi?" I whispered, nudging against the IV cord—it was moving in my arm again and pinching my skin.

"You had that pregnancy scare a few years ago—remember?" she asked incredulously. "With that woman from New York—the one from the research firm who came out for meetings once a month and slept with you."

I recalled the woman from New York—her name was Claire Braxton. She was young and blonde and eager to get me into bed. We did it in the Bentley several times. I had the apartment in Brentwood at the time and we had sex on the floor of my living room and once on the kitchen stove. I pretended I was making pancakes and slapped her naked ass with a spatula while she screamed and moaned with pleasure. We went at it like rabbits until she reported to me her period was late. She insisted the condom broke and I got her pregnant. She intimated she would file a paternity suit. She was hungry for money. I must have been so worried, I resorted to confiding in Bobbi. It turned out she was not pregnant, and I quickly dumped both her and her firm.

"If you had a vasectomy, you wouldn't have been able to get her pregnant either," Bobbi continued, as though she were uncovering a murder case.

I said nothing, just listened to Bobbi's big revelation.

"What I want to know is why you would tell Jane that?" Bobbi's cross-examination continued. "I mean, what if you *are* the father of her child, Craig? Why would you lie and play games with someone's life?"

Before I could comment, Bobbi continued.

"And you know what else?" she persisted. "Something tells me *you're* in love with *her*."

"And why would you think that?" I realized Bobbi must have picked up on my feelings for Jane a long time ago—likely when we all worked together at my old agency. Bobbi's status as the office barometer made it easy for her to decode my relationship with Jane—she probably spotted it the first time she was in the room with us both.

"I knew it a long time before Jane said anything to me," Bobbi confirmed. "You want to know why I always gave you details about Jane's personal life? It's because I knew you wanted them—you lived for them because you have feelings for her. Strong feelings."

I didn't get a chance to answer because Alonzo burst in the door, phone in hand. "Boss—your parents just called me—they let themselves into your house to drop their bags. They're on their way down here now." Alonzo looked pleased with himself as he made this announcement.

"Thanks, Alonzo," I mumbled, thinking about Jane and my last conversation with her in the bar in Santa Monica. I also thought about her sitting there during the Our Vows Dot Com meeting—how confused and dumbfounded she looked when I delivered my love lecture directly to her. I closed my eyes. *Jesus, Craig, what have you done?*

Dr. Gonzalez rapped on the door and then entered. "I hope I gave you enough time to chat," he said to Bobbi. "But it's time for your friend here to get some sleep." He turned to me. "I'm going to administer a dose of pain medication and I'd like you to close your eyes."

I felt like I had somehow been saved from Bobbi's inquisition and discovery of my intense love for Jane—I was just too weak physically to address the whole issue. It would have to go on the back burner until I healed.

Bobbi nodded and stood up. She peered down at me and pursed her red chapped lips, still chewing the Nicorette gum. "We're not finished," she warned. "I'll be back when you have more strength." She put her hand on my face and patted it gently. "Get some rest, *Sheyna*."

As everyone exited the room, Dr. Gonzalez handed me a thimble-sized container with pills in it and a plastic cup of water. "This is Vicodin—it will help with the pain in your head and eye," he offered. I gratefully accepted the pills and swallowed them with the water.

Several hours later, I woke up to my parents sitting in two chairs observing me anxiously. I blinked my eye but said nothing. For some reason, I was not ready to see them.

"Son," Don said to me in his loud crunchy voice with the Irish accent. He stood and put his hand on my shoulder, gently rubbing it. It was the first time he touched me affectionately since I was a child.

Julia looked near tears. "Craig, darling," she uttered, voice quavering. "We were sick with worry."

"Have you talked to my children?" I asked Don, ignoring Julia.

"We spoke to Alessandra as soon as we heard from your work colleague," Julia answered before Don could say anything—a first.

"You mean Alonzo," I remarked, thinking Julia never liked to acknowledge the names of people she felt were beneath her.

"Yes," she responded. "Alessandra chose not to share the fact that you were missing—she didn't want Axel and Anabel to worry. We all decided it was best to tell them you were in an accident and in the hospital, which is what she did as soon as she heard from us."

I was irked by this information, even as I lay helpless in a strange hospital bed after losing several days of my life and waking up with unmanageable pain. Of course, Alessandra would not tell the kids I was missing or even care what happened to me. She probably wished I wouldn't resurface, so she would never have to be reminded of the man she married and who fathered her children. I was sure my permanent disappearance would free her in some way.

"How's that eye doing, son?" Don interrupted Julia impatiently. "The doctor told us you'd be blind if it weren't for his steady hand in surgery."

"I've been incredibly lucky," I said, feeling the pain in my head returning.

"You know, the police want to question you," Don stated firmly. "I staved them off for a few days but, eventually, you're going to have to answer questions related to this incident. For one, what were you doing in this part of the city in the first place?"

"Yeah, I know," I answered. It's like Don was questioning one of his mob clients—trying to find out what nefarious activity was at the root of the situation, so he could formulate an argument and get me out of trouble. I rolled my head to the side and glanced at Julia. "Can you please get Dr. Gonzalez? I need pain meds."

Julia rose and exited the room hurriedly.

"Now, son," Don said, throwing me a solicitous look. "I don't know what happened here, but whatever it is, we'll fix it. All the material items—your car, cash, clothing, jewelry—it can all be recovered through an insurance claim."

Naturally, that's what Don cared about most—he had no thoughts or questions about what drove me into this situation in the first place. He would never understand. And I was too exhausted to explain. Don would always be Don and Julia would always be Julia—the two people who least understood me on this earth. They would never comprehend their alienated son—the ever-disappointing Craig Keller.

# Twenty

D<small>R. G</small>ONZALEZ RELEASED ME to go home the week before Christmas. My eye had healed to the point where I could see, but there was a deep scar above it. The Doctor told me that time would eliminate the scar without the help of plastic surgery, and he gave me a salve to put on it several times a day. The wound to the back of my head was almost completely healed; my hair was growing back.

While I was in the hospital, Meseret-Mary visited me every day and we became fast friends. She was twenty-seven and had been homeless since she was ten. I couldn't imagine growing up on the street, but she had somehow triumphed over incalculable odds—she had survived. She calmed me with her stories of living on Skid Row and the freedom of being homeless. I often asked her what her aspirations were, but she didn't seem to have any. She was comfortable in the discomfort she had known her whole life. I was astonished. I grew fond of her—so fond, I promised to return to the mission to see her. And I meant it. It was a bittersweet parting when I was finally discharged from the hospital to return to my old life—or some version of it. I had no idea what I was in for.

Alessandra brought Axel and Anabel to see me at the urgent request of Don and Julia. Don had long since flown back to San Francisco to handle his court appearances, but he left Julia behind at my house to get things in order, assist with acquiring a replacement for my destroyed vehicle and a new phone, deal with insurance adjustors, etc. The police questioned me, but I feigned complete amnesia about what happened. I told them my only memory was of stopping in the area because of car trouble but that I recalled nothing after. So, there were no charges to file. All I wanted was to put the incident behind me.

Axel and Anabel took turns visiting me. Alessandra, of course, only dropped them off, refusing to see her ex-husband in such a vulnerable state. The kids were fascinated with the scar above my eye and wanted to touch it—to know all about how it happened. Alessandra had told them I was in a car accident—not that I'd been beaten to a pulp by homeless people. It was all such a charade. Always with her.

Mitchell Keller Vance & Mercer—with the missing partner—had sent a bouquet of flowers, with a note that said, "Get well, Craig—we miss you." I pictured Pearl trying to figure out what to say on the card because, as Bobbi explained, Warren had been tight-lipped about what happened to me—he really didn't know much anyway. Bobbi had shared that I was recuperating from an accident and unable to see or talk to anyone. She only shared my location, so they could send me something. She said Warren was surprised that I was so close to downtown and Skid Row, but he didn't question it in the end. He told the office and public I had taken a medical leave of absence following a serious accident.

Bobbi came to see me several times during my convalescence at Temple Medical Center, but she stopped badgering me about Jane. I told her, emphatically, that she was not to reveal to Jane anything related to my 'vasectomy.' I did promise her I would address Jane when I was well. That was a deal we made but I still had no idea how I was going to do that.

With Jane, I was numb. I felt immobilized—unable to see her as the woman I loved and the mother of my unborn child—and unable to accept that I would never see or speak to her again. I felt like I was in a bubble—some impenetrable place where I didn't really exist anymore. I was no longer Craig Keller, the ad guy. I was some poor sad bastard who had been brutally beaten and robbed on Skid Row—now unemployed, untethered to any work or personal situation. Some part of me was disappointed Jane didn't bother to call or try to see me—I had a secret wish she would turn up if only to tell me to fuck off. It would have helped rectify the feelings of emptiness and ignorance—the wondering about how she was and what she was doing—the feelings which permeated my heart throughout the entire tragedy.

I had a lot of time to ponder my life while I was in the hospital—to reflect on why I chose advertising as a profession. I realized that I never really chose advertising; rather, it chose me. Advertising campaigns worked to manipulate others into specific behavior. Photos and words needed to be manipulated in just the right way to create the desired effect. That's why rough concepts contained copy and images that were for position only—waiting for the exact right combination that would resonate on both a psychological and emotional level with the consumer. It struck me that my whole life was a series of vignettes that were for position only—nothing was complete—nothing finished.

But I was home now—home and ensconced in my own bed, in silk pajamas with Julia waiting on me hand and foot. She had purchased a Christmas tree and decorated it herself. It was fifteen feet tall and stood in the living room, near the windows that led to the pool. She had chosen a pale shade of green for all the decorations—Julia was a monochromatic kind of woman. She liked things just so. Still, it was a majestic tree and symbolized so many things this year. It represented both an ending and a beginning—something shining and new—something aching with nostalgia—a wound from youth that would never heal—and yet it was healing. I was healing—gradually, like a slow-rising sun.

ADELE ROYCE

The second night I was home, Julia had baked Irish butter cookies for Christmas, and we sat on the couch crunching away and just observing the tree, lit up without any other lights on in the house. I had poured us each a Scotch, so we could relax.

"I wrote some poems while you were in the hospital," Julia revealed, eyeing me uneasily and taking a sip of Scotch. She set her glass down on a coaster. "Would you like to hear one?"

"I would," I answered, suddenly seeing her face. It was lit by only the flickering lights emanating from the tree. She pulled a notebook off the coffee table and held her smart phone flashlight in front of it, so she could see well enough to read.

She cleared her throat. "It's called 'Forgiving Nature,'" she said and proceeded with the poem:

> "The wind glides its hands over you as if to say,
> 'You are not at fault; you are not to blame.
> The clouds were only joking last night when they
> showered you with tears and told you it was okay to
> melt.
> I howled and transformed you into a fierce, red-eyed
> swan
> Who sailed out into the night,
> A frantic cavalier, who dared stretch his neck above the
> stars.
> What did you see there?
> Did you notice the gods shaking their fists in glorious
> victory?
> Or did you get lost in the sweltering caves?
> The darkness you fear despises your willful ways,
> But cannot escape the chains of light surrounding it.
> So, do not be frightened; come out again.
> The sun needs you and the trees want you here.
> Look! The flower with the shock of red petals
> saw you last night and still holds out her generous
> hand.

*She knows you have ceased to breathe.*
*She knows you have lived and died.*
*She knows you have broken into shards of green light*
*And she still has not said a word.*'"

When Julia stopped speaking, she paused for my reaction. I felt tears in my eyes, remembering the depth Julia had in her and knowing this was one of those moments for us. The poem was moving and prophetic at the same time. I don't know how Julia could have known what happened but, in some magical mother-son way, she was able to intuit the feelings and pour them onto a page with her beautiful words, woven into a lilting melody.

I reached for her hand and she accepted it. She moved closer to me on the couch, and we embraced. I inhaled the scent of her hair and there was something so familiar about it—a feeling from childhood—a feeling I needed desperately but had not felt for so long. I realized then that I did love Julia—I loved her in the purest way a son could love his mother and I no longer wanted to hold it back.

When we finally withdrew from the embrace, I kissed her on the cheek and whispered, "I love you, Mom."

Her look was briefly one of surprise, but she smiled, eyes wet with tears and nodded. "I love you."

THE NEXT FEW DAYS were spent getting ready for Christmas. It was on a Tuesday this year and it was already the Friday before. Don was scheduled to fly in that night and spend the holidays with us. It was my weekend with the kids, and Alessandra, through some sudden spell of magnanimity, decided to leave them with us through Christmas morning. They would return to their mother's home Christmas day through New Year's to be with Alessandra and her family, who were visiting from Italy.

Julia was busy making dinner arrangements, doing last-minute gift-buying, and decorating the house.

Bobbi called unexpectedly Friday afternoon while I was

walking on the beach. I sent the call to voice mail and then listened to her message. She said she just wanted to wish me a happy holiday and see how I was doing. I dialed her number and listened as it rang.

"I'm glad you called me back," she said immediately. "Are you okay? I never heard from you."

"I'm still recovering—I'm much better but not one hundred percent yet. How are you?"

"You know—they're closing the office on Christmas Eve until after New Year's—I always get bored at this time of year. There's not much for a single Jewish woman to do at Christmas."

"I'm sure you have friends who would love to see you," I returned, not taking the bait of Bobbi's guilt card.

"I have to tell you something important, Craig," she said in a serious tone. "I'm assuming you never had a conversation with Jane because she came to me yesterday and told me she's proceeding with the divorce and now planning to … planning to …" Bobbi hesitated.

I thought about Jane—impossible, impenetrable Jane, and had no idea what to say. I obviously wanted to know what Jane was planning but the prospects frightened me—I almost didn't want to hear what Bobbi was about to say.

"Craig—are you still there?" she asked.

"Yes—I'm here."

"She's planning to terminate the pregnancy," Bobbi revealed. "She doesn't want a baby and especially as a single parent."

I felt my heart race. Jane was going to abort my child at Christmas—how rich and just at the same time. I didn't know how to respond. I had heard about abortions—mostly from my former partners, who were stupid enough not to use protection during their endless office conquests. I just imagined Jane in stirrups, gazing at the ceiling in some dank, fluorescent-lit office, the obnoxious glare of light blinding her beautiful green eyes while she was prodded with a metal instrument between her legs, the sound of a vacuum humming, sucking the life out of the fetus we created—sucking it into a tube where it would be disposed of with the rest of the dead embryos. Maybe Jane would go out afterward and celebrate her lightness—the weight of this burden finally disappearing—never again having to think about the coward who made her that way—the coward who sat comfortably ensconced in his Malibu home, with his wealthy family and hardship-free children. I said nothing.

"Craig," Bobbi said, voice now rising. "Did you hear what I said?"

"Yes."

"What are you going to do about it?" she demanded. "You want to see your child literally flushed down the toilet?"

"You know what, Bobbi?" I burst out, suddenly furious, even though I knew I was shooting the messenger. "I'm done talking to you—it's none of your business—do you hear me? Jane can do what she wants with her body—it has nothing to do with me and certainly nothing to do with you. So, mind your own business, Bobbi, and go back to smoking cigarettes and chewing your nicotine gum—you'll be alone on Christmas, just like you always are—because you're a nosy busy-body."

With that, I hung up on Bobbi. My jaw was tight, and my hands were trembling. I felt a tingling sensation throughout my body—it was pulsing with fear—fear of what I was doing and not doing—fear of my unshakeable immobility and intractable refusal to do the right thing. It took me several minutes to catch my breath.

When Don arrived, it was close to 7 p.m. I had been silent most of the day, thoughts of Jane pervading my mind—images of her haunting me like an impetuous phantom.

Don wanted to have dinner out, so we made reservations at 9 p.m. at Mélisse on Wilshire Boulevard in Santa Monica. It was the first time I drove the new Bentley—the first time I drove at all since the accident, and I was apprehensive. It felt weird and unfamiliar, but I knew I had to get past the first ride to feel comfortable driving again.

Don was chattering about work and his cases, delivering blistering asides and commentary on his sketchy clients and their endless lists of felonies. I wondered how Don could take it still, at his age, but he always seemed to thrive on the chaos. Julia sat in the back seat, quiet and contemplative, just listening to Don's bombast.

When we got to Mélisse, we took our seats and ordered drinks. It wasn't until the drinks were delivered that I spotted her and almost gasped aloud. It was Jane sitting with Marisa and Kat. I froze with some strange terror. Jane was sipping what looked like champagne out of a flute and I realized, with extreme dread, she could have already ended the pregnancy. Maybe this was her celebration—she could now drink alcohol to her heart's content and bash me freely with her two best friends, who hated me anyway. Jane was facing my direction and would likely see me at some point.

My eyes shot nervously across the table at Don and Julia, sipping martinis and I knew what I had to do.

"Excuse me a moment," I said to them in a monotone, like an android being controlled remotely—drawn into the circle of contempt—where I would have to face my demons head on. "There's someone here I need to say hello to." I slowly rose from my chair and made my way toward Jane, my heart beating faster the closer I came.

Before I reached her table, she looked up and did a double take, her eyes widening like she was catching sight of the spirit of Christmas past. I just stared at her without saying a word, suddenly tongue-tied. She was as beautiful and radiant as always, wearing a midnight blue velvet jacket over a white button-down shirt.

She looked uncomfortably at Marisa and Kat and then back up at me. "What do you want?" she asked in a flat tone.

"I'd like to talk to you. Will you please step outside with me for a minute?" My voice was calm, although my heart was pounding in my chest. I was petrified she would say no and slay me right there in front of her best friends.

Marisa spoke before Jane could answer. "You have one hell of a nerve interrupting our dinner," she exclaimed. "If I were Jane, I'd call security."

"You're not Jane—and I'm not talking to *you*." I turned

to Jane, whose mouth had dropped open at my bluntness. "Will you please come with me?" I repeated.

Our eyes locked and some unspoken dialogue occurred. She finally placed her napkin on the table and stood. "Excuse me," she said to her friends. "I'll only be a minute."

Marisa and Kat exchanged glances and shook their heads, but they let Jane go.

We silently made our way out of the restaurant and stood on Wilshire Boulevard under the lights of the Mélisse logo, near the flower beds, which were overflowing with succulents. Jane tossed her long hair and glared up at me reproachfully, hands on her hips.

"I—um—it's been so long," I began. "A lot has happened."

"I wouldn't know, because you never contacted me again," she replied with sharpness in her voice. "Bobbi told me you were in an accident."

I nodded. I could tell she was examining the scar above my right eye and a look of compassion briefly crossed her face. "Are you okay?" she asked.

I inhaled the night air. *No, Jane, I'm not okay because not only was I assaulted and damaged but I lost you and, therefore, my whole world was destroyed.* "I'm better. How've you been?"

She lowered her eyes to her feet. "How do you think I've been?" she said glancing up at me again. Her eyes were now watery.

"Jane—are you—did you …?" I bit my lip nervously. I simply could not complete the sentence.

"Did I—what?" she asked, eyebrows furrowing slightly.

"Are you still pregnant?" I asked, feeling my heart sinking at what her response might be.

"Why would you care about that?" she asked, defiantly. "You made it clear you wanted nothing to do with me anyway. I think the words you used were that you were incapable of feeling *anything* for me."

"Are you still pregnant, Jane?" I pressed, swallowing hard. "I need to know."

She stared at me, cocking her head to the side, lips

pursed. "You need to know because?"

"I need to know because I could be the father," I finally admitted, waiting for her to shred me to pieces right there in front of Mélisse.

Her expression turned to one of shock. "But," she stammered, "you said you had—what are you saying, Craig?"

"I'm saying I lied, Jane. I lied because I didn't want to hurt you—I didn't want to ruin your life. I didn't want you to destroy your marriage—for me—for us. So, I lied—I lied about the way I feel about you and I lied about having a vasectomy. I thought it would make life less complicated."

Jane's mouth gaped wide open and she looked as though she might faint.

"Are you all-right?" I asked, taking her hand in mine.

She wasted no time in yanking her hand away. "You fucking *lied* to me?" She glared at me in anger and disbelief. "You told me you couldn't possibly be the father of my child and now you just happen to run into me at a restaurant and tell me you lied—that you played God and did what *you* wanted?"

"Jane, please—I didn't know what I was doing—I was mixed up." I tried again to touch her, putting my hand on the sleeve of her velvet jacket, but she recoiled.

"You manipulated the situation to your own end game, without a thought of what it might do to me," she accused, voice shrill. "Tell me this, Craig Keller, what would you have done had you *not* run into me tonight? Huh? Tell me that."

She was now screaming at me, her eyes flashing with rage. I looked around, feeling pitiful at the shameful scene unfolding. A couple was entering the restaurant, gawking at us with their eyebrows raised. I waited for them to be out of earshot before responding to Jane's understandable tirade.

"I'm sorry," I mumbled. "I'm sorry, Jane—but I have to know—are you still pregnant or did you do something?"

"You mean did I have an *abortion*? That's what you mean, right?"

She was so indignant—her green eyes were aglow with outrage. I took a step back.

"You have no right to know anything, now," she fumed. "You gave up that right the night you lied to me."

"No, Jane—please—*please* don't do this. I want to make this right—I was a mess then—I thought I was doing you a favor—I made a mistake. Please don't push me away."

She looked up at me, a disgusted frown on her face and just shook her head. "Stay away from me. You're a monster and you have no place in my life now."

With that, she turned and retreated inside the restaurant, letting the door close behind her. I just stood on the sidewalk staring out into traffic, not knowing what hit me. I was tempted to wander out into the street and stand in front of an oncoming bus, but knew my parents were waiting inside. And my death would ruin Christmas for Axel and Anabel. I took a deep breath and entered the restaurant, purposely averting my eyes from Jane's table. I seated myself with Don and Julia, doing my best to act like nothing happened.

"Wow, that was some long hello," Julia remarked. "We weren't sure whether to wait for you, so we ordered appetizers—Don's starving."

I didn't comment. I just sipped my martini and tried to erase the ugly scene from my mind. It was over with Jane. She hated me—and rightfully so. I was a horrible spineless bastard with no redeeming qualities. It was obvious she had taken care of her problem and there was nothing more between us—nothing growing, nothing left. Just like Dr. Truer had predicted: I had lost her for good.

AT HOME THAT NIGHT, after the children had arrived, I asked Julia and Don to keep them occupied because I was exhausted and still reeling from the earlier scene with Jane. I sneaked off to bed early after an intensive shower. Before I put on my silk pajamas, I stared at myself naked in a full-length mirror. I looked like my own skinny, disheveled twin. I had not worked out in weeks because of the injuries, and my body was thin, my face pale and gaunt. I had lost at least fifteen pounds in the hospital. I quickly covered my skeletal frame with the pajamas and pulled out my Scotch. I lay in bed, taking slow sips and remembering Jane. I thought about being in bed with her, touching her body, feeling her soft skin and taut muscles. I recalled the conversations we had—so hopeful and romantic. I thought of Jane as a complete person—her robust work ethic and brutal honesty. She was a real woman. And I screwed her over—I screwed her over and she crushed me.

By sip number three, I heard a knock at my door. I glanced at the clock; it was after midnight. "Yes," I called. "Come in."

It was Julia. She opened the door a crack and then popped in. "May I speak to you?"

"Of course," I responded, setting my Scotch on a red coaster that sat on my nightstand.

She was in her robe and slippers, padding along my bedroom until she got to the bed. I sat up uncomfortably, it was so seldom Julia entered my bedroom. "Is there something you need?" I asked with profound curiosity.

She didn't answer. Instead, she sat on the edge of my bed like she did when I was a little boy, tucking me in for the night before reading me a bedtime story. She had a contemplative look on her face. "Craig—what's wrong with you tonight?" she asked, tentatively. "What happened at the restaurant to make you so somber?"

I studied my mother's face and saw that DJ/Anabel earnestness. I smiled but said nothing.

"Craig, please talk to me," she pleaded. "Who did you see at the restaurant and what happened? You seem terribly upset right now."

"That's because I *am* upset," I answered, realizing I was confiding in Julia, which I hadn't done since I was a child—back when DJ was there, and I trusted her with my life. "Something happened—with a woman—someone I loved—love," I disclosed, feeling relief at expelling the story.

Julia cast her honey brown eyes downward and then flashed them up at me again. "Is it Jane?"

"Um—I—how did you know?" I queried, feeling strange that she had guessed correctly.

"I saw her enter the restaurant right before you did. I recognized her from the night I met her at your house. She looked troubled. What happened?"

I shrugged. "I messed up, Mom. No, I really *screwed* up."

Julia nodded her head in empathy. "I like when you call me Mom," she said softly.

There was a silence between us.

She stood and came closer, put her hand on my arm, patting it gently. "Is there anything I can do to help?" she asked.

I shook my head. "It's over. I have to accept it and move on."

"Craig ... um, whatever happened with Jane, it doesn't change who you are. I, for one, think you're extraordinary. I love you, Craig, no matter what you've done to screw up anything."

She leaned over and kissed me on the cheek, then put her hand under my chin, lifting it slightly. "Everything's going to be fine. You'll see. Good night, darling."

And she walked out of my room, closing the door behind her. I had a sudden epiphany that I was the one who had built a wall in the relationship with my parents. I created the rift that kept us apart all these years; I had assumed they felt a certain way about me; however, the greatest realization of all was that I could change it.

# Twenty-one

*C*HRISTMAS EVE WAS UPON us, and the house was buzzing with activity. Julia had Christmas music playing non-stop and spent most of her time in the kitchen with the kids, engaging them in cookie-baking and other holiday traditions.

I reflected on the past few weeks of my life and felt like I had taken a long, arduous journey but had not yet returned. My mind was consumed with thoughts of Jane. I had several dreams about her since that night at Mélisse. The dreams were always of us walking on the beach like we did that rainy day. I no longer kidded myself that she would ever be with me now. My thoughts were more about what I had learned from being in love with her—from finding out what love really felt like. It was everything I said in the Our Vows Dot Com presentation. It struck me that the only way I was able to give that presentation in the first place was from knowing real love with Jane. She had educated me.

I also understood now what it was like to be hurt by a woman—hideously and mercilessly heart-broken with no way to leap over it and put it behind me. I would have to wallow in the pain—wade deep into a dark and murky well and wait it out, day after day, taking a small step up, one at a time, clutching at the slippery stones with all my might—desperately searching for a light at the top to find my way out. It abruptly hit me what all those sentimental love ballads were about—the grief that inspired the lyrics of so many songs I had heard before, but which, pre-Jane, meant nothing and resonated in no way, unless they somehow directly reminded me of DJ. This had all changed after being with Jane.

I sat on the couch and sipped a cappuccino, thinking that Christmas dinner would just be Don and Julia and me, as the children would return to their mother's house after they opened presents in the morning. Camilla was staying at the house and preparing for the small celebration. I recalled the huge holiday feasts we had in San Francisco when I grew up and how those celebrations had diminished over time. When DJ was alive, it was always festive and carefree—so many family members enjoying each other—the season felt magical. It was DJ's favorite holiday, and after he died, the enchantment disappeared, replaced by an air of melancholy. The joy had been emptied like a deflating balloon, deprived of the oxygen it needed to keep it buoyed up in the air.

Julia's voice interrupted my thoughts. "Come see what the kids are making," she called excitedly from the kitchen. The divine scent of butter and vanilla filled the house as I followed Julia's voice into the kitchen.

"What have we here?" I asked, watching Anabel draw eyes on a sugar cookie using a pastry bag with green-colored frosting.

"It's you, Daddy," she replied grinning.

I moved so that I was looking over her shoulder. She was squeezing out long green eyelashes. "Is that what I look like to you?" I asked with amusement. "A pair of eyes?"

"I'm not finished yet," she declared.

Axel was busy making his cookie look like a basketball, using a pastry bag filled with red frosting.

"Axel let's trade colors," Anabel ordered. Axel handed his bag to Anabel while she gave him hers. Then, she did something so hilarious, I could do nothing but laugh. She squeezed out a glob of red frosting in a crooked line above my right eye.

"Now, I'm done," she said proudly, turning her cookie so I could examine it properly.

"I look pretty scary, Anabel—this is Christmas, not Halloween." I rested my hands on her shoulders from behind. She tilted her head back to look up at me. She had a mischievous smile on her face that reminded me of DJ—she was irresistible. I kissed the top of her head and then turned my attention to Axel, who was now creating a Lakers logo with purple frosting.

"That's some ball," I remarked.

"Thanks, Dad," Axel responded with a slight smile as he continued drawing the logo.

I patted his shoulder and rubbed it. "Maybe I should hire you as a graphic designer—you're pretty accurate with that logo."

"I know it by heart," he answered proudly, blinking his green eyes at me. His voice was still in the transition phase, so he sounded half-boy, half-man.

Don waltzed in at that moment barking orders into his cell phone. "Fuck's sake, it's Christmas Eve and I need an answer before sundown."

Don liked to use lines like that from old Westerns—it added to his often eccentric and comical appeal—especially with the Irish accent. One thing Don never did was temper his language in front of my children. I had long ago gotten used to it—I always reminded the kids that those words were to be used sparingly and by grownups only. It was all I could do because Don was not about to change his habits.

"That sleazy bastard won't know what hit him," Don growled into the receiver before ending the call. He then pocketed his cell phone and smiled at his grandchildren fondly. "Something smells mighty good in here—what are you cooking, young lass?" he asked Anabel, who was happy to display her portrait of Daddy.

He burst into a fit of laughter and slapped me on the

back. "Now that's an accurate representation of your old man," he chortled. "You, poor bastard."

"Don." Julia shot him a mildly scolding glance, putting her index finger to her lips as a warning about his language.

Don just laughed and gave her a casual wave of his hand. Don was in an unusually good mood and I wondered if he had been hitting the eggnog early. He danced around the kitchen, tapping his cane to the holiday music—a rendition of "Jingle Bell Rock" was playing, and Don was doing some sort of Irish jig, singing the lyrics but getting them all wrong. I stood back and observed the scene.

As soon as he danced his way out of the kitchen, I was alone again with Julia and the kids. Julia was busy pulling sheets of baked cookies from the oven and replacing them with sheets of cut out dough.

"How many cookies are we baking?" I asked, thinking we hardly had enough people to eat them and that I'd be throwing away the majority unless we sent them home with Axel and Anabel.

"About five dozen," Julia answered, and after seeing the surprised look on my face added, "It's Christmas, darling— don't worry—someone will eat them."

That's when an idea came to me. "Mom," I began, thinking it had become so easy to start calling her Mom and that I really didn't want to go back to calling her Julia ever again. "Would you be opposed to me adding a few dinner guests for tomorrow night?"

"Like whom?" she asked, looking pleased that I was still calling her Mom.

"Just a few people who don't have families or dinner plans," I answered, thinking of Bobbi, Alonzo and Meseret. "Three people, to be exact."

Julia looked thoughtful for a minute and then responded. "I think that would be lovely. I'll let Camilla know she'll need more food."

I smiled at Julia. "Great—I'll call them now."

With Bobbi, it was going to be tough, because our last conversation involved me insulting her and hanging up.

I simply had to apologize and hope she wouldn't hold a grudge against me forever.

I dialed her cell number and let it ring, knowing she would be wrapping up things at work to close the agency. She answered on the fourth ring.

"Bobbi," I started sheepishly.

"Yes, Craig," she stated with a cool professionalism that was not at all characteristic of the way she usually acted with me.

"Listen, Bobbi—I'm calling to apologize for what I said on the phone last week."

There was silence on the other end.

"Look—I know I was awful, but I was not in my right mind—I was so stressed out and—maybe the pain meds affected my behavior. But I never should have taken it out on you. I'm sorry, Bobbi. Will you please accept my apology?"

There was another awkward silence, but she finally spoke. "Craig, there are some lines you should never cross and that was one. I was only trying to help." Her voice still rang with a distrustful coldness.

I sighed. "Come on, Bobbi—let's put this behind us. We've known each other too long."

"I can't help it, Craig, I'm still mad at you. But I do forgive you and I'll accept your apology."

I breathed a sigh of relief. "Are you too mad to have Christmas dinner at my house?"

She suddenly let out a cackle. "Are you sure you want a nosy *yenta* in your home? I might bring gossip back to the office." The last line dripped with sarcasm.

"I'm sure. Listen—it's going to be a small group but Don and … I mean, my mom and dad will be there. They're looking forward to meeting you. Six-thirty?"

"And they know I'm Jewish, right? I mean, I was just planning on getting some Chinese takeout and staying in tomorrow night."

"I promise they won't force you to go to midnight mass with them," I answered, grinning into the phone.

My next call was to Alonzo, who accepted the dinner

invitation with enthusiasm and promised to pick up Meseret from the Union Mission on Skid Row and drive her to Malibu.

I AWAKENED EARLY ON Christmas Day, brewed coffee and began getting things set up to make the kids pancakes. Today, instead of blueberries, I would add fresh strawberries to the mix—something different for Axel and Anabel. Don staggered into the kitchen, stubbing his toe on the leg of a bar stool.

"Oh, bloody hell," he screeched in pain, bending forward to examine his injured toe. He was wearing a long, crimson silk robe with black lapels, cuffs, and belt. It resembled something a prize fighter would wear to a match. His matching slippers were open-toed, hence the stubbed toe. "I should have grabbed the cane," he complained, "especially since I was fairly ossified last night."

"Good morning, Don," I greeted him while slicing strawberries. "Merry Christmas."

"And a Merry Christmas to you, son," he said, sounding faintly like the Lucky Charms leprechaun.

"How about some coffee?" I asked, turning, and getting a cup for him.

He just nodded as I poured coffee into the cup and pushed it across the kitchen island.

"Thank you, son," he said, grabbing the cup and immediately taking a sip. "I might need a naggin' of whiskey, if you know what I mean." Don never put anything in his coffee, except Irish whiskey but, even for him, it was too early to hit the sauce. He studied me thoughtfully. "So, Craig, have you given any thought to when you might go back to work?"

I obviously had not shared my discussion with Warren, nor my abrupt departure from the agency. He never asked. "I suppose after the new year and when I've fully recovered," I answered, thinking I had no idea what I was going to do with my life moving forward.

"That's good, you know, because you've one hell of a gig

over there in Santa Monica," he remarked, leaning against the island, and watching my face. "It'd be a shame for you to give that up."

I tried to stay calm because I wasn't sure whether he knew anything about my recent decisions or anything about my life as it stood. I didn't comment.

"I didn't raise you to be anything but a winner, son," he continued, running his hand across the top and sides of his grey hair to tame its mischief. "I know you cleaned up with all those advertising awards recently."

"What are you getting at?" I demanded.

He shrugged. "I just know how one bad decision can affect your whole life—your whole career."

"You needn't beat around the bush—just tell me, Don. You think I'm a failure, right?" I realized Don must know the whole story about my leaving the agency, but he had waited until I was stronger before springing it on me.

"Not at all, son," he protested, those light jade eyes focused on mine. "I just think there are times in life when you hit a breaking point. You're in the middle of your career and, I hate to say it, son, but you're having a mid-life crisis."

He paused to take a sip of his coffee. "I had one. You probably don't remember it, but I bought that race car— what was it—a Ferrari, I think? A red one, of course—what a clichéd bastard I was," he admitted, shaking his head at the memory. "I had an affair with this woman from work—a secretary. She was a fine lass, son. You know," he added, whistling, and drawing an imaginary hourglass with his index fingers for emphasis.

Don had never come clean with Julia or anyone about his extramarital affairs. Julia had to have known, but she looked the other way. I remembered running into him all over the Bay area, at dinner with different women. I wouldn't have dared question Don's behavior. It was something I took in stride—behavior I then repeated in my own life and throughout my ill-fated marriage.

"What does any of this have to do with me?" I asked, feeling a lecture coming on. I pulled out the pancake ingredients and preheated the oven to cook bacon so I wouldn't just be standing there fidgeting nervously, awaiting his next precautionary words.

"Son, I know what happened at work. I spoke to Warren when you went missing and he shared it with me. He said you had an affair with some secretary in the office and then quit your partnership."

Of course, Warren would have told Don the story, like co-fathers sharing the wayward missteps of their hapless son. I took a deep breath and blew it out slowly, waiting for Don to continue.

"And, son, while I have to say it's never smart to dip your pen in company ink, you're a chip off the old block." As he said this, he adjusted his robe proudly, like he had done something exceptional in raising a son who would screw his secretary.

"Dad, she wasn't my *secretary*, okay?" I insisted, without thinking.

Don stopped cold and stared at me with his eyebrows raised. "What did you just say, Craig?"

"I called you Dad," I responded looking him square in the eye. "I'm calling Julia 'Mom' now, too. You know why? Because you're my parents and parents should allow their kid to call them Mom and Dad."

Don sighed and shook his head. "You sure *are* having a mid-life crisis, son. I called that one right, indeed."

"So, what?" I argued, feeling the veins in my temples throb. "You just said you did the same thing."

"But I didn't quit my job, Craig—there's a limit to the self-destruction, you know—you put the heart crossway in me, son. Do you know how worried your mother was?" His face was now contorted with emotion, something I rarely saw.

I was fascinated. "Really?" I responded sarcastically. "Is that why you stayed in San Francisco the entire time I went missing?"

He eyed me anxiously. "We weren't sure what to do."

"You didn't care," I countered, voice raising. "If it were DJ, you would have been on the first plane out here. But you didn't care enough about me—you waited to see if I were alive first before you'd commit to the cost of plane ticket."

"Don't you," Don shouted, suddenly out of control. He limped around the island like a fleet God, barreling toward me. He grabbed me by my pajama top and twisted the material under my throat, thrusting his face right up to mine. "You take that back right now or I'll rip this jumper right off," he threatened, staring ruthlessly into my eyes. His look reminded me of the many times right before he would get out his belt. "Take it back, Boy."

"Oh, come on, Don—Dad—or whoever you are to me," I yelled back at him. "Admit it—I've always been a failure to you—I'll never be DJ and you'll never forgive me for that."

Don just twisted my pajamas tighter under my throat and breathed heavily into my face, the sour smell of last night's Scotch commingled with the morning coffee and steamed into my nostrils. I realized in my current condition, I might not be able to take Don down, even though before my 'midlife crisis,' I could have flattened him in two seconds.

"You're a goddamned liar and a coward, for fuck's sake, Craig," he ranted, twisting my pajamas further and putting his free hand around my neck, clamping down hard as though he were trying to strangle me. I heard the seams of my pajama neckline splitting. "And DJ has nothing to do with this. You can blame him all you want, but you're responsible for yourself, you goddamned pussy bastard."

I grabbed his hands and attempted to release my neck from his grasp. At that moment, Julia soared into the room, face white as alabaster. When she saw Don with his hands around my throat, she screamed, "What in the *hell* is going on here?"

Don didn't loosen his grip nor take his eyes off mine. Instead he was now shaking me violently. My body bumped up against the oven several times.

"For goodness sake, Don, take your hands off our son—it's Christmas Day and our grandchildren are in the house," Julia scolded, running up to Don and attempting to pull him off me. He had me cornered against the hot oven, which was now scorching my back.

"Stop it, Don," Julia commanded. "This is insane."

He suddenly loosened his grip and backed away from me, the penetrating stare still focused, relentlessly on me. "Go cry to your mother," he scoffed. "Go hide behind your mother's skirt, why don't you—pussy bastard. I'm not staying around to watch this Donny Brook."

With that comment, he limped away, muttering, "Merry fucking Christmas."

BY BREAKFAST, JULIA HAD calmed Don so he could be civil toward me in front of his grandchildren. Although he didn't address me directly, he fawned over Axel and Anabel, who were delighted to be served 'special Christmas pancakes'.

After breakfast, we sat in the living room and watched the kids open their presents. I had bought Anabel a gold necklace she wanted, along with an assortment of gift cards so she could buy and listen to music of her choosing. Alessandra had forbidden a smart phone for obvious reasons. Anabel also requested a book-binding kit because she loved to both write and draw. Don and Julia threw in gift cards for her favorite clothing stores.

Axel was much easier. He wanted a world and constellation globe because his greatest wish was to travel; the latest Kindle reader with a Lakers logo case because he loved books; and a 20" mountain bike. He was set.

When it was time for the kids to leave for their mother's house, I felt a twinge of emptiness. Julia offered to drive them to Bel Air in my car, and I accepted, thinking it would be one less awkward moment with Alessandra, even though I didn't relish the thought of being alone with Don. But I knew once the kids were gone, I would be left with Don and Julia until they headed back to San Francisco the next day. I would again be alone and faced with figuring out what to do with my life. I wished it were as easy as Don had positioned it, but there was no way I could go back to Warren and reinstate my partnership now—especially while Jane was still working there.

My thoughts went to Jane and I almost choked up. I wondered what she was doing today. I knew she would not be celebrating Christmas, but I hoped she was at least with her grandmother—maybe her friends. I secretly hoped she was not with her husband but had a feeling she had patched things up after everything that happened between us. It was the most practical thing for her to do, given the circumstances. Still, I somehow wished she were still thinking of me—that maybe she came to the realization that I did what I did because I loved her. It was my only hope for her now, knowing I'd never see her again.

I remembered the many moments of our relationship over the years and, while most of it involved me manipulating and controlling Jane, the feeling I had when I was with her won out in the end. She made me a better person and the brief time we were mutually in love was enough to carry me through until I might find another woman like her. Deep in my heart, though, I knew I never would. Jane was one of a kind in every way.

AROUND 5:30 P.M., I realized our guests would arrive soon and Julia had still not returned from Bel Air. Camilla was busy with her staff in the kitchen and I was beginning to worry about Julia. I even resorted to speaking to Don about her whereabouts.

"Have you heard from Mom?" I asked when I saw him tinkering with the well-stocked bar cart in the living room. He was tugging at the glass stopper of the Scotch decanter, helping himself to his first drink of the day. I was surprised he waited this long.

"No," he replied, not even looking up at me.

"It's been quite a few hours since she left. Do you think we should call her?"

"Nah—maybe she headed into town to do the messages," he responded grabbing the tongs, dropping ice cubes, one at a time into his glass. 'Messages' was an Irish term for groceries. I doubted anything was open on Christmas day, but I didn't challenge Don. "She'll be here soon, son."

At least he sounded congenial. He usually did as soon as the liquor touched his lips.

"Can I fix you a Scotch?" he offered. "You need one, lad."

"Thanks, Don," I responded, "but I'll wait until our guests show up."

"Come on, Craig," he urged. "We deserve to get a little wrecked tonight, don't you think?" Don poured the Scotch into a glass and handed it to me. "Cheers," he said, clinking his glass against mine.

"Now, let's go outside and watch for the first star," he ordered, grabbing his cane, and limping his way to the back patio, which I had opened to the night air. It was a beautiful evening and, at Christmas, every year when DJ and I were kids, Julia always sent us out to look for the first star—only on Christmas Eve, not Christmas Day. I didn't have the heart to correct Don. It was a family tradition and what I thought to be a way to keep us occupied for an hour or so.

When we were outside, Don turned his face up to the sky. "Do you see anything?"

"I think it's too cloudy of a night to see much," I replied, searching the sky myself to make sure I wasn't missing something.

"You know, son," Don began, now shifting his eyes toward me. "I never considered you a failure. You got a lot of things wrong."

Before I could say anything, he continued. "When we filed a missing person report, we were beyond devastated. My heart seized up in terror because I was reliving what happened to DJ. I was paralyzed—that's why we didn't come to L.A.—we were frozen in time—back to the hellish trance of that day you boys were on the yacht."

He turned away from me so that I could no longer see his face. We were at the rails leading out to the ocean and Don leaned against it, stretching his body as far as he could over it. The sun was setting, ushering in the end of Christmas Day.

"Don," I said, moving nearer so I was standing right next to him as he continued to lean over the rails.

He suddenly turned to me and said in a voice so wracked with emotion, I could barely understand him. "All I could think is that I couldn't lose my boy again—my only boy. I simply couldn't go through it—I'd rather die than go through that again."

I saw tears in his eyes as he uttered that last line. He turned his head in the other direction, so I wouldn't see him cry. It was then I realized how selfish and unkind I'd been to assume my own parents didn't love me—all these years thinking they were against me, evaluating me, comparing me to my saintly brother. They just never got over losing their child. It had nothing to do with me and everything to do with their grief—their abject grief over losing a son.

I put my hand on Don's shoulder. "It's okay, Dad," I mumbled as the sun began to quickly disappear—casting a silvery gloss on the dark, rippling, infinite depth of the ocean. He turned to me finally, and I gripped my hands on either side of his shoulders. "I understand," I added.

Our identical pairs of eyes—one older and wiser—met, but we didn't say another word. There was no need. I knew he loved me and that was all I wanted—after all these years of wondering what went on in Don's complicated mind, it was simple. He loved me.

I heard Sylvia's voice calling from the open glass patio doors. "Mr. Keller, your guests have arrived."

I patted Don's arm and excused myself, re-entered the house and saw Bobbi in the entryway, all dressed up in a long flowing navy dress. Her hair was pulled into a slick bun, with only a few loose silver strands hanging around her face and neck. She wore long dangly earrings which sparkled when she moved her head. I grinned. She was a sight for sore eyes.

"Bobbi," I greeted her. "I'm so glad you made it—please come in."

She took a good look at me and smiled. "May I have a hug?" she asked, like I might say no.

I grinned again. "Of course." She threw her arms around me and planted a kiss on my cheek. I heard her murmur, "My *sheyna punim*." She smelled like cigarettes and Shalimar.

When we withdrew from our embrace, I welcomed her into the living room. "Would you like a drink?" I asked.

"Sure," she replied with a smile in her voice. "After all, it's Christmas." She was now staring at the huge Christmas tree in fascination. "Wow—that's one heck of a tree you've got there."

"Thank you—my mom actually found it, decorated it, lit it—you name it."

I escorted Bobbi outside to where Don was standing, still staring at the sea.

"Don," I called to get his attention. It took him a moment before he slowly turned in our direction. His expression was still somber. "Don, I'd like you to meet someone. This is Bobbi Silverstein. We—um—work together." I wasn't sure what to say now that I no longer worked for the agency.

"It's a pleasure to meet you, Don," Bobbi said, holding out her hand.

Don's face suddenly relaxed into a huge smile. "Bobbi," he returned, shaking her hand. "It's a pleasure." They began chatting and I could tell Don took an immediate liking to Bobbi.

Alonzo arrived shortly thereafter with Meseret and I welcomed them as I had Bobbi. "This is some house, Boss," Alonzo exclaimed, mesmerized at his surroundings as he walked past me. I was surprised that the usual gust of pot smoke was for once not following him. Meseret looked like she might have been in a different universe. Alonzo must have told her to dress up because she was wearing a smart white blouse with a black skirt and flat boots. I sensed her shyness about being in my house, so I went overboard to make her feel comfortable.

"What's your poison, Meseret?" I asked playfully. "Would you like a glass of wine?" Then I realized she had once been on drugs and I felt guilty for even offering.

"Mary likes juice," Alonzo interjected before Meseret

could respond. "She likes good old-fashioned OJ, if you have it."

"Coming right up," I replied as Meseret gave me her biggest toothless grin.

Julia showed up shortly thereafter, making excuses about getting lost on her way back to Malibu from Bel Air.

We had a pleasant dinner and over drinks afterward, Bobbi and I caught a few moments alone. I was aching to ask about Jane but was not sure how to bring it up and, for once, Bobbi did not bring it up herself. Finally, I couldn't hold back. "How's Jane?" I asked, expecting the worst.

She cocked an eyebrow at me like I had brought up a taboo subject. "She's fine. She's back with Derek, you know. It happened over a week ago. They went to Seattle together to celebrate Christmas with his family."

My heart sank at the thought that my prediction was accurate. Jane and the violinist were back together. I didn't have it in me to ask anything further. I didn't want to hear it. "Well, I guess that's good news," I responded after a long pause. "That's what she always wanted—you know, to be married and have stability."

Bobbi studied my face with a frown. "Now, Craig, I know you don't believe that bullshit for one minute. Tell me," she said facing me squarely. "Did you ever talk to her again?"

I thought back to our unfortunate final conversation in front of Mélisse, and a chill ran up my spine. Jane was so angry with me—she acted like she wanted to kill me. In fact, I don't think I'd ever seen her so infuriated. "I didn't," I lied, thinking it was better that Bobbi remain ignorant of that scene. "Why do you ask?"

"Well—it's just that something happened to turn her completely away from the idea of divorce—it's like it happened overnight. One day she was ending her marriage and terminating the pregnancy; the next she was back with Derek. I thought maybe you talked to her or something."

I gulped hard, wanting to ask about the baby. But I did not. So that was it. It was just not in the cards for Jane and me. It was over, and just like I told Julia, I needed to move on.

# Twenty-two

*N*EW YEAR'S EVE CREPT over me with the lonely revelation that I had no real friends except Bobbi, Alonzo and Meseret. I had spent most of my unoccupied time with my previous lineup, or some version of it—a group of women I had no interest in contacting now, and I had no interest in recruiting new ones. They just all seemed so unremarkable in comparison to Jane. I compared every woman with her—even women I saw on the street—women who would have been attractive to me before Jane. I spent the evening on the couch reading Kurt Vonnegut short stories from *A Man Without A Country*. I knew the stories had a lot of material that sketched out the differences between men and women. I stretched out on the large sectional and read story after story until I became sleepy and retired to bed. I skipped the Scotch and shut off the lights. For the first time in years, I retired before midnight.

THE FIRST WEEK OF January, I received a call from Warren. After some pleasantries, he got to the real reason he was calling—to ask when I was planning to come back to the agency.

"Keller, we've missed you," he stressed in a voice that told me he meant it. "I know you said you violated your contract but now I don't know what to believe."

"You think I made that up?" I asked, wondering what Warren was getting at.

"Veronica interviewed every female employee at our agency, and they all denied involvement with you. In fact, they were mostly complimentary and, I'm sure this won't surprise you, find you the most charming and attractive partner at the agency."

*Of course, they did.* I had only expressed interest in Jane, so the rest of the women at the agency would naturally think me an elusive gentleman. *Laughable.* Veronica would not have thought to interview Jane. I wondered what Jane would have said had Veronica brought it to her attention. Maybe she would deny it, given I was effectively out of her life and she was back with the violinist. I suddenly had a painful vision of Jane and the violinist going at it in bed—having makeup sex. I pictured his limber violin-fingers all over her breasts, and in other places mine had been, and I felt nauseated.

"Did you hear me, Craig?" Warren asked. I had been silent on the line for a while.

"I did," I finally responded, now pacing in my entryway.

"As far as I'm concerned, nothing happened, so there's no reason for you not to return as full partner, under your original contract," Warren added, emphatically.

I sighed. "I need to think about it, Warren. I'm technically still recovering from the accident." I studied my reflection in the hallway mirror as I paced by it. The scar was healing but it was still visible. I remained on the thin side, but my appetite had returned. I had even started slowly incorporating a light gym routine back into my life. But I just wasn't ready to face the agency again. I was still in limbo about what to do next.

"How much time do you need?" he pressed.

I hesitated. "I'm not sure—maybe another month or two."

"Then why don't we say March first is your return date,"

Warren suggested. "We'll call it a medical leave of absence. I kept your email address active. So please plan to review your emails throughout your leave—you'll help us end the first quarter strongly."

I reluctantly agreed, and we hung up.

AFTER ANOTHER FEW WEEKS of bumming around the house, walking on the beach and spending an increasing amount of time in the gym, I felt back to normal. But I was bored—bored off my ass. I needed a change of scenery and, one day, as I perused the numerous Chagall paintings in my private collection, I decided to divest myself of some of the paintings. It would necessitate a trip somewhere—probably Europe.

After some research and phone calls, I decided London was a perfect place to meet with qualified, financially solvent art brokers and find my much-needed escape from L.A. London was a city where I could be anonymous—live like a local but not be one. I was ready for this change.

I SPENT MY FIRST week in London getting re-acquainted with the city. There was a time when I visited London at least once a month to meet with an airline client. I remembered seeing a British girl named Nicola, who lived in the West End but always met me in my hotel room. She had long blonde hair and was white as a birch tree. I recalled biting her for the first time and seeing lingering bruises a full month later when I returned to London on business. Her skin was so fair, the bruises took a long time to heal. That was when Alessandra began to suspect my London trips were not spent alone and wanted to come with me on every visit. I tried to stay in touch with Nicola and even made an excuse to see her while Alessandra was with me—lying about having a late dinner with a client. I remember seeing Nicola's tiny, stinky flat for the first time and was so disgusted, I broke things off with her. She had miserable habits like leaving underwear all over the floor and keeping a week's worth of dirty dishes in her sink. I vaguely wondered what became of Nicola—if she had found a proper British gentleman to marry, perhaps had a couple of children.

I was staying at the Dorchester in Mayfair, which was centrally located and within walking distance to all the areas I wanted to visit. I bought several bespoke suits on Savile Row, traversed Hyde Park and spent a lot of time drinking tea and reading. I set up appointments with a variety of art dealers and contracted to sell eight of my Chagall paintings. I had fourteen left and they were my favorites; however, a few days before I was ready to leave, a dealer expressed interest in the one painting I never wanted to part with, one with an estimated value in the ten-to-fifteen-million-dollar range—the average value of Chagall's most important works.

*Lovers in the Red Sky* was a masterpiece I had first acquired in London at the height of my Chagall obsession. The painting represented so many things to me now, with its fiery crimson smear of a sky. I had always imagined the man in it was me, with magical powers to float—staying anchored to my lover—naked—yet protected by a compassionate universe. To let the painting go would mean letting go of a larger part of myself. It was a part that obstinately stayed to remind me that even if I were alone, I would never be without hope.

I decided I would put the dealer off until I made a final decision.

WHILE IN LONDON, I received a call from Warren asking me to meet with one of our clients—British fashion designer Noel Marques. I was surprised that Warren even knew I was in London and wondered how he found out. Warren claimed there was no one else available to lead the meeting and that since I was in London anyway, it would be a perfect segue back into agency life. March first was now less than a month away.

I was to meet Noel Marques at St. Martin's Lane Hotel, which was situated near the bustling theater district in Covent Garden. I decided to walk from the Dorchester, which was a little over a mile away. The morning was cold, and the cloudy grey sky pissed rain intermittently. I wore a black wool peacoat and carried a black umbrella. It felt odd to be attending a meeting without a suit on, but Warren didn't seem to mind. Plus, if everything I knew of Noel Marques were true, he would want the meeting to be more informal. I reached St. Martin's Lane and found the hotel entrance. Once inside, I dropped my wet umbrella in a nearby stand.

I was looking for The Den, which was tucked away off the lobby. I entered the room and saw small groups of people sitting around drinking tea. The Den was a classically British, oak-paneled, snug with a grand sofa and cozy tables. The art on the walls animated the space with spirited, larger-than-life portraits. One that immediately caught my eye was of Anne Boleyn. The entire painting, including the frame, had been cut in half at her throat, the two pieces hanging on the wall jaggedly apart. I considered the cruel fate of Henry VIII's second wife, who was beheaded on false charges of witchcraft and adultery, among other things.

My eye was drawn to the back of someone who happened to be viewing the same artwork. It was a silhouette I recognized with heart-stopping familiarity, appearing an otherworldly specter—not even real. I froze, staring at her back until she turned around, so I could see her face. It was Jane or someone who looked exactly like Jane. Maybe it was the British version of Jane. When our eyes met, an electric current pulsed through me. I knew right away it was the real Jane, gorgeous and serene as ever. We faced each other silently. Jane wore a sleek black wool coat that almost reached the floor.

"Jane," I uttered softly, taking a few steps toward her.

"It's you." She looked as though she had seen a ghost. "What are *you* doing here?" she asked in a curious voice, approaching slowly until we met in the middle of the room, where the grand sofa was.

"Primarily selling some of my Chagalls," I answered. "What are you doing here?"

"I'm here for Fashion Week—Noel's line's being featured. I'm meeting with him in a few minutes."

"Then I guess we're in the same meeting. Warren asked me to attend."

"What?" she asked, blinking at me incredulously. "Why?"

"He asked me as a favor since I was in town anyway. He didn't tell me you were going to be here—he said no one else was available." I got the feeling Jane was not at all happy to see me, especially since I was slated to horn in on her meeting.

"Really?" she continued with the grilling. "That's interesting. He never said anything about sending you."

"If you'd like, I can leave now," I suggested. "Because there's no reason for the two of us to attend—I don't want to step on your toes."

"Oh right, then I'll look like the bad guy," she argued. "I'll be the one who prevented the hero from saving the account."

I wasn't sure if it were my imagination, but Jane seemed more emotional than I'd ever seen her in the past—more insecure—more volatile. "Is there a problem with the account?" I asked, more out of inquisitiveness than anything else.

"Not that I'm aware of—but if Warren sent you, I'm assuming something's up … unless he just doesn't trust me—I'm sure that's what it is—he sent you to make sure I don't mess this up." She shook her head in frustration and stared at the floor.

"Jane," I said gently. "I'm sure it has nothing to do with your competence—you've been on this account for years. I honestly don't know why you're so upset—he probably just forgot you were here."

"There's no way he forgot," Jane countered angrily. "He's been calling me every day to check up on me. Believe me, he knows exactly where I am."

I stayed silent for a moment, just studying Jane's face. Her skin was luminous even while expressing resentment and exasperation.

"You know what I can't believe?" she continued with the same level of scorn in her voice, upper lip curled in contempt. "I can't believe Warren would ask *you*, someone who hasn't set foot in the agency for three months, to pinch hit for me—*me*, who hasn't taken a day off since you left. I mean, seriously, have you even *seen* the campaign?"

Before I could respond, Noel Marques entered the room. I recognized him from the time I'd met him once before—a tall British gentleman around my age, with a billowing mane of ginger hair that grazed his shoulders. As I had predicted, he was dressed casually—in dark blue jeans with a pullover sweater and checked wool overcoat. He was holding a red umbrella, which dripped on the floor. A young woman approached him and took his umbrella to dry in a nearby umbrella stand.

"Jane Mercer," he said, breaking into a huge smile as soon as he spotted Jane. "Come here, you."

They embraced and Noel kissed Jane on both cheeks. "You look smashing, as always," he commented, looking Jane over from head to toe. "May I help you with your coat?"

As Noel helped Jane out of her long black coat, my eyes instinctively lowered to her abdomen. She was wearing a baggy sweater dress, the color of slate blue and tall, black over-the-knee boots. It was not an outfit a woman in her second trimester of pregnancy would be wearing. I felt the same sick feeling that she'd aborted our child because I didn't have the balls to tell her the truth.

"Noel," Jane began, immediately changing her tone to signify the fresh torture of posturing was about to pour over the room. "Have you met Craig Keller? He's a senior partner with the agency." She finished the sentence with her fake work smile.

Noel turned and gave me the once-over with an approving grin. "Mr. Keller—what an unexpected pleasure. I do believe we met years ago—you're an advertising legend."

We shook hands.

"The pleasure's all mine," I returned, smiling back at Noel. "I don't mean to infringe on your meeting—I know

Jane has everything covered. I just happened to be in town and Jane invited me." I knew putting Jane in the driver's seat would relieve her of her concern that I'd really been sent by Warren.

"Of course," Noel responded pleasantly. "I'm honored to have you join our meeting. Please sit down." Noel gestured to a corner with a couch and two leather chairs. "Would either of you like tea? I believe they have Earl Grey and Darjeeling."

"Either sounds great," I responded. Noel signaled one of the service staff. I removed my coat and caught Jane's eye. She looked slightly calmer than she had earlier. Perhaps I'd put her mind at ease.

I sat in one of the leather chairs while Jane and Noel took seats side by side on the couch. I figured it was best for me to be slightly separated from them, so Jane wouldn't think I was trying to interfere. It did make me wonder why Warren sent me when Jane was already in London, servicing her account. Warren never did anything without a specific objective.

I leaned back and sipped my tea, watching Jane lead the meeting. I had no idea why she was so insecure because she was smoother than I'd ever seen her. I decided I was not going to interject unless specifically invited to comment.

The print ad campaign Jane presented was interesting, slated to be placed in the usual suspects: British, French, and U.S. Vogue, Elle, Harper's Bazaar. The current line was rock 'n' roll themed, so showed a lot of black leather, metal zippers, stilettos, and glittery sneakers. Jane presented like a champ, noting the film-noir-style photography and gritty, purposely un-posed models, seemingly engrossed in street scenes.

At one point, Noel turned to me. "Craig, what do you think of this campaign?"

I leaned forward, and Jane turned her tablet toward me, so I could study the ads more closely. I immediately noticed the diamond wedding set had been returned to her ring finger. She eyed me cautiously.

"Well, unlike Ms. Mercer here, I'm not an expert on women's couture," I began.

"There's no need to be modest, Craig Keller," Noel replied with a grin. "I've seen plenty of pictures of you with gorgeous, fashionable women."

Jane looked away uncomfortably as he said this. Noel didn't want to stop there.

"You also have impeccable taste in men's fashion and you're one of the most respected ad men in the industry," Noel said while giving me another once-over, pausing at my Grenson leather boots. "I'd like your opinion."

I observed the ads again and then my eyes moved to Jane's. She seemed nervous that I was going to undo her pitch. *You'll just never trust me again, will you, Jane? I can't say I blame you.*

"I think the campaign does an excellent job of showcasing the fashion without being too frivolous," I finally responded. "The photography feels more documentary-style—authentic and experiential—like you're peering into someone's stylish life, rather than dissecting the clothes themselves."

Jane's eyes widened with relief.

"I couldn't agree more," Noel replied and then turned to Jane. "Great job. You have my buy-in."

Jane beamed. "Thank you, Noel."

When the meeting had concluded, and we said goodbye to Noel, the room had completely cleared out and Jane and I were alone in The Den at St. Martin's Lane. She gathered her coat and stood awkwardly, like she didn't know what to say.

"Where are you headed off to now?" I asked.

"Up to my room—I'm staying here at the hotel—one more night and leaving out of Heathrow tomorrow morning."

"What a coincidence—I'm leaving in the morning, too." I was thinking about how incredible it would be for Jane to invite me to her room, but I knew there was no way. I was quickly reminded of the time only a few months ago when I was inside her—gliding my hands over her body—feeling her flesh from every angle. It seemed like years had passed since then. "You know, Warren asked me to return to the agency March first," I told her, anticipating a reaction of some sort. "How do you feel about that?"

She shrugged. "When has it ever mattered how I feel about anything?"

"But it *does* matter," I countered, attempting to keep my voice measured and my intense feelings for her in check. "The last time we talked about this, you made it clear you'd find it difficult to see me in the office after everything that's happened between us."

"Oh, right, you mean when you dumped me in that bar in Santa Monica. How could I forget?" she spat out with sarcasm. "For some reason, I was emotional that night. But the reality is, *everyone* wants you back."

"What's that supposed to mean?"

"It means nothing's been the same since you walked out." Jane put her hands on her hips. "There's no motivation with the clients—no spark among the colleagues. Alonzo's almost suicidal. Bobbi couldn't care less about anything other than her paycheck. And Warren—well, Warren would give anything to have you back—he told me a flame was extinguished when you left. And that's a quote." Jane's expression was one of defeat.

"I don't care about any of them—I'm asking what *you* want."

"And why are you choosing to ask me what I want *now?*" she returned, defiantly. "You got what you wanted. Your master plan materialized."

"What master plan?" I inquired, truly not getting what she meant.

"Your plan, Craig—you wanted a fling, you had it, and then when things got messy, you sent me back to my husband."

My eyes again lowered to her hands; she was twisting the bands around her ring finger. "I only wanted you to be happy, Jane."

"*Happy?*" She repeated in sarcastic disbelief, tossing her long hair in disgust. "You *crushed* me. It must have been such an ego stroke for you to watch me beg—knowing you'd tear me down within five minutes and leave me to deal with everything alone. It must feel good to be so omnipotent—to have so much power over so many lives."

I took a deep breath and tried to center myself. It was killing me to listen to all the anger and hurt pour out of Jane because of my actions. "I just wanted the best for you—that's all I want for you now."

"Well—then I guess you got what you wanted," she shot back, this time stepping around me and heading towards the Den's exit. "Safe travels," she muttered.

I sailed after her. "Jane, wait," I called.

She stopped just short of the door and turned back. Her eyes were wide with pain. I proceeded toward her and wrapped my arms around her body, pulling her close. I put my hand on the back of her head and stroked her hair. She was crying now. I could feel her body shivering and her breath becoming labored. She withdrew and looked up at me, tears streaming down her cheeks. I pulled her back toward me and held her with all my might, rocking her from side to side.

"I never meant to hurt you," I whispered, my lips tasting her hair as I moved them. "I only did what I did because I … I love you."

She suddenly pushed me away and stared up at me. "What did you just say?" she demanded, tears still flowing down her face.

I looked her directly in the eye. "I love you, Jane. I've always loved you. How could you *not* know that?"

Her mouth dropped open like she was trying to decipher what I had really said. Then, without a word, she abruptly turned and walked briskly out of the room and into the hotel lobby. I followed her as she marched towards the elevators. I stopped in the lobby and let her go. I watched as the elevator doors opened and she stepped inside, keeping her back turned to me until the doors were safely closed.

THAT NIGHT, I HAD a tough time sleeping. I had finally told her. But, like everything else in my life, it was a little too late. I tossed and turned for hours, thinking about what would happen when I got back to L.A. I would get my act together and return to the agency. I would work alongside Jane and, at some point, we would settle into a comfortable friendship. We had to. It would be the next phase in our work relationship—one without secrets and games. She now knew I loved her. She could move on with the violinist, knowing the one man she slept with outside of her marriage loved her. And maybe that would be in some way comforting—maybe it would make up for a fraction of the pain and anguish I had caused her over so many years.

THE NEXT MORNING, HEATHROW airport was packed. It was a Saturday and there was traffic from every direction. After I checked my bags and made it through security, I pawed my way to the Virgin Atlantic Lounge 'clubhouse' and found a seat in the plush dining room, just a few feet from the bar but hidden in a booth near the stairwell.

I ordered a cappuccino and a bowl of fruit, pulled out a copy of the *London Times* and began to sift through it. After about twenty minutes, I heard familiar voices at the top of the stairwell. I cautiously lifted my gaze in the direction of the voices and realized it was Hayden and Jane. Hayden must have been in London for Fashion Week, too, likely sniffing around Noel Marques and anyone else who would give her the time of day. I tried to inconspicuously eavesdrop on their conversation, which required me to lean far right so ambient noise wouldn't disturb the clarity of the discussion.

"Oh, come on, *everyone* knows," Hayden scoffed. "And the most hilarious thing of all is that you think it's a secret."

"I don't like what you're implying," Jane retorted. "My husband and I have been trying for a long time."

"Well, it looks like your rich, sleazy boyfriend took care of it for you. Your *husband* told me *everything*."

"What are you talking about?" Jane demanded.

"Are you really dumb enough to believe Derek and I slept together only once? As soon as you went back to him with your phony story about having his child, he did the math and knew you were lying. He was on my doorstep the very next day."

I slowly rose from my booth and sneaked a peek around the banister of the stairwell. Jane was standing at the top stairs, leaning against the rail and I saw it for the first time—her baby bump. She was wearing a snug-fitting navy dress and I could see it plain as day. She hadn't had an abortion. She had done exactly what I had advised her to do—the safe choice—which was saving her marriage and lying to her husband about the pregnancy—about her affair with me.

"I don't believe you," Jane objected. "There's no way he would be with you again—after you drugged him and pretended to be with him in order to wreck what we had."

"Oh, please," she snorted wickedly. "You were just waiting for an excuse to jump back in bed with Craig. Everyone knows that—especially your husband. You made a fool of him, but he made an even *bigger* fool of you."

I watched Jane's expression turn from anger to shock. "You're ... a liar," she managed to stammer out. "You'd say anything to hurt me—but I know it's not true. I—I know my own husband."

This time Hayden laughed right in Jane's exasperated face. "You know *nothing*," she shrilled. "And if you don't believe me, I'll remind you of that little wheezing noise Derek makes right before he comes. It sounds like a little wheezy tea kettle, ready to explode."

Hayden then made a noise that sounded the way she described the violinist's ejaculation technique and took a step forward, putting her face right up to Jane's. "Sound familiar?" she demanded in a vicious tone.

Jane recoiled so vehemently from Hayden, she backed up and missed the step behind her. It was like watching someone in slow motion—she stumbled in her high heels, desperately grasping for the stair rail, and missing it. My heart seized with adrenaline and, from all the years of running on the treadmill, holding enormously long planks, and lifting heavy weights, I lunged up the stairs with the force of a freight train at full speed.

Just as Jane was about to topple headfirst down the length of the stairwell, I dove toward her, grabbing hold of her waist with both hands to break the fall. Once I had her gripped in my arms, I felt my body sway erratically. I had to squat down low and steady my legs, which were three full steps apart, so I wouldn't tumble down the stairs myself.

As soon as my balance returned, I slowly carried Jane down the stairs to where I had been sitting. Her hands were tightly clasped around my neck and her face buried between the lapels of my jacket, like she was clinging to me in shock, afraid to let go.

"I got you," I whispered with relief. "I got you, Jane." I squatted down so her feet would touch the floor, but she gripped me fiercely, like a frightened animal. "Hey—Jane—you're okay. You're going to be just fine."

She slowly moved her face from between my jacket lapels, pulling back to look me in the eye, still clutching me around the neck. Her look was both astonished and enlightened, like she was seeing me for the first time. "You … where did you come from?" she asked breathlessly.

"I was there the whole time," I answered, staring into her beautiful eyes. "The minute I saw you falling, I …"

"You were watching over me," she interrupted softly, eyes suddenly wet with tears. "You saved me—you saved *us*."

I nodded slowly. Jane was right. I did save her, and I saved our unborn child. But what she didn't understand is that she saved me a long time ago. It had never been so clear to me before this moment what it meant to be emotionally rescued. And our mutual salvation was something that would last a lifetime—through the many weathered, obstructed, and twisted roads that led us to each other's emotional doorstep—tirelessly knocking until there was finally an answer—an open door to walk through—a warm, well-lit room to be welcomed into—a place to finally rest.

# Twenty-three

"**W**HAT DO YOU THINK, Boss?" Alonzo asked as he spread the last of the ad layouts before me. "We don't have much time on this one."

I sighed. It was just like Alonzo to wait until the last minute on something this important. The truth was that the concepts were great. I could tell he was inspired.

Warren and Jeffrey suddenly appeared in the doorway of the war room. "Craig, do you have a minute?" Warren asked.

I glanced at Alonzo, who was looking for a quick approval—on something—anything—so he could in turn get client approval. I turned to Warren and Jeffrey. "Of course, but I'd love your opinion on these concepts."

Warren sauntered over to the table with Jeffrey in tow and they both looked over my shoulder. "Ah, Kenton Fox again. Which one do you like?" Warren asked me.

I shrugged. "I think they're all effective, but this one seems to stay with me," I responded, tapping my fingers on one of Alonzo's creations.

"Then, let's go with that," Warren responded. Jeffrey immediately nodded in agreement.

"Do we need to check with our other partner first?" Warren asked.

"Normally, I'd say that'd be a wise move; but since she's off today, it's Friday after five and we're backed up to a drop-dead deadline …" I shook my head and shot a look at Alonzo. "You have your approval."

"Thanks, Boss," he chirped before scooping the pages from the table, long black hair undulating as he flew out the door to make deadline.

Warren and I exchanged wry smiles as we exited the war room, walking down the hallway, side-by-side.

"Have a good weekend," Jeffrey called to us as he headed in the opposite direction toward his office.

"What was it you wanted to see me about?" I asked, glancing at Warren as we walked.

"I found out today Towne Ink is officially dissolving," he began, giving me a devious smile.

"Really?" I asked, thinking I knew all about Hayden's demise and who helped cause it.

"Yeah," Warren responded. "Heard it was pretty ugly."

I just smiled, not volunteering anything. We passed my office and exited the building, each heading in a different direction toward our cars to depart for the evening. I slid into the seat of the Bentley, turned on the ignition, leaned over, and put the convertible top down before I pulled out of the agency parking lot. My phone was ringing; it was Don.

"Son," he started loudly as soon as I answered.

"Yes, Dad," I responded, grinning. He sounded like he had time on his hands.

"First of all, are you alone?" he asked warily.

"I am," I answered, adjusting the Bluetooth volume so I could hear Don clearly.

"Good because I have some valuable information for you, son," Don confided.

"What about?" I asked interested. "Is it about a certain ad agency that's closing its doors?" I suggested, knowing Don would never mention Hayden's name in my presence. Once he found out what Hayden was capable of, and how she almost killed a Keller, he vowed to never bring her up again. But I knew he would seek vengeance, especially given his relationship with her father.

"She's done. And her father's facing thirty-five years in prison for tax fraud, money laundering, and bank fraud. He'll be lucky if they don't throw the book at him, that crooked son of a bitch."

"What's going to happen to her?" I asked, thinking of all of Hayden's unspeakable acts and wishing for her to hurt as badly as those she had hurt throughout her life—I wanted retribution.

"She'll be run out of town—she was funding her agency with her crooked bastard father's dirty money. Now that it's all out in the open—she's facing RICO charges. She'll be lucky if she gets a job at the local strip joint, the lousy trollop," he sputtered bitterly. "You know, karma's a nasty bitch when you have to lie with her, son."

"Well, I couldn't agree with you more," I commented, gazing out the window as I hit the Pacific Coast Highway. I had just passed a crowd of women whose heads turned as I drove by. I smiled, thinking it had been a long time since I played the counting game. None of that mattered anymore. I was suddenly reminded of Dr. Truer, whom I had not seen since my total melt-down in her office. "Dad, do you ever hear from Dr. Truer?"

"Oh, that's a good story, son. I got a post card from Janice a few weeks ago. She ran away with her lover—some female psychiatrist she worked with when her patients needed prescription medication. They were both in horrible marriages to men, and they decided to shut down their practices and move to the island of Santorini."

I almost chuckled out loud. That's why Dr. Truer always pushed me to follow my heart. She must have been living vicariously through me, waiting for an opportunity to follow her own heart. "Good for Janice," I responded after a long silence.

"What made you think of her, son?"

"Oh, I don't know," I answered, still smiling at the

thought of Janice with her female lover on a Greek island, drinking a Campari and soda, batches of frizzy blonde hair sticking out from underneath a straw hat.

"Will you do me one humongous favor, son?" Don asked with a smile in his voice. "Will you give your beautiful lass a big kiss for me?"

"I will, Dad."

I reached my home in Malibu and parked in front, waiting for the wrought iron gates to close behind me. I breathed a sigh of relief, looking forward to a relaxing weekend.

I entered through the front door and stopped by the mirror hanging in the entryway to examine my face. I evaluated my light jade eyes—the slightest trace of a scar above my right eye—there to remind me of what it's like to be miserable—to feel hopeless—to throw everything away because continuing seems impossible—incomprehensible. But one thing I had learned over the past year was that everything *was* possible. It was possible to have everything I always wanted, and not just in material possessions. It was possible to love and to be loved—to have family and friends and people who depended on me—people I could depend on, too.

The biggest surprise turned out to be Warren, whom I had once thought to be my enemy. He deliberately sent me to the meeting with Noel Marques in London—not because he wanted to check up on Jane, but because he wanted to help resolve my conflict with her. He knew what would make me happy and it was important for him to help me get there. Warren later revealed that Julia had personally visited him on Christmas Day to inquire about Jane—about our relationship—wondering if there were anything he could do to intervene. They had exchanged cell phone numbers when I went missing. That's why Julia was late for our Christmas dinner. Once she had expressed how despondent I was without Jane, Warren connected the dots and figured out with whom I had violated my contract. Veronica had never really conducted any interviews with the other female employees. There was no need.

The best part of the story is that I realized *I* was the

biggest obstacle in finding happiness. And once I figured that out, it was so simple to break through it—to shatter it forever. The one shining element in my reflection was happiness—it was joy and, as trite as it may have sounded to my earlier self, it was love—love in its truest form.

I turned away from the mirror and called out, "Hello— anyone home?" The house was perfumed with the savory scent of garlic, olive oil, and thyme. I beelined for the kitchen and found Camilla, with the oven door open, basting a roast chicken. "Where is everyone?" I asked her.

"They're outside," she answered. "You're right on time."

"Come with me for a minute." I gestured to Camilla, who shut the oven and followed me.

I led her into the living room, stopping briefly at the fireplace where *Lovers In the Red Sky* glittered above, its dark red essence splashed against the wall, almost the color of claret in the glow of the late-afternoon sun. I smiled, thinking how easy it would have been to let the painting go, but how elated I was to keep it at my hearth, knowing it would be there every day to remind me of my own mystical, magical powers. I approached the window to the patio and pool, putting my hands up against the glass and leaning forward. My heart was bursting with pleasure at the scene before me.

"Wait here for a second," I told Camilla. I opened the door and stepped through it, feeling the cool dusk air as it floated into the house. It was already November. I took a deep breath.

There she was—my beloved wife, sprawled out on one of the daybeds, wearing a floor-length emerald green dress, looking majestic as ever with her long auburn hair rippling wildly in the ocean breeze. She was holding our son, Jackson Brady Keller, who had just turned four months old. This would be his first holiday season. I approached Jane and she looked up, smiling.

"You got out early," she exclaimed, standing, and then crouching down to transfer Jackson to his swing, which looked more like a stereotypical space-age pod from the seventies. Jane had convinced me that it was the only baby chair/swing to own because of its special gliding motion properties. I had never considered such things before. I never really cared—before her. Once Jackson was safely ensconced and fastened into his pod, Jane bounded toward me.

"I wanted to play hooky with you," I teased. "Everyone at the office was jealous that you had the day off."

"Do I have you all to myself this weekend?" she squealed playfully as I dove down and swept her up, kissing and hugging her—twirling her around the pool. She clinched her hands around my collar, tugging at my silk tie to loosen it.

After I set Jane down, her green dress fluttering around her, we held hands and I led her back to the daybed. I knelt and kissed Jackson on the forehead. He was just about to fall asleep, vibrating in his gliding space pod. I sat next to Jane on the daybed and put my arm around her.

"You have me all to yourself forever," I finally answered, observing Jane's eyes, reminded that Jackson's were similar. He was going to look just like her—or a mixture of her and me as Jane had predicted. I hoped it would be more her, but time would be the measure. "What would you like to do this evening, Mrs. Keller?" I asked as we laid back and settled onto the daybed, remnants of the sunset lingering on the horizon.

She inhaled deeply and turned her eyes to the sky. "I don't care as long as I'm with you."

"I have an idea," I suggested mysteriously. I rose from the daybed and signaled Camilla, who was standing near the window. She knew exactly what I wanted. A minute later, she brought out two champagne flutes and an open bottle of Dom Perignon.

"Are we celebrating anything special?" Jane asked, giving me a curious glance.

"Us," I answered, watching closely as Camilla carefully filled the glasses, a flurry of bubbles soaring infinitely within each. Once she was finished, we picked up our flutes and clinked them together. "We're celebrating *us* tonight because there is no other *us* in the world and that's *incredibly* special, don't you think?"

"Yes," Jane responded, nodding, her eyes becoming slightly misty. "Oh, *yes.*"

I leaned over and kissed Jane softly on the lips; she smelled crisp and alluring. The sun was gone now; the ocean became a dark mass. The dim patio lights flickered on and the pool suddenly glowed with its deep green essence. Jackson continued to sleep contentedly, and we just lay there, sipping champagne, with nothing more to say or do. We were together, the sublime warmth of our bodies fused together comfortably, heavenly.

—*Craig Keller*

# Playlist

Find "For Position Only" on Spotify.

"Choke" by I Don't Know How but They Found Me
"Longshot" by Catfish and the Bottlemen
"Your Dog" by Soccer Mommy
"Carnival of Sorts (Box Cars)" by REM
"1950" by King Princess
"Ain't Talkin' 'Bout Love" by Van Halen
"Miracle" by Chvrches
"Dennis" by Roy Blair
"Up All Night" by Beck
"California Dreamin'" by Sia
"Happier" by Marshmello & Bastille
"Blur" by MØ featuring Foster the People
"Jumpsuit" by Twenty-One Pilots
"Down to Earth" by Flight Facilities
"Skin and Bones" by Cage the Elephant
"Half the World Away" by Oasis
"Home" by morgxn

# Acknowledgments

Thank you to my first readers, Mom, Shirley, Doug, Pat, Jenni, and Pam, and to my critique partners, Lori, Don, CarolJean, and Phil. Your honesty, enthusiasm, and candid advice drove me exactly where I needed to be with this book. I'd also like to acknowledge the South Florida Writers Association for providing the resources that led me to Don's critique group.

A huge round of applause goes to photographer and friend Merrell Virgen for creating yet another beautiful cover—the image says so much about the story. Your talent is unmatched.

Thanks to my brother for adding color to chapter 18, due to his tireless efforts volunteering in Skid Row. I couldn't have made that so real without a crucial interview with you, Bo.

Many thanks also to Dr. Monte for teaching me the medical terminology and procedures necessary to create a very realistic scene.

Special acknowledgment goes to my sister for connecting me with Chris at Dagmar Miura Publishing in Los Angeles. Thank you, Missy.

And to the other Chris in my life, owner of Gotcha Mobile Solutions, thank you for your insight, careful guidance, and smart marketing.

# About Adele Royce

Adele Royce was raised in Los Angeles, and graduated *magna cum laude* from Arizona State University with a BA in English Literature. She survived the insanity of the Las Vegas Strip, where she worked for many years as an advertising and PR executive. Ms. Royce's personal experience with the industry's creativity and chaos gave her inspiration for her multiple-book series titled *Truth, Lies and Love in Advertising*. She lives with her husband in South Florida, where she is active in the writing community. Her short stories have won numerous first place awards.

Connect with Adele Royce online at adeleroyce.com.

Made in the USA
Middletown, DE
04 January 2021

30750509R10168